A MINDHUNTERS NOVEL

DARK DEEDS

AWARD-WINNING ROMANTIC SUSPENSE

ANNE MARIE BECKER

ALSO BY ANNE MARIE BECKER

The Mindhunters Series

Only Fear

Avenging Angel

Deadly Bonds

Dark Deeds

Acceptable Risk

End Game

The Mindhunters Novellas

Christmas Stalking

Until Death

Wicked Night

Deadly Holidays (A Collection of Mindhunters Holiday Novellas)

A "Nico & Eve" Short Story

Deceit in the Desert

The Redemption Club Series

Stacking the Deck

Sleight of Hand

Raising the Stakes

The Redemption Club Collection (Books 1-3)

DARK DEEDS

THE MINDHUNTERS, BOOK 4

ANNE MARIE BECKER

For Andrea—beta reader and alpha sister.
You are amazing.
I love you.

P.S. I only used "crushed" twice.

CHAPTER 1

Friday, 4:03 p.m., early February
Hoboken, New Jersey

Becca followed the instructions—both parts—to the letter. She'd told no one, and she arrived at the diner alone. The window that separated her from the sleet-slick street outside proclaimed the breakfast specials in ketchup-red and mustard-yellow stencil, which only accentuated the day's shades of gray.

Then again, it was February. In Hoboken.

"Another refill?" The waitress's attitude had gone from cheerful to weary over the past hour.

"No, thanks." Three cups had already shifted her usual state of heightened awareness into downright jittery territory. It went against all her self-protective instincts—and in a personal security specialist and bodyguard, those were strong—to continue to sit and wait, but she wanted this interview. Had worked for months to chase down this lead that might provide new information about Samantha Manchester's disappearance. The trail had been cold for twenty years, which was why Becca needed Selina. So she didn't protest when the tired waitress misheard her and moved to top off her cup yet again.

Her hand shook slightly—adrenaline and caffeine were a potent mix—as she lifted her cup to her lips. She set it down too hard, sloshing a bit over the rim, splashing droplets onto the table. As she reached for the napkin dispenser, the tiny diamond stud in her nose reflected in the metal surface, winking at her like sun on snow. During the weeks they'd exchanged emails, Becca had learned that eighteen-year-old Selina loved piercings, extreme hair color and all things city-chic, so Becca had opted to wear the stud she normally removed for her daily job. Her nearly white-blond hair was a constant. Still a year shy of thirty, Becca was short enough, her appearance young enough, to get away with wearing ripped jeans and a T-shirt advertising a popular punk band.

Another minute ticked by. Resigned, she took out her phone and sent the text she'd been composing in her mind. *So sorry. Going to miss rehearsal but will be at party. Will make it up to you.*

She was, technically, in New York City to serve as a bridesmaid in a wedding, but the proximity to this lead in Hoboken had been crucial to her decision to fly in early. However, she hadn't counted on her lead being late for their appointment. She was going to miss the next train back to the city.

A moment later, Vanessa texted a reply. *Because of Diego?*

Becca's body went still. Months ago, she'd reconciled herself to seeing her ex-lover again, since Diego was the groom's best man. She was dreading it, but she would pull on her big girl panties for the sake of her friends' wedding. Vanessa and Noah deserved happiness.

She texted back. *No. Work.*

I know this weekend is tough for you. If you want to talk, I'm here.

Though Becca appreciated the offer, sharing wasn't in the cards. Her two-week affair with Diego last summer would be forever locked away in a vault in the back of her mind. Unfortunately, her masochistic side occasionally whipped out those memories like little jewels and re-examined them in all their sparkling, stunning detail.

A young woman peeked through the diner's ketchup-and-mustard window and Becca hastily returned Vanessa's text. *See you soon.*

Swallowed up by a trench coat that appeared secondhand, the woman looked all of twelve years old, especially when she rapidly blinked away snowflakes as if she were lost and confused. But the highlights in her hair were expensive—not homegrown, but from a quality salon. She winced as the tinkling of a bell announced her entrance, then she spied Becca in the corner.

With halting steps, as if she were facing a firing squad, she made her way to the table. "Becca?"

"That's me." Becca smiled warmly and gestured to the opposite side of the booth. "Thank you for coming."

After another glance around, Selina slid onto the bench. "I almost didn't, but I had to meet the woman who thinks she can take down the Circle." Selina's gaze flicked over her. "Kind of small, aren't you?"

"The best things come in small packages." It was something Becca's brothers used to say to her, before ruffling her hair. Or trying out the latest wrestling moves on her. Not that they'd dared to attempt such a thing in years, not since she'd shown up to a family dinner wearing her black belt in Tae Kwon Do. "I'm tougher than I look." And at five and a half feet tall, she wasn't *that* tiny.

"Me, too." For an eighteen-year-old, Selina's eyes were hard with life experience, her jaw set in concrete.

"You'd have to be tough, to survive what you've been through."

The waitress approached, some semblance of her cheerful smile back in place at the prospect of another paying customer. Selina ordered a cup of coffee, then waited until the waitress was at the other end of the diner before speaking. "How'd you find me?"

"I'd been looking for anything about the Circle. You were mentioned in a police report."

Selina stiffened. "There's not supposed to be anything to connect me to them."

"It was under your previous name, not your new one. That took some more digging. The rest you know." "You bribed my friend for my email address."

"Pretty much." There had been weeks of trust-building there, too, during which they'd exchanged increasingly lengthy emails until Becca had convinced Selina she could be trusted.

Selina ducked her head, pretending to be absorbed in stirring her coffee. "You believe the police report?"

Becca sensed her response was critical to the success of this interview. "There was very little to it, which surprised me. You were a witness, a survivor, one of a kind, who could have testified against a major crime syndicate. But then you disappeared. I'm guessing the former is the motivation for the latter."

Selina set aside her spoon and met Becca's gaze. "I'm only here because you think you can take those monsters down. I want to help, but..."

"But you're afraid. I don't blame you for not trusting anyone. I know what the Circle is capable of. I've been gathering information on them for months now. I've read every police report I could get my hands on from Chicago to New York to Las Vegas."

"To find out if they took this Samantha Manchester girl like they took me."

"Yes, but she was taken in Chicago, so it's a little different. My boss at SSAM—"

"Damian Manchester. He's Samantha's father?"

Becca nodded. "Sam was thirteen years old when she was taken from a mall in the North Shore area of Chicago twenty years ago. A year later, they found her skeletal remains in a wooded, rural area outside of the city."

Selina shuddered. "That could have been me. If I hadn't been rescued, death would have been the easy way out."

"Except she might not have died."

Selina looked up sharply. "What?"

"Recently, we found evidence that suggests it might not have been Sam's body in that shallow grave after all. The Circle may have taken her, then faked her death and identification to throw the police and Damian off the trail." It was precious little to go on, but it was something new, when hope of finding justice had nearly been lost.

Becca waited a moment and watched Selina absorb her words before she continued. "From what I've learned, I believe the Circle deals in the trading of human flesh, including sex slaves and children for pornographic purposes. You were almost one of their victims." That was only a part of their extensive operation, and looking for information about Samantha had been like trying to chip away at an iceberg, searching for that one bit of helpful information.

"Help me stop them," Becca pleaded when Selina remained quietly thoughtful.

"You don't know for sure that the Circle was involved in Sam's disappearance."

"True. That's why I need your help. You're the only person known to have escaped the Circle and survived." Others had been killed before they could testify. Selina had taken off before she could suffer the same fate. And the police report had been notably vague.

Selina seemed to weigh this, then sat back, her shoulders dipping a notch as she made her decision. "It's not a pretty story."

"In my line of work, few stories are."

"You see this kind of thing at SSAM often?"

The acronym for Damian's agency, the Society for the Study of the Aberrant Mind, was a tribute to his daughter Sam. SSAM's clientele enlisted Becca and her fellow agents to hunt violent repeat offenders when local law enforcement agencies or FBI failed to apprehend the criminals, for whatever reason—often a lack of resources or a case that had gone cold or fallen out of the public eye.

Like Samantha Manchester's case.

Becca leaned forward on the tabletop scarred by water rings and knife marks. "I can teach you ways to protect yourself. You're doing a good job hiding, but I have a lot of experience in staying safe." And plenty in getting hurt, too, and how to avoid it in the future. "My job, my entire world, is all about personal security."

Selina pressed her lips together, then shook her head. "I'm here now, and I'll talk. But then we can't meet again. I can't risk it."

"I understand." Becca hoped to get what she needed and leave this woman in peace.

"I hope so, because it's a matter of life and death—and not just mine." Absently, Selina's left hand rubbed her upper right arm as if warding off a chill.

Who else was she protecting? "I made sure nobody followed me," Becca assured her. "I haven't told anyone I'm here. Not even my boss."

Selina stared out the window for so long Becca wasn't sure she would share her story after all. When she spoke, it was in a bitter, miserable tone. "I was at a party where there was alcohol. I was out beyond curfew. My parents didn't care. I'd run away so many times, they'd stopped trying to get through to me. Besides, I was going to be eighteen in a month. An adult." She huffed out a breath. "As if I knew what that meant. I was an idiot."

Stealing Selina's innocence was yet another of the Circle's crimes.

Selina shook off her self-flagellation and refocused. "My phone's battery died so I went to the car to charge it while I called a friend who was supposed to meet me. Before I could dial, two guys opened my door and yanked me from the front seat." She paused and swallowed. "It was dark, and everything happened so fast. They put something over my head and tied me up so I couldn't see or move. In a matter of seconds, they had me. It was all so efficient. I was scared, but that was just the beginning." Remembered fear contorted her face.

"It must have been horrible." Becca resisted the urge to reach out and comfort with a touch of the hand. Her source still looked as if she might bolt at the slightest provocation.

Selina's lips pressed into a hard line, and a flash of warrior-like determination glinted in her eyes. "It was a fucking nightmare. But I got away. And then nobody believed me. Do you know what that's like?"

"Yeah, I do," Becca said quietly. Inside, her heart rate spiked with memories. Years of repressing fear and anxiety, pleading with the authorities to listen to her story. Years of being dismissed. Just when she thought she'd moved past it, the horrible memories would pop up again. And now that the man who starred in her nightmares had been released on parole, those moments had occurred more frequently.

Selina must have seen the truth in Becca's face. She took a deep breath, then continued. "When they pulled the bag off my head, I was in a basement with no windows and barely any lighting. There was a row of cells, maybe four or five metal doors, side by side. They—" She broke off and put a hand to her opposite shoulder, the same one she'd been rubbing earlier. Tears shimmered in her eyes. "They branded me."

"Branded?"

Selina traced a circle on the table. "With a hot iron. A symbol that I was theirs. Then they put me in a cell with nothing but a cot and a scratchy blanket. One guy tried to touch me, but the other guy stopped him. Said to save me for the clients. I'd bring in more money if I was pure." Her laugh hitched in her throat. "The other guy said I was nowhere near pure. Assholes. Later, a third guy came to film me. I was so scared they were going to send it to my parents or something."

"What did they film?"

"That's just it. I wasn't doing anything interesting. They encouraged me to plead with them, like they enjoyed seeing me begging for my life. It was bizarre."

An introduction to the merchandise, possibly? Something to show potential clients? No doubt, interest from buyers would have led to worse scenarios for Selina. Chills ran down Becca's spine at the thought of what could have happened if the teen hadn't escaped, and what had probably happened to many similar girls, maybe even Sam.

"If Sam was a victim, do you think she could still be alive?" Becca asked. "Or maybe she escaped like you did?" And somehow didn't find her way back home. If there was hope for Selina, perhaps there was hope for Sam, though she would be in her mid-thirties by now. She'd be an entirely different person than the daughter Damian remembered, but at least he'd have closure.

"I don't know. Part of me hopes she isn't alive if she didn't escape early on." Selina's eyes met Becca's. "The things I've read online about human trafficking, these people have to be animals. Fucking monsters." Selina glanced away to compose herself, but she couldn't hide a shudder. "When they were taping me, the camera's light was bright. It lit up the walls of my cell. There were names everywhere, like a warning or something. It didn't matter what we did—or who we were before—now we were *theirs*." Her hand moved to her arm again. They'd marked her as Circle property, but she'd reclaimed her life.

Goosebumps erupted on Becca's arms. Had Samantha's name been on that wall? She'd been taken in Chicago. Would they have trafficked her through New York City, maybe to keep the authorities from locating her when Damian was putting the pressure on?

"How did you get away?" Becca asked.

For the first time, a small smile curved Selina's lips. "I was lucky. I had a guardian angel who let me out. Told me to be quiet and follow him. The guard was passed out, snoring. I think my angel might have drugged him." Selina's gaze flitted away from Becca's. "And don't ask me any more about my angel because I don't know. And I wouldn't tell even if I did know. He took me to another man who helped me set up a new identity. He saved my life."

Someone in the Circle risked his life for this one young woman? It had to be an undercover agent. The Circle was known for a wide range of crimes in a number of big cities—New York, Chicago, Miami, Dallas, Las Vegas and Los Angeles were all infected with their influence. This man could be FBI, CIA, ICE or DEA. Or maybe he worked alone.

"The police report says you couldn't remember where you'd been held," Becca said. "Or how you got out."

"That was for my own protection. I was stupid."

"How so?"

"There never should have been a police report. The guy who helped me, my angel, told me to forget everything I'd seen. To run like hell and start a new life. But I went home to get some things I thought I couldn't live without. And to say goodbye to my parents. I told them what had happened, hoping they'd care." She pressed her trembling lips together and looked away. "Stupid."

When Selina looked back, she'd wiped her expression of all emotion linked to the memory. "My parents called the police while I was up in my room. Just in case I wasn't lying, I guess. Or maybe they wanted me admitted to the loony bin. I wasn't home more than fifteen minutes before a cop was there, asking me questions. Almost like he'd been watching for me to pop up somewhere. That's when I knew my angel was right. I should run.

"I told the officer I couldn't remember anything. As soon as I could, I snuck out my bedroom window and never looked back. Started a new life with my new identity." She met Becca's gaze. "Until you found me, I had become Selina. Now I'm back to dealing with the old me again."

"Sorry about that."

"I thought I could keep in touch with a friend or two from high school, but I guess I should stop that, too." Selina's anger faded quickly. "If telling my story will save someone else from the Circle, I'm happy to help. But if you tracked me down via a police report and figured out how to get my email address, then the Circle can do it, too. Or the NYPD mole."

"Mole?" Becca was sure her eyes had gone as wide as the rims of their coffee cups. A mole working on the force was leaking vital information to a crime ring? It would explain why the police closed Selina's case so quickly. And why the Circle had operated for decades, seemingly without interference from law enforcement. They were usually one step ahead of police raids. It made sense that they might have a reliable source of information within the NYPD. Besides, money could buy almost anything.

But an undercover agent *within* the Circle *and* a police officer leaking information *to* the Circle? As this investigation proceeded, Becca would have her work cut out for her figuring out who was friend or foe.

"My rescuer said that there was a cop who was dangerous and might kill me to keep me quiet. At the very least, I was afraid the Circle would come looking for me, especially if they thought I'd testify."

"Let me assure you, you're difficult to find."

"And yet you found me."

"I'm very careful. I know my words might not be worth much, but I promise you can trust me. You call me and I'll come running to help." This time Becca did reach out to touch Selina's wrist lightly. She was encouraged when Selina didn't pull away.

"But how can I help you?" Selina's eyes brimmed with misery and regret. "I won't put myself at risk again."

"Do you remember where you were held?"

"I do." Selina took a napkin from the dispenser. "Got a pen?"

Becca promptly handed her one, and a moment later, Selina pushed the napkin toward her. She'd written down an address in

Brooklyn. Below it was a name that froze the air in Becca's lungs.

"What's this name at the bottom?" Becca asked, hoping her words sounded normal when she was nearly choking on them.

"That's the name of the mole. My angel warned me not to talk about it, but I figure you'd better know who you can or can't trust."

"Diego Sandoval? You're sure that's the name your angel gave you? That's the name of the guy working for the Circle, betraying the NYPD?" Becca's stomach twisted.

"No way I could forget it."

And there was no way Diego would sell out his brothers in blue. No freaking way.

The Diego she'd known, the man she'd held in her arms, the proud NYPD detective who'd vowed to rebuild his career, would never accept bribes from a crime ring. Unless she'd never really known him at all.

Friday, 3:12 p.m. Central Time
Chicago

DEATHBED CONFESSIONS WERE RARELY LIGHT. OFTEN, THEY WERE heavy, like "Jane is adopted." Or "I stole that silver from Grandmother's cabinet before my sister could get her grubby hands on it. It's in the attic." Where, over the past fifty years, the silver had probably served no purpose, denied the warmth of some relative's fingers pulsing around it because of the dying person's greed.

Light wasn't what he craved, anyway. Dark was more his speed. Dark was *real*.

Which was why he had the woman in his basement.

He tightened the noose around her neck, ignoring her whimpers and focusing on the thundering in his ears. Blood, adrenaline, endorphins—a cocktail that produced a natural high. And if it was natural, it was right.

"What kind of name is Fanta, anyway?" he asked his victim. "Your mother had to have been a crack addict, too, to choose a god-awful name like that. Was she a whore like you?"

The woman moaned a response. Probably because she couldn't do anything else with duct tape across her mouth. Her mascara smeared as tears and snot ran down her face. He reached for a tissue and gently wiped the mess, then checked the bandage on her upper arm. The wound wouldn't completely heal in time but the symbol he'd branded there was legible.

"It's not your fault. Destiny is predetermined by genetics, then shaped by environment. You were at a disadvantage in both areas." He adjusted the chair she was strapped to, balancing it on two legs against the wall so that if she tried to shift, it would slide out from under her, the noose would engage, losing its bit of slack, and she'd be gone within minutes. No muss, no fuss.

"You should be thankful." He reached for his camera. "Nobody noticed you before, standing on that street corner. Not the real you. But now they will. Thanks to me. Your contribution to society will go down in history."

Her deathbed confession—that she was a drug addict and a prostitute, which he already knew, since he'd used both to lure her into his basement—was certainly no ray of sunshine. But her lifestyle ensured he could get what he wanted without repercussion.

More important, it would prove his loyalty to Tony.

He shifted the camera to the side so that he could look into eyes wide with surprise. "I've even written a glowing obituary for you. And once I talk to people at the church, you'll be considered a victim of society, ignored and neglected. I'll make sure you get a proper funeral."

Tears of gratitude streamed down her cheeks. Again, he dabbed at them around the duct tape.

"It'll be beautiful. The organist is a friend of mine. I'm sure she'll donate her time. I bet I can even get a couple of choir people. Mother is a member of the ladies' ministry. There'll be casseroles

and cakes. I'll make sure people notice you. Understand you."
Nobody had given her a second look before—unless they'd been
looking for a cheap quickie in the alley.

He would make Fanta fabulous. He'd also satisfy his cravings
and ensure Tony's continued cooperation. *Win-win-win.*

He snapped a few more pictures. "Now don't you move, or
this'll be over too quick. Although, I do have to be kind of quick. I
have places to be."

The airport, to be exact. He'd have to leave Mother alone for a
day or two, but it would be worth it. He had a job to do.

He grinned as anticipation fizzed in his blood, adding to the
addictive natural mixture already pulsing through his body and
making him lightheaded. It was the same kind of buzz he got pre-
kill, though he was a man of caution and had restrained himself
from killing as much as he would like. Nobody seemed to understand that burning need.

Except for Damian Manchester and his agents. At the wedding
this weekend, he would be among people who understood the
necessity of death, the beauty of it. He strived to be like them, to
channel his urges—his *gift*—to better society. This weekend, he'd
be among the SSAM group, even if they didn't know about him.

Or what he did in his basement.

In New York, he might even get a hint of what the SSAM
agents' consciences hid. Certainly not prostitution or drug addic-
tion. But every conscience had burdens to bear.

CHAPTER 2

Friday, 7:08 p.m.
Harlem, New York City

Herrera got the drop on Diego just outside his Harlem apartment, stepping out of the stairwell to confront him as he slid his key into the first lock. This conversation had been building for months, so, without a word, Diego let the man follow him inside. Whatever Herrera had to say wasn't something the neighbors needed to hear, anyway.

"What's the problem?" Diego read tension in every line of his fellow NYPD detective's body.

Herrera paced the small living room in short, jerky strides. Diego was seriously regretting his decision to wait until after the wedding rehearsal to change for the rehearsal party. If only he'd come in his tux, he could have driven in the rented luxury cars with the rest of the family and bridal parties. But he couldn't stand wearing the monkey suit any longer than necessary, and he'd nearly been late because of work.

Herrera was usually calm seas and smooth sailing. Now, he

abruptly halted in his pattern and spun to face Diego, his large nostrils flaring with irritation. *"What's the problem?* You're giving guys like us—like me—a crap name."

Diego forced his jaw to unclench and his muscles to relax. "I doubt your ego is that soft." He let his gaze drop to the man's paunch and raised his eyebrows.

And hated himself for it. He had to bite back the apology that sprung to his lips. *This isn't me,* he wanted to explain. Of course, that wasn't possible. It would endanger the mission.

As was intended, Herrera backed away, disgusted and maybe a little hurt. "You're walking a thin line, Diego. I get any hard proof of what I suspect you're doing and I'll have to go to the lieutenant."

"I'd expect nothing less from such an upstanding detective." His sarcasm only deepened Herrera's scowl.

Too bad. Even if Diego had been sloppy enough to leave behind hard evidence of working with the Circle, their lieutenant couldn't do anything. Diego had assurance from higher up in the food chain that he'd be protected. Unfortunately, that didn't keep Diego's coworkers from wondering what the hell was wrong with him. Then again, that was the point.

Didn't make it hurt any less.

"Good luck with finding that evidence." Diego turned away, unable to make eye contact with Herrera any longer. Being a dirty cop twisted his insides into knots, but it was a necessary evil.

"It's only a matter of time. Your reports have been late, you've had a suck-ass attitude, nobody trusts you enough to ask for help with a case, and, well, we know what else."

"What else?"

Herrera flicked a finger at Diego's tux, where it hung from the back of his barstool. "You've been high-rollin' it these days." His mouth turned down at the edges. "Guess shiny and bright attracts guys like you. Got tired of slumming with the rest of us, huh?"

Diego's teeth ached with the effort of holding his tongue in check.

Herrera blew out a breath. "Fuck, man. I know what you went through when your niece died. Losing her, especially that way, must have been hard. We all understood the fuck-up at the scene. You shouldn't have been the one to discover her body in the first place."

Don't go there. Attitude, he could use to his advantage. Accusations, he could withstand. But compassion? That made his knees buckle.

Diego laughed shortly to cover the moment of weakness. "I came to terms with my mistakes. And I learned who I really am, and who I want to be. As for the rest, you have no proof."

Herrera's mouth twisted in disgust. "I thought I could talk to you, man to man. Detective to detective."

"A man has to choose whatever path is right for him, and live with the consequences." Diego shrugged as if he'd made peace with that, when in reality he struggled with it daily.

Herrera growled in frustration and turned on his heel. The apartment door shut with a snap behind him.

Diego looked to the ceiling and prayed for patience. He'd done a lot of that these past few months. It went against his nature not to defend his honor. But Herrera lying in wait on a Friday night didn't bode well. Or maybe it did. It fell in line with Diego's cover. But didn't work so great for his day job—or his daily life, for that matter. Lying to everyone had been hard as hell. The only saving grace was knowing what he did was for a higher purpose.

At least Herrera had approached him before the party. Diego wanted to keep this filth away from his friend's wedding. Noah was like a brother to him, and deserved happiness, as did his bride, Vanessa.

As did Becca.

His heart sped as he thought about seeing her again, even as his brain told him it was a bad idea. His life was enough of a mess. He didn't need to drag her into it again. She'd proven she didn't want to be involved. And she definitely wouldn't want a man who was working with the other side. He wanted to be a good guy. He wanted to be the *best* guy.

But, for now, it meant working with the bad guys.

He hurried to change into his tux for the fancy post-rehearsal party. On the counter, his phone vibrated with an incoming text message.

Shipment. Saturday, 6 a.m.

Tonight, he'd be friend, brother and best man. Tomorrow morning, he'd be the bad guy again.

Friday, 8:42 p.m.
Chelsea district, New York City

A POSH ART GALLERY SERVED AS A BACKDROP FOR THE POST-rehearsal gathering. Diego's large Puerto Rican family would have set up a buffet in someone's home and had a loud, boisterous affair with plenty to eat. The Sandovals didn't do subtle. The bride's family, on the other hand, consisted of blue-blood, old-money New Yorkers. So, elegance, neck-choking ties and tiny appetizers were the norm. At least there was an open bar.

The high-ceilinged room was filled with beautiful people whose imperfections were softened by the lighting and dull personalities brightened by alcohol. The delicate strains of a string quartet and a setting of eclectic paintings, sculptures and pottery lent everyone—even his jaded, NYPD-detective hide—an air of sophistication.

Spying the groom standing near the makeshift bar, Diego headed that way. He needed something to take the edge off. As Diego approached, Noah's gaze flicked from his soon-to-be wife Vanessa, who was talking with her family across the room, to Diego.

"Phase One complete. Nothing left but the wedding and recep-tion. Would have been nice if the *entire* wedding party had been able to make it." Noah narrowed his eyes at him. "You know anything about that?"

"I had nothing to do with Becca not being there. Haven't talked to her, let alone seen her, in months." Seven and a half, to be exact. Casually, he surveyed the room, but didn't see Becca.

"You didn't scare her away?"

Diego released a gruff laugh and motioned for the bartender to bring him a beer like Noah's. "As if anyone could." Becca was the most fearless woman he'd ever met. She'd saved Diego's sanity last summer. Then she'd disappeared without so much as a Dear John letter. Even a Dear Schmuck text would have sufficed. Still, she'd braved his prickly defenses for a while. She sure as hell wouldn't cower now.

Noah grinned. "So you didn't bump into her before the party and maybe lock her in your bedroom?"

"Nope." Despite his casual response, the image of smooth white skin against his silver sheets and the knowing smile of a fallen angel filled his brain, and he had to swallow to refocus. He changed the subject before it could catch him off guard again. "That was some poker game last night. I, for one, contributed heavily to your honeymoon fund. You're welcome."

Diego had even come away with a nice little souvenir from the bachelor party. The stripper had insisted on tossing him the sexy red garter. But damned if he hadn't pictured it wrapped around Becca's creamy thigh. His mouth watered at the image, and at the thought of kissing his way upward, along the curve of her hip, to the little butterfly tattoo just above her panty line. He could almost taste her.

Again, he forced the memories from his mind. Despite the way she'd left, he respected Becca. Hell, he owed her. She'd kept him on his toes, had pushed him back to the surface when he was drowning. Had pushed him to reach for higher ground when grief and frustration had nearly done him in.

But then she'd left him dangling at the edge of the cliff.

What would she think of the choices he'd made since? He cringed at the thought.

He'd been tempted to make a fool out of himself and chase after her, or at least demand an explanation. It was a good thing they lived eight hundred miles apart. In the long run, it had worked out for the best that she'd left him in her rearview mirror. He was no good for anybody right now. Besides, they came from totally different backgrounds—his Puerto Rican Catholic and hers... Hell, he didn't really know. In the two weeks they'd gotten to know each other—in the Biblical way—they hadn't gotten around to talking about religion at all, though she'd called out to the great deity a few times in the heat of the moment.

"What?" Again, Noah narrowed his eyes on Diego.

"What, *what?*" Diego rounded his eyes in what he hoped passed for an innocent expression.

"You're grinning."

Diego looked away from Noah's perceptive gaze. They were both detectives—Diego with the NYPD and Noah in Chicago with the CPD—and knew how to break each other down with just a look. They'd met in the second grade and had been like brothers ever since. Thirty years of history gave Noah unique insight.

"I'm just happy, man." For a few hours, anyway.

Noah looked over Diego's shoulder and frowned. "Hold on to those happy thoughts. Becca's here. And she brought a plus-one."

Diego shifted so he could see the doorway and was rewarded with a swift kick to the chest at the sight of her. Becca's short white-blond hair gleamed like a halo as a dress the color of a ripe, juicy plum displayed devil-may-care curves. She smiled as Vanessa welcomed her—and her date. A tall, broad-shouldered man with dark blond hair, reminiscent of a Viking god, stood at Becca's side, handing their coats to a waiting attendant in a gentlemanly way. The Viking leaned down and said something in Becca's ear. Her lips parted on a wicked smile.

Mine. Hot jealousy slammed into Diego's gut. He nearly bent over from the unexpected force of it. He clutched his beer like a lifeline.

As if she felt his eyes on her, she suddenly looked his way. Hell, she probably *had* felt him. His flash of lust burned as bright and hot as the rays of the sun. Her gaze connected with his, then shifted away as if she hadn't recognized him, which pissed him off. But it also gave him free rein to observe her again.

Upon closer inspection, she was slimmer, if that was possible. Her petite frame and heart-shaped face had become streamlined, as if she'd shed any trace of dead weight. Which probably included *him*. And her eyes... Behind the careful distance in their mocha depths was a sadness that hadn't been there before, almost as if they'd switched places and she was now the lost one.

He neutralized his expression. He wasn't supposed to feel anything toward her, anyway. Nothing but tenderness for the time she'd soothed his pain. And he should sign up for some of that oceanfront property in Arizona, too, while he was deluding himself. Loss swamped him and his entire body clenched as if trying to hold off emotions suspiciously akin to grief.

Beside him, Noah nudged his arm, then looked pointedly at Diego's hand. "You may want to switch to something harder. And not in a glass container."

"I'm fine." And definitely delusional.

"Just talk to her."

Diego's mouth went dry. He'd love to do more than talk. Anything but talk, actually. He and Becca had always communicated just fine between the sheets. But, words? There hadn't been any need. She'd seemed to understand what he was thinking and feeling, without even asking. He couldn't say the same on his end.

No wonder he'd avoided serious relationships. They were hard work.

Noah smirked. "I'm sure she doesn't bite."

The image that slammed through Diego's brain like a charging rhino brought a grim smile to his lips and heat to his groin. Becca had bitten him once, but it hadn't been in anger or defense. And she'd quickly licked and kissed the tender area. "I'll think about it."

"Think fast, big boy. Incoming at eight o'clock."

Sure enough, Becca was headed his way.

BECCA THREADED HER WAY THROUGH THE CROWD AND STOPPED TWO feet from Diego. Noah greeted her, but quickly excused himself, probably sensing the tension between her and Diego. The noise level prevented her from keeping any more space between them and still having a conversation. His coffee-brown eyes were impenetrable.

"Glad you could make it," he said.

Was he being sarcastic because of her tardiness? She couldn't tell. Which shocked her, since she'd always been able to read him. In her head, Sulu's voice from *Star Trek* ordered, "Shields up." His distance was her fault, entirely, after how she'd left things. Part of her was relieved. This was how it had to be—shuttered expressions and inane chitchat. At least it was better than the uncontainable grief she used to see in his eyes.

In fact, he was looking good, his honey skin practically glowing. Gold and diamond cufflinks flashed as he lifted his beer to his lips, reminding her of the other reason she was sticking to safe topics. Was he living the high life with payoffs from the Circle? Could he really betray his fellow officers for money? She hadn't thought so, but he certainly looked tougher, edgier. Harder.

"Wouldn't miss this," she said.

"Guess something held you up, then?"

"Guess so."

And she might have dragged her feet a bit once she'd returned to her hotel room. Selina's words naming Diego as a Circle minion within the NYPD had plagued Becca for the entire train trip back to the city. Selina had sounded so certain about the name, but she had to be wrong.

Unless Becca didn't know Diego as well as she'd thought. After all, they'd only had two weeks together and the defensive, emotionless man standing before her now wasn't the man she'd known. The man who'd cried in her arms, mourning his niece's death. Besides, it wasn't as if it would be the first time Becca had been dangerously wrong about a man.

Her nerve faltered, and she almost looked back at Matt for help. But Brother Number Four was on the opposite end of the room, chatting with SSAM's receptionist. Matt would have Becca's back in a New York minute—if she'd told him anything about Diego and her weakness for him. But she hadn't. Back in college, she'd shed that young, naïve woman who depended on her family for backup. Now she played things close to the chest. Still, her parents and four older brothers were there for her when she needed them. Matt certainly hadn't given her any issues when she'd asked him to fly out to accompany her to the wedding festivities this weekend. Then again, he might be sticking close to her given the release of her Colossal Mistake from jail last week. Matt was the only person on earth who knew about it.

"You look well," she admitted to Diego. Did her voice sound over-bright? Was her smile shaky? Lord, she'd imagined seeing him again so many times, you'd think she'd have it down pat.

You're an actress playing a part. Saucy. Confident. You've done this before. She was so good at pretending everything was okay. She'd even psyched herself up to approach him immediately, rather than spend the entire weekend waiting, wondering if he'd talk to her.

"Time heals all wounds, right?" His voice was melted chocolate drizzled over her body. Her skin prickled painfully as it awakened like a numb limb—her body, asleep for months, shaken to full awareness.

She looked toward the bartender as he came to their side of the bar. "A shot of *anejo*."

In her peripheral vision, Diego raised his eyebrows. If he

thought she needed the hard stuff to steel her nerves, then too bad. Something had to get her through this interminable weekend.

"So, what kept you?" Diego asked.

"Duty called."

Something that might have been concern flashed in his eyes. A second later, it was gone. Maybe she'd imagined it.

"What job are you working in New York? Or maybe it was a different kind of duty that kept you." His gaze slid to Matt and he slugged back a swallow of beer.

Jealousy or disdain? Whatever it was, Diego's assumption gave her a layer of protection from him. Let him believe her brother was a romantic interest. She could keep this friendly yet impersonal.

"I should get back." She'd take the out he'd given her.

He raised his brows. "So, that's it? That's all you have to say?"

You scare me. Or, rather, the hormones that slammed through her when she saw him scared her. "I'm fresh out of chitchat."

He wouldn't like the questions burning in her brain. *How the hell did your name come to be associated with the Circle, especially when you're trying to rebuild your career at the NYPD?* She wanted to shake the answer out of him, but there were so many reasons to hold her tongue. She didn't have that kind of connection with him anymore, for one. Not after how she'd left. And she needed to talk to Damian about this new information first. Besides, this wasn't the place to address things with Diego, and if he was a mole, she certainly didn't want to tip her hand. She'd rather do some poking around to confirm or deny the accusation without his input.

"Then I suppose you should just disappear. That is your MO, isn't it?"

Ouch. Where was that damn tequila? The bartender was busy filling a server's tray. Becca was ready to turn and abandon her quest for alcohol when Diego leaned close and spoke again, his voice warm with shared secrets. "I remember a time you couldn't get enough of me."

She jerked back. "You want to go *there, now?*"

He shrugged. "I'm fresh out of *chitchat.*"

"I'm surprised you noticed I left. What we had was a nice bit of fun, but that was all." The hitch in her voice belied the casualness of her reply. And she was having trouble meeting his intense gaze. Thank God her tequila had arrived. Rather than take her time sipping it, as she would have liked, she decided to shoot it and retreat. But she caught a glimpse of Diego's face as she turned to leave. His honey-toned skin had flushed pink. His attention was locked on her throat. What had she done wrong now?

He blinked and his shields slid back into place. "Yeah, fun. Nice catching up with you." He toasted her with his beer and meandered away.

She should be happy he was letting her off the hook by not grilling her for answers she wasn't prepared to give. So why did she feel so damn disappointed?

When Becca returned to Matt's side, he frowned toward Diego but quickly regained his easygoing manner. "Catherine's been keeping me entertained while you were chatting up that Dwayne Johnson lookalike."

Becca stifled a snort. Diego wasn't that muscular. Sure, he was hard in all the right places, and, physically, a close second to the hunky actor but... She pulled on a mask of indifference as she realized what Matt was doing. Fishing. Ever the protective older brother, Matt was trying to get a reaction out of her, to judge how much she cared about Diego and probe for information on her love life.

Ex-love life.

She turned to Catherine, looking for backup. "Be careful. My brother thinks movie heroes should be worshipped. Action movies are his passion. He can recite every line from *Aliens*. Is that what he's been boring you with?"

Catherine herself had a certain movie-star elegance about her.

Tall, willowy and strawberry-blonde, she could have been Nicole Kidman's younger sister.

"Hardly," Catherine said. "He asked me about SSAM."

"Ah," Becca said. "Your favorite topic." If Damian was the brain of the operation, Catherine was the heart. She lived and breathed her job and cared for all the employees like family.

"She was full of useful information." Matt's eyes were concerned as they shifted to Becca. "She told me what you do on a daily basis." Catherine blushed guiltily.

Becca frowned. "I've told you what I do."

"Yeah, but I guess I never really listened."

She scoffed. "Well, there's a shocker. I should have put you in a headlock while I recited my job description."

But Matt wasn't in the mood for her teasing. "It's not like you willingly share the details of your life." A look passed between them and Becca knew he was thinking about the nightmare he'd helped her with in college. He was privy to that experience only because she'd been desperate for help, the kind of legal help her newly minted lawyer-brother could provide. "But I can see why you downplay the risk level. Mom and Dad would have had simultaneous coronaries if they'd heard about some of the risks you've taken."

She'd definitely been gone talking to Diego too long. How much had Catherine told him? The tequila rolled in her empty stomach and she reached for an appetizer off a passing tray. "Well, security experts—"

"Or bodyguards," Catherine added.

"—have to be prepared for anything," Becca finished. "It's my job. But Mom and Dad don't need to know what I'm truly up against. Really, it's not that dangerous on a daily basis."

"Just on occasion." Matt's knuckles brushed her neck as he reached out and affectionately tugged on the end of her hair. He'd teased that she'd cut it short so that her brothers could no longer use it against her. He was only partly wrong. The haircut had been a reflection of her transformation. The new Becca had emerged from a cocoon, and only she knew what it had cost her. Well, Matt had some idea. He knew about the man who'd been released on parole last week—and what that man had done to her life, shaping it irrevocably.

Concern etched her brother's forehead. As a lawyer, he was likely considering what he knew about her past and how it connected with this new information about her career choice.

Becca's chin rose into the air. "I can hold my own."

"I don't doubt it," Matt said with all seriousness. "I'm still glad I'm here, though, after the week you've had."

Becca shot him a meaningful look, using nonverbal cues to tell him to shut up. She didn't want to discuss this in front of Catherine.

Mischief sparked in Matt's eyes, but he backed away from the subject. "I'm certain you can take care of yourself. Speaking for all the Haney men, we've taught you well, grasshopper."

At the familiar reference, Becca smiled. But when Vanessa's melodic laugh drew her attention to a group of people several feet away, Becca's gaze collided with Diego's and her smile faded. When Matt tugged at her hair again to get her attention, Diego's mouth tightened.

Matt eyed his empty drink. "I think I'll get a refill. Anything for you two?"

Catherine shook her head.

"Tequila shot," Becca called as he walked away.

"Diego looks like he wants to devour you," Catherine said. "Or beat up Matt."

"Maybe he just ate a bad shrimp."

"He doesn't know Matt's your brother, does he?"

"No. And it works for me, so let's just let it go." Deep down, Becca felt pathetic. Juvenile tricks weren't going to satisfy the hunger. That beast wanted to be fed and had developed a taste for one man, and one man alone. Now that the man was near, nothing else would do. She'd have to stuff the beast back in its cage until she left on Sunday.

She snuck a look toward the circle of people chatting around Diego. He was immersed in conversation with Noah. Diego's mother was nearby, too, which reminded her she should have asked Diego how his family was coping, but doing so would have admitted she thought of them more often than she was comfortable with, or opened her up to rejection.

The past was best left in the past. They'd found mutual satisfaction—Diego had used her, she had used him. And when her heart became involved, it had been time to skip town.

Bodyguard, protect thyself.

A hand at her elbow brought her attention back. Her boss had approached without notice. "Could I have a moment alone with you?" Damian Manchester's gaze was apologetic as it landed on Catherine. "It'll just be a moment."

Catherine waved them away. Sixty years old and still trim and fit, Damian Manchester cut a fine figure in his tuxedo as he led Becca to the fringe of the room. He turned to face her, the lines around his eyes and mouth more pronounced than usual, likely due to the added stress of the past couple months, when old wounds that had long scarred over had been freshly sliced open.

A shadow lurked in his eyes. "Sorry to pull you away."

"It's okay. It sounds important."

"We seem to have acquired a unique type of fan. In fact, that's what he calls himself. The SSAM Fan." His gaze swept their surroundings.

Becca dropped her voice. "Is someone stalking you?"

"Not really stalking. I'm not sure how to categorize him. He's contacted me repeatedly—text messages, emails, news clippings..."

"How long has this been going on?"

"A couple years, but it always seemed harmless, until this past week."

"*Years?* What happened this past week that was so different?"

"He mentioned you in his last email."

"Me?"

"Let's talk at breakfast tomorrow," he said hastily as Vanessa and Noah made their way to them. "I wanted to give you a heads up, just in case." Obviously, Damian wanted to keep the SSAM Fan low key for now, probably out of respect for the happy nature of the weekend's events.

She smiled and talked about the wedding with Vanessa and Noah while her mind raced with Damian's new information. What exactly had the SSAM Fan said that would involve her?

"What's the scoop?" Catherine's brow knitted in concern as Becca rejoined her minutes later. As their mother hen, she had a sixth sense for whenever one of her chicks, including Damian, was in trouble. "Is there something new in Samantha's case?"

"I wish, but no." *Except my ex-lover might be accepting bribes from the organization involved in her disappearance.* Becca wouldn't tell Catherine about that yet, however. Technically, there wasn't anything new in the investigation until she got the facts straight.

The tinkling sound of a fork against glass brought the crowd to silence as Noah claimed everyone's attention. "I'd like to make a toast to my bride."

"She's not married yet," someone in the crowd shouted and everyone laughed.

"She will be." Noah's gaze turned hot as it landed on Vanessa. "I know a good thing when I see it and she's the best thing that's ever happened to me. There's no way I'm letting her go."

"And there's no way I'd leave you," Vanessa replied.

Becca's heart clenched as she recalled how she'd snuck out of Diego's apartment all those months ago. Leaving as if they'd done something criminal. As if what they'd shared were dirty.

But it was *her*, and her conscience, that was dirty.

CHAPTER 3

Despite his best efforts to remain disengaged, Diego was aware of every move Becca made. Every inhalation of breath, every curve of her lips, every subtle glance in his direction was on his radar—including the three minutes during which her boss pulled her aside. Damian Manchester had come to New York to help Diego catch Natalee's killer last summer. The man was typically intense, but tonight his body language indicated something more was going on. Had Becca truly been working a case earlier?

During Noah's toast, Becca seemed melancholy. The speech touched Diego, too, and he wanted... Hell, he didn't know what he wanted. To say the words that would clear the shimmer of tears in her eyes? To pull her to him and console her in the way they'd always communicated well? His body rejoiced at the thought, cheering him on, knowing what lush comfort lay in her arms. Not that she'd want to rekindle what they had, or that it would comfort her in the least.

She didn't want *him*, period. Not anymore.

Besides, his blood turned to lava whenever he touched her, so embracing her, holding what he wanted knowing he'd have to release it again, would be the equivalent of masochistic torture. Jesus, the woman tied him in knots. Yet, the moment she moved with a hurried gait toward the ladies' room, he followed as if drawn to her by an invisible string.

He lingered outside the restroom door, pretending to examine the artwork on the wall when people walked by so he wouldn't look like a total creep. Finally, Becca emerged. Shit, she had been crying. Most of her mascara had been wiped away and her lashes were spiky. She still looked like sex on a stick, and he berated himself for even thinking about that at a time like this. But with Becca, it had always been that way. Instant chemical reaction.

She came to a sudden stop when she spotted him. Her surprise dissipated as she stiffened her spine. "It's just allergies. Something's in the air."

"Good to know. Can we talk?"

"Sure. I'm sure there'll be some down time at the reception tomorrow night."

He knew that trick. Had used it on women to distract them or put them off, and then they never talked because he'd found a way to leave by then. The irony that the tables had been turned was not lost on him.

"Now's good for me." He arched a brow in challenge. He'd never known her to back down from a dare, but maybe he didn't really know her. Still, she'd been there for him in those awful, dark days following Natalee's death. And he'd been a dick to her when she finally showed up tonight. He'd pulled on his tough-guy cloak and acted like he was done with her. She deserved better, despite the way she'd left him. At the time, he'd called and left her a message after she returned to Chicago, but she hadn't called him back. Ever. What if she'd changed since then? She definitely seemed to have sharper edges. The thought saddened him.

Becca looked toward the party. "Now's not good for me. Besides, we already talked."

"Not really. A few minutes are all I'm asking for. Unless you're afraid." Goading her was a sure way to invoke her stubborn pride. "Or I could show up at your hotel room later, if that's more convenient."

She scowled. "Fine. You have two minutes, but outside."

"It's cold as a witch's teat out there."

"It's that or nothing."

"I get it. You don't want your date to see us alone together, even if it's just talking." The thought both pleased and irritated him in equal measure.

She opened her mouth to reply, then snapped it closed and strode to the hostess by the door. Diego caught up to her as she handed over the claim for her coat. He reached around her to do the same, catching a whiff of Becca's citrus scent. It immediately transported him back to a night they'd spent in each other's arms at a cheap motel—and the early-morning shower that had left the tantalizing smell of her soap filling the tiny room. His mouth watered, remembering the creaminess of her skin, richer in flavor than the gourmet appetizers they'd just indulged in. Other parts of him grew uncomfortably hard with awareness. He distracted himself by observing the playful way the light gleamed like white flames against the tips and curls of Becca's hair.

The attendant returned with their coats and Diego held the front door open for Becca. "After you."

She narrowed her eyes at him. "Why do I get the sense I'm Little Red Riding Hood? Lose the wolfish grin, baby cakes. I pack a silver bullet, just in case."

She sauntered ahead of him. Because her coat only extended to her waistline, he enjoyed a nice view of her tight ass.

"You might have to use that bullet," Diego muttered to her backside. He hadn't yet applied himself to scaling the walls she had erected, but she'd called what they'd shared *fun*, downgrading their time together to a quick fling. If that was the case, why not have a bit more *fun* this weekend? Remaining aloof sure as hell wasn't working.

Once upon a time, they'd had a special connection— one he hadn't had before and definitely not since. Was there a way to get that back? His colleagues viewed him as a slug, treated him like dirt, and Herrera's judgmental grimace had haunted him all evening. Diego was tired of people not seeing the real him. Becca had given him the freedom to be authentic last summer. Maybe he could find that again, maybe she could save him again, even if just for a couple nights.

It was even colder than he'd predicted. Inside his coat, he hunched his shoulders to trap the warmth. Becca stopped several feet away from the front door, within a ring of light from a street lamp, her moist breath creating a fog. She would be frozen solid soon, and was probably banking on that as an excuse to get away from him faster. On the plus side, the cold kept down the pedestrian traffic, so they were alone.

"Okay, so, talk." She tilted her face up to him, the city lights giving her skin an ethereal glow. Her expression was guarded, but she'd clearly been hurting earlier.

"I'm sorry I was an ass," he said.

Surprised, she laughed. "Okay."

"I don't even know why I acted that way. I didn't know what to say, I guess."

"I know the feeling." Her muttered words gave him hope. If he could raze her defenses, maybe he'd get to the truth.

"What happened between us last July? I thought we were having a good time, and then you were gone before I could blink. You didn't even return my call."

She frowned. "And you would have preferred a clingy girlfriend? I had to get back to work in Chicago, you had to get back to your life here in New York. We both knew going in that what we had was a temporary thing. A distraction. That we would eventually walk away. No harm, no foul."

Diego fisted his hands in his pockets as she rattled off cliché after cliché, making their affair into a moment in time that was a cliché. Walking away had always worked for him in the past, but not now. Not with her. He might not be doing much right lately, but everything with her had been perfect. How could he make her remember how good it had been? All he knew was her lips were turning blue and, despite his frustration, he wanted to kiss the rosy warmth back into them.

She shook her head. "That's not the answer."

"What?"

"Falling into bed. Sex. The way you're looking at me. Now that we're within fifty feet of each other again, I'm supposed to help you scratch some kind of itch?"

Something like that. He'd never craved a woman like he craved her—her body, her mind, her smile. Hell, he'd missed her. Missed what they'd shared.

"You don't feel this...whatever it is...between us?" Maybe she hadn't been as attracted to him as he had been to her.

"Arousal is a temporary condition. You'll survive. And you'll get over it." Something chimed in her coat pocket and she reached inside, pulling out her cell phone. "I've got to go." Staring down at the screen, she moved past him.

Sensing he had to say more or he'd never get another opportunity, he reached out. "Wait."

But she'd already frozen, so when he tugged on her arm, she stumbled backward into him. She quickly pushed away and regained her feet. But it wasn't him she was looking at. She was staring at her phone, her breathing irregular as the color drained from her cheeks. Her instant alarm was so un-Becca-like that adrenaline pumped into his system, preparing him to face the unknown danger.

As if reorienting herself to her surroundings, Becca whipped her head left and right, glancing down the sidewalk, then narrowed her gaze at the door to the gallery. The tiny furrow that always made him want to kiss her between the eyes deepened as she concentrated once more on her phone's screen. As he moved to look over her shoulder, she shoved the phone into her pocket and out of sight.

"What's wrong?" he asked.

"I have to find Damian."

"He left the party shortly after your discussion." Mentally, he kicked himself for revealing how much he'd been keeping tabs on her, but she didn't seem to notice.

She raised her hand as if she could flag a cab on the deserted side road. Realizing the futility, she spun on her heel and walked with purpose toward the main street a couple buildings away, where there was actually some traffic.

"Talk to me, damn it." The very bad feeling expanded and, along with the icy air, filled his chest as he jogged.

His strides were twice the length of hers, yet he had to hustle to keep up. Tension radiated off her. Her cheeks were flushed now from running, her breath clouding the air in quick puffs. Her eyes were bright as she stopped suddenly at the next street and held up a hand to flag a cab.

Diego maneuvered her so she wasn't so close to the curb, where cars were zipping by fast enough to pull her into traffic. He stood in front of her, forcing her to notice him. "What's going on?"

"Nothing." She exhaled and quivered.

Diego sensed it wasn't due to the cold, though a distinct chill was seeping into his limbs. "Bullshit. Show me."

She must have heard the determination in his voice because she reached into her pocket and held out the phone. There was a text message from an unknown sender.

My admiration for you knows no bounds. We're on the same team, fighting the good fight. Keep doing your important work for Damian, and for Sam, like this afternoon. Ever yours, The SSAM Fan.

A picture was attached, but before he could click to enlarge it and get a closer look, she jerked the phone from his hands.

"Who's the SSAM Fan? What's in the picture?" All he'd seen was what looked like red and yellow writing on a window. Clearly, it meant something to her.

Seemingly oblivious to his questions, she pushed past him as a cab pulled up. She climbed in and gave the driver the address for the hotel where she and the other wedding guests were staying.

Becca scowled at Diego as he slid in beside her. "Nobody invited you."

"I'm not sure what just happened out there, but I'm not leaving you alone. You're shaking like a leaf." He yanked the door closed and the cab driver zipped into traffic.

"Suit yourself. Crap. I need to call my...date."

The fact that the fight had gone out of her told him all he needed to know. Whatever the message meant, she was rattled. But she wasn't leaning on the guy whose ear she'd whispered in at the gallery. In fact, she'd forgotten all about him. Diego's concern for her stifled the fleeting triumph.

"I'm surprised he didn't come out to check on you." He looked out the back window at the sidewalk where they'd stood moments ago. No sign of the Viking.

Ignoring his jab at her date, she dialed her cell phone and held it to her ear. "Hey, I had to head out... Yeah, I'm fine. Just something work-related. Sorry I had to ditch you." Her voice had turned soft.

Shit. Maybe he had competition after all.

Competition? Was he really thinking of pressing his luck with Becca and pursuing a fling? Deep down, he realized he'd been hoping for a chance to recapture that happiness, even if only for a couple days.

"I'll call you later," Becca said into the phone. "It would be better if you met me there."

Met her where? At her hotel room? He gritted his teeth as jealousy reared its ugly green head.

"Love you, too," Becca told the Viking.

Diego's heart plummeted. So much for competition. He wasn't even in the race.

BEFORE THE CAB PULLED UP TO THE HOTEL, BECCA MADE A QUICK call to Damian to let him know about the text from the SSAM Fan. Aware that Diego was listening, she left out the part about the attached photo. Her heart was still pounding with the image she'd glimpsed. The message was extremely personal. The Fan had obviously known about her meeting at the diner earlier. Which meant Selina could be in danger and Becca had no way to warn her except via email. *Shit.*

Could it have been Diego? Did he know Becca was investigating the Circle and was meeting with the one woman who'd escaped the crime organization's grasp? But he'd been at the wedding rehearsal while Becca was returning from Hoboken, and he'd been standing right in front of her when she'd received the text. Then again, he could have alerted somebody within the Circle. The pressure behind her eyes built to a crescendo as scenarios played out in her head.

She and Damian had arranged to meet in her room, so she had to ditch Diego. She opened her door the moment the cab came to a stop.

"Take him wherever he wants to go." She handed the driver some cash and bolted from the car.

"Like hell." Diego followed her onto the sidewalk and the cab pulled away, leaving them standing there. Together.

"I'm safe. It's been a long day, so I'm tucking in for the night. You can go home now."

But his feet were planted in a determined stance. "You must have forgotten to engage your cone of silence in the cab because I overheard everything you said to Damian. I know you're meeting him. So I know you're lying to me about *tucking in for the night.*" He took a step closer to her. "I hate lies."

And yet her source had named him as a mole for the powerful organized crime ring, which meant his career, his white-knight charade, his dedication to family and a better society, and his entire life was a lie. Her brain refused to wrap around the consequences of her misjudgment in character.

She held her phone up. "You didn't have someone send me this." It was half statement, half question, and her doubts were clear.

Diego frowned. "No. Why would I? Tell me what's going on."

"It's none of your business."

"It is when you're accusing me of something, something that obviously scares you." He stood there, arms crossed, feet spread wide, as immovable as a boulder.

She took a deep breath and blew it out, the heat of her breath mixing with his. "I don't know what's going on."

"But Damian does?"

She hoped to hell he did. At least he'd be able to tell her whether this latest message matched the characteristics of the SSAM Fan who'd been sending him things for years. How had he known about Hoboken, and that the meeting with Selina had been about Samantha?

Seeing her shiver, Diego reached out to take her arm and turn her toward the door. "Let's go inside. I think we both need to talk to Damian."

She didn't want to stand in the cold arguing with Diego any more than he did. Besides, even if he barreled his way past all her roadblocks, by Sunday afternoon she'd be back in Chicago and he'd go on with his life here.

He reached ahead of her to hold the glass door to the hotel open. She walked past him, through the lobby and to the elevator without looking back, but she felt him behind her the whole time.

She pushed the up button. "You can walk me to my room, but you're not staying for the meeting."

"We'll see."

The confidence in his voice, reinforced by a layer of steely determination, told her she wouldn't be getting rid of him easily. She knew that tone, and resigned herself to letting Diego stick close until Damian showed up and asked him to leave.

Once inside the elevator, she tried to ignore Diego's warmth. His familiar spicy, masculine scent had filled the cab, now it filled this small space. It seemed to fill *her*, more with each breath. Like sweet torture, it was both soothing and arousing.

As the elevator continued its ascent, a flash of memory hit her. They'd been on their way to a penthouse apartment. Adrenaline had been running high all day as they set a trap for Natalee's killer. Alone together in that elevator, Diego had turned to her and pressed her body into the corner, his hands pressed against the wall on either side of her head as his lips brushed her neck, her pulse point, along her jaw, until she was begging him to take her mouth with his. When he obliged, she plunged her fingers through his thick hair and held on for dear life. As the elevator approached its destination, he'd pulled away long enough to look down into her eyes. Something had passed between them, something unspoken and intangible that had warned her she'd better guard her heart.

For all the good it had done her.

Running had saved her, but in the short term she'd paid the price. Months later, the passion had become a dulled memory. Or so she'd thought. Her skin flushed with heat. She glanced to the side and saw a tight smile pulling at Diego's lips. Was he recalling the same moment?

The doors slid open and she moved down the hall to her room. Once inside, she hung her coat in the closet but kept a grip on her phone. She purposely avoided looking at the king-size bed that dominated the room like the elephant nobody wanted to acknowledge. She'd try like hell to ignore it, and the memory of things they'd once done in a similar bed.

She spun to face him, her hands on her hips. "See? No boogeymen here. You can leave now."

"I think I'll stick around. Besides, we never finished our conversation."

Becca shrugged as if it didn't matter, hoping Damian would arrive soon. Her defenses had taken a beating tonight, barraged with memories, hormones and more time with Diego than she'd bargained for. She needed an opportunity to regain her footing. She met Diego's gaze in the mirror above the desk. "So, let's finish it."

His eyes sparked with something unidentifiable. "Are you done avoiding me yet?"

"Avoiding? Hardly. You're standing in the middle of my hotel room." She edged past him, past the elephant of a bed, to the closet and snagged her yoga pants and a T-shirt. No way was she going to be any more uncomfortable around this man than she already was. And she was tired of the looks he was giving her attire. As if he wanted to peel her dress off and lick her from head to toe like a popsicle.

"I'm going to change," she announced.

Despite his knowing laugh, she disappeared into the bathroom to search for her sanity. And to check the text message and picture again without Diego hovering. The Fan had definitely known about the Hoboken diner. The window was unmistakable proof. She quivered with anger, wondering how she could check up on Selina to be sure she remained unharmed. Hastily, she typed an email on her phone, asking Selina to let her know ASAP that she was safe. Then she hurried to change, knowing Damian would arrive at any moment. As she stepped out of the bathroom, she might as well have been naked. Diego's gaze swept her body like a security scanner.

"I'm ready. Talk."

He surprised her with a sigh of defeat. "We can't go back, can we?"

"To last summer? That was one of the worst times of your life."

"On some levels, yes. On others..." His voice drifted off and his gaze grew hot enough to melt silver. "At least we were comfortable with each other. We could communicate back then. Or maybe I was wrong about that? Maybe I read too much into what was just sex, just *fun*."

Now he was throwing her words back at her. It stung more than she'd admit.

"No, we can't go back."

He stepped closer. "What about forward?"

"What do you mean?"

"We were good together. We could be again, even if just for a little while." The heat in his eyes showed he was serious. A couple extra nights in Diego's arms? It sounded like heaven—and hell, if he turned out to be a dirty cop.

A knock sounded at her door, saving her from making a decision. A grim, haggard Damian stood at her door in jeans and a polo shirt. It was startling, as she was used to seeing him in his tailored suits, a uniform of sorts, a carryover from his corporate days when he'd become wealthy and had everything a man of power could want—including a beautiful wife and child.

Diego's heat warmed her back as he shifted to stand behind her. Damian's gaze slid to the other man before he turned a questioning look on Becca.

She shrugged. "Diego was there when I received the text. Haven't been able to shake him since."

"Good to see you again," Damian said to Diego.

"Good to see you, too, sir." Diego shook the other man's hand.

"Your family well?"

"Thanks to SSAM's help, we're doing better. Still dealing with the grief, but it's a bit easier knowing we brought Natalee justice."

Damian's eyes flickered. He knew all about dealing with the heartbreak left behind when some monster stole the person you loved. He was still due his share of justice.

"I'd like to stay, if you don't mind," Diego said.

"I think your expertise would be helpful," Damian said. "Especially since you were there with Becca tonight."

"Not exactly *with* me," Becca said.

"Still, I saw the message." Diego raised his brows at her, daring her to argue against him *and* her boss.

She turned to the more reasonable of the two men. "You sure you want to share what you know about the SSAM Fan with an outsider?"

"I'm sure," Damian said. "It's time to lay it all out on the table. Especially if the Fan's starting to contact my agents."

She wanted to hear Damian's story, but if talk came back around to Selina and the Circle, and what the Fan might know about her meeting today, including that Diego might be a Circle informant, she'd have to find a way to deflect. Something told her to hold on to that nugget.

"Have a seat." Resigned to having Diego sit in on at least part of the meeting, Becca gestured to the desk chair and the only other chair in the room—right next to the bed. Damian took the one at the desk. Unfortunately, that left Diego to take the other one. She sat down on the bed and crossed her legs under her.

Becca handed Damian her phone with the anonymous text loaded. "I'm glad you mentioned you had a stalker who called himself the SSAM Fan or I wouldn't have known what to think of this."

"Stalker?" Diego echoed.

"He's been more fan than stalker, so far." Damian reached into the pocket of his jeans and pulled out a folded paper, then handed it to Becca. "This is a copy of his latest email. I've been documenting everything he sends, keeping copies in a file so I have them handy, if they're ever needed."

Becca met his steel-gray eyes. "As in, if he turns out to be one of those serial killers who likes to follow the investigations of the crimes they've committed?"

Damian nodded. "Sometimes they even contact the people hunting them, which is why I kept track of everything from my—our—*fan*. But I didn't sense malicious intent until recently."

"What changed?" Diego asked.

He gestured to the paper in Becca's hand. "That was sent to me a couple days ago. In the past, he's sent me emails and clips from news shows or blog posts, usually trying to help solve murders he'd seen in the press or heard we were working on. But this...this is different. Much more personal."

Becca unfolded the paper and read the note. Diego shifted closer to read over her shoulder.

Life is not always roses...especially white ones... sometimes it's just thorns. But then, you, of all people, know that. Justice, God's will—those are the real reasons we continue on.

Your SSAM Fan.

Though the words were relatively innocuous, the hairs on the back of her neck stood at attention. And this time, it wasn't due to Diego's proximity. She passed the note to Diego so he could get a closer look.

"Does anybody else know about this?" she asked.

Damian looked troubled. "A couple times over the years, I've shown the communications to Lorena. We agreed to keep a close eye on the level and type of contact from him. But, frankly, it wasn't worth our time to follow up until now."

Lorena was a veteran profiler, or mindhunter. Her psychology training and years of experience with the FBI Behavioral Analysis Unit prior to her work for SSAM gave her unique insight into the minds of criminals.

"What does she have to say about this note?" Becca asked.

"On the surface, the words are supportive, but there's a dark undercurrent. And he's obviously been following me, and now, you."

"Following you?" Diego asked. "How do you know?"

Something shifted in Damian's eyes. "The reference to white

roses... I leave white roses on Sam's grave every weekend before church."

Becca's heart squeezed for him. "So this guy really is a stalker, not just a fan?"

"With this note, and now yours, I'm starting to think so. He would have had to follow me from where I live now, close to the Loop, to where I used to live. Sam is buried in All Saints Parish near Kenilworth. But I haven't gone to her grave in at least three weeks." A flicker of pain tightened his features.

He'd petitioned to have Sam's body exhumed to do further testing, to determine if the previous identification had been falsified. Through business and through SSAM, Damian had extensive connections in the Chicago area and was able to get the exhumation approved. Years ago, a positive ID had been made based on the clothing scraps that had been found on the skeletal remains. But now, DNA testing would be done. The current theory was that once the Circle had realized they'd taken a girl with a powerful father, they'd covered their tracks in a hurry by making it look like a serial killer who'd been active in the area had killed her. As to whether they'd killed Samantha, or some other girl they'd dressed in her clothes, it would be several days before Damian saw any definitive results.

Damian's gaze was miserable as it landed on Becca. "This person's been watching me for a while, and now it seems he's expanding his scope to include you."

Diego scowled at Becca. "What does he mean by the text he sent you, when he refers to where you were this afternoon? Is that what the picture's about?"

She'd wondered how long it would take before they'd focus on that. And she didn't want to share her thoughts until she knew where Diego stood with the Circle. "The picture is the outside of a diner I was in earlier today. I was following a lead."

"For a case you're working here in New York?"

"It's for Sam's case, in Chicago, but my lead was here." And that was all she'd give him.

His frown deepened as he realized she'd just erected a roadblock.

Damian cleared his throat to break the sudden tension in the room. "Maybe you should stop. It's too dangerous to investigate—"

Becca threw a hand up to halt him. "I don't want to go into that until we're alone. Maybe at our breakfast meeting?"

Damian must have sensed something in her tone or nonverbal cues, because he immediately stood. "Yes, let's plan on that."

Beside her, Diego had stiffened as if his whole body was going into red-alert mode. "What aren't you telling me? What's too dangerous?"

Finding out your ex-lover may be working for a violent crime syndicate.

Damian stood with a grim smile. "I'm sure Becca will fill you in if she feels it's necessary. Good night."

She lifted her brows at Diego, an invitation to follow Damian's example and leave, but he remained stubbornly in his seat. At six-foot-two and at least two hundred pounds of solid muscle, she'd have to call hotel security to budge him unless she could convince him to walk out on his own.

"I'll see you tomorrow, sir," she told Damian at the door.

"Keep your wits about you." His gaze shifted to Diego and she knew he was advising this in all areas of her life.

"Always." She closed the door behind him and turned to Diego. "It's been a long night and I'd like to get some sleep."

Diego ignored her suggestion. "What aren't you telling me?"

"Nothing you need to know about." She shrugged, hoping it was true, hoping he didn't have a connection to the Circle.

He rose in one fluid motion and practically stalked toward her. Her pulse thumped so hard in her ears he could probably hear it. "You helped me once. I want to help you. *Let* me help you."

She read the earnestness in his eyes and nearly caved. But there was no way she could work with him. Not when she didn't trust him. And she damn sure couldn't trust herself around him. "I'll be fine. Thanks for the offer, but—"

He reached for her and laid a palm against either side of her neck. Surely he felt her pulse racing beneath his fingers. Contrary to the messages her brain was screaming, his warmth soothed the stiff muscles there. "Just accept the help." His gaze moved to her lips.

Her will was weakening. *A good offense is the best defense.*

"I can't accept help from someone I can't trust." Calmly, she issued her ultimatum. "If you want to help, first tell me how you're involved with the Circle."

CHAPTER 4

Diego had once been jolted with a Taser as part of his training at the police academy. Being on the receiving end of Becca's doubt and insinuation was ten times the shock. Her question arced through him like electricity, stunning him with a pain like no other.

He jerked his hands away from her neck and stepped back. "The Circle?" How the hell did she know about that?

But Becca, being the headstrong woman she was, didn't back down under his glare. The subtle point of her chin shot up a notch. "The group has recently been connected to Samantha's disappearance—and you've recently been connected to *them*."

He flexed his muscles, fighting not to react beneath her judgmental gaze. From any other person, he could take the accusation. Hell, he'd held up under Herrera's criticism. But not from her. They'd shared too much. More than most people shared, even if she did want to label it just plain *fun*.

You shared nothing but your grief and a passion that was bound to burn out sometime. Apparently, he'd been wrong to think they knew each other just because they'd had a few intense days together. She didn't know him at all, and he'd been desperate to see a connection that wasn't there.

She was watching him closely, her eyes widening with every second that went by, judging him unworthy. Guilty. Hell, he was, but not in the way she thought.

He took a step toward her, closing the gap. "Connected? Why would you say that?"

"I have my sources." She sank against the wall behind her. As if she could get away. As if she was afraid—of *him*. The thought halted him in his tracks and sat like a cold rock in his belly.

"I have the right to know my accuser's name."

"You do know of the Circle, then?" Her words were quiet, emotionless. As if he'd burst her last bubble of hope. He knew the feeling.

"No NYPD detective worth his salt can function without running up against them at some point." Like cockroaches, the Circle's henchmen lay low, lived in the shadows and were impossible to extinguish. Plus, they had the strength of money, international resources and decades of established trade patterns. And they were dangerous as hell. Damian was right to suggest she halt her investigation. But, God...*Sam?* Damian thought his daughter was taken by the Circle? He could only imagine the continuous loop of horrible scenarios playing in the man's head. No wonder he'd looked so tired.

"My source named you, specifically, and says you're on the Circle's side. A mole." Becca's voice faded to a whisper. Fear flickered in her eyes, wounding him to the core. She swallowed nervously.

He huffed out a humorless laugh. She believed he was involved with the worst crime ring to hold New York City—and many other cities—within its deadly grasp. Unfortunately, she was right, and he couldn't tell her the real story. Especially not if she already

distrusted him. He saw the judgment in her eyes and her precon-
ceived notions shredded him.

His words came out as a growl as he pushed them past the
tightness in his throat. "Heed Damian's advice and back away from
the Circle. Bad things happen to people who come near them." He
should know.

That little crinkle formed between her eyes. "That's it? That's
all you're going to say?"

That was all he could say, so he did the only thing he could. He
walked out the door.

LIKE A DIEHARD GEEK AT COMIC-CON, THE FAN TREMBLED WITH
the excitement of being so close to Damian and Becca, even if just
for a few moments. From the bar just off the lobby, he'd seen them
return from the rehearsal party, about a half hour apart, dressed to
the nines and looking even more amazing up close.

Had Becca received his text? He'd simply captured a photo
from the diner's website since he hadn't been able to make it to
observe the meeting itself, but the message should be clear. He
knew where she was. He wanted to help. They were in this
together.

He was dying to know what she was thinking. He only had
access to her email, since he'd paid a hacker for access to the
SSAM accounts. What had she learned at the Hoboken diner about
Samantha Manchester's disappearance? If Becca would work with
him, he could help, and become the ultimate hero in Damian's
eyes, and in hers.

But she couldn't accept his offer to partner just yet. He wasn't
making it that easy to find him. He had to protect himself, too. He
wouldn't let her find him until the conditions were just right, until
he knew beyond a doubt that he could trust her with his own
secrets.

In the meantime, he would build their anticipation until Becca and Damian were eager to receive more from him. Eager to meet him. He was tired of being behind the scenes. He wanted to belong.

He'd stumbled across the stories of SSAM's triumphs years ago. And become intrigued long before Becca had made her contributions to the team. Now that he'd watched her in action for a couple years, this little pixie seemed to be the strongest of them all. She'd get knocked down, and get right back up. He might have summoned the nerve to get on the elevator with her when she'd returned to the hotel—she seemed friendly enough that he might have been able to talk to her—but she hadn't been alone. She'd walked through the hotel entrance with a man whose glare could melt an iceberg. NYPD Detective Diego Sandoval, whom Becca had helped on a case months ago. Sandoval was also best man at the wedding, so it made sense that Becca would know him.

The twin fangs of jealousy bit him in the belly. Becca was *his* partner. It was *his* gifts that allowed him to do this, to be here, and he'd embrace them.

Just as he was about to abandon his post at the bar, Sandoval came out of the elevator, crossed the lobby and put his hand on the front door, bracing to push out into the cold, dark night. Suddenly, he dropped his hand, detoured and headed straight for him.

DIEGO TRIED TO OUTRUN THE SHARP-EDGED BETRAYAL RIPPING UP his insides, but when faced with the cold blackness outside the hotel windows, he decided getting a drink while he thought things through might be a better idea than letting adrenaline control his actions. And if Becca happened to come downstairs to do the same thing, maybe they could hash this out.

He couldn't stand her thinking the worst of him, but what would telling her the truth do? Maybe build her trust, but for what? She'd be leaving to return to Chicago in a little over twenty-four hours. Telling her could possibly ruin his cover, a cover he'd spent months building. Why couldn't she just trust him? Had he done something to make her leave last summer, something that had destroyed their connection?

He took a seat at the end of the bar where he could have some privacy, laying his coat over the barstool next to him to ensure nobody would sit beside him. "Scotch, neat," he ordered.

Since it was Friday night, the bar was relatively busy though it was near midnight. But the crowd was sedate, the music mellow jazz, which suited his mood. Tomorrow, he could blast his hard rock while pumping iron, but tonight he had to get through this anger and focus on the shipment coming at six in the morning.

He pulled his phone out of his pocket and dialed the number he'd memorized for emergencies only. He didn't want to scare her, but with Becca's reference to a *source*, he had to be sure. It rang several times before a sleepy voice answered on the other side.

"Hello?"

"Selina?" A breath of relief whooshed out.

"Who's this?" Selina's voice changed to slightly alarmed.

"It's me. The guy you called your guardian angel."

"Because you wouldn't give me your name," she said, a softness in her voice now.

"I still can't. I just needed to see if you're okay."

"Yeah. Had a visitor today."

"That's why I'm calling. If she tracked you down, I'm worried other people can, too. People who aren't as nice as Becca."

"So you're on a first-name basis, huh? I'm glad to know I was right to trust her."

"You were right." Even if Becca couldn't trust him. "But please be extra careful. Call me at this number if you're not sure whether you can trust someone. I'll check them out for you."

"Why didn't you give me this number before?"

Diego took a swig of the scotch the bartender sat in front of him. "It's risky to talk to me." And he risked his own life contacting her. "What else did you tell Becca today?"

"She wanted to know my story, and I told her what I could."

Including his name, but only as a mole within the NYPD. "What, specifically, did you tell her?"

"Why? Was there something I shouldn't have?"

He sighed. "No." He hadn't told Selina his true identity all those months ago, preferring to remain her anonymous savior in case the Circle tracked her down. He never expected the person to track her down would be Becca. The attempt at misdirection had failed. He'd assumed, if the Circle got a name out of Selina, his name would only be connected with the crimes they already attributed to him. If anything, it was meant to strengthen his cover story. Instead, it had broken his tenuous bond with Becca.

"She wanted to know the details about where I'd been held, and how."

"Did you give her the address?"

When Selina spoke, he could hear the frown in her voice. "You sound worried. I checked her out. She even gave me references. She's legit."

"Oh, I know." He knew how capable Becca was of investigating, and what she'd do with that information. She'd also go to hell and back to solve a case, to catch a monster. Apparently, he was now the monster. If she was planning to visit the building where Selina had been held, where the Circle held their human trafficking victims, he'd have to ensure that she'd find nothing. And that the Circle didn't find her. "Did you meet Becca at a diner?"

"Yes. I thought it'd be safe to meet in public."

That had to be the meaning of the photograph Becca had been sent, but why would the SSAM Fan send her that, with such a note? Someone was following Becca's every move. "I strongly suggest you leave town for a bit. At the very least, mix up your routine."

"I thought you said I could trust her."

"You can. But someone else found out about your meeting."

Selina cursed. "I shouldn't have taken the risk. I just wanted the Circle taken down."

"That'll happen. In the meantime, be extra vigilant." He hated scaring Selina. She'd been through so much, but a bit of fear meant to ensure survival was better than being dead.

"I will. But what about Becca? Have you warned her?"

"Let me worry about her."

He finished his call with Selina, then his drink, and scooped up his coat from the stool. A piece of paper slid to the floor and he bent to pick it up. It was a four-by-six-inch glossy photograph. The contents had his gaze snapping up to survey the people in the bar. Nobody was watching him. Nobody seemed out of place. When had this been placed here? He'd only been there ten minutes.

He gestured to the bartender. "You remember anybody coming near this area?" He indicated the two stools where he'd been sitting.

The bartender shook his head. "No, but it's a busy night."

"Thanks." Diego pulled his coat on and tucked the photo in his pocket, not taking it out again until he was on the subway. The image was of a black woman tied to a chair with duct tape over her mouth. She'd obviously been crying and had a look of such despair that Diego knew she'd been killed. She'd been aware of what was coming. He could see it in her eyes.

But where? How? Who? And why would anybody want to give this to him?

Diego turned the photo over and read the careful block writing on the back.

Unburden your conscience. Tell me no lies. A circle binds her forever...

Circle? He looked closer at the woman's upper arm, which was bare. And there was the thing he sought, the thing he feared he'd find... the circle tattoo, ringed in flames. It looked freshly imprinted, as it had been on Selina the night he'd found her in that cell. The Circle's emblem. Diego had encouraged the Circle to discontinue the human trafficking after Selina had escaped. So what was it doing on this woman? And who had left this for him?

BY THE TIME DIEGO TOOK A CAB FROM THE PARK AVENUE HOTEL TO East Harlem and walked into his apartment, he'd made the toughest decision of his life—one he hoped would protect both his career and Becca. He dialed his liaison at the Circle. The phone was answered immediately, despite the fact it was way after midnight and an important shipment was expected in less than five hours. But then, cockroaches did their best work at night.

Had the photo been left by them? Was this a test? Was he supposed to prove his loyalty by coming to them first, instead of his brothers at the NYPD?

"You've been compromised." Diego's skin crawled as it did with every tip he revealed to them.

"What?" There was a note of alarm on the other end.

"The cops know you've reopened the Cattle Call. I got a tip this evening."

"Shit, no. We haven't done that in months."

This couldn't be a dead end. "You sure?"

"Positive. You got your wires crossed. I'd know if we reopened trafficking routes. Boss has been grumbling daily about the loss in revenue. Why? What'd you hear?"

"I must have been wrong, then."

"Yeah." His liaison's laugh was like ragged stones in a rock tumbler. "You need new snitches. Guess dirty cops don't get no respect after a while, huh?"

Diego gritted his teeth and wished he could punch the guy in the face. "Yeah, well, without this dirty cop, you wouldn't have traded several million dollars in guns last week."

He'd chewed his tongue to a pulp trying to keep from saying things that would ruin his undercover mission. Part of the task force's goal was to get to the people at the top of the Circle, which meant letting their operations continue as smoothly as possible without police interruption until everything was in place. His one exception had been Selina. She had been a moment of weakness, but he didn't regret saving her. One day he wouldn't have to put up with creeps like this and he'd have the satisfaction of seeing them behind bars because he'd bitten his tongue when it counted.

The liaison grew quiet for a moment. "Boss liked what you did for us there. You'll be rewarded, especially if tomorrow goes through without a hitch."

"Now we're talking." Diego let the greed come through in his voice. "I appreciate the rewards. I'll keep the NYPD away from the shipment in the morning."

"Everything will be fine. Relax."

"I get paid not to relax when I'm on watch. Just let me know if you hear the Cattle Call is starting up again so I can watch for trouble on my end." The Cattle Call was Circle slang for human trafficking, and for the way these victims were put on display for potential buyers. The women, and sometimes children, were even branded like cattle. "In the meantime, if you have any operations going down in the Brooklyn building, I'd start the move."

His contact sighed. "Your intel's that reliable?"

Diego pulled the picture out and stared at it again. If the Cattle Call was out of commission, what was this woman's story? Though only a photo, the fear in her eyes was palpable. He thought of Becca receiving the same treatment for getting too close to the Circle. "It's reliable," he confirmed.

"I'll order them to clear out. See you at six."

Saturday, 12:25 a.m.
Chicago

As a responsible, single, attractive woman, Eve Reynolds

knew showing up at murder scenes after midnight by herself wasn't smart. But as an investigative journalist, such risks often came with the job. Besides, the scene was already populated with a couple of CPD's finest. Watching from her car as they taped off the alley across the street, she dialed her partner in crime. She nibbled on a thumbnail as she waited for him to answer.

"Yeah?" Patrick answered. "What's up?"

"Where are you?" she demanded. There was the soft sound of music in the background. Was he on a date? "I think I've got a lead on a good story. I need you here now."

"What?"

"Focus," she hissed impatiently. "I've been snapping pictures on my phone, but I need my cameraman."

"What's the story?"

"Dead prostitute in an alley."

Patrick snorted. "Doesn't sound like breaking news."

She ignored his jaded tone. "The Circle's involved."

"The Circle?" Finally, Patrick seemed to give her his full attention. "What the hell are you doing in their territory in the middle of the night?"

"Following a lead." Eve had to bite back impatience.

"I can't make it," he said. "We can cover the story later. You don't need pictures from the scene."

"Bullshit. It's not that far from your house and it'll take them a while to process the alley for evidence. This story is big. National-news-network big. Nothing about the Circle has popped up in ages." Her reputation as a don't-take-no, tough investigative journalist wasn't for nothing. She'd built it from the ground up, taking shit assignments and paying her dues. After years of hard work, pounding the pavement for stories and making contacts, she'd finally started getting recognized for her work. One of her stories had even won a national award. But the Circle? They'd been untouchable. Nobody would talk on camera, and certainly not to her. Breaking this story was going to blow her competition out of the water.

"How'd you find a lead on the Circle?" he asked.

She resented the doubt she heard in his voice. After two years working stories together, one would think he'd trust her instincts. "You're not the only one with resources. I know someone inside. He gives me tidbits now and then, asks me to sit on them until he's done with his work." But this one, he'd let her follow up on.

"Who?"

No way was she going to reveal her source. Besides, what she had with Nico was between the two of them. "Not important."

"If you're chasing after the Circle, it damn well *is* important. I'm not putting my neck on the line until I know who's giving you tips. Besides, it's not like you needed me when you accepted that award last month all by yourself."

Now Patrick was going to grow a pair? She liked him so much partly because he was malleable, agreeable—and a damn good cameraman.

"Never mind," she said. "I'll cover this. You hug your teddy bear, or your blow-up doll, or whatever, and go back to sleep."

He sighed. "Good night, Eve. Let me know how it works out."

Eve got out of her car, squared her shoulders and crossed the street. Thankfully, she remembered one of the CPD officer's names. "Hey, Phil. Tough night to be out on the streets."

Phil's eyes widened in recognition. "Cold, but no snow, thank God. What are you doing here?"

"Looking for a story, of course. Girl's gotta eat." She winked and smiled with satisfaction as male interest sparked in his eyes. Eve had used her long dark hair and movie-star smile to her advantage before. It looked like it would come in handy tonight, too.

His gaze slid over her and she mentally winced. The cold had prevented her from wearing a skirt and heels, as she would normally do. Instead, she was in sweats and boots.

"Yeah, I'm hoping to get my story and call it a night. Maybe a hot bath with plenty of bubbles to warm up first."

At this image, his cheeks flushed pink in an adorable way. "Detective's been held up, but he'll be here in thirty."

"*Minutes?* Geez. Good thing I brought coffee. Want a cup?" She pulled out the Thermos she'd lugged from the car. You never knew when you'd have to bribe a cop, or any other potential source. She had everything from chocolate bars to cigarettes in her backseat.

Phil rubbed his hands together, then nodded. She touched the thermos's cup to her lips, then held it to him. He picked up on the sensual vibe she was going for. Nico would have smirked at this guy's gullibility, but Phil was a valuable resource. Something to be respected and rewarded.

She leaned into him a bit, dropping her voice to a whisper. "Can't you give me something to tide me over?"

His gaze slid across her face, then to his fellow officer, who was pretending to tape off the other end of the alley but was shooting them curious glances.

Eve caught a glimpse of legs covered in fishnet stockings sticking out from behind the Dumpster, and her stomach flip-flopped. "Who is she?"

Phil seemed to soften. "We don't know yet. A prostitute, judging by her extreme clothing, especially in this weather."

"Nothing to identify her?"

"Only a strange tattoo on her upper arm. Well, not really a tattoo. Almost as if it had been branded by a hot iron. It's a little bigger than a cigar burn, so maybe it could be something like that." He looked around nervously, as if realizing he shouldn't be talking to her.

"What was it?" She nudged the coffee cup to Phil's lips again.

He took a sip, then responded. "A circle, with jagged triangles shooting outward. Almost like a sun, or…"

Eve's heart galloped, spurred by the image. "Like flames." Like the Circle's brand.

She'd only heard rumors of how the organization marked its victims and property. Had this prostitute been both? Officials claimed the Circle's reach had been cut off in Chicago over a decade ago. So who was this woman, and how was she connected to the defunct organization? Eve's scalp tingled, sensing the beginning of a major news story.

CHAPTER 5

Saturday, 6:00 a.m.
Brooklyn

The freezing pre-sunrise temperatures lent a bite to the air that Diego appreciated. It cleared his brain, wiping away the final vestiges of sleep. The shipment was on time, the transfer completed before the sun's rays softened the dark, dirty street near the dock. Diego had smoothed the way, contacting his task force coordinator at the FBI and making sure the NYPD hadn't caught wind of the delivery.

The bad guys win again.

Several crates of weapons that had been brought in by boat were now disappearing by truck as the sun broke over the nearby buildings, turning the dusting of snow to chips of diamonds reflecting the light.

"That couldn't have gone better," his liaison said. He handed Diego a wad of cash before striding off toward his car.

Diego wanted to argue. It could have gone much better if he'd been able to get the name of the Circle's main guy and bust this investigation wide open. Unfortunately, the multi-agency task force had been in place for years and weren't ready to take the whole organization down yet.

Diego jogged after his contact, who preferred to remain nameless. "Can I catch a ride with you? I wanted to check out the Brooklyn building."

"I told you I passed your message along."

"I just want to know what someone would find if they went digging there."

The guy squinted. "Sure. Hop in."

The sight of the building where he'd found Selina always turned his stomach. At least he'd been a part of ending that particular nightmare. The Cattle Call had ended. Still, there was an unlabeled white delivery truck parked outside the building when nobody should be here. The neighborhood was still quiet at this hour, but more lights were on. Most people in this crime-ridden area of Brooklyn kept to themselves, however, and the building the Circle rented was surrounded by vacant or repurposed old factory buildings.

His liaison gestured to the truck. "Satisfied? They're loading it today."

Sure enough, a man who was coatless despite the cold morning, his sweat-soaked shirt plastered to his body, wheeled out a filing cabinet on a dolly. It appeared Diego's warning had been heeded. He squashed the guilt he felt that Becca would find nothing if she came here searching for answers, reminding himself how relieved he'd be when she left New York City in one piece. She was tenacious and would find answers elsewhere, outside of his turf.

Diego nodded. "Satisfied. The boss won't regret it."

"What made you think this building was at risk?"

Diego had weighed the consequences of keeping the picture he'd received to himself, but his liaison could have valuable information. He pulled out the picture of the mystery woman. "I received this."

The other man's eyebrows lifted. "A warning?"

"I don't know, but I figured it was worth mentioning."

He handed the picture back to Diego. "She wouldn't have been from here, anyway. You needn't have worried."

"What do you mean? She's got the Circle's mark.

She's part of the Cattle Call."

He pointed at the symbol. "The *C* in the middle indicates she was Chicago's problem."

Diego squinted, just making out the *C* in the center of the circle on the woman's arm. "She's from Chicago?" Alarm welled up inside. That meant this could touch Becca's investigation. What was she stumbling into?

"Maybe, but they haven't had a Cattle Call in years. That brand looks fresh. If this was taken recently, then either the Circle is starting up again there or someone's copycatting."

Either option was bad.

"Thanks for the info, anyway," Diego said.

"No problem. Just as long as you continue to keep the NYPD out of the loop." With a sly grin, the other man left, not bothering to offer Diego a second ride.

Saturday, 8:34 a.m.
Manhattan

"You're sure about this?" Damian's expression was doubtful.

Becca let the waiter take away her nearly untouched plate. Her stomach had been tight since Diego abruptly took off. When the waiter left, she nodded in response to Damian, then followed it with a shake of her head indicating the opposite.

Damian chuckled. "Well, as long as you're in agreement."

"I don't know what to think." Or whom to trust. Despite her impeccable track record as a SSAM agent, she hadn't always made the wisest decisions, especially about men. "All I know is that my source—"

"Whom you believe is trustworthy," Damian interrupted.

"—who I deemed trustworthy, yes." Selina was a victim, and Becca was certain she hadn't made anything up. "My source named Diego, specifically, as a mole for the Circle."

"It sounds unbelievable."

She blew out a breath. "Thank you for that bit of validation, at least. Now, if I could just make sense of why his name would be connected that way."

"Why don't you ask him?"

"I tried." Becca was still wondering if she should have run after Diego last night. It would have been a bad idea. He'd been furious —in a quiet, controlled way that chilled her to the marrow—when he'd walked out of her room. In his eyes, she'd seen sparks of anger and hurt, but not directed at the entire world this time. They were aimed solely at her.

She feared he'd never forgive her. Which was ridiculous. Either he was guilty of working for the Circle and she didn't want his forgiveness because she was going to have to take his ass down, or she didn't care about him and didn't need his forgiveness.

So why did she feel like such a bitch?

"I take it that didn't go so well." Damian's frown was sympathetic.

"He walked out. I don't know what to do, sir. I have to stand across from him at the altar today and smile like the world is a beautiful place and love is possible." All the while, she'd be wondering if Diego worked for the Circle. And he'd know it. He was too perceptive not to notice her distraction, or her doubts.

"I can have SSAM resources check into a possible connection, but it might backfire and hurt his career."

She frowned. "I don't want to do that, unless he deserves it."

"What does your gut tell you?"

She was afraid her hunches were tainted by her heart's desires.

"Based on what I know of Diego from last summer? That there's no way in hell Diego's involved with the Circle. But he seems different."

"Losing someone you love does that to a person." A shadow flitted through Damian's eyes. "You find ways to move on. Ways to cope."

"What if his way to cope was working for the other side?"

"What if there's another explanation?"

Becca sighed. "That's what I'm hoping."

She couldn't blame him for walking out on her last night. Regret had gnawed at her, keeping her awake until dawn cracked through the small gap in the blackout curtains. Something about the accusation against Diego didn't ring true. At her core, she recognized he was a good man. He wouldn't hurt anyone. And he certainly wouldn't work for an organization like the Circle.

So why hadn't he stayed last night to fight for his honor?

Maybe because he shouldn't have to.

She had difficulty trusting people. That much, she recognized. It required a gamble, and as with any bet, one had to be prepared to pay the price if one lost. But the payoff could be big. Maybe she should take a chance.

"Give him a chance to explain, or find another way to determine the truth," Damian said. "A careful way. In the meantime, let me know if you hear anything else from the Fan. I've got Einstein trying to trace where the text came from."

"I'm not sure that'll work. When I tried to text him back, it wouldn't go through."

"Might have been a throwaway phone. Don't block any numbers. Our Fan might try to reach you again on your cell phone."

Breakfast wrapped up and Becca went up to her room and retrieved her gun from the safe. Matt had plans to sightsee with Catherine today. Becca's agenda included some sightseeing, too, but of a different sort. She only had today to track down the

Brooklyn address Selina had given her. She glanced at the napkin she'd stashed in her purse, eyeing Diego's name in Selina's scrawl, beneath the address.

She memorized the number and street, then balled it up and tossed it into the wastebasket. Having his name linked to that location seemed unfaithful. The man had her feelings twisted up like a complicated braid, one that gave her the mother of all headaches.

It didn't help that she still hadn't heard back from Selina to make sure the woman was okay. Not that she'd expected to. Sometimes it took days to get a return email. The one bright light from her inability to sleep last night was that, on closer inspection of the photograph the SSAM Fan had sent, it was evident that the photo hadn't been taken yesterday. There was no sign of sleet or wet streets. In fact, there had been a flowerbox on one window. So, while the SSAM Fan had known she'd be there, and that it had to do with the investigation into Samantha's death, he might not have been there at the exact time Becca was meeting with Selina. Maybe he hadn't seen the young woman, or followed her home, or harmed her in any way.

So why did he care about that meeting? What was he trying to prove? That he could track her anywhere? But why?

These questions hounded her as she stepped off the elevator and into the marbled lobby. And nearly plowed into a man.

"I'm so sorry," she said, jumping back. But in doing so, the item in the man's arms, which had become crushed to his chest when she'd plastered herself to him, succumbed to gravity. She caught his camera—an expensive-looking one, at that—just in the nick of time and handed it back to him.

"No harm done." He grinned good-naturedly and juggled his camera until he could hold out a hand to shake. "No need to burden your conscience. You must be with the wedding party?"

"How'd you know?"

Vanessa stepped away from the counter where she'd been

talking with the concierge and joined them. Her smile was bright, her skin glowing. She was every bit the blushing bride-to-be.

"Great timing," Vanessa said. "I see you've met our photographer. I gave him an advance copy of the guest list."

Becca grinned at the man who was prematurely balding and rather frumpily dressed but had a pleasant demeanor. He seemed friendly, in an odd-duck kind of way. "I'm sure I'll see you there tonight," she said. "Excuse me..."

"Wait." Vanessa caught up to her a few feet later. "Are you meeting me and the girls at the salon?"

"If I can't make it, will it ruin your day?" Becca itched to follow this lead, but she was supposed to be there to support the bride, so that came first. Although since Vanessa's mother had become a dragon about taking over all the planning, Becca had been informed that her official duties wouldn't start until just before the six o'clock wedding.

Vanessa tipped her head thoughtfully. "You've got that look."

"What look?"

"Like you've got saving the world on your mind. Noah gets the same expression when he's working a case. Is this about the work you were doing yesterday?"

Becca pulled Vanessa even farther aside, out of the high-traffic area near the front doors. "I'm sorry, but there's this lead, and today is my only chance..."

Vanessa held up her hand. "Don't worry about it. Just be safe, okay?"

"Always. And I *will* make this up to you. Out of curiosity, what is Noah doing with the guys?" She could file the information away for later, in case she chose to seek Diego out for questioning—or apologies.

"I didn't ask, but they're probably just hanging out somewhere, shooting pool, or hoops, or something. They don't get to see each other much anymore, living so far apart." Her gaze was speculative. "Are you and Diego reconnecting? I could find out where he'll be today."

"No, don't bother," she hastened to say. The last thing she needed was Diego thinking she was looking for him. "I was just curious."

"Just be ready to leave for the church at five. Mother's hired cars to transport the wedding party."

"I'll be there." That should give her plenty of time to investigate the building in Brooklyn.

Saturday, 10:30 a.m.
Manhattan

DAMIAN HADN'T EATEN MUCH BREAKFAST DURING HIS MEETING WITH Becca, both because he had a brunch to attend shortly after, and because he had no appetite. The restaurant Damian chose for brunch was a safe, neutral location—one that would subdue his ex-wife's reaction to what he had to say. Priscilla would never permit a public display of emotion.

"Glad you could make it." He rose to kiss Priscilla's cheek when she approached his table. His gaze swept over her in appreciation. She'd always been an elegant, charming woman.

Her smile was hesitant. "I was surprised to get your call yesterday." She sat in the chair he pulled out for her, then craned her neck to look up at him as he pushed her chair in again. "Are you healthy? Is anything wrong? You might as well tell me now rather than sugarcoat things with an expensive champagne brunch."

Her concern touched him, and he felt a stab of regret for the news he was going to have to break.

"No, no. I'm fine." He sat opposite her and the waiter automatically appeared to fill their water goblets and champagne flutes, informing them that the buffet was available whenever they were ready. Once that business was out of the way, Damian braced himself for what he knew would come.

"Is there news about Samantha?" Her question was no less full of hope than it had been every time he'd seen her over the past twenty years. Admittedly, that had been less and less frequent, but they'd stayed in touch, talking at least a couple times a year. While she had relocated to New York City and started a new life, he'd stayed behind in Chicago to pursue resolution from their old one. At times, he'd been jealous of her resilience. Yet when he saw her, the same shadows of grief lurked in her eyes.

They each missed their daughter in their own way.

"When we talked last month," she said, "you mentioned you might have a lead. You wouldn't give me the details."

"I didn't want you to be disappointed if it didn't pan out."

"*If?* Does that mean..." She leaned forward, sucking in a breath just before the words rushed out in a whoosh. "Did you finally find Sam's killer?"

"Unfortunately, no." And the investigation into whether the Circle had been involved could become a danger to his employee if he didn't end the search. His body tensed at the thought of abandoning the best lead he'd had in years. The best in decades, in fact.

Get your agent off the Circle case or someone will wind up dead.

The email he'd received just an hour ago, after his breakfast with Becca, had been pithy and to the point. And enough to scare him. The threat indicated Becca could be on to something valuable in Sam's case. Or they could just be getting too close to something else the Circle was hiding. And it wasn't signed by the SSAM Fan, which meant a couple of unknowns knew about Becca's investigation. He needed to talk to her again about this, but she hadn't been in her room so he'd left her a message on her cell.

Though he wanted justice badly, if this threat turned out to be serious, he'd find another way—one that didn't risk the life of one of his best agents. Becca was a living, breathing person and his daughter was, most likely, gone. He'd protect the person he still could.

"Damian?" Priscilla asked, bringing his attention back to her. "Are you sure there's nothing new? Why did you want to meet before the wedding? I would have seen you in a few hours." Priscilla, a patron of the arts, had helped the bride during last summer's investigation and was an invited guest.

He drew in a breath and exhaled before continuing. "I had Samantha's body exhumed."

Priscilla's jaw dropped, but she promptly recovered, pressing her lips together with such force they turned white around the edges. He could sense the explosion building.

"*You what?*" When she could finally speak, her words were a hiss of breath to avoid anyone nearby sensing her anger. But Damian felt the blast of it. "Can you even do that without my consent?" She laughed harshly. "Of course you can. You did."

"The lead I received indicated our daughter might not be dead. I used the information to petition the courts." And he might have had a friend who served as judge to help push things through. "I would have told you, but I didn't want to get you involved unless... I had to be sure."

Tears sprang to her eyes as her lips quivered. "Samantha might be alive? You didn't think I'd want to know that?"

"No, I didn't. Because it would have meant getting your hopes up when the odds are against us getting our daughter back." He sighed and reached for her trembling hand. It was a good sign that she let him take it. "I don't think she's alive, but I'm exhausting all the possibilities. I want to make sure we haven't missed anything."

Her blue eyes, so like Samantha's, blazed as they met his. "Was it our daughter's body in that grave?"

"I don't know yet. They're still doing an analysis. I wanted to tell you face-to-face while I had the chance. And they might need some information from you, possibly a sample of DNA. Right now, I have them comparing mine to the body."

"The body? God, you really do believe it might not be her, after all these years."

He could no longer protect her from hoping against hope that their daughter was alive. A year after Sam's disappearance, the police had only recovered a skeleton and some clothing remnants that matched what Sam had been wearing when she disappeared. They'd used dental records to confirm her identity, but those could be faked, for a price.

"If it's not Sam..." Priscilla's statement dropped off sharply.

Damian sighed as she reached the conclusion that had haunted him for the past couple months. "Then she might still be alive."

"Where? Where would she have been all these years?"

"That's why I don't think she's alive. She would have come back to us if she could." He wouldn't tell her that the rest of the tip he'd received had involved the Circle and human trafficking. It had been sheer torture to imagine his sweet Sam living in that world.

Priscilla dabbed at her eyes. "Well..." She fidgeted with her champagne glass, then took a big sip, clearly at a loss for words. "I had no idea this was the news you'd have for me today. One of these days, I hope you'll have some good news."

"I will. I'll never give up. I promise." He reached across the table and squeezed her hand in reassurance. One day he would have the news they needed to put this horror to rest forever. Or he'd die trying.

CHAPTER 6

Saturday, 10:45 a.m.
Brooklyn

About the time she was scaling the seven-foot chainlink fence in the freezing cold, Becca began to think this might not be one of her better ideas. Breaking and entering. Trespassing. She was now guilty of both. But she needed the opportunity to peek inside. She'd find no better time.

The square red-brick building used to be a factory, but a few broken windows and an air of eerie quiet indicated it was abandoned. Probably should be condemned, too, by the looks of it.

Her feet hit the ground inside the fence. It was a cold day, but some sun struggled through the clouds. It was the middle of the day, but this wasn't a main street, and certainly not the type where kids played freely. In fact, most of the neighboring buildings were fenced off, too. So far, she hadn't seen a soul, as if the entire block were a ghost town. But most of the Circle's covert activities were likely done under the cover of night.

Once beyond the fence, she rounded the side of the building

that was less visible from the street. The thin layer of snow had become a muddy mess here. Still, she detected tire tracks and a boot print. Someone had been doing some early-morning delivering. Or extracting.

Becca touched a gloved hand to her waist, feeling reassured that, beneath her coat, she had a weapon at her disposal. Thankfully, the snow underfoot was too wet to crunch as she made her way to the door. There, a four-inch-diameter bit of graffiti in the form of a circle with flames painted around it proclaimed who used the building. The Circle. She was certain it was meant to strike fear into the hearts of anybody who didn't belong on the property. It worked. But the building really did appear to be empty, and Becca desperately wanted a peek at the wall of names Selina had mentioned. She wasn't going back to Chicago empty-handed.

The cold metal of the doorknob refused to turn under her gloved fingertips. Locked.

She bit the tip of her glove to pull it off, then unzipped her coat and reached into her inside pocket. She withdrew a small leather pouch, then opened it to reveal her lock-pick set. A moment later, under her ministrations, the lock gave way.

The gray hadn't penetrated the thick brick walls, leaving the interior dark. Reluctant to alert outsiders to her presence by turning on the lights, she pulled a small penlight from another pocket. The air was thick with dust motes, tickling her nose and winking in her flashlight's beam. She took shallow breaths. When she exhaled, they made puffs of clouds in the cold air.

There were no furnishings in this large, empty room. The building had been gutted. But the tracks outside and the stirring of dust inside indicated someone had been here recently, so she drew her weapon, keeping the light in her other hand. Her beam fell across another Circle emblem. This one loomed as tall as she was on the wall in front of her. Three doors led into smaller rooms, which presumably had been offices once upon a time. But the last door was locked. Using her mouth to hold the penlight, she went to work on the lock, while mentally replaying her interview with Selina, who said she'd been held in a basement. She fully expected to find stairs on the other side.

Becca opened the door and directed the light inside. Stairs led downward. *Bingo.* She was surprised at the warmth of the room, having expected the basement to be cool, especially with its concrete walls. Once the door shut behind her, she flicked on the lights. At the base of the stairs was a space heater. The metal wasn't cold to the touch, but wasn't hot, either. It hadn't been turned off all that long ago.

She swept the room with her weapon, trying to focus on the adrenaline coursing through her, to channel it toward what the discovery of Samantha Manchester's name on the cell wall Selina mentioned would mean for Damian. But fear fought for a place of prominence in her mind. She was, after all, trespassing on a deadly crime ring's turf.

To her right was a series of thick steel doors, each with tiny rectangular windows cut at about eye level. The place definitely had a prison vibe.

The cell doors were unlocked. Thank God, they were empty. No prisoners here, though she'd welcome the satisfaction of rescuing a victim. She pushed the last one open, imagining Selina trapped here. Her breath caught at the sheer volume of names listed there. There had to be dozens—some scratched with finger-nails or whatever utensil might have been available to them, others penned in blood. Where were all of these women now? Who had hurt them? And how many names were in the other cells?

She scanned as many as she could, not seeing any that might be Samantha, but a sixth sense warned her to hurry. She holstered her weapon to pull out her phone and take several pictures of the wall. She did the same with the other cells where she found more names, then hurried upstairs. The chilling discovery that so many women had been held here had the hair on her neck standing at attention. Her thoughts were in a whirl when she reached the top, pulled out her penlight again, turned off the overhead lights, and opened the door.

"Seen enough?"

Her heart leaped to her throat at the unexpected question. Diego stood in the center of the large, empty room, seeming to fill it with his presence. The Circle emblem on the wall behind him nearly glowed as her light hit it.

She'd holstered her gun, so she'd have to use other weapons at her disposal to talk her way out of this. "Enough to know some very bad things happened to some very innocent people here."

Diego's jaw twitched. "I know."

She froze. So he *had* been here, had seen the names on the walls, and done nothing about it? Gooseflesh raised her skin. Selina had been right. Diego *was* the mole.

"Jumping to judgment again, I see." Diego's tone was flat, but something flashed in his eyes, warning her that his emotions were running deep and strong enough that he had to hide them from her. He was practically vibrating with the effort to control his anger.

Which was fine, because she was angry, too. And disappointed. Diego was affiliated with the Circle. How else had he known where to find her? "You tell me then, what am I supposed to think? You knew to find me here, which leads me to believe you work with the Circle. How else would you know about this place?" Her arm gestured to the darkness and her heart sank to her stomach. "You warned them, didn't you? They cleared out because you told them I might be coming."

His face contorted as she searched his face for the truth. "Shit, Becca, I thought you were smarter than this."

His words had her trying to refocus, but it all felt just out of her grasp. The pain of realizing she'd misjudged him. The sense of betrayal. And the fear she'd made a dreadful mistake.

No. There had to be another explanation.

Diego took a couple steps toward her. "Coming here by yourself? Entering private property uninvited?" He shook his head as if he couldn't believe her stupidity, which was like a cattle prod, finally breaking through her shock. "It's dangerous. Not to mention illegal."

She glared at him. "So is selling women and children on the black market, but that didn't stop these assholes. *These* are the kinds of people you want to protect and serve? It's dangerous. Not to mention illegal."

He schooled his expression into perfect blankness, turning him back into the emotionless drone he'd been a moment ago. "Contrary to what you believe, I'm not the bad guy here. But the law is the law. You're under arrest."

He'd hoped she was sticking close to the hotel today, like any sane person would. He'd assumed she'd be too occupied with the salon spa day stuff and bridesmaid duties—whatever those might be—to get into trouble. Plus, Damian had warned her about the danger of the Circle investigation.

Once again, he'd underestimated how well he thought he knew her. Hell, she'd tracked down Selina, hadn't she?

He rubbed a hand across his face. Becca obviously wasn't going to take a break. Not even for one damn day. She couldn't rest. Like a dog protecting her owner, she'd clamped down on a lead for Damian and wasn't opening her jaws for anything.

As angry as he was at her, as much as he wanted to strangle her right now, she had no idea what danger she could be in. So while she hit him with scathing remarks, he took her weapon, cuffed her and read her the Miranda rights. Outside the building, he'd parked close to the doors so he could get her out of there fast and unseen —if she hadn't been seen already. He ducked her head to put her in the back of his car.

"You can't do this," she tried, calming a bit.

"I just did." And he'd do it again if it meant keeping her safe.

Saturday, 3:37 p.m.
NYPD's 23rd Precinct, East Harlem

BECCA GRITTED HER TEETH AS SHE WAITED FOR DIEGO TO determine her fate. "The wedding's coming up fast."

He looked over briefly from where he sat, leisurely drinking coffee with a uniformed officer, at a table too far away for her to reach because he'd handcuffed her to his desk. *Smart.*

She hadn't been processed yet. Still, as her eyes met those of a woman in a skimpy sequin-and-fringe dress and heels she couldn't possibly walk in—especially if, as her behavior indicated, she was stoned out of her mind—Becca didn't think she could be any more humiliated.

Then again, she'd been through this before, and with much less understanding detectives. She simply had to appeal to Diego's common sense. If he had any. Because if he was working with the Circle, he probably didn't. But in the hours she'd had to sit there and think, she'd realized that, if he were truly a dirty cop, he wouldn't have brought her here. He would have dumped her dead body in the Hudson River or called on his Circle cronies to do it for him. No, if he were working for the Circle, why would he bring her here, to his home precinct, where everyone could watch what he did with her?

Either way, Diego would pay. But her main concern at the moment was getting to the wedding on time. Wait until she had to explain *this* delay to their friends. Or to Damian, whose voicemail earlier had ordered her to proceed with caution on this investigation. Maybe she'd get lucky and Diego would release her, wouldn't say anything, the wedding would go off without a hitch—except the hitching of the bride and groom—and nobody would be the wiser.

Or maybe she'd made her own luck. When Diego had left her with her thoughts, presumably to let her stew in her guilt, she'd put a sequence of events in motion that could be his undoing.

Oblivious to his impending doom, Diego popped a mint into his mouth and took his sweet time crossing the room. He leaned down into her face. Damn, he smelled good, and it wasn't just the mint. The scientists had it right when they discovered pheromones and their powerful link to attraction, because—*God*—being anywhere near this stubborn man sent her hormones into overdrive, even when he had her handcuffed to his desk. She held her breath and refused to breathe in any more of him. Except that he wouldn't get out of her face.

"Have you figured out how many ways you almost died today?" he asked.

"I believe I'm entitled to a phone call." She ignored his question. Not that she needed the phone call—she hoped. Diego had taken her weapon and shoved her into the back of his car like a real suspect but hadn't taken away her phone, and she hadn't brought that fact to his notice. She'd already texted the one person she thought could get her out of this mess and give Diego a taste of his own medicine. She just hoped that person showed up soon.

Diego sighed and leaned against his desk, his hip brushing her arm through his jeans. "You're not really under arrest, Becca."

"Good to know you haven't lost all of your faculties."

He dropped his voice. "I had to get you out of there. Had to show you what could very well be in your future if you pursue the Circle. Except it'll be much worse. It won't be a jail cell you'll be locked in. It'll be a coffin."

Words escaped her, floating somewhere in the ether beyond the red haze that had fogged her vision. She fought through it to bite out her response. "I'm sure it's the same end result when you work for the Circle. Did you warn them?" Hurt and mistrust strangled her words.

His face turned to stone, but she was saved from whatever reply he'd been about to issue by the arrival of the cavalry.

"*Dios mío!*" Estella Sandoval's eyes widened as she took in what had to be a surprising sight...her son leaning over Becca, who was handcuffed to his desk, as his eyes shot brimstone at her.

Diego jumped to his feet. "Mama? What are you...?" His question trailed off and he narrowed his gaze at Becca, who tried to hide a satisfied grin. "I thought, if I left you your cell phone, you'd contact Damian to get you out of this mess. Guess I was wrong."

"Guess so," Becca said, smiling sweetly. "I went straight to the top on this one."

Estella embraced her in a hug, her warm, plump body practically engulfing Becca. They hadn't had a chance to talk since Becca had helped solve the tragic case of her murdered granddaughter, but that was the great thing about Estella. She had a way of making everyone feel like family, and like you'd never been apart.

"So good to see you again, *hija*." Estella brushed Becca's cheek with a kiss. The woman must have been baking one of her famous specialties today. She smelled of cinnamon. "I didn't get to talk to you at the rehearsal party last night."

"I had to leave early. Thank you for coming. I wish it was under better circumstances." Becca had been counting on the woman who had borne Diego, who had put up with the stubborn male all his life, to have some sympathy for her.

"Should I get a bail bondsman?" Estella managed to send an angry gaze at her son before softening her face for Becca again. "What did you do?"

Becca opened her mouth to speak but Diego butted in. "She broke the law. I'm actually going easy on her."

"How much money do you need?" Estella opened her purse as if she would write a check right there. Becca was touched, and a little ashamed she'd brought Estella into this mess. But only a little. Diego deserved some of the recrimination his mother was sending his way.

"No need, Mama." With a heavy sigh, Diego bent to unlock Becca's cuffs. "She's not under arrest. Unless they made being stupid a crime in the past few hours."

The fact that he really wasn't going to arrest her, or turn her over to the Circle, spoke volumes. Maybe he was a good guy after all, even if his methods were misguided.

"Not to my knowledge." Estella gazed bewilderedly between the two of them. "What's going on? Noah's getting married in an hour. You're supposed to be there. This is *his* day."

Becca rubbed at her wrist as if it hurt, milking the sympathy. "I was worried your son wouldn't come to his senses in time for the wedding."

Estella's jaw dropped. "You're not even dressed yet."

"That's why I need to get out of here." Becca shot a look at Diego. "*We* need to get out of here."

"I'll take you. St. Paul's is just a couple blocks from here. We can walk it, and maybe someone is still at the hotel and can bring your things."

Diego huffed out another sigh. "No, Mama. I'll drive her back to the hotel."

Estella nodded sagely. "Now you're making sense. With the lights on, we'll get there sooner. Add the sirens and we'll have plenty of time."

Diego glanced at the ceiling as if he could find patience there. "No lights. No sirens."

"No fun," Estella muttered, preceding them to the doors of the precinct.

As his mother stepped out of hearing range, Diego helped Becca into her coat, then bent to speak into her ear. "Next time you pull a stunt like today's, your sweet ass *will* end up in jail. Because I'm not going to let you get yourself killed, even if you tell my mother on me."

CHAPTER 7

Saturday, 8:46 p.m.
Manhattan

"At least tell me if you were with her," Noah said. "Then it wouldn't be so bad that we were nearly late to the altar because our wedding party was missing."

"We made it in time." Diego didn't take his eyes from Becca, draped in a rich red bridesmaid dress that rippled and slid across her curves as the Viking dipped her on the dance floor. The man was elegance and charm. Diego ignored the twinge of jealousy. Where the hell had that guy been while Becca had been risking her neck that afternoon? If Becca were Diego's, he wouldn't have let her out of his sight after realizing how much danger she was putting herself in to pursue these various investigations. But maybe Becca didn't share that part with him. The thought made him feel a little better.

"We?" Noah asked with unconcealed interest. "So you *were* with Becca?"

"Yeah, I was with her. At the station. The woman is in serious need of a babysitter. She's too damn dedicated for her own good."

Apparently sensing the fear behind Diego's words, Noah didn't laugh. "It's her job," he reminded Diego quietly.

"Yeah, well, what she was doing was illegal." Diego snorted at Noah's raised brows. "I don't know why you're surprised. I arrested her, or gave the impression of it, anyway. Just wanted to shock some sense into the woman."

Noah grunted. "Bet that went over well. Thanks a lot for stressing my wife out, man." But his words held no heat as he gazed across the tables to the dance floor, where Vanessa's dark hair slid across her shoulders as she looked up at her father.

Beside them on the dance floor was Becca with her Viking god. *Fuck it all.* Why did he care? They hadn't reconnected, and she'd be leaving for Chicago tomorrow. His life would go back to what it had been without her. That shouldn't leave a sour taste in his mouth, but it did.

"Don't worry," Noah said when he caught the look on Diego's face. Luckily, he misinterpreted the source of Diego's frustration. "You gave a hell of a toast, so all is forgiven on my end. Even Becca was forgiven for dashing into the pre-wedding prep at the last second. She pulled it together pretty damn quick."

That was because Becca was capable, efficient and gorgeous. Tired of feeling frustrated, Diego jerked his gaze away from her. "You and Vanessa may have forgiven her, but I haven't."

"No harm, no foul," Noah insisted.

"She called my *mom.*"

Their gazes simultaneously shifted to the woman who'd given birth to Diego and had treated Noah as if he were just as much her son since the day Diego had brought him home from school. Estella was dancing with Damian. "She didn't."

"She did."

"Well, good for her."

Diego gave Noah a look meant to quell any more discussion on the matter. "She doesn't know what's good for her. She's messing with the Circle."

Noah let out a low whistle. "I didn't realize that's what Damian had her working on these days. But it makes sense. A buddy from the CPD called to congratulate me, saying it was a good thing I was leaving for my honeymoon, because the shit just hit the fan back in Chicago."

"What do you mean?"

"The body of a prostitute was found in an alley. She had the Circle's mark on her."

"What?" Diego's skin prickled. "Who was she? What did she look like?"

Noah's eyes narrowed. "Why?"

Diego patted his pockets before he realized he was in his tux and hadn't brought the picture with him. "Someone sent me a picture last night. A woman with the Circle's brand on her shoulder."

"Why would someone send that to you?"

Diego shrugged, not wanting to reveal his dirty cop status to his best friend, whom he looked up to and admired as a fellow detective. "A case I'm working on. It involves the Circle, too, but here in New York. I'll fax the image to the CPD, see if it's the same woman."

"I'll let them know to expect it." Noah's brows were drawn together in concentration, not at all what a groom should be doing after his wedding.

"Go dance with your wife," Diego suggested.

Becca was grasping at straws if she hoped Selina could give her a solid lead on Sam's murder. The two instances were separated by two decades and hundreds of miles. Had she seen the names on the basement cell's wall? He'd already given those names to his task force leader to investigate months ago, when he'd been able to go back for close-up pictures. So far, they'd matched the names to numerous missing persons cases, but many other names hadn't yet been matched. They'd probably been young women and children who were lost ones, runaways and strays nobody would miss. Diego wanted to grind these monsters into the pavement with his boot.

"You going to tell Becca about the picture?" Noah jerked his head toward the dance floor, where Becca was leaving her date in favor of the bar. The Viking stayed behind, engulfed by the gyrating masses in a group dance.

Diego's eyes tracked the woman who was the source of his current frustration. Damn it, he was the one who deserved to hold Becca in his arms. He'd been the one to protect her today. The one to put his career on the line to save her.

"She'd understand," Noah said. "She can even help."

"She's in enough danger." She was up to her beautiful neck in it, in fact. And it troubled him. He wanted to wrap Becca in bubble wrap and tuck her away—maybe in his bedroom—for a good long while.

Not that she would appreciate the sentiment.

BECCA WAS HAPPY TO SEE MATT FIND ANOTHER DANCE PARTNER. He'd been a great escort, but after her long ordeal today, she craved peace and quiet, away from the prying eyes of family. He was too aware of her distracted demeanor and full of questions she'd evaded. At least she'd made it through the ceremony without scowling at Diego.

The bartender handed her a cold bottle of water. Absently, she thanked him while contemplating how long she'd have to wait before she could slip away from the reception and up to her room to regroup. After the wedding and pictures at the church, they'd moved back to the hotel for the reception. The toasts and first dance were over. The cake cutting had to be soon...

A tingle of awareness signaled Diego had come up behind her just a moment before she felt his tuxedo jacket brush her bare arm. Her nipples hardened in automatic response. *Damn pheromones.*

"Show you forgive me with a dance?" His voice was next to her ear. A rush of heat ran over her like warm bath water, making her relaxed and susceptible to his influence.

"No, thanks." She tipped the water bottle to her lips, hoping to cool her reaction. Her body didn't care that Diego had embarrassed her, nearly arrested her, and might be in league with criminals. Her heart argued that she didn't have the whole story. She'd obviously need to keep her brain in charge. "I've had enough dancing."

"How about other stuff?"

She turned to face him, to see if he was joking. A teasing light danced in his dark eyes, but she saw heat there, too. They could so easily fall back into bed together. They'd been good there.

But it was the *together* part that worried Becca. Even after the anger and resentment of what he'd put her through at the station, a connection flowed between them, apparently unstoppable. Certainly unexplainable. It didn't help that he'd been one-hundred-percent within his rights to arrest her, yet he hadn't. His actions only confused her more. And it certainly didn't help that she suspected he'd been trying to protect her, genuinely concerned about her safety. That was the romantic side of her brain talking.

"Because falling into bed together would solve everything." She pulled sarcasm around her like a protective cloak—one that would hide how much she wanted to take him up on his offer and screw him until the constant ache inside disappeared.

His gaze flicked to her lips. "It would solve *some* things."

"I don't think so." But the way her body tingled belied her rejection.

"That's not a very firm no. Besides, I get the sense your date can't keep up with a woman like you. I'd wager he has no clue what you were up to today, or how to take care of you."

The multiple implications of *take care of* were not lost on her.

She couldn't deny that Diego was oh-so-capable of taking care of her physical needs. Apparently, nobody had told him yet that Matt was her brother. She wasn't about to enlighten him and remove one more barrier between them.

She leaned away to put a couple inches of distance between them. Not that it helped. "How about *hell, no.* Is that firm enough?"

He sighed. "I don't have a room to invite you to, anyway. I'm headed back to my apartment after this is over."

Disappointment caught in her throat. Damn. She should be excited she'd be free of him again soon. Free of the temptation, and the reminder of past mistakes. "Back to your real life, away from troublemakers?"

"Something like that." His tone had turned sour, as if he was disappointed, too. Didn't he want to be rid of her? Earlier, he'd acted like he wanted nothing more.

"Well, it's been fun." She set her half-empty water bottle down.

"*Fun?*"

In two blinks, he'd grabbed her hand and tugged her off the stool. He pulled her with him to the coatroom near the main entrance, just at the end of the bar. He didn't speak, didn't slow down, until they were tucked into the rectangular room, away from everyone. The disco beat muted as he shut the door. The room was a closet, really, and the leather, suede and faux fur of a multitude of coats made their surroundings cozy. Even the lighting was dim enough to be welcoming. Diego was anything but.

"*Fun?*" he asked again. Anger flickered in the deep pools of his eyes. She'd passed some invisible line with him.

"I was just being snarky."

He stalked forward, shoving several hangers full of coats to the side and backing her up until her rump hit the wall. "Snarky?"

"Is there an echo in here?" She tried to laugh, but it caught in her throat at the ominous look he gave her.

"Don't act like you didn't feel anything, like nothing fazes you."

His eyes blazed, definitely fazing her. His hands moved to her waist, his thumbs stroking her abdomen in an up-and-down motion that was hypnotic. "It's that cocky attitude that gets you in trouble."

It had also saved her ass, and her sanity, on more occasions than she could count. But it wouldn't save her from her feelings for Diego. The heat of his hands made her abdominal muscles tighten and she nearly gasped with pleasure. She kept her fists at her sides, though they itched to grab him and hold on.

God, one touch and she was ready to go up in flames. His pupils dilated in recognition of her reaction. She looked away to avoid discovery, but he stood so close that she ended up staring at the button on his tuxedo shirt—the button directly over his heart. She remembered laying her cheek there for a long time after one of their aerobic sex sessions had left her sated and boneless, listening to the rapid thump-thump that had gradually steadied to a constant rhythm. The soothing pattern still echoed in her head some nights as she tried to fall asleep.

She swallowed and her gaze traveled upward again. A muscle jumped at his jaw, as if he were keeping a tight rein on his temper. His hands squeezed her waist lightly. If she laid her palm against his chest now, would she feel the passionate jungle beat or the calm, steady Diego? It didn't really matter. They both drove her wild beyond reason.

What did matter was who he was, deep down. And what would happen if she allowed herself to trust him.

"Tell me how you're connected to the Circle." She hoped the pleading note in her voice would defuse his anger about the topic in question. "I want to understand."

"I was going to tell you." His mouth turned white around the edges.

"But now you're not? Because you're angry at me? You're trying to punish me?"

After a moment, he looked away. She was shocked at the

discouragement she'd read in his expression, but he didn't let go of her. "I'm not angry at you, just the situation. You don't trust me, and I'm beginning to realize that I don't trust you. Why did you run away last summer?"

She stiffened. "You're changing the subject."

"So are you. I want to understand you as much as you want to understand me. Tell me what I did to hurt you."

The fist around her heart squeezed. "You didn't hurt me. Nothing happened that we didn't want to. It was mutual."

"And the leaving part? That wasn't mutual. I thought you had a couple more days in New York, but then you were gone."

She'd left in the early morning hours, without so much as a phone call to say she was heading back to Chicago. She'd had to fight heartache the entire time. Hell, she was still fighting it. "You were grieving. You had a career to rebuild. I was a distraction."

"A welcome one." His gaze moved over her face, as if trying to read her thoughts.

"At the time. But that would have changed. I was a temporary fix."

He stiffened, his mouth forming an angry slash. "It was pity, then, because of what I was dealing with?"

"I don't give myself away that cheaply." She hadn't been with a man in months before Diego, and hadn't been with anyone since.

"Then what made you give yourself to me and then leave? Was I getting too strong? Maybe you prefer a weak man, crippled with grief, someone you have to heal?"

She felt the sting as if slapped, and would have taken a step away if she could. She lashed out with her tongue instead. "Maybe your fragile ego simply can't take the truth." And her ego couldn't take much more, either. She'd had her reasons for running away last summer, and they were none of his business.

With one hand, he released her waist to stroke a long finger across her collarbone. Her pulse at her neck leaped as if it wanted to be held in the palm of his hand.

"You don't need me," he said. "I get it. You'd rather be needed. I get that, too. Maybe you even get off on it. But maybe you should let yourself stick around long enough to lean on someone. Otherwise, you'll end up alone."

"I suppose that's my choice." Alone was better than making a painful mistake. Better than counting on someone and having them fail you in the worst of ways. Better than ruining his life and watching his love turn to hate. She couldn't stand the thought of the heat in Diego's gaze hardening to ice.

He studied her a moment, then dropped his hands. She nearly swayed toward him, hoping to regain his touch. "I suppose it is," he said. "I hope you meet someone who's worth the risk someday." He reached into his pocket, then held out his phone to her. Confused, she took it, noticing that he'd loaded it to dial a phone number she didn't recognize. All she had to do was hit Send.

"Who...?" When she looked up, the question died on her lips. He was already out the door.

DIEGO COULDN'T GET AWAY FROM BECCA FAST ENOUGH. DESPITE HIS frustration and confusion, the urge to kiss the forlorn look from her face nearly had him doing something stupid. Something that would unleash the tension inside him in a most delicious, but ultimately unsatisfying way.

Because complete satisfaction would only come from Becca's trust, her coming to his bed, or inviting him into hers, willingly and with nothing but total honesty between them.

The little tremble of her lips haunted his thoughts as he made his way to Damian's table, deciding to do one more thing to protect her. What he was about to do would kill every last ounce of trust Becca had in him—if she had any left—but it could also save her hide.

"She's not listening to reason." Diego pulled out a chair and sat next to Damian.

Damian's salt-and-pepper brows went up. "Becca?"

"Who else?" He leveled a gaze at the other man. "And I know she's investigating the Circle. You don't want her anywhere near that group."

Damian's finger absently traced the stem of his wineglass. "I know. Just as I knew she wouldn't listen to me."

He was surprised. "What?"

"Someone warned me she'd get hurt."

"No offense, sir, but if you knew she was determined to crack this case, and you knew she was in danger, why would you let her go?"

"I knew she wouldn't be alone. I knew you would follow. She's got a big heart, and she wants to help me find justice, no matter what the cost." Damian looked over at him speculatively. "But I think I know a way to ensure her safety."

"How?" Diego would do anything to ensure Becca would be safe once back in Chicago. "I'm going to hire you."

DAMIAN HOPED TO HELL HIS INSTINCTS ABOUT PEOPLE WERE SPOT-on tonight. He'd suspected for a while now that Becca cared for Diego. What else could have changed her demeanor so suddenly last summer? And now he knew Diego cared for Becca in return.

"Hire me?" Diego asked.

"To protect Becca."

Diego's laugh was part exhalation, part groan. "She's a personal security expert, a bodyguard. Not to mention the most stubborn woman I've ever met. She won't let anyone protect her. Least of all, me."

"Unless I say so. As a condition of her employment."

"You'd fire her?"

No, but he couldn't let them know that. Becca could be head-strong—an admirable quality in some instances, but not this time. "I want to keep her. She's a phenomenal agent, but, as you pointed out, she's a wildcard sometimes, and she needs someone to stabilize her."

"And you think I'm the man to do it?"

"You may be the only man who *can* do it. Her specialty is security. As a detective, you'd bring a special skillset to the investigation. Besides, if what Becca told me this morning is true, I'm certain you have knowledge about the workings of the Circle that could help."

They sat in silence for a long moment. Finally, Damian had pity on him. "I believe you care about her. Or am I wrong?"

Diego looked at Damian's glass, probably wishing he had a drink in his hand. "No, sir. You're correct."

"And your intentions?"

Diego sighed. "Before the last thirty seconds of our conversation, I'd intended to return to my life, my job, and forget about her."

"How'd that work out for you before?"

"Not so well." Diego looked like a man who'd just faced his future, and it looked like a million shades of gray. Drab and boring without the color and life Becca would add. "But I have a job to do here. I can't take off for Chicago on a whim. Although, there might be a connection to my case." Diego looked thoughtful.

"Take a personal leave, if you can. It's a win-win proposition. Becca will have added protection, I'll have peace of mind, and you'll...well, I suspect you'll figure out the next step. It would be worth the time and effort."

Misery mingled with amusement in Diego's gaze. "I know we have sparks, for sure." He gave a gruff laugh. "Hell, we could set the city on fire. And I have to admit I am worried. I recently received a new lead. An unexpected one, that leads to Chicago, of all places."

"Care to explain?"

"I received a picture last night, of a woman who was obviously a captive."

"What?" Damian was alarmed. "From the Circle?"

"I don't know. It's not really their style, and there was a cryptic message on the back, kind of like the ones your SSAM Fan likes to send. It wasn't signed like your notes, or Becca's. But it was the brand on the woman's arm that caught my eye. It was the mark of the Circle."

"What else?" He could see there was more.

"There was the letter *C* inside. It indicates the Chicago arm of the organization. But my sources say that arm shut down years ago."

Damian felt chills go up and down his arms. Had Samantha been branded in a similar manner? "Take my offer. Come to Chicago and investigate, alongside Becca. How about committing to one week?"

Long enough for Damian to figure out who was threatening Becca because of her investigation, and why. And to make sure the SSAM Fan wasn't going to hurt her. He had his best computer guy, Einstein, working on tracing the various texts and emails they'd received.

But that wasn't Damian's only agenda. He hoped Becca would find someone to settle down with for a lifetime. Diego could be her anchor, if she'd let him. She deserved that, especially after all she'd been through—and what she'd be going through now that James Powell had been released from prison. He knew all about that part of her past, though Becca was unaware he knew. He kept tabs on anything, or anyone, who might harm his agents. Which was how he also knew about the emails she'd received from James over the past few days. There were many reasons he wanted Diego around.

"Can you get a week off from the department?" Damian asked Diego.

"I'm just getting off probation," Diego admitted, scowling. "Not sure they'd appreciate me leaving."

"Find a way. Tell them about this photograph, and maybe they'll push you to go to Chicago."

"Becca won't appreciate my interference, I'm afraid."

"Find a way to work with her. You'll have to be persistent. She has some serious walls around her heart."

Diego's eyes narrowed in suspicion. "You know why, don't you?"

"Yes. I thoroughly inspect the backgrounds of all of my hires, though she doesn't know I know. But I recommend you get her to tell you, don't dig it up yourself. You're looking to build trust, after all. It'll take patience." And maybe a bit of cunning.

Diego looked concerned, but the glint of challenge lit his gaze. "I'm your man, sir."

CHAPTER 8

The SSAM Fan slipped the rectangular gift onto the table, slightly apart from the rest of the silver-and-white-wrapped wedding gifts, then merged into a group of guests before anybody noticed. He was enjoying this cloak-and-dagger stuff, sneaking around right under the SSAM agents' noses. With each successful covert contact, he was proving himself worthy.

He wanted to find Samantha's killer just as passionately as SSAM did. Even if they went about it in extremely different ways. They took a psychological approach to studying their prey, just like him, but where they focused on one murderer at a time, he looked at the bigger picture. Why people like him were compelled to kill.

His gaze surveyed the room, but nobody seemed to pay him any attention. And if a pair of eyes happened to land on him, they usually moved on within seconds. Anonymity was probably the sole advantage to being a slightly overweight, balding man in his late thirties who lived at home with his mother. And to having a camera in front of his face most of the time. Unless his subject was a drama queen looking for attention—and those people didn't notice him because they were so into their own worlds—people tended to look away from cameras.

Even if anybody noticed him, this was his life, his destiny, and he was determined to embrace it. Why else would his job allow him to be here? He had a unique skillset, perfect for today's festivities.

And perfect for helping Becca. He'd already set up a couple of special interviews when he got back to Chicago that would be invaluable to her. He was certain of it. She would soon be begging to meet him and express her appreciation.

And with the picture he'd left for Diego, the man would see his value, too. He'd see that the SSAM Fan was a better partner for Becca than Diego could ever be. The Fan had access to clues Diego never knew were there.

He hadn't gotten up the nerve to approach Damian with his ideas yet. He was too imposing a figure. But perhaps he could talk to Becca. He looked for her, moving among the guests as he did so, but she wasn't in the big ballroom. Diego was seated with Damian. Becca's date was on the dance floor, with someone else. His eyes narrowed as he saw how close the man was holding the woman in his arms. Catherine Montague. She wasn't a SSAM agent, but as Damian's administrative assistant, she was an integral part of the organization.

And she was having way too much fun with Becca's date.

Outrage and protectiveness—on Becca's behalf—rose up, filling his chest. She was a sweet woman, an agent of justice, like him. And, like him, she deserved to be treated so much better.

After Diego left her in the coatroom, Becca stared at his

phone for a long while. If she pressed Send, who would be on the other end? And would she want to hear what they had to say? Curiosity ultimately got the best of her.

"Hello?" Selina's voice answered.

Becca was flooded with relief. "Selina? You're okay?"

"Who is this?" Her voice was wary now.

"It's Becca. I was just calling to check on you."

"How'd you get my number?"

"I guess we have a friend in common."

Selina's voice softened. "He's wonderful, isn't he?"

Becca was starting to realize just how wonderful. Diego must have kept his identity a secret from Selina, only giving her the Diego Sandoval name as it was connected to the Circle. Not revealing his identity as a true hero.

Becca had shown Diego nothing but doubt, but he'd given her the gift of knowing Selina was okay.

After a couple minutes of checking in with Selina and reminding her of precautions she should take to be sure she wasn't followed, as well as leaving her phone number again for emergencies, Becca gave herself time to regain her normal rhythm before leaving the coatroom. Diego's rapid retreat had left her stunned, not only because it had sounded like he was saying goodbye forever, but because he'd finally given her the last piece of the puzzle. His gesture had gone a long way toward proving she could trust him. Was he asking for her trust in return? He had saved Selina, so whatever his purpose in posing as a mole for the Circle, her gut feelings had been confirmed. Diego Sandoval was a good guy.

Which left her with muddled emotions.

For a while after hearing Diego's name connected with the Circle, she'd been flooded with memories of a time she'd been so involved with a man that she hadn't seen the truth staring her in the face. The trauma with James Powell had impacted her entire adult life. Though she was proud of who she had become since, she'd never again open herself up to that kind of hurt, the kind that came from letting people get too close, too fast.

In the ballroom, she spied Diego and a jolt of awareness went through her like electricity, quickly followed by alarm when she realized he was sitting with her boss. With heads bent close together, the two of them looked to be discussing something serious. Diego had left her hormones in a twisted mess. What was he up to now? Telling Damian about her investigating the Circle this afternoon? If so, she'd kill him. He might be a good guy, but he wasn't allowed to interfere with her career—just as she didn't want to interfere in his.

She walked past the gift table, and a photograph nestled beneath the ribbon of a silver-wrapped package caught her eye. She moved closer, making out the details without touching the package or shifting the ribbon. It was a picture of a wall—the wall with the six-foot Circle emblem painted on it.

Prickles of alarm moved through her. Such a *gift* was too subtle for the Circle. Would the SSAM Fan leave this among the wedding gifts? Why?

To show that he can. To get your full attention. To prove he can be as up-close and personal as he wants, whenever he wants.

She angled her body so she could survey the room. In her absence, she'd missed the cake cutting. People were milling about or seated with plates of cake. The dance floor was half-full. A photographer stood on the sidelines, capturing the energy on film. She recognized him as the man she'd bumped into in the lobby earlier, just outside the elevators. A bartender remained at his station, scowling as he wiped down the bar. A couple hotel staff members were collecting empty plates and glasses off of the tables. But she didn't see anyone who didn't belong. Of course, there were nearly two hundred guests, so she could easily miss an important face. Hell, she didn't even know what, or who, she was looking for.

Becca headed toward Damian's table. Diego still sat at his side, apparently lost in thought, but his earlier anger and frustration seemed to have dissipated.

"Sorry to interrupt," she said as both men looked up.

Damian's welcoming smile slipped as he noted the expression on her face. "What is it?"

"I think he's been here, sir. I think the Fan left a gift on the table over there."

As she and Diego followed Damian to the table, she slipped Diego his phone. "Thank you for Selina." *For giving me peace of mind, and for reminding me I can trust you.* All of that was too much to say with her boss within hearing.

He acknowledged her gratitude with a nod. A small smile reassured her that he was close to forgiving her for her doubts.

At the table, Damian examined the box without touching it. Becca stopped by his side. "That's a picture of a wall inside the building where the Circle holds the people it steals for human trafficking."

"Here in New York?" he asked.

"Yes." Apparently, Diego hadn't told Damian where she'd been that afternoon. She felt more gratitude toward him.

"But you think this is from the Fan."

"It's his style." And if this was from him, the Fan had been at the factory sometime that day. Suddenly, she was glad Diego had shown up and dragged her ass out of there. She might have expected to run into Circle thugs, but this Fan was unpredictable. What did he want? "Should we open the box?"

Damian looked to Diego as if he should be included in the decision. What had transpired in those few minutes she'd delayed her return? Sure, Diego knew about the SSAM Fan's notes, and he was linked to Selina, but he was ultimately an outsider, not a part of the agency. Like Cinderella, he'd be returning to his apartment, to his life, at midnight, when the party was over. Part of her hoped he'd turn into a pumpkin. She hated pumpkin. It would be easier to leave him behind tomorrow.

"Yes," Diego said. "But be aware that he might be watching."

Becca let her attention slowly wander the room again, as if she was just interested in observing the party. Again, nobody seemed to be paying particular attention to her or their table.

Damian turned his back to the room so that he could pull a handkerchief from his pocket, using it to keep his prints off the package as he discreetly slipped off the bow. He read a note carefully scripted on the back of the photo. *"Congratulations to the happy couple. And congratulations to Becca for this lead. It's been a pleasure, even from afar, to watch the SSAM family celebrating how life goes on, even when those lives are painted with death and destruction. You give me faith in happy endings, and justice for all.* It's signed *The SSAM Fan."*

"Creepy," Diego commented.

"Even more personal than before, though, at least for him," Becca said. Deep in thought, she nibbled on her bottom lip. When she caught Diego watching her with interest, she promptly ceased. *"Painted* might refer to the case that Noah and Vanessa were involved in. In addition to knowing about my meeting with Selina, he knew about the wedding this weekend." And somehow he'd followed her to the building today. She certainly hadn't seen anyone there except Diego. She caught his gaze and knew he was thinking the same thing. This man was watching her every move. Fan, indeed. The man had definitely crossed the stalker line. He was familiar with past operations. And he had an inside track to their personal lives.

"How did he immerse himself in all of these places, leaving the notes, without notice?" Becca asked.

"There are a couple hundred guests here," Diego pointed out. "It wouldn't be so hard to blend into a crowd, or even just slip in and out, if nobody was watching for you."

"I'll ask the hotel for any video surveillance of this area," Becca said. "Maybe we can see someone delivering this *gift.*"

At the mention of the package, Diego handed Damian a pocketknife to carefully slit open the tape. Again, Damian used his handkerchief to handle the box. The gift had been meticulously wrapped. Inside, there was what looked like a CD case with a printed cover that was a collage of familiar faces.

"These are all SSAM agents," Damian told Diego.

The title printed across the middle proclaimed the disc a *Salute to SSAM Heroes.*

"I'll schedule a meeting at SSAM first thing Monday morning," Damian said. "That should give me some time to view this and Lorena can put together a profile. I'll see you both at the airport in the morning."

Becca looked from Damian to Diego, alarm blooming and bouncing around like a fireball in her stomach. "*Both*, sir?"

"All indications are that the Circle is too dangerous to investigate alone, so I've hired Diego to come to Chicago and help out."

Becca gaped at Diego. "And you accepted the job?"

Why? The word was on her lips, but she pressed them together rather than air any more of her personal issues with Diego in front of her boss. Not because he would hold it against her, but because, in his quiet, protective, fatherly way, Damian would do everything he could to help smooth things over.

But when Damian's attention was elsewhere, Diego leaned in close to her. "I can see the wheels turning. Give the hamster a break and just accept that I'm your new partner."

The goodbye he'd said in the coatroom apparently hadn't been real. Becca let her confusion show. "Why would you accept this position? You could easily go back to your life and I could go back to mine."

"Where you'll continue to risk your neck for the people you care about." The hardness in his voice softened with a sigh. "I know you mean well, but you don't seem to give your own safety much credence."

"And if I promise I'll put my safety first?" She was desperate to get him to back off. Before this trip, knowing she'd spend a large portion of this weekend in his company, she had reinforced her defenses. They'd taken a beating over the past twenty-four hours. But working together for a whole week? Those walls would buckle. And she couldn't let him in. Too much was at risk. So much he didn't even have a clue about.

"No deal. You always put others first. So I'm going to be there to put you first. I'm going to stick very, very close to you, Becca Haney."

Saturday, 10:18 p.m.
Manhattan

"Aren't you going to say anything?" Becca asked as Diego followed her into her hotel room and started poking around, assuring himself the place was empty of boogeymen. He'd been quiet since their encounter in the coatroom, and they finally had a chance to talk about his work with the Circle, and why he accepted Damian's proposition to spend the next week in Chicago. Instead, he seemed to have retreated within himself.

"All clear." He handed her the key card, then the gun he'd relieved her of when he'd fake-arrested her. "Keep it near you during the night."

"The Fan hasn't seemed dangerous. His notes seem to indicate he wants to help. I'm not sure I need a bodyguard."

"He's a stalker, Becca," Diego said with infuriating patience, as if talking to a child. "And that doesn't even include the risks you're undertaking with the Circle investigation."

"Maybe I should hire the SSAM Fan as my partner," she teased. "He seems to want to help, and he won't demand to be near me twenty-four/seven. And then we'd know who he is. Everything would be wrapped up with a bright red bow."

Diego stepped close. "You may get your wish if we don't figure this out together. But for the next week, I'm your partner. Your *only* partner." His gaze touched on her lips before he took a step back. She licked her lips, wishing she could taste him there.

You are in such trouble. Forget keeping Diego away with her defenses. She'd have a hard enough time keeping her hands to herself.

"We have to talk." Diego moved away from her and sat in the chair in the farthest corner from her. Out of reach. This was going to be a serious talk.

"Yeah, we do." She plopped down on the bed. "You basically admitted you work for the Circle, but are actually undercover for law enforcement."

"A special task force, actually. Inter-agency. I only know my supervisor, FBI Special Agent Todd Garrison, but there are apparently several officers—FBI, DEA, ICE, local law enforcement and possibly others—working different angles in various cities to figure out who's at the top of the pyramid. We could have taken out several operations, arrested dozens of criminals, but our objective is to get to the head of the snake. Unfortunately, the man is secretive as hell, and his lackeys refer to him only as *Boss*. I don't know anybody else in the group except my supervisor, who you talked to, and the same goes for each member."

"So you can't hurt each others' covers, but you also can't determine friend or foe."

"Exactly."

It sounded so lonely. Becca's heart twisted for what he must have been going through these past few months. Despite his large family, he'd felt alone last summer, when she'd met him, because his mistake had nearly cost the Sandovals justice in Natalee's murder case. Their affair had been a brief reprieve from reality, but when she'd left, he must have returned to work under a dark cloud of suspicion based on the mistake he'd made, which was further compounded when he'd purposely perpetuated the dirty cop image.

"I imagine it was hard for you, having to lie to your coworkers," she said.

He shrugged as if it were nothing, but something dark, something like pain, moved across his features. They'd been rough on him, then. *Shit.* She didn't want to feel sympathy for him.

"If you hadn't accepted this job, you wouldn't have been there to save Selina. You gave her a new life." Becca hoped reminding Diego of the good he'd done, saving someone's life, would obliterate the pain in his eyes.

"I could have ruined everything, but when I saw her there...she looked so much like Natalee."

"That must have been hard." Becca wanted to go to him, to hug him to her, but she sensed he didn't want that.

"At least I could save her, you know?"

Yeah, Becca did know. She hadn't been able to save herself, or her friend, from pain years ago, but she'd dedicated every waking moment to helping others avoid similar fates.

"Did you tell the Circle I'd be coming to Brooklyn? Is that why the building was cleared out? Did they move more girls?" The hurt at his decision to go behind her back stung like betrayal, but she couldn't blame him. She was doing the same thing to him.

Diego shook his head. "It was all for your own safety...and I needed to see if they'd resumed the Cattle Call."

"Cattle Call?"

"Their human trafficking operation. They put their victims up on display like cattle."

"Display how?"

"Usually private chat rooms or video viewing sites that are by invite only." His face was set with determination. "You asked me why I took this job to work with you? I've seen what the Circle can do. I won't let them touch you like they do their other victims. I'll protect you."

His words pulled at her, making her want that connection again. She stood and moved in front of his chair until his knees bumped hers and he was looking up at her. She ran a hand over his soft dark hair. "And you? Who's going to protect me from you? You make me want to make bad decisions. I can't do that again."

His pupils dilated ever so slightly. His nostrils flared as if inhaling her. His hands came up to her hips, and her body screamed an affirmative response. She leaned toward him, wanting him to yank her dress up and over her head and press his hot mouth to her belly.

But he didn't. His fingers dug in slightly—just before he gently nudged her away and got to his feet. The rejection stung.

"When's the flight tomorrow?" He gave her a wide berth as he moved toward the door.

She swallowed her disappointment at his all-business tone. *You wanted this. You wanted him to stay back.* "One o'clock. If you can get tickets."

"Damian said Catherine would take care of it."

"Then it's as good as taken care of." She couldn't meet his gaze, humiliated that she'd nearly thrown herself at him. She'd read the signals wrong. Apparently, she'd learned nothing in the past eight years.

"Are you sure you want to come to Chicago?" she asked, hoping to create some distance again. "You have Circle contacts here in New York City. You could just send me any information you find that might pertain to Samantha's disappearance. Besides, you're working hard to get your reputation on track. Surely, you don't want to jeopardize that now just to babysit me."

He stalked toward her but stopped just out of reach. Restraint was etched in every taut muscle. "I would do anything to protect you. Including keeping my hands off you when all I want to do is rip that silky dress in half, toss you to the bed and not let you up for a week, maybe longer. But we can't." His words became strangled, as if torn unwillingly from his throat.

"We've worked together before, and were able to keep sex and work separate."

"You weren't in immediate danger then. And we know how that time ended. I don't want to go through that again."

Had he actually been hurt when she'd left? She'd assumed he'd slip right back into his life and forget about her, other than some fond memory. She'd needed to get out before the pain began.

"We both need to keep our heads for this one," he said. "I'm focused solely on keeping you safe. Which is why I need to move into your apartment for the week."

"What?" What would it be like to have Diego Sandoval to herself, nonstop, uninterrupted, for an entire week? And what would it be like not to touch him? Sheer hell.

"It's the best way to make sure you're safe, and to make the best use of the short time we have to investigate together." He moved to the door before she could form a logical argument against such torture. "Good night, Becca. Don't let anyone in."

A groan escaped as he shut the door behind him. *Words to live by.*

Saturday, 11:42 p.m.
Auburn Gresham neighborhood, Chicago

Eve was on her own again. But she was used to that. If you couldn't count on yourself to get things done, who could you count on?

Patrick wasn't answering his phone. Nico wasn't answering his phone. But she had a story to tell, so she'd tell it without them. She unloaded a couple bags of groceries from her car and made her way to the steps that led up to her apartment.

"Midnight snack?" Nico's shadowy form emerged from the dark area beneath the stairs.

She dropped a grocery bag on her foot. "Son of a—" She clutched at her chest a moment, then rubbed her sore foot. "Anybody ever tell you not to sneak up on a woman in the middle of the night?"

Nico bent to scoop up an apple that had rolled away. "Anybody ever tell you not to come home alone, near midnight, in one of the toughest neighborhoods in the city? Why the hell do you live here, anyway? With your looks and talent, you could have some anchor-woman's job behind a desk in a cushy studio, living far away from the south side of Chicago."

She ignored the delight she felt that Nico found her attractive. She'd had recurring sex dreams about him for months, but wasn't sure if she'd been imagining the spark between them. Instead, she focused on the more important part of his statement. "You think I'm talented?"

He narrowed his eyes in disbelief. "I wouldn't have chosen you otherwise."

Chosen you. The words sent a thrill through her.

"Yeah, well, it would be nice if you'd call first. And if you'd let me air the story you've been giving me, maybe I would land one of those *cushy* jobs." Not that she wanted a desk job. It sounded boring.

Nico lifted the bag she'd dropped and gestured to the stairs, indicating they should continue their conversation inside. On the second floor, she balanced the other bag as she unlocked her door, leaving it open for Nico to follow her in. As on his previous few visits, awareness of him heated her skin. She set her bag on the counter, then turned on a single lamp, which created the illusion of intimacy. It was only the two of them, and the rest of the world didn't exist. Except it did.

Nico set the bag on the counter, then rinsed the apple and took a bite. "You didn't answer my question."

She cocked her head, trying to remember. "Why I live here?"

He nodded, then poked through her groceries, separating them into perishables and nonperishables as if he were Joe Homebody.

"I grew up here. It's where the stories are."

His gaze pinned her. "And?"

She grinned, loving that he seemed to know her, to know when she was holding back. "And I want to make a difference here. Give back, you know?"

His eyes darkened. "Again, that's why I chose you."

"So can I tell your story yet?" Her breath caught at the possibilities. The networks would be scrambling to air her pieces. Setting up a rogue website that reported gritty stories and aired video clips of her on the scene, wherever the news was, was her idea of an audition tape, and she'd finally been gaining some recognition in the field. But she wasn't at the pinnacle yet.

"Not yet."

He worried about the Circle finding out he'd been talking to her over the past few months, feeding her information, so their deal meant she couldn't reveal a shred of information until he gave her the go-ahead. She'd have a front-row seat when the Circle went down in flames. For now, he showed up out of the blue every few weeks with some tidbit about the Circle's activities in town. The group had supposedly disintegrated a decade ago, but rumors on the street over the past couple years indicated they were gaining a foothold again. And in her neighborhood, no less. What she couldn't figure out was Nico's agenda. To know what he knew, he had to work for them, which begged the question, why was he biting the hand that fed him, which also meant screwing over the most dangerous people in town? That was why Eve hadn't revealed his juicy stories yet. Because she knew the moment she did, he'd be dead.

"Did Becca Haney back off?" Nico asked.

Eve shook her head. "I sent an anonymous message to her boss, but I'm not sure it worked. They're not even in town at the moment."

"Thanks for trying." Nico's scowl deepened. Eve had done some quick investigative work after he'd contacted her yesterday. He'd tipped her off to the dead prostitute, and asked that, in exchange, she find a way to get Becca to back off with her investigations.

"Why is she so important?"

"I need her to back away. She met with someone recently, a victim I don't want the Circle to recover. Becca's getting too close to the truth."

Which meant she was putting his mission in danger. "She's supposed to be back in town tomorrow, according to my source. I'll see what I can do."

"Thank you." He finished the apple, but instead of tossing the core in the trash, he tucked it in his pocket. The man didn't trust easily. Then again, she had considered sending the core to the lab for DNA testing to find out who her mystery man really was. For all she knew, Nico could be a murderer.

"The woman from the alley, Fanta, what do you know about her?"

Nico rubbed a hand against the shadow of stubble on his jaw. "Someone mentioned that a body had been found. It had been branded with the Circle's mark, and left in their territory, but it wasn't done by us."

Us. He identified with the Circle, yet was betraying them. There was a deeper, grittier story here, she was certain. "You're sure the Circle had nothing to do with it?"

"I'm sure. What they can't figure out is why someone would use their brand. A copycat? A taunt? One thing is clear—women with their brand don't usually get thrown away like that."

"What usually happens?" Eve wasn't sure she wanted to know, but the journalist in her was screaming at her to follow up. She sensed a major story.

"They're sold on the black market. And not just women, either. Children, too. Like pieces of meat."

Eve's stomach churned with the dual impact of a revolting scenario and an exciting lead. She had to find Patrick and get a formal story together about human trafficking. She'd leave Nico out of this, of course, and rely on digging up other sources to find answers.

"I should go." Nico stood.

Eve felt a pang of loneliness. He was going to leave, and she was going to make a sad, late-night microwave dinner for one.

"Stay for dinner," she said. "I can whip up some pasta and sauce in no time."

He laughed. "It's nearly time for breakfast."

"I work odd hours. We can have an omelet instead."

"And I thought I was the only crazy one." Nico eyed the groceries on the counter, then her. His gaze hesitated on her mouth, her best feature. It was wide, with straight white teeth.

"I can't," Nico said.

It was the same response he always gave, despite the hunger— and not just for food, but for companionship— she read in his eyes. What inner prison kept him from accepting a simple kindness from a friend?

She shrugged as if she wasn't hurt. "Maybe next time."

Regret flitted across his face before he pulled on his steel armor. There would be no dinner the next time, or the time after that. He was using her for some purpose. Had chosen her to help him in his cause.

She was just a means to an end.

Maybe she'd skip the dinner and head straight for the bag of Oreos.

CHAPTER 9

Sunday, 2:08 p.m.
JFK International Airport, New York City

"**B**reathe." Diego's command was whispered in Becca's ear from the seat next to her on the plane.

"Easier said than done," Becca said.

"The Fan probably isn't on the same flight."

Just in case, though, they'd carefully scanned faces in the boarding area and as people got on the plane. Nobody looked familiar or overly interested in Becca.

Diego sighed. "Look, I'm sorry I took your boyfriend's seat."

Oh, for heaven's sake. She wasn't moping about him trading seats with Matt so that Diego could stick close to her. "His name is Matt and he's not my boyfriend."

Diego glanced toward the first class area where Matt was sipping a Bloody Mary. "So who did I give up my choice seat to?"

"My brother."

Diego's eyes widened, and he laughed. "I should have seen that." But when passion interfered, sometimes people were blind to the obvious. Which was why Diego's decision to keep things platonic was wise.

Before the doors closed and electronic devices were stowed, she checked her emails on her phone. And stiffened as she hastily scanned one that had come from James.

We're bound to bump into each other, living in the same city. Hope to see you soon, and finish where we left off.

Part of her hoped she'd bump into him—in a dark alley where she could show him what she'd learned since he'd last taken advantage of a half-dozen young women who'd attended the same university. But the grown-up, responsible part of her knew that would be a bad idea. Continuing to ignore him was the best plan. She wouldn't respond to his provocation.

Becca switched off her phone before Diego saw the email, then tried to do as he'd recommended, taking a deep breath, even though it went against every warning in her head. She didn't want to relax or be reasonable around him. She wanted to throw a full-on fit, like some toddler who wasn't getting her way, and insist he stay behind in New York City. Because if she couldn't have him in her bed—*another bad idea*—then her frustration would keep building, and she'd rather not have him around at all.

A flight attendant announced the closure of the cabin door and insisted they prepare themselves for takeoff. Becca took another breath and braced herself for two hours hip-to-hip, shoulder-to-shoulder, in a metal box, several miles in the air, with the biggest temptation to face her gender since Eve was offered the apple. The heat of Diego's body engulfed her in a way that wasn't so much uncomfortable as comforting—which made her *uncomfortably* aware of him. Now that he'd committed to keeping his hands off her, she seemed even more aware of her aching need to have his hands *on* her.

He grinned as if he knew exactly what effect his body was having on hers. "Need some air?" He reached for the nozzle above their heads, but increasing the airflow only seemed to send his scent her way.

One hour and fifty-eight minutes to go.

Becca gritted her teeth as Diego stretched out in his window seat, aligning their legs from hip to knee. She caught Catherine sending her an amused look from across the aisle. As Damian's ever-efficient assistant, Catherine had made the travel arrangements and ensured that Diego could join their flight at the last minute. He'd been at her door at nine this morning, packed bag in hand, ready to escort her to breakfast.

After the plane leveled off and the seatbelt sign turned off, Matt appeared at their row. He asked the stranger on her left if he could trade seats with him for a moment. The man gladly retired to the First Class cabin. Matt had sent several curious glances Becca's way since they'd left the hotel, but hadn't asked any questions when Becca explained Diego would be coming home with them. Which shocked the hell out of Becca. Her brothers weren't known for their silence, or their tact, especially where she was concerned. It looked like her reprieve was over.

She sighed, realizing one more of her defenses was about to be razed. "Matt, this is Detective Diego Sandoval. Diego, meet Matt, Brother Number Four."

"*Four?*" She felt a smidge better at Diego's expression of horror.

She nodded. "Four. All older."

Matt leaned across her to hold out his right hand to Diego. "I take it I'm allowed to talk to you now."

Diego shook her brother's hand. She didn't like the look the guys were sending each other. As if they were about to share their *Becca stories* and commiserate over a cold beer.

One hour and forty-nine minutes left...

Sunday, 3:53 p.m.
O'Hare International Airport, Chicago

Becca survived the flight, but the worst was yet to come. She'd be spending an entire week with Diego.

"You doing okay?" Catherine sidled up to her as the group watched the baggage carousel for their luggage.

Matt, Diego and Damian were all within hearing, so Becca couldn't very well complain. "With all the attention I'm getting, how could I not be okay?"

Concern crinkled Catherine's forehead as she caught the sarcasm. "Attention?"

"Someone who calls himself the SSAM Fan, who's been sending notes, pictures and links to Damian, has recently started sending things to me as well."

She paled, her eyes going wide. "I think he sent me something."

"What?"

"I found a copy of *The Scarlet Letter* outside my door this morning. I thought a hotel guest had dropped it, so I checked inside for a name and found a strange inscription. Didn't make sense to me, but I didn't think it was important at the time, either."

"Where is it now?"

"It's in my carry-on." Catherine reached inside the bag at her shoulder and pulled out the tattered book.

"Read it," Damian said, pulling in closer. Catching the tension, Diego moved directly behind Becca.

Thankfully, Matt was distracted with a phone call.

Catherine opened the cover and read the inscription. "*You might as well wear a scarlet A on your chest. Don't hurt her again.*"

"Any idea what it means, or who you hurt?"

"No. But if I'd known we were watching for notes from a stalker, I might have paid more attention to my surroundings last night." Catherine's tone turned accusatory. Her feelings were hurt, Becca realized. Catherine viewed SSAM as her family, and she'd been left out. "Why me, and why the reference to a scarlet letter? Who is the woman I supposedly hurt?"

"His sights have been set on Becca lately," Diego said. "Maybe he thinks you hurt her?"

"Maybe he thought you were stealing my boyfriend, when you danced with Matt at the reception," Becca explained when Catherine's confused gaze shifted to Diego. *Not that boyfriend.* He had only been a temporary indulgence. And she hadn't danced with him. That would have had her body in a tempest of hormonal need.

"I wondered the same thing at the time," Diego said. "How Becca's date could be dancing so close to another woman like that. Before I knew Matt was her brother."

Diego had been jealous. The thought sent a thrill through Becca that she had no right to feel.

"At least now we know a bit more about our Fan," Damian said. "He's expressing a loyalty to Becca. That's one more thing we can use to identify him."

Diego pulled a picture out of his pocket. Beside her, Catherine inhaled sharply, taking in the image. It was a woman, tied up and duct-taped across the mouth.

"Who is this?" Becca asked Diego.

His shoulder bumped hers as he shrugged. "I received it Friday night, after I left your room."

She looked up sharply, meeting his gaze. "And you're just now showing it to me?"

"He showed it to me," Damian said. "We were going to discuss it at the meeting."

On Friday, after she'd practically accused Diego of working for the Circle, and he'd left, the Fan had sent him this? How had the Fan known? "What does it mean? And why do you think it's the Fan?"

He reached to turn the picture over in her hands.

Unburden your conscience. Tell me no lies. A circle binds her forever...

"Sounds like some kind of riddle," Becca murmured.

"I wasn't sure it was from your Fan," Diego said. "He didn't sign this one like he did the others."

"He didn't sign mine, either," Catherine pointed out.

"Maybe he reserves the Fan designation for those things he sends you two." Diego gestured to Becca and Damian. "The reference to the Circle, and the branding—" he pointed to a mark in the picture, on the woman's shoulder, "—originally made me think someone from the Circle had sent this."

Which must have alarmed him to no end, Becca thought.

"But the riddle," Diego continued, "sounds more like the Fan."

"But how would the Fan know about your work with the Circle?"

"He might not have," Diego explained. "He knows about *you* looking into the Circle, and he's probably seen me with you."

Becca shuddered. "If he took this picture, he might have done this to the woman."

"I'm waiting for confirmation from a detective at the CPD, but I'm certain this is the woman they found dead in an alley a couple nights ago. Your fan has gone from friendly to stalker to killer in a very short amount of time."

Sunday, 4:05 p.m.
Metropolitan Correctional Center,
Van Buren Street, Chicago

IT WAS A SHAME TO MISS A CHANCE TO RIDE ON THE SAME FLIGHT AS Becca and Damian, but it was necessary for his plans. The Fan had opted for an early morning flight, giving him plenty of time for the interviews he planned in Chicago. But his mind kept going back to his time among the wedding guests. He'd rubbed shoulders with his idols. And soon he'd be one of them. He wondered if Damian and Becca had viewed his SSAM Heroes DVD yet. There were more gifts to come.

The first was entirely for Becca. James Powell wasn't going to leave her alone. The Fan had hacked into Becca's email account once more, wondering if he could gain a clue as to what was next in her investigation, or what she'd learned from Selina. Perhaps the building in Brooklyn had been it. He'd followed Becca there from the hotel, careful not to be noticed. The moment he'd seen her lurking near the fence from down the street, he'd turned and walked the other way, knowing he could get a closer look at the building later. Sending her the picture of the inside wall had been his way of telling her he could hold his own in the investigation, hinting at what they could accomplish if they worked together.

Soon he wouldn't have to resort to hacking her emails. She'd give him access to all of her information willingly, because that's what partners did. They were there for each other. Just like he was there for Mother.

But before James, he had Tony Moreno.

He'd need to clear prison security to gain the next gift he'd send to the SSAM family. *His* family.

"The reason for your visit?" the prison guard asked.

"Interview. Part of the documentary." He gestured to the camera case hanging at his shoulder, then set his bag down for inspection. He passed the new guy the documents that the warden had signed off on months ago. The Fan had been here often enough that any other guard would recognize him and buzz him through, but he didn't usually do interviews on weekends. That was time reserved for Mother. Luckily, expecting him to be out of town all weekend, Mother had taken on extra shifts at the hospice where she worked as a nurse, so he had time to spare.

After the guard examined the document thoroughly, the Fan was buzzed through and made his way down the familiar hallway to an interview room. Tony Moreno sat, his leg jostling under the table and his hands clasped in front of him. The guy was jonesing for nicotine.

He tossed the carton of Tony's favorite cigarettes across the table, where it slid to a stop at the man's hands. Tony grinned, revealing two gold teeth among the tobacco-stained others. He was brown all over, except his soul. That was black as midnight.

"Ready to unburden your conscience?" the Fan asked, sliding into the chair opposite Tony.

"Aren't I always?" Tony had already unwrapped the carton and was tapping a cigarette free of one of the packs.

The Fan spent some time setting up the camera and making sure it was ready to film. He sat down out of range of the picture and slid the match he'd smuggled in across the table to Tony, who snatched it up greedily.

Tony took several long puffs before meeting his gaze through the haze of smoke. "What do you want to know today?" The nice thing about Tony was that since he was serving several life sentences for rape, assault and any number of other offenses, he wasn't going anywhere. And he liked to talk. Especially about the things he'd done.

"Good versus evil," he said.

Tony grinned. "The usual, then?"

"Actually, today I'd like to know more about the Circle." They'd been dancing around the topic for months. Last week, Tony had finally told the Fan about the Circle's brand. The one Fanta's dead body bore.

Tony's smile faded. "Can't. They'd kill me."

"I think I've proven my loyalty to you by taking care of Fanta." Fanta had seen Tony driving away with his last victim. She hadn't come forward to testify—*because, let's face it, who would trust her?*—but Tony didn't want to leave her as a loose end and the Circle had pretty much written him off. "You asked me to destroy her and I did."

"Using the Circle's logo. Fuck! They know about my concerns about that whore."

"You're in prison. Why would the Circle think you were involved? I'm not going to tell them."

Tony jerked his head toward the camera. "You wouldn't have to. Broadcasting that movie you're putting together would be enough to condemn me."

"What have you got to lose?"

Tony took another long drag on his cigarette. "Shit. I haven't even told my lawyer about the Circle. Could probably have got my sentence reduced if I'd talked then."

"All five sentences?"

Tony smirked. "Drop in the bucket. It could have been much, much worse if the cops were any good at their jobs."

"They caught you, didn't they?" Actually, it had been Becca who'd caught Tony, with the cops' help. It was part of what had drawn his attention to her, and what had led him to interview Tony.

Tony's eyes narrowed. "What do you want to know?"

"Just one little thing." He pulled a second carton of cigarettes out of his bag and set it at his elbow. Tony's eyes went to it like a mother's to her baby. "I want to know anything you know, or may have heard, about a particular event that went down twenty years ago."

Curiosity sparked in Tony's bland brown eyes, giving them new life. There was nothing Tony liked more than having valuable information to impart. After all, everyone wanted to feel his or her life was worth something.

"Something twenty years ago, involving the Circle?" Tony shook his head. "I would have been twenty-five. I had just started working with them."

"But you might have heard something."

Tony shrugged. "What about?"

He slid the carton toward Tony, but left his hand on it in the middle of the table. "Samantha Manchester. What did the Circle have to do with her disappearance?"

CHAPTER 10

Sunday, 4:17 p.m.
O'Hare International Airport, Chicago

After Catherine left with Damian, Matt hoisted his bag.
"Dinner's at six-thirty."

Becca sighed. "I'll be there."

"We'll be there." Diego arched a brow that reminded her he was going to be there, wherever she was going.

"Fine." It wasn't worth the argument. And if he wanted to spend the afternoon with her family, it was his funeral. "Let's go."

"Where, exactly, are we going?"

"My parents'. Be prepared for some serious interrogation." Though her tone was sarcastic, inside she was worried. She'd never brought a man home before. There was sure to be a barrage of questions and curious looks aimed her way as well.

"At least there will be one friendly face." Diego watched her brother head through the doors to the taxi stand. Giving up his seat in first class had won major brownie points with Matt.

"And it won't just be my parents. All of my brothers live within a short drive, so they'll be there."

Before she could reach for it, Diego grabbed her bag along with his. "Did you park?" At her nod, he maneuvered their way through the crowd to the sliding doors that led to the shuttles. A short ride later, they were in the lot where she'd parked. A half-inch of snow crunched beneath her shoes as she led Diego to her sky-blue VW Bug. She popped the trunk so he could load their bags while she dusted accumulated snow from the windshield.

In the driver's seat, Becca bit back a grin as Diego folded himself into the passenger seat of the small car. It was cold in the short-term parking lot and she held her hands up to the vents, praying the heater would kick on soon.

Diego caught her watching him trying to shift his long legs into a less awkward position and winked. "I'm more man than your car can handle." He was eyeing the situation with uncharacteristic good humor. Or maybe it was characteristic, and she hadn't seen it much behind his grief last summer. There had been hints of his humor at times, and Becca had responded to it, trying to provoke more laughter from him when she could, like a junkie looking for a fix.

"How far to your parents'?" His question pulled her back from distraction.

"About twenty minutes. I'm sorry, but we won't have time to stop by my apartment first since it's not on the way." And because she didn't want extra time with him, alone in her apartment. She eyed his long legs. The denim stretched to outline his thighs and made her own thighs clench with the desire to wrap them around him. "You're going to regret inviting yourself along, and not just because of the muscle cramps."

"Why? What kind of torture do they have in store?"

"An anniversary party. It's a special occasion, otherwise I would have begged off after the wedding and the travel and..." And having

Diego glued to her. "My family values commitment. It's what makes us a unit, so we celebrate anniversaries together."

"That's nice."

She shot him a sideways look. "Yeah, it is." His family was the same way, which was why Natalee's death had hit them all so hard, like a ripple extending outward and touching everyone.

"So, an investigation, an anniversary and a wedding all in one weekend?" He sounded impressed.

"Yeah, life's just ducky lately." Especially with James Powell out of jail and this new Fan up to who-knows-what.

"Sarcastic much?"

"You left out the part I spent in an East Harlem precinct because someone didn't have his priorities straight."

It was his turn to ignore her jab. He glanced out his window as she pulled into traffic. "How many years of marriage?"

"Forty."

He whistled. "Quite a milestone."

"Lucky you, you get to be a part of it." She gripped the wheel tighter as she entered the freeway that headed toward her parents' home. They still lived in the house where she grew up. And Diego would soon be standing inside it. With her family. Making chitchat. *Lovely.*

"Do you ever want that for yourself?" he asked.

"A family?" She did. Badly. But history had warned her it might not be in the cards. "Do you?" she tossed back at him.

"I wasn't sure, but..." His words drifted off. She was surprised at how desperately she wanted to know the conclusion of that sentence. But when he spoke again, he'd changed the subject. "They sound like wonderful people. They put up with bossy little you all these years, didn't they?" He grinned and her breath caught. She quickly looked away.

Maybe she should let her brothers have a go at him, just to put him in his place. One evening of their incessant grilling and he'd cower in the corner with his thumb in his mouth and beg to be put on a flight home.

"Does your family know about you and me?" he asked. "About our past?"

"I didn't tell anyone."

"Because you were ashamed?"

Startled, she glanced at him. "No. Because I was moving on."

"You did a good job of it."

She had to have imagined the hurt in his tone. He was looking out his window, so she couldn't see his eyes. Not wanting to deal with the pain she might have inflicted, she chose to remain silent and think of what was to come. She remembered her familial duty. "Damn. We'll have to make a stop. I'm supposed to bring the appetizer."

"You're going to buy something from the store for your parents' fortieth anniversary celebration?" His look of horror amused her.

"You've never tried my cooking. Trust me, my family is expecting store-bought from me. In fact, they're probably praying for it."

"This is the year you'll surprise them."

In many ways.

An hour later, Diego was lugging several grocery bags and a bottle of wine up the stone path to her parents' brick four-bedroom home in Jefferson Park, and Becca was steeling herself for the barrage of questions that was sure to follow this impromptu change in plans. The most disconcerting issue would be explaining the ruggedly handsome man she'd brought home with her from New York.

"I hope they don't mind us arriving a little early," Diego said.

"Not at all," she assured him, touched that he'd care what her parents thought. He'd even thought to add their favorite wine to their purchases as a gift. "They're not stuffy. Besides, you said that mysterious thing you're making will take about thirty minutes.

That's perfect." Everything felt just a little too perfect, when deep down she knew it would never be. *Don't fall for him again, it'll hurt even more the second time.*

Her mother and father opened the door together, looked their fill at Diego, and their shock quickly turned to delight.

"Well, hello." Her mother's smile was warm, her blatant inspection approving. Dolly Haney was a former beauty queen from the farming area of Illinois. Rumor had it, the moment Donald Haney had laid eyes on her, he'd known what he'd wanted for the rest of his life, and lured her back to Chicago where he was practicing law. So far, things had gone swimmingly for Dolly and Don.

For Becca, not so much.

Her mother turned a questioning look on her.

"Mom, Dad, this is Detective Diego Sandoval. We worked a case together in New York last year, and he was Noah's best man. He's in town for a few days."

And yes, I know I've never brought a man home before. And no, having him here, now, during a very important family event, shouldn't seem odd or at all significant.

Despite a hole in her story large enough to float a cruise ship through, Becca continued with the charade. "He found himself with nothing to do today, so I thought we could take the poor stray in."

She couldn't tell them the truth. They barely had an idea what she did for her daily job. Matt was the only one who really knew, thanks to Catherine.

Diego lifted the grocery bags in his hands and turned his most charming smile on her parents. "I know this is an important event for you, and I'm honored to be here. I'm also happy to earn my keep."

"He cooks?" You'd think Dolly Haney had been notified the Rapture was upon them, so great was the glow of admiration in her eyes. When Diego handed her the wine with wishes for a happy anniversary to her father, her mother practically snatched his hand and dragged him inside. "Come right in."

"Apparently, food isn't the way to just a *man's* heart." Becca's grumbling went unheard as her parents were quickly pulled into Diego's orbit, hovering about him in the kitchen. Still, some of Estella's cooking skills might have rubbed off on him, and the thought of tasting an authentic Puerto Rican dish had her stomach rumbling. She followed the trail of happy conversation to the kitchen, where the heavenly, memory-evoking smells of her mother's pot roast already filled the air.

"I thought I'd make something easy, but delicious." Diego was emptying the bags they'd filled at the grocery store, pulling forth ingredients with strong, sure hands. "Fried plantains, or *tostones*, and a sauce called *mojo*."

"Well, aren't you a sweetie-pie?" While Dolly's question was aimed at Diego, her look was turned in Becca's direction, as if asking who this anomaly was and where she had found him.

"I'll pour us some wine," Donald offered, adding to the intimate celebratory vibe that was starting to rub Becca the wrong way. Diego's role in her life was suddenly a little too familial.

Ever prompt, her oldest brother Seth was first to arrive at the scheduled time. He bent to kiss Becca's cheek as he strode into the kitchen, which suddenly seemed tiny with him, Diego and her father filling it. How her brothers had ended up with all the height in the gene pool, leaving none for their youngest sibling, was beyond her.

Dolly stepped next to Diego and laid a hand on his shoulder. "Becca brought a friend."

Seth's survey of the other man was quick, but comprehensive. Becca grinned, anticipating a sarcastic comment.

"Nice apron," Seth said.

She bit back her disappointment. Diego indeed wore the frilly thing well. His mother had insisted, and apparently Diego was amenable to anything Dolly suggested. Which only made Becca more cranky.

"Thanks." Diego's left hand held a knife while he shook Seth's hand with his right. "Nice to meet you."

The two seemed to silently take each other's measure. Michael and Billy chose that moment to walk in together, carrying an enormous bouquet that they presented to their mother with a flourish. The kitchen was now overflowing with people, but Becca felt warm inside, happy to have her family around her.

Her middle two brothers were only a little over a year apart in age, but had always seemed to have the ability to communicate silently, as if they were identical twins. As one, they turned their attention to Diego and gave the same arched-eyebrow look.

Seth grinned. "Allow me to introduce Diego. Becca's *friend*."

Michael made as if to bow down to Diego. "Becca's obviously been sharing her secrets with you."

Becca nearly choked on a sip of wine. Thankfully, nobody seemed to notice her awkwardness. Except Diego, who grinned at her in amusement. "Secrets?" he asked.

"How else did you know the way into our inner sanctum is food?" Michael leaned over the counter to take a peek at the sauce Diego was stirring, which was emitting a wonderful garlicky smell reminiscent of aioli, and grinned. "Yep, you definitely know the secret."

Warm conversation flowed as much as the wine, and Becca soon lost her irritation as laughter filled the kitchen. Diego's fried plantains and dip served as an appetizer while Dolly supervised the setting of the table and seated everyone, ensuring that Becca was squeezed in at Diego's side. Matt arrived late, just as they were sitting down to eat. He winked as he spied Diego beside her.

"Hello again," Matt said.

Becca sent him a look set to stun. She'd dial it up to kill if he went into any detail about their weekend in New York.

"Again?" Dolly asked, never one to miss a significant part of her children's conversation. "Have you and Diego met before?"

"At the wedding," Matt said.

"You look refreshed," Becca said, hoping to throw attention to him. By the looks of the pretty pink box with a designer logo, he'd brought a fancy cake for dessert, which had given him time to enjoy a nap and a hot shower.

Diego's knee rubbed against hers under the table. On purpose? He'd decided they'd work better together if he were hands-off. She jerked her leg away and clenched her thighs together. Unfortunately, she could still feel the zing of his touch radiating through her body. With her peripheral vision, she tried to detect if he'd intended to touch her, if somehow he'd changed his mind about wanting more, for just this week. Instead, she became distracted by the dusting of dark hair on his muscular forearms. He'd rolled his sleeves up while he was cooking. She had a flash of memory—his forearms on either side of her head, supporting his body above her as he slowly made love to her. Her skin heated involuntarily.

"How was the wedding?" her mother asked. Dolly passed her the platter of pot roast at the same time Diego tucked his napkin in his lap. His fingers brushed her hip. Her hands were suddenly full and her brain empty.

"It was great to catch up with everyone." Becca's response seemed to gush out of her. Thankfully, nobody seemed to find that odd. Conversation turned to other things, and she relaxed enough to enjoy hearing what her brothers were up to. While their family dinners had become more sporadic as everyone's lives became busier, no matter how much time passed between gatherings, crowding together around the dinner table was like slipping into a comfortable robe. Even Diego seemed to appreciate her family's laughter and camaraderie.

After dinner, they settled in the living room in front of the fireplace with their wineglasses. Diego had charmed them with conversation, warmed their bellies with good food, and been the perfect guest. And he'd kept his mouth shut about his past relationship with Becca. She owed him a debt of thanks.

"I should start the dishes," Dolly said. It was their usual cue, and Becca and her brothers immediately put up a protest.

"Not on your anniversary, you don't." Don began to rise.

"We got this," Matt said. "You two lovebirds enjoy the fire. Becca will bring you coffee and dessert here. I brought the cake—chocolate—as promised."

"Best do as they say," Don said with a wink. "They outnumber us." He put his arm around Dolly as the rest of them stood to return to the kitchen.

At the sight of her parents' love, Becca felt a twinge of longing. Would she find that kind of deep love one day? That kind of bond required trust, and she wasn't sure she was capable of letting go enough to believe in another person that much. To have faith he would be there for her, no matter what.

After she'd delivered cake and coffee to her parents, she returned to overhear the men conversing.

"You're a guest," Matt was telling Diego. "And you cooked. I can't let you clean up, too. You're making us look bad." His words were spoken with good humor. "Hey, Becca, why don't you give him a tour of the homestead?"

"I don't think he'd be interested," Becca said.

"I'd like to see it," Diego said. "I don't know a lot about your past." He gave a long-suffering sigh. "But if you don't want to share your kittens and unicorns..."

Didn't he see what a mistake it would be to be alone together? She was feeling soft and vulnerable after an evening in her family's company, creating a longing for what she couldn't have.

CHAPTER 11

Diego's guess had been stated in jest, and couldn't have been further from the truth. Becca's room wasn't pink frills or kittens and unicorns. It was rock star posters and a corkboard filled with pictures of family and friends.

"I went away to college," Becca explained, looking slightly embarrassed.

"And didn't come back?" Diego picked up a small box on her dresser and opened it. A single diamond earring glinted inside, next to a class ring.

She snatched the box away and set it back on the dresser with a snap. Definitely special, or he'd touched a nerve. She seemed to rethink her action and put it in the top drawer instead. Diego got a glimpse of something hot pink and lacy. Against Becca's satin skin, it would be absolute sin.

"I never moved back, if that's what you mean," she said.

"Never moved on, is what it looks like."

Becca bristled. "Just because my parents kept my room like this doesn't mean I didn't mature. I've grown up in more ways than any of you will ever know." She pressed her lips together as if holding in the rest of her statement.

Once again, Diego sensed a mystery behind her words. Something held her distant from others, even from her family. As if she wasn't fully sharing herself with the people she was closest to. He felt a sudden desperation to reignite her temper and erase the sadness and regret in her eyes. Even better, a spark of passion would burn off the sexual tension brewing between them. But he'd established that no-hands rule to save his sanity. If he had a boundary firmly in place, it would be clear when he was crossing it. At least, that was the theory. His body clearly didn't want to obey his brain.

He took a step closer. "Did you go far for college?" He was going to leave in six days. There was no reason to press for information, but the more he knew about her, the better he could protect her. At least, that was what he told himself.

She shrugged. "Far enough that a commute home on the weekends required planning."

She didn't mention where. He found that interesting. Most people were proud of where they'd attended school. Had it been her college class ring she'd wanted to hide in the drawer? "Was SSAM your first job?"

She nodded. "When I was done with school, I'd heard of them and knew what I wanted. It was a perfect fit."

Done with school. Again, an odd way to phrase—or not phrase— her words. Most people would say they'd graduated with such-and-such degree. And why had an agency like SSAM been a perfect fit for a young girl graduating from college? From what he'd seen, most of Damian's hires were experienced professionals, having worked in the field before coming to SSAM.

Diego didn't like that Becca was holding back or keeping secrets. Had a man hurt her? "You're leaving a lot out."

She turned away.

"Don't hide from me," he said. "We shared more than most people."

"That was a controlled environment. In the real world, it's different."

He didn't want it to be different. He wanted to recapture what they'd had. "What if there's more?"

She took a step back, out of his reach. "You said we shouldn't be together, in that way, especially while working together."

He moved forward. "That doesn't mean we can't give it a try after the investigation is over. After other distractions are out of the way."

She retreated again, her rear coming into contact with her desk. "There can't be anything."

"It's as if you don't even want to see if the spark is still there." He could see it was there. He just wanted her to admit it.

"Because I don't."

He lifted a hand to brush his thumb over her lips—her lovely, lying lips. They trembled. He'd wanted to kiss them ever since he'd seen her across the gallery at the rehearsal party. "You react to me...the same way I react to you."

"That's just basic human nature. Physical lust."

He stiffened. "The 'it was only a bit of fun' line again? What are you afraid of?"

She gave a harsh laugh as he leaned closer, his hips leaning into hers. He only had to tilt his head to capture her mouth.

"I'm not afraid." Contrary to her statement, her voice hitched.

In the depths of her wide brown eyes, he saw a mixture of anxiety and hope that mirrored what he was feeling. He closed the distance. *Just one taste.*

As his lips touched hers, sensory memories consumed his brain, dashing his thoughts into incoherence. Her flavor on his tongue was like coming home. He knew her mouth, recognized the part of her bottom lip that, when kissed, plumped like a ripe cherry but tasted even sweeter. Her little moan of surrender unhinged something inside him. How could she insist that physical desire was all they had?

Why bother pushing for more, especially if she'll run away from you again? It would be torture, working with her but not touching her. But if he could prove to her that what they had was worth fighting for after this case was over...

It won't be enough. Whatever's got her running scared will keep her away.

His subconscious fought to be heard, but he smothered it as, like a flower unfurling its petals, she opened her mouth to him. His hands found her hips and held on for dear life as her tongue swept inside his mouth.

God, he'd missed her. Fiery, bright and beautiful, she was like a sparkler on the Fourth of July. Bringing happiness and a bit of awe into his life. Emotions that had lain dormant for months awakened at her touch.

Her fingers dug through his hair. His scalp prickled deliciously at the contact. He groaned and hiked her up until she wrapped her legs around his waist, her bottom resting on the desk behind her. His erection pressed painfully against his jeans as he leaned over her, intent on devouring as much of her as he could, for as long as he could.

Unable to resist touching her skin any longer, he dipped a hand under the edge of her blouse, then edged beneath the satin bra to cup her breast. Her flesh filled his palm, and he brushed a thumb across the nipple. She arched against him, moaning into his mouth. Her pelvis pressed harder against the ridge in his pants. God, he loved how responsive she was to his touch—like the motor of a high-quality racing machine, just waiting for his foot on the pedal to rev its engine.

"Becca?" Dolly's voice called from down the hall. "Your phone's ringing in your purse. I didn't know if I should answer it."

Becca ripped her mouth from his. His moist lips grew cold as her irregular breath blew against them. She unwrapped her legs from his waist, then pushed him away and dropped her feet to the floor.

"I'll be right down," Becca called back before her mother could appear in the doorway. Thank goodness. Diego didn't want to scandalize the sweet woman who'd welcomed him into her home.

Becca started straightening her clothes, which he'd shoved this way and that in a frenzy to get to her skin. She turned to the mirror to finger-comb her hair. He wondered how she'd hide her swollen lips and pink cheeks.

He stepped up behind her, planting his hands on her waist as he bent to place a kiss on her neck. He liked her short hair—easy access to more skin. "See? We're good together. Too good. You make me lose my head."

She stiffened, then wriggled out of his grasp and moved toward the door. "You'll regain your senses soon enough."

Confused by her cold tone, Diego wanted to tug her back into the room and question her until he understood what the hell had her defenses rising up again. But she was already halfway down the stairs, acting as if he had no effect on her world at all.

Sunday, 8:10 p.m.
Chicago

THE FAN TOUCHED THE NECKLACE IN HIS POCKET. WITH A PROMISE of more cigarettes and star billing on the documentary, Tony had come through, giving him what he needed to prove his value to Damian and Becca. He'd held the little butterfly charm up to the light at least a dozen times since he'd retrieved it from the storage room where Tony had said it would be. He couldn't wait to share his find. But there was much to be done before then.

It had been a busy day, but he'd finished his interview at the prison in time to do some research and ensure that Fanta's body had been found where he'd dumped it in a South Side alley—her home turf. He'd contacted his church to start funeral arrangements, and received kudos from the pastor for his involvement with the downtrodden. If only Pastor Bob knew how involved he really was, he thought with a grin. And he'd even put in a couple hours at work to make up for lost time.

He had more yet to do tonight, but *that* meeting was best done during the darkest part of the night, when evil reigned.

He finished unpacking his suitcase, started the laundry, and went upstairs to put the kettle on. Mother would be home from her job at the hospice soon, and she'd want a cup of chamomile before bed on this cold, damp night. He'd reserved a bit of time to chat about her weekend.

From the cupboard, he removed her favorite teacup with the gold-plated rim and delicate pink roses. He stood on tiptoe to reach the top of the fridge and pull down the Crown Royal, poured a shot into his mug and replaced the bottle. He'd have a quick nip to celebrate his recent accomplishments, and those yet to come, but he'd be discreet about it. Mother didn't like seeing him drink. It reminded her too much of the Colonel, which is what she'd called his father. The Colonel had insisted on the title, and on respect. Even if he'd had to beat it out of them with his leather belt. Even if the infraction was small and the rules rigid.

The only time the Colonel hadn't touched him was during his illnesses. It was almost a blessing that the Fan's childhood had been full of them. He'd spent so much time in the hospital that Mother had practically moved in there. In fact, it was when he was about ten that she started studying to be a nurse.

But the Colonel—a nasty, raging drunk a majority of the time—had died of liver disease years ago. And sometimes a guy deserved a drink. Just one, though, because of his DNA.

Was the desire to kill genetic, too? The Fan had often wondered if the Colonel's violence had ever led him to kill a person. Or if the urge to kill had led to the violence of other sorts. Or maybe he'd found other ways to deal with the urges.

These were the kinds of questions that had instigated the documentary...good versus evil, light versus dark... He was determined to find the answers to why he felt the urge to kill. And whether a good person still lived inside him. Because he felt like a good person. He made good choices. And if he had to make a bad choice, it was for the greater good. He had subdued his urges for years, channeling his quest for understanding into his interviews. But one day, he'd decided enough was enough. He'd begun killing, but only when justified—even if most of society couldn't comprehend those reasons.

Then he'd seen the story about Tony, a seasoned gang member who'd raped and killed several women and had been taken down by SSAM Agent Becca Haney. She'd looked into the camera and given a brief statement to the effect that all types of people existed in society, and understanding them was SSAM's goal. The Fan had begun his documentary that day, petitioning for access to Tony. On their first interview, Tony had looked him in the eyes, his tattoos rippling with life as he leaned forward on the table and looked into his video camera, and given him the answers he'd been searching for.

"You see, God gave us each certain gifts," Tony had said. "Some of them don't fit society's idea of normal, or right, but if you're good at it, if you crave it, there must be a reason. Fighting it only makes it worse in the end. Feed the beast."

Oh, he had been. But it seemed he'd finally found people who understood why. He'd made the best of what God had given him. He'd decided that he could help himself, society and even Mother at the same time, though he limited his release to only a few victims a year. Feeding the beast too much would become sloppy, and he'd get caught.

The front door opened and closed. The familiar shuffling sounds of Mother hanging her coat and scarf sounded from the front hall. He poured her tea and met her at the small kitchen table, dipping his head to kiss her cheek.

"Good evening, Mother. How was work?"

She didn't smile, didn't lift her head to meet his eyes. Her thin lips barely moved as she answered in a thin voice. "Tolerable."

His chest tightened with the familiar feeling of drowning in darkness, a feeling he'd experienced regularly. The depression cycle had begun again. He would fix it as only he could. It was his gift. He was always fixing things for the women in his life.

Sunday, 9:12 p.m.
Lakeview East, Chicago

EVE LAUGHED AND TOSSED HER HAIR OVER HER SHOULDER, THE signal to Patrick to start filming. It was a tiny hidden camera, but he knew how to get the best angles in the worst situations. Even when he was sitting at a table a few feet away.

Trusting he was capturing the interview on film while she recorded the audio, she worked to keep the prick sitting next to her talking. Coaxing information out of a subject was what she did best. Mining for the gem of a story hidden beneath the bullshit. Flirting was her pickaxe. Stroking egos was her shovel. With these tools, she often unearthed information more valuable than diamonds.

Of course, James Powell was leaving out his recent incarceration for raping several of his female students nearly a decade ago. She swallowed her disgust and nodded as he spoke, laughed when appropriate and mentally created a checklist of talking points for her news segment. He went on and on about his impressive attributes, including his exalted Stanford education and prowess with the ladies. But her thoughts were on Nico. In the time since he'd appeared at her apartment, she'd done little but think about their recent encounters. If he was seeking her out for help, he was somehow in danger because of Becca Haney sticking her nose into the Circle investigation. Eve had become convinced, as she dug into Becca's past, that this man held an important key to knowing what made Becca tick—and therefore, could provide valuable insight into how to get Becca to back away.

Except the more she sat with James, the more she realized what a sleaze he was, and how right Becca had been to make sure he was locked up.

As if he read her thoughts, James reached over and trailed his finger down her arm from shoulder to wrist. "We could go somewhere more private and continue this discussion."

Eve forced herself to smile seductively. "Sounds like an offer I shouldn't refuse. But that's not what I'm here for. I want to work with you."

James lost some of his verve and pulled his hand away. "Work with me on what?"

"I want to bring down Becca Haney."

His lips curved upward again, this time with a calculated gleam in his eye. "Why didn't you say so?"

"Before this is through, I'll make you a legend." And Becca Haney would be too caught up in the public backlash and a slander lawsuit to quietly pursue her investigation into the Circle. Nico would be safe and Eve would have the glory of releasing a story that would rock Chicago to its foundation.

CHAPTER 12

Sunday, 9:30 p.m.
Jefferson Park, Chicago

The rest of the night at the Haney household had been a blur, but somehow, Becca and Diego had eaten their cake, kept up their conversation, and issued an intelligible goodbye. All while Becca's mind was whirling.

You make me lose my head.

Diego's phrasing had been so eerily similar to what James used to tell her that it had stunned her, slamming her with memories that were inconveniently timed. James was out of prison, on the streets, possibly telling his sappy lines to a new woman. Same song, different verse.

"So the call wasn't important?" Diego held out her coat.

"What?" She brought herself back to the present and the people around her. She'd hugged her parents, wished them a happy anniversary, and she and Diego and her brothers were walking to their cars.

"The call. The one your mother mentioned. You've been distracted ever since."

"It wasn't that."

He narrowed his eyes on her as she refused to continue. "Was it me? I was trying to prove a point. For the sake of the investigation, I can back away."

Backing away wouldn't help. Moving forward wasn't possible. It seemed there was no answer. She turned from Diego's questioning gaze as Matt stopped beside her car.

"You'll keep her safe?" her brother asked Diego. "Because, despite whatever she's said about me, I would never let her go with anyone I didn't trust. Something tells me I can trust you."

"You can." Diego shook Matt's hand. "I promise. My sole purpose for existing this week is to protect your sister."

A shiver of anticipation ran through Becca.

Matt walked away and Diego held out his hand to her. "Keys." It wasn't so much a demand as a request.

Because she didn't want to argue while her family could still be watching, and, frankly, she was tired, Becca handed them over. Diego moved around the vehicle and opened the passenger door for her.

"Such chivalry," she muttered, not sure why she was feeling so pissy about his sweet behavior. Maybe because it was battering at her already weakened defenses.

"You look like you could drop at any minute." He halfway lifted a hand as if he might comfort her. Rethinking it, the hand fell again.

She got in and buckled up. Feeling like a popped balloon, she slumped further into her seat.

Diego squeezed himself into the driver's side and extended the seat back as far as it would go. He pulled the car out of the driveway, glanced at her, then back at the road. "Rest. We have a lot to talk about when we get to your place."

And a strategy to develop. One that had to take into account so many items that Becca was weary just thinking about it. So she closed her eyes and pretended she could quiet the thoughts in her head long enough to rest.

Several minutes later, she woke up, startled to realize she'd been able to rest after all. Diego was parking in the lot of her high-rise building near downtown. Perhaps it had been a bit longer than a few minutes.

She frowned. "How do you know where I live?"

"I have my sources," he said. "Besides, it's my duty to know these things."

"As my bodyguard."

"Right." In the dim light of the parking lot, his teeth flashed in his amusement. "And as your partner."

"And was it your duty, as my bodyguard *or* my partner, to stick your tongue down my throat?"

"I didn't hear any complaints."

"Hard to talk with a tongue down your throat." She sighed through her crankiness. "Okay, partner, so where do we go from here? I thought we'd selected the hands-off plan."

"That'll be tough for a week, especially now that I've had my hands *on* you again." He was staring straight ahead through the windshield, but the huskiness in his voice told her just what he wanted. And it was what she wanted. But his next words shattered the delicious images. "But I can't sleep with a woman I don't trust."

Her jaw dropped, though what he suspected was true. She was keeping something from him. "You don't trust me?"

He finally turned to her, regret in his eyes. "I want to, but I know something more is going on."

Oddly disappointed at his ability to turn on and off the professional aloofness, as well as the thought that he'd only kissed her to break her down, Becca slipped back into evasion mode. "Let's get settled. It's late."

She got out of the car and he followed with their bags. In the elevator, he handed her the keys and pushed the button for the tenth floor. He really had done his homework.

The slide and snick of her key in the door seemed to echo in the empty hall. She pushed her door open and stood there, suddenly uncertain. This was her last chance to back out. Once he was inside her place, this would be *real*. For a whole week. Unless she could solve the case sooner. That thought, and the knowledge that he might be able to leave before a week was out or she lost her sanity, got her moving again.

"Need anything?" she asked.

"Maybe a cup of decaf if you have it?" He set their bags down just inside the door. "Unless you want another shot of tequila to get you talking." His bottomless brown eyes seemed to dare her to pick the latter, knowing it would loosen her inhibitions.

"I'll start the pot," she said.

"I'll check the nooks and crannies."

He was gone in a flash, making sure no stalkers—fan or foe— lurked in her bedroom and bathroom. The thought of him in her personal space sent a wave of longing through her. She needed to keep up those defenses, so, rather than run her own security check, she went the opposite direction and entered the kitchen, with a quick check of the pantry, just in case.

Diego returned a moment later. "All clear."

There hadn't been anybody hiding in her tiny pantry, either, but she'd caught sight of the salt-and-pepper shakers she'd stolen from the delicatessen where she'd first talked with Diego. A little memento of their time in New York together. Silly, since they were nothing special, but just looking at them reminded her of their first conversation, and the strong but emotionally complex man she'd fallen for in those moments when he'd talked about his dedication to justice and his love of family.

From across the tall bar counter, Becca could watch Diego move about her living room. Though she'd chosen comfortable, functional furnishings in simple, muted earth tones, he roamed her small square footage as if he were at a museum full of priceless art. His fingers lingered on a piece of pottery her mother had made, he gazed at the framed black-and-white scenic photographs of Lake Michigan—the real thing could be seen in full color out her windows—and then he peered at family photos on a bookshelf.

Diego Sandoval is in my apartment.

She feared she'd never be able to look at the place without imagining him here. Her nipples puckered, her hair raised as if sensing danger, or the possibility of pleasure. It seemed the two were separated by the thinnest of lines when it came to Diego.

He picked up a four-by-six frame. The picture was one her father had taken of her and her brothers just a couple months ago, immediately after their annual Thanksgiving flag football tournament. Their faces had been flushed with exertion and the November chill.

"You look happy." He turned from the photo to her. "Are you?"

She avoided his gaze by looking at her hands as she scooped coffee beans. "Sure." She resisted the urge to cross her fingers behind her back. Detective Sandoval would have noticed that.

Besides, she *was* happy. Most of the time. Except when she missed Diego, or longed for someone to come home to or share her day with. Someone she could count on, when the exhaustion of being the person others counted on weighed her down.

She should get a dog.

"As you found out tonight," she said, "in order from oldest to youngest, that's Seth, Michael, Billy and Matt."

"And then you."

"And then me. We're each within a couple years of age of the next one in line."

He set the frame back on the shelf, making sure it aligned with the others, and joined her in the kitchen. He leaned a hip against the counter, facing her. "You deliberately misled me to believe you were in love with another guy."

Her eyebrows rose so high, she felt her hairline move. "In love with?"

"I heard you on the phone with Matt, when we were in the cab in New York. You told him you love him."

"I do. He's family. Don't you have to love your family?" Her tone was teasing, but this talk of love was meandering into dangerous waters.

"No, you don't." He was perfectly serious and she looked up in surprise. "Not everyone has a solid foundation they can rely on. You do, yet I get the sense you're holding back from them. Just like you're holding back from me. Love scares you."

She stiffened. Suddenly, the atmosphere was much too intimate. He'd sliced through her defenses to her core, where she'd buried the truth. He seemed determined to exhume it and breathe new life into it, which was impossible because love did scare her. Being that open, that vulnerable, was a dangerous place to be and went against her instincts as a security expert.

"Maybe we'd better call it a night and talk about the investigation in the morning," she said.

"Is that what happened last summer? You couldn't deal with the intensity between us so you ran rather than face it?" When she didn't answer, he sighed and went to sit on the sofa, giving her some breathing room.

Becca busied herself with pouring coffee, ignoring how her body shook with a multitude of emotions. She should never have agreed to this. He was too close. Too aware. Too desirable. Too *everything*.

Last July, his grief had taken over his thinking. He probably wouldn't have turned to her for comfort if she hadn't been handy. And boy, had she let herself be handy. There'd been an undeniable chemistry between them, but she shouldn't have acted on her impulses.

Pathetic, Becca. When will you learn?

Apparently, she had a pattern of letting men who needed her

get under her skin and into her heart. Then let them use her until she had nothing left to give. James Powell had been a dangerous example of that.

This time, she'd been smart enough to get out, leaving Diego before extensive damage had been done. Except here he was again. Up close and personal. Ready to do serious damage to her heart if she let him in.

Her eyes narrowed on him as she joined him in the living room. She set their two cups on the coffee table, then sat at the other end of the couch, tucking her feet under her. He sighed as if amused at her attempts to remain distant in her tiny apartment.

"I heard the pity in your sigh. Don't feel sorry for me." That was the one thing she couldn't abide. Sure, she could feel sorry for herself on occasion, but pity from others, especially Diego? Not allowed.

He shook his head. "I could never feel sorry for you. You're the strongest woman I've ever met."

How little he knows about me. The thought brought a crushing pain to her chest, and the overwhelming urge to unburden herself, to share that part of herself with him. But that would let him close, not keep him away. It would create a vicious circle—her giving in to her desire for him, that desire blossoming into a feeling that threatened to swamp her good senses, her giving too much until she was wrung out, and then running away.

And then the pain would start again.

Better to break the cycle now.

DIEGO SENSED THE MOMENT HE'D LOST HER. HELL, THERE HAD BEEN so many of those moments lately. But this time, he could almost see her slamming a metaphorical door shut in his face.

"Don't do that." Frustration tightened his throat, making his command nearly a growl. She was too far away to touch, but the need to reach for her, to reestablish some kind of connection, nearly overwhelmed his good sense.

"Do what?" She fluttered her eyelashes in innocence.

"Shut me out. We have work to do this week. It'll be easier if we can talk freely. And the more I'm around you, the more I think the only way we can do that is to get the past out of the way. You can talk to me about anything. God knows I leaned on you. Let me repay the favor."

She seemed to weigh his words. When she spoke, it was nearly a whisper. "I'm not sure how."

He figured she had defenses a mile high, so simply dropping them wasn't an easy option for her. Remembering the deck of cards he'd spied on the bookshelf, he had an idea. "How about a game of strip poker?"

She nearly choked on her coffee. "Sure. That'll help."

He ignored her sarcasm, warming to his idea. "A modified form of it, where we remove barriers instead of clothing."

She sent him a wary sideways look. "I may need that tequila after all."

"I want you sober for this." He rose and retrieved the cards. "Though I'd love to see you naked again, I have a different form of stripping in mind."

A baring of their souls. He'd gotten a glimpse of the real Becca tonight, the one she kept hidden from him. Her family, her childhood bedroom, her apartment—hell, even her tiny, feminine car. All these things were clues to who she was and why. The brief taste was just enough to whet his appetite for more. He wanted to know all of Becca Haney—head, toes and everything in between.

"What do you mean?"

He sat back down on the couch, a little closer to her this time. "This game is more like truth or dare, mixed with strip poker." He'd make up the rules as they went, but definitely come out the winner.

Her eyes lit with cautious intrigue. "If the player doesn't want to answer a question, he or she has to remove an article of clothing?"

"Exactly." He was at an advantage, having still kept his shoes and socks on. She, on the other hand, had discarded her boots and socks sometime after they came home. He also had a belt. He figured she had four items of clothing, at most, before he'd have her completely exposed—either physically or emotionally. And it would be her choice which option she chose. She had the power.

"We can give it a try." Her voice hinted at her reluctance, but she leaned forward to scoop up the cards he'd dealt. By the end of the round, he'd arranged to lose to her, hoping a taste of victory would relax her.

She pursed her lips in thought. "Do you regret what you had to do to gain the Circle's trust?" She seemed to hold her breath as she waited for his answer.

"No." Technically, he didn't. Because he'd kept his resurrected reputation as a good cop in sight. His dirty cop image was a step that had to be made to get his career, and his life, back on track.

She seemed disappointed by his answer. "It has to be the truth, remember?"

"The answer is still no. No regrets."

"That's what I get for asking a yes-or-no question, I suppose. I'll deal the next one." She reached to take the deck of cards from him and his fingers brushed hers. She fumbled a bit as she shuffled.

He won the next hand. Her gaze was wary, but he'd ease her into this. She wasn't yet relaxed enough to answer the tough questions.

"Why do you feel such a need to help others, even if it puts you at risk?" he asked.

She let out the breath she'd been holding and sank back against the cushions. "Same reason you do, probably. I want to help other people find their way, find justice. If I can't have it for myself..."

She stopped abruptly and her gaze flew to his, narrowing as if he'd tricked her. "I enjoy helping people."

So, there *was* something in her past that motivated her now. What was that event that shaped her life? He took the cards from her and dealt another hand. Again, he lost.

"I didn't phrase my question correctly before," she said, thoughtfully. "And my new question is similar to what you asked me. You work with the Circle, but not *for* them."

He grinned. "Is there a question in there?"

"Why did you help Selina? It must have put you at risk." She chose to use his same words.

"I was in a position to help her. I was the only person who could, or would." He sighed, seeing the disappointment in Becca's eyes. She wanted more. "And I'll only tell you more if you forfeit a piece of clothing."

Flames erupted in her eyes. After a moment's hesitation, a wicked grin bloomed and she peeled off her shirt, revealing the satin bra he'd had his hands beneath earlier. Her breasts were on the small side, but they fit his palms perfectly, as did all the curves on her slender body. With the buttercream color of her bra, it appeared as if the tender globes were dipped in frosting. His mouth watered.

"Well?" she asked when he couldn't find the words to speak.

He cleared his throat and brought his thoughts back to the present conversation—which took him down memory lane, past some not-so-happy memories. "I told you how Selina reminded me of Natalee. I couldn't leave her to the fate the Circle had in mind. But saving her saved me."

Becca reached out and squeezed his hand, then let go. It was a brief gesture, but he knew she understood. "You help the ones you can," she said. Again, he wondered who she hadn't been able to help. Had it been herself or someone else?

"And knowing I was able to help someone get away from the Circle helped me get through the ugly assignments." He'd had to do things that turned his stomach while he'd been working to earn the Circle's trust. Things like ignore criminal activities, tip them off to police routines, and even help them plan a bank heist. He'd done it with the blessing of his task force leader, but Garrison didn't want to know the details—only Diego had to live with those. He hoped the sleepless nights and added stress paid off in the end.

"I imagine acting as a dirty cop is tough."

"Yes. I've lost the respect of pretty much all of my friends on the force. It helps to remember that one night I made a difference in someone's life. I was visiting my Circle contact that night, hoping to build some trust with them by delivering information about an upcoming police raid on a drug shipment. It was the first time I'd seen the basement of the Brooklyn building."

"They must have come to trust you, then. Did you know about the Cattle Call?"

"That's a bonus question," he pointed out. "You owe me one."

"Put it on my tab," she said, gesturing to him. "Tell me the whole story. Please."

"Well, since you asked so nicely..." His tone was light, but the shock of finding a woman in a cage that night was burned into his brain. The only thing that could combat it was imagining her living her new life, far away from whatever had been in store for her. "I'd heard of the Cattle Call, but hadn't seen any signs of it."

"Seeing the cells must have been a shock."

"At the time, I acted like I didn't even notice Selina was there, or didn't care. But, she looked out at me through the tiny window in the cell door. Didn't make a sound, just watched me. Like she was trying to be brave, but was really young and scared inside." So much like he'd imagined Natalee in her final hours.

"I delivered my message and left," he continued. "I'd learned something about my Circle contact. He liked to party. So when I saw him entering his favorite club late that night, I took a gamble and returned to the building. I was able to sneak in and get her out of there." He blew out a breath, feeling a little looser in the chest after sharing his story with someone. No, not just someone. *Becca*. "It felt so damn good to see her escape. To see her so...alive." He hadn't been able to save Natalee, but he'd saved one young woman.

"That was very risky." The words held no judgment, only concern.

"I know someone else who takes those kinds of risks." He hated knowing that she could be hurt on any given day, with any number of investigations that he knew nothing about. It must be what a cop's spouse felt like on a daily basis. He wanted to *know*, to be there to protect her. From everything, always. It was a pointless desire.

She straightened and snatched the deck from him. "My turn to deal." But after the hand played out, she'd lost.

Diego sorted through the myriad of questions he wanted answered, which ranged from easy stuff about her childhood or current favorite music, movies, or colors to the tough ones about how she'd been hurt in the past and why she'd walked out on him in July.

She must have read his choice in his eyes because the moment he opened his mouth, she reached out and took his hand, then pressed his palm to her bra-clad breast. "You could exchange your question for a touch," she offered. "A onetime offer."

His breath hitched at the feel of her vibrant skin, where his fingertips stretched over the top of her bra. There, she was just a shade softer than the satin material. But the question on his mind burned hotter than the skin-to-skin contact.

"Why did you leave me, Becca?"

CHAPTER 13

B ecca wished away the past few seconds. Maybe Diego hadn't gone there. Maybe she'd misheard his question. But, reading the doubt and frustration in his gaze, of course he had.

"I thought everything was going well between us at the time," he said. "Did I say something? Do something wrong?"

Had he really thought that? "No," she hurried to assure him. "It was all me. My issues."

"What issues?"

She clamped her lips together. That question led down a path she was trying to avoid. In a sudden movement, he whipped his shirt over his head and tossed it aside. She looked her fill at the strong, wide chest she remembered, at the triangle of dark hair spread across his pecs, then upward to the broad shoulders that surely were molded like those of Atlas. And she knew exactly how that spot at the base of his throat, where his collarbones met in a V, tasted.

He was as fit as ever, and had even bulked up a bit. He probably worked out more since he had to deal with the Circle.

He'd want to be in top shape to face them down...if it ever came to that. If he couldn't help bring them down, would he have to serve in this role indefinitely? And how long could he continue to deceive the crime ring? She shivered at the thought of the danger he had been taking on daily since she'd seen him last.

"The shirt is payment for my question." His gaze held hers prisoner. "Now tell me what I did wrong."

"Nothing. I swear. It really was my stuff that got in the way."

"Is that *stuff* between us now?"

"Yes." As if strangled, the word came out half moan, half plea to let things alone. "That's all you'll get."

With jerky motions, he dealt a hand and they played it out. The cards she held shook as she realized he was going to win. She stood and unbuttoned her pants, then, with a wiggle of her hips, pushed them down her legs and to the floor, where she kicked them away. She'd choose physical nakedness over emotional any day of the week.

Her breathing hitched as his gaze slid over her like a caress, from her feet to her stomach to her chest, then finally to her face. He reached out and took her hand, then tugged her into his lap. With his free hand, he traced the line of her neck, continuing down along the top of her bra. As if in a trance, he journeyed up again to trace her lips.

His gaze found hers, his eyes lit with desire. Becca didn't even try to resist as he shifted her until she was straddling his lap and her lips were an inch from his. Through his jeans, she could feel his arousal, could feel her own body answering the primal call, readying herself for him. Sex, she could handle. Revealing her past mistakes, not so much.

"You said no touching during this op." Her words were a whisper against his lips.

"I must have been insane. No more boundaries, Becca. Let me in."

The pleading in his voice undid her. Wordless, she bent her head to his.

With a hunger that matched her own, he closed his mouth over hers. The heat and fervency with which he claimed her pulled a whimper from deep in her throat. She put a hand against his chest for balance, but soon found the appendage had a mind of its own and began exploring the expanse of caramel skin dusted in dark hair. The heat, the memories, the months of loneliness, the want...God, the constant, aching *want*...it all exploded in a fireball behind her ribcage, incinerating the pain.

There was only heat, only Diego.

His hands slid from her shoulders to her waist. He slipped his fingers beneath the edge of her panties. She ground her pelvis into the hard ridge beneath his zipper. His fingers cupped her bottom, then one hand slid up again, his thumb brushing against a spot just below her waistline.

Her butterfly. Though he couldn't see it, it was as if he was tracing her tattoo. The one that symbolized the change she'd strived so hard for in her life.

With every lick, nip and shift, he was only feeding the flames that would consume her. And she couldn't let that happen. It was what she'd been fighting against since she'd met him, and it was why she had to be strong now. For the changed Becca that she had become. Because if he broke through her remaining barriers as if they were spider webs, he'd hate her. She'd hate herself.

With a burst of will, she put both hands against his chest and pushed away. And nearly fell backward out of his lap, but his hands were there to catch her. She took some small satisfaction in his irregular breathing.

His eyes searched hers. "This, between us, isn't just going to go away. We have something."

It was that *something* that had her running scared. The last time she'd thought she had *something* with a man, she'd been horribly wrong—with disastrous consequences. Though she'd only half succeeded, she'd done despicable things in her efforts to put James Powell behind bars. Things that could now hurt Diego's career and family.

Not to mention the shame she would feel. He would never look at her the same. It had taken herself years to look in the mirror again, and she'd recreated herself in order to do it. But Diego? He would walk away and never have to look back. And she'd have to rebuild herself again. It was best if they went their separate ways in a week. And even better if she could keep her hands off of Diego in the meantime.

"If you're so worried about why I left, why did you take Damian's offer? Is it so *you* could leave *me* this time? The joke's on you. You'll soon find that being around me is more trouble than it's worth."

She was surprised when his mood didn't shift to the anger she expected, but to pity. It pissed her off.

She climbed off of him and gathered her clothes from the floor. "I'll grab some sheets and a blanket for you. If you want something to eat or drink, help yourself. I'm heading to bed." *Alone.*

She went into the bathroom and retrieved linens from the cupboard, taking deep breaths as she tried to regain her equilibrium. When she returned to the living room, Diego had stripped down to his boxers and was turning out the lights. The deck of cards remained spread out on the table.

She stopped in her tracks and swallowed hard, then forced herself to turn to the couch and set down her bundle. "You should have everything you need."

"Becca," he called, stopping her retreat. "You asked why I took this job?"

"Yeah?"

"Because you're worth it."

Sunday, 11:06 p.m.

As Becca crawled into bed—alone, but very aware of the man settling on her living room couch—she received a text.

I did it all for you. We're in this together. Come see, and hurry. Lakeview Luxury Apartments, number 1203. —Your Fan

She swung her feet to the floor and immediately ran to Diego, who was lying on the couch, his hands tucked behind his head as he stared up at the ceiling in the moonlight. His gaze smoldered as he watched her cross the room, probably thinking she'd changed her mind and was coming back for seconds.

She handed him her phone. "It's him. The SSAM Fan is back in Chicago."

"He seems to be everywhere you are, and now he's signing it directly to you." Diego's eyes sparked with something unreadable.

"Let's go. I'll be dressed in one minute."

"Whoa." He was on his feet and taking hold of her shoulders before she could walk away. "Shouldn't we call for backup first?"

"They can meet us there." She turned, freeing herself of his large, warm hands, but immediately wishing they were on her body again.

Diego began pulling clothes from his duffel bag in the corner. "Too bad Noah's on his honeymoon. We could use some friendly CPD backup."

"We've got SSAM," she said. "In fact, we've got you. That's why Damian hired you, right?"

Diego didn't look so certain.

"We'll call the cops," she assured him. "But if we beat them there, I'm not going to just stand around."

Thirty minutes later, she and Diego found themselves outside a posh high-rise in the Lakeview East community. Becca and Diego headed for the elevator. On the twelfth floor, the door to apartment 1203 was slightly ajar. Nobody answered her knock.

"No sign of the CPD," Becca said. "We should see if anyone needs our help, right?"

Diego nodded. "I've got you covered."

Both Diego and Becca drew their guns and edged their way inside, covering each other's backs. The inside was furnished in leather and rich, glossy woods in a modern style. Everything smelled new and looked untouched, as if they'd walked into the floor model.

Except for the open front door, all seemed normal. Still, the hair on Becca's neck was standing at attention.

"Hello?" Becca called out, moving farther into the apartment. At the open door to the bedroom, she froze. The dead, naked body of James Powell lay on the bed. His arms were spread-eagled, handcuffed to the wrought-iron headboard. His blue lips and the garrote wire around his neck indicated strangulation was the cause. A vase on the nightstand held a dozen yellow roses.

As bile crawled up her throat, the image of another room flashed in her mind. A rundown motel room set for a romantic rendezvous...and resulting in murder. The similarities here were so stunningly vivid, down to the smallest detail, that Becca was speechless. Which was a good thing, because she was afraid if she opened her mouth, she might vomit. The room blurred and shifted and she forced herself to inhale, then exhale. Repeated the action until the room righted itself. But nothing was right about this room.

Diego checked the bathroom directly off the bedroom for signs that an intruder was still there. *Shit.* She hadn't even thought of that. All her training, all her common sense had flown out the window. Her world had come to a standstill upon finding her ex-lover murdered.

"You know him." Diego returned to her side after ensuring the apartment was empty except for him, Becca and the body. His words were more a statement of fact than a question, since it was obvious by the way Becca stood just inside the doorway, shaking and staring in shock, that she'd had a personal reaction to the dead man.

Or maybe she was reacting to the fact the SSAM Fan had finally crossed the line. While they'd suspected a criminal vein in his words before, and that he might have killed the prostitute in the picture left for Diego, this was clear proof the Fan was involved in something illegal, and definitely deadly.

But what Diego was most worried about was how pale Becca had become. The Fan had left this body specifically for her, as if it were a gift to murder this man. His detective instincts screamed that the corpse—whoever he'd been—had something to do with her past.

"This wasn't your fault," he reminded her, trying to break through the haze of shock. "You didn't kill him."

"But the Fan did it for me." There was a hiccup in her miserable sentence that told him just how close her emotions were to the surface.

"Who is this man?" His eyes narrowed on her. "And don't lie to me. It's obvious that you know—knew— him."

"James Powell. And it's just like before, except he's the one who's dead."

Prickles of foreboding stabbed at his gut. Someone had died in a similar way in her past? He took out his phone and dialed the police again. After he was assured they were almost there, he pulled Becca into the other room, where she couldn't see the body. She was shaking beneath his hands as he directed her to an armchair in the living room and gently pushed her into it.

"It'll be okay," he told her.

The assurance was as much for him as for her.

It wasn't okay. The CPD arrived, followed by a Detective Wells who spent a long time questioning them. They discovered that this was, indeed, James Powell's apartment. A laptop sat open on his desk, open on an email he'd sent Becca earlier that morning —an email that sounded like a threat.

An hour later, Wells made the decision Becca had known was coming, to bring her to the station for a more formal interview. Diego protested but she acquiesced, letting the detective slide her into the backseat of his car. At least this time there were no handcuffs. But it was no less humiliating because her experience was compounded by Diego witnessing her downfall.

She handed Diego the keys to her car.

"I'll meet you at the station," he said. The bite in his voice could have been disgust, fatigue or concern. Becca was too numb to decipher it.

"Call Matt. He'll know what to do." She could see the confusion in his eyes as Wells nudged him out of the way so he could close the car door. Another barrier between them.

It didn't matter anyway. By morning, Diego would be so through with her that he'd catch the first plane back to New York. Whether the SSAM Fan had meant to help her or frame her, killing James Powell was about to make things very, very bad for her.

Her fan had gone to great lengths to recreate many of the details of the scene she'd walked in on eight years ago, in a motel room. Only this time, there was even more reason to suspect Becca had committed the crime. Her motive was well established.

At the station, Wells escorted her to an interview room, sat her down at a metal table, and gave her a bottle of water. All she could think was thank God Diego didn't have to witness her total decomposition.

"You have a criminal record." Wells said. "You didn't tell me that at the scene."

The matching chair across the table from her screeched as he slid it out to take a seat. His statement didn't require clarification, so she remained quiet.

"I should arrest you," Wells continued, his eyes narrowing on her. "You were arrested before for a very similar crime."

Should arrest her? That meant he wasn't going to. Becca immediately perked up at the thought of a reprieve. She kept quiet, though. Last time this had happened, she'd talked, and nobody had listened. Nobody had believed she hadn't been integral in the death of a friend. Of course, James had set the stage well, twisting the circumstances of Amy's death to make Becca look like a jealous bitch, capable of murder.

Wells's concentrated gaze was meant to tear her down. "You broke into a man's home, and that man is dead."

"The door was open when I got there." Becca and Diego had already been over this with Wells, but they had only each other to corroborate. He was trying to punch a hole in her story.

"Why were you there in the first place?"

Again, these were questions she'd answered on the scene. "If you'll check my phone, you'll see a text inviting me to the location."

"You could have arranged for someone to send that to you."

"I could have. I didn't. Is my lawyer here yet?"

Wells leaned forward. "Lucky for you, your friend swears he's been with you nonstop for the past eighteen hours."

She never thought she'd be thanking God for having Diego as a constant shadow, but she did. When she'd discovered Amy, she'd been alone...until her screams had brought the night manager at the motel running to the scene.

A calculated gleam entered Wells's eyes. "But Detective Sandoval doesn't know about your record, does he? He might not be such a willing alibi once we notify him about your previous arrest."

She pressed her fingertips to her tired eyes. What she wouldn't give for two aspirin. But she didn't dare ask for anything. Her heart squeezed painfully at the thought of Wells showing Diego her file. Diego was a detective trying to rebuild his reputation and she was a woman with a police record. Even if their passion had a future, she'd be holding him back. He'd made a big mistake and was making amends, but if he were involved with her, she'd undo all of his hard work. Sure, she'd had her reasons for what she'd done, and Diego might understand, but she couldn't expect him to excuse her past behavior. Just as she hadn't expected her family to have to deal with her mess. She loved them too much for that.

"I'm here."

Becca looked up at the familiar face in the doorway and had to restrain herself from jumping into her brother's arms. He read the emotion in her eyes and nodded his understanding, then turned to Wells. "I'm Matt Haney, Becca's attorney."

"Haney?" Wells said, taking the business card Matt held out to him. "You're related?" He shook his head. "It doesn't matter. Things look bad for your client, Mr. Haney. I'd advise her to talk."

"Which is why *you're* not her lawyer." He shut the door behind him and pulled a chair from a corner to sit next to Becca. "You okay?"

She nodded wearily. "As well as can be expected. I *want* to talk, Matt. I have nothing to hide." She looked at Wells. "I didn't kill James."

Wells's thumbs tapped together as if he were transmitting a message in Morse code. "It's not like I feel sorry for James Powell. He's a parolee who served time for other charges. He wasn't totally innocent."

Not even close.

"I'm not stupid, Detective Wells," Becca said. When she'd seen the vase of yellow roses on James's nightstand tonight, and the way he'd been sprawled naked on the bed, his inbox exposed with the recent communications, she'd known exactly how this was going to look. *Ugly.* "I wouldn't set up the scene to look exactly like it had at the scene of Amy's murder. It would be like hanging a neon sign over my head saying I did it."

"Becca—" Matt's voice held a warning to stop talking.

Wells looked up as someone knocked on the door. "Come in." A desk officer delivered a note and, after a furtive glance at Becca, quietly left. Wells looked up from the scrap of paper, his expression dark.

"Talk to your commander," she told Wells, fearing the note involved some kind of evidence against her. She didn't like the way he was viewing her as if she were lower than dirt. "He knows the whole story." He'd been in charge of her case when Becca had tried to help take James Powell down. She'd been a squeaky wheel, so she was sure he'd remember.

"Oh, I already know about your assistance with Powell's arrest." His eyes flashed wickedly, and Becca had no doubt the man knew all the dirty details. Had read about them and probably watched the evidence for himself. She flushed red with shame. Wells's gaze moved over her body and she fought to contain her anger.

Matt stiffened beside her, ready to leap to her defense. "Is my client under arrest? If not..."

"Your client's help is why she's not under arrest...yet," Wells said. "You're free to go, as long as you stay in the area and continue to cooperate. I'm sure we'll have more questions. In the meantime, I suggest you tell your boyfriend out there to calm the fuck down. I hear he's looking like a mental patient ready to chew through his straps to get to you."

Becca shivered. Was Diego eager to protect her, question her or throttle her?

Diego was in the waiting area for over an hour, pacing like a caged tiger while a million possibilities ran through his head, each more alarming than the last. At least her brother was in there with her. She wasn't totally alone.

When Becca finally emerged from the interview room with Matt, she wouldn't meet his gaze, and his detective instincts were going wild—as were his Becca instincts. He wanted to demand she talk to him, after he grabbed her up against him and held her for several long, stabilizing moments.

He did neither. Something in her guilty expression told him neither strategy would work.

"She's free to leave," Matt said. His emotions were unreadable.

"You can go," Becca told Matt. "I'll be okay."

"Call me first thing in the morning." Matt pressed a kiss to her temple, nodded a goodbye to Diego and left.

"Did you book your trip back to New York yet?" Her tone was self-deprecating, but it wasn't what Diego wanted to hear. Since he couldn't trust himself to convey his thoughts and emotions in a calm manner, he turned on his heel and walked out the door.

"Hold up, would you?" Becca jogged down the stairs to catch up.

He shortened his strides to let her come even with him, but continued into the parking lot until they'd reached her car.

"Wait, Diego," she pleaded, putting her hand on his arm.

He swung around to face her. Puffs of breath escaped from her parted pink lips, fogging the darkness and catching the moonlight. A shiver of desire rippled through him. Damn it. Even when he was pissed off at the woman he wanted to toss her over his shoulder like a Neanderthal, head to the nearest cave and feel her hot breath against his skin, the rumble of her sexy moans beneath his lips.

He scowled as he tried to control the tempest of emotions inside him. "You want to talk *now?* Here, on the street, in the middle of the night, with the police still inside praying for you to confess to murder so they can wrap this case up in a shiny red bow? I've been trying to get you to talk for days. Hell, I've been hoping to hear from you for months. I simply got used to the disappointment. But, damn. I can't continue like this."

She looked away. "You're right. There's a lot you don't know. I didn't know how to tell you." Her lips twisted in a grimace. "That's a lie. I didn't *want* to tell you."

"And?"

"And this still isn't the right time or place."

Anger vibrated through every nerve ending.

"That doesn't mean I won't talk," she hastily added.

He wanted to hold on to the anger. It kept him warm, kept him sane, kept the fear at bay. God, she could have been locked away for breaking and entering, murder and who knows what else over the past couple days.

She stepped up close and wrapped her arms around his waist, then tucked her head against his chest. The gesture was so gentle and surprising, such an unconscious admission of fear and need, that it caught him in the throat.

"I *am* going to tell you everything," she said against his coat. "*Everything.* I promise. When the time is right."

"Is the time going to be right soon?"

"As soon as you get me home."

He brought his arms around her. "I called Damian and told him what happened. He didn't ask any questions, just said he'd make some calls on your behalf."

She sighed against him. "Thank you. I'm not sure I could have handled that conversation right now."

"You're shaking," he said. "Let's go home."

"It's not the cold. That's kind of refreshing."

"Then what is it?"

"I'm afraid." She pulled away to look up at him. "My past is catching up to me and I don't want to ruin your life."

Ruin his life? What could be that bad? "You brought me *back* to life. There's no way you could ruin it."

She gave a short, humorless laugh. The glow of the parking lot lamp cast a bluish tinge to her face. Her brown eyes were dark, her blond hair nearly white, giving her an ethereal fairylike quality. Her gaze was locked on his. Tension radiated off her. Her fingers were curled tightly into the fabric of his coat.

Fear. She was worried he would hate her for whatever it was in her past. That he couldn't forgive whatever transgressions she'd made. That she gave him that much power over her feelings was an honor he wouldn't put into words. If he did, she'd no doubt circle the wagons or retreat again. She didn't seem to realize how vulnerable she was making herself right now.

He touched a finger to her cheek. "Do you have an arrest record?"

"Yes, sort of."

He'd already guessed as much. The *sort of* part he'd figure out later. "Did you kill someone?"

"No."

"Kidnap?"

"No."

"Rip someone to shreds?" He could picture that, if they deserved it. Becca's heart burned for justice. She wouldn't do anything that didn't serve a higher purpose. And though he'd meant his comment in a teasing manner, she didn't smile.

"No."

"Do anything that someone didn't deserve?"

She blew out a breath. "No."

He searched her eyes, and she seemed to be searching his right back. "Were you even guilty of what you were arrested for?"

"No. The charges were eventually dropped."

Except something had her feeling guilty. But if she hadn't done anything illegal, it was a crime of the conscience. He frowned. "Hell, Becca. Anything else we can get past."

She lifted her arms and wrapped them around his neck, hugging him with a fierceness that spoke of her relief. Again, he was struck by her vulnerability. Perhaps she was coming to trust him, after all. She stood on her tiptoes and brushed her lips against his. The icy touch of winter retreated as liquid heat flowed through his veins, the kiss spreading through him like hot chocolate, warming him from the inside out. He tightened his arms around her. At least something good had come from tonight's horrible events. All her defenses were down and he was finally —*finally*—seeing the passionate, sensitive Becca he'd fallen for months ago. She pressed into him and slid her hands up his chest to his face, cupping his cheeks.

Reluctantly, he ended the kiss. "You're freezing." Pulling her hands from his face and curling them inside his palms, he tried to infuse heat back into her.

"Thank you." Her eyes had a dazed look that made his chest ache. Had he put that contented, awestruck look on her face?

He grinned. "For the kiss? There's more where that came from."

She laughed, a puff of hot air in the darkness that hit his bare neck and sent a shudder through him. God, he wanted this woman. Every damn inch of her.

She grew serious again. "No. Thank you for staying while they questioned me, though you might wish you'd walked away when you hear my story."

"We're in this together. Partners. Besides, Detective Wells didn't really let me stay with you."

"I felt you with me the whole time. Take me home, Diego."

CHAPTER 14

Monday, 1:48 a.m.
Becca's apartment

Becca owed Diego so many things, but right now she owed him the truth. Once inside her apartment, he grabbed a couple sodas from the refrigerator and gestured to the couch, indicating she should take a seat.

"Hungry?"

Her stomach clenched. "No, thanks."

He sat down close to her but kept a few inches of breathing room, which was just what she needed. The cards from their strip poker/truth-or-dare game were still spread across the coffee table. Beneath her, the soft blanket she'd given him to sleep with was warm and comforting. He handed her a soda. She took a swallow, struggling to find the words to express the myriad of emotions that surrounded the memories of her past.

He waited patiently for several long minutes before speaking up. "Don't get shy now, Becca. You've seen me at my worst."

"So now you get to see me at mine?"

"I'd be privileged." The words, spoken quietly but honestly, gave her courage.

She reminded herself she wasn't going to be scared of anything —of him, or his reaction. This was Diego, who'd told her everything about the niece he'd lost, and how much he ached for his family's loss. She'd felt that ache, too.

She set her soda on the table. "You once told me you felt responsible for Natalee's death."

He stiffened at the mention of his niece's name but didn't dispute her statement. "I was wrong to feel that way."

"Feelings don't always have rational reasons behind them."

"True. And it took me some time to realize that."

Becca nodded. "I've felt ashamed for so long now—since I was twenty years old. I made so many mistakes."

"In college?"

"Yes. I was trying to help a friend."

He smiled softly. "You're always helping friends."

"Yeah, well, I didn't know what I was doing back then." She'd been incredibly naïve to think she could take on a serial criminal and find justice for Amy. Then again, she hadn't known at the time that James Powell was a repeat offender who'd never been caught.

"During the fall of my sophomore year, I took an upper-level English lit class. It was my major at the time." So many things changed that year. In fact, her entire life changed. "I guess I caught the eye of my professor, James Powell. In the spring, when I was no longer in his class, he let me know he was interested...and not just in my brain."

He turned toward her slightly, his bent knee almost touching hers. "I take it we're talking about the same James Powell who was found murdered tonight."

"Yes. He was released on parole this past week."

"What did he do?" Diego's question was quiet, with an undercurrent of alarm. "And what did you do to him that got you arrested?"

"Wow, cut right to it." She took another swallow of soda. The bubbles burned a trail to her gut and she promptly set the can down. "He murdered Amy. I was arrested for it."

Diego went completely still. She couldn't blame him. She remembered that time, the craziness of it. *Stunned* pretty much summed it up.

She forced herself to meet his gaze, but rather than the condemnation she expected to find there, she saw confusion. "I didn't lie when I said I didn't kill anyone," she said.

"I didn't think you could. Not without a damn good, life-or-death reason. I'm simply shocked anybody could think that of you. What evidence did they find? Set the scene for me." He'd switched to detective mode, which somehow made her retelling easier.

"Amy Sturgeon was the victim's name. She was my sophomore roommate, and she was found naked, lying face-up on a motel bed just a mile from campus. There was a vase of yellow roses on the nightstand, with a card addressed to her, signed *from James, with love.*"

"Similar to the scene of tonight's murder."

"I'll admit I had flashbacks when I saw the flowers." And chills. *Déjà vu.* A bit of raw panic. "And there are other similarities, which is why Detective Wells was only doing his duty when he interviewed me. Both times, I had reason to be angry with the person who died."

"And your supposed motive in Amy's murder? Jealousy?"

She crossed her legs under her, snuggling further into the blanket. "Yes. Amy apparently dated James the semester before we were in his class. What I didn't know when I was dating him was that he had a habit of pursuing his female students, putting them on a pedestal, and making them feel like he needed them in order to feel whole. When she realized I was dating him, Amy came to me and told me what he'd done to her. When I confronted him, he laughed it off, saying she was jealous because he'd dumped her for a better woman."

"You."

"Yes."

"What did she say he did to her?" Diego's face was dark as a storm cloud, anticipating her answer.

"Rape. Apparently, he liked to get rough."

Diego opened his mouth, as if he'd ask a question. Then closed it again, apparently deciding to let her tell the story at her own pace.

"I chose to believe James over Amy, since we'd been together a couple weeks at that point and he hadn't tried anything with me."

"Did Amy go to the police?"

"No. Later, I learned James had convinced her she'd be a pariah. That she would lose her scholarship, that people would treat her differently, that nobody would believe her." In the end, it had been Becca nobody believed. "My failure to believe her must have hurt her so much. We stopped talking. I broke up with James not long after that, when I realized how manipulative he was. Since Amy's accusations, I'd begun to get a creepy vibe from him. The night after I told James we were through, Amy died and there were things that made it look like I murdered her."

"The police believed you had motive and opportunity."

"Luckily, there wasn't enough evidence against me, so the DA decided not to prosecute. They found James's DNA on Amy."

"Because he'd raped and killed her."

"That was my theory. But James painted a different scene. Said *he* had dumped *me* to go back to Amy. That he'd left Amy that night at the motel room after they'd had consensual sex. He told the police he'd called me to tell me he was going back to Amy. He presumed I must have gone to confront her. One of my earrings was found at the scene...one he'd given me as a gift a week before, then torn out of my ear the night before, when we'd fought."

"When *you'd* broken up with *him*." He narrowed his eyes on her. "The earring at your parents' house."

"I keep it as a reminder." Not to get too involved, not to trust too much, or love too hard. "He made me out to be a jealous bitch, capable of murder." The word still left a bad taste in her mouth. "I have no doubt he did it. Maybe Amy was going to go to the police. I don't know. For some reason, he had to get rid of her. The CPD found her laptop on the motel desk—another similarity to tonight's scene. It showed her inbox, and James sending her an email declaring his love and asking to meet her about three hours before she died. And it showed an email from her to me, telling me she'd reunited with James, that I wasn't enough woman for him, etcetera."

"He could have sent that easily if he had access to her laptop."

She nodded. "I agree. But in the eyes of the police, it also gave me a motive—jealousy. Combine that with the fact I'd been alone in my dorm room, studying, and I also had opportunity and no alibi."

"James was never investigated as a suspect?"

"You have to understand James was a guy blessed with an unusual abundance of charm. He had that charisma that politicians and cult leaders have. It made you feel good to be near him. It was like basking in the sun when he turned his smile on you. Until you got to know him and realized the beauty was only skin-deep." She picked at an invisible piece of lint on the blanket between them. "He chose his victims well. Young women who were star-struck by his professor status. Pretty, but not beautiful. Lonely. Naïve."

"None of this sounds like you."

She smiled wryly. "Not anymore. I toughened up a lot after him, though there was a distinct stage where I had to find my inner strength by trying on different exteriors. My hair was even purple at one time. And then there was the nose piercing."

"The butterfly tattoo." His gaze shifted to her hip, not that he could see the mark.

"I'm sure I left my family speechless for a full year. They certainly didn't push me too hard for answers. Then again, maybe Matt covered for me."

"Your brother? That's why you had me call him tonight."

She nodded. "He's not just my lawyer, he's the only one who knows what happened."

"You didn't tell your family? Didn't you think they'd support you?"

"I was too ashamed. And they would have been crushed to hear about the murder charges. I didn't think I could deal with the worry and disappointment in their eyes."

"So the charges against you were dropped. How did James get arrested? Since he was released, I'm guessing it wasn't for murder."

She looked away, knowing Diego would hate her for what she'd done after. But that part she'd keep to herself, buried down deep inside.

DIEGO'S GUT TWISTED AT THE PAIN AND GUILT ON BECCA'S FACE. NO wonder she'd been afraid to love a man again. James Powell had dragged her through hell. It seemed that hell continued.

Becca pulled her knees up to her chest, hugging them. "There wasn't enough evidence to prove, beyond any doubt, that he'd murdered Amy. But after he became an official suspect, other students came forward to tell their stories. He was arrested on several charges of rape. But Amy's murder was never resolved."

"That's why you work at SSAM," he guessed.

"I changed my major to Criminal Justice the next fall and heard about the work SSAM was doing to catch the criminals who fell through the cracks. I knew that was the place for me."

"Why couldn't you tell me about this? Did you think I wouldn't understand?"

"It's not something I talk about. Ever."

She hadn't even told her family. She'd carried this around for years, channeling it into her work. Diego understood that, as he had done the same thing for months now, working to put his past mistakes behind him. But that had been different. He had made a mistake and had to repair the damage. Becca was paying for James's actions. She carried the shame.

"None of this was your fault," he told her.

"It seemed nobody listened to my side of the story. Or nobody believed it."

"You didn't think I'd believe you," Diego said quietly.

"I didn't want you to have to make the choice. I made peace with myself years ago, but to this day, my past still pops up to haunt me on occasion, usually hurting the people I love."

Diego's heart shifted and lost ground. He was falling hard for this woman who had given him so much of herself in his time of need but couldn't trouble anyone with her own pain.

He reached for her hand and linked his fingers with hers. "You're an amazing woman. Thank you for telling me."

She looked up in surprise, obviously expecting the opposite response. Did she think he would walk out on her? Probably. Her past lover had framed her for murder and left her out to dry.

He cupped her cheek with his free hand. "It's a wonder you trust men, after what you went through. It's a testament to your inner strength and resilience that you ever trusted me."

"What do you mean?" Her words were whisper-soft.

"I'm a man and a cop. Double-strike."

"Even when Selina dropped your name as a Circle mole, I trusted you. It took me a while to sort that out, but deep down in my gut, I knew you weren't a bad guy."

His chest tightened with an onslaught of emotions. Relief. Gratitude. So many things went through him at once. Mostly, though, Becca had given him what he'd needed for months. She believed in him and recognized that he was more than the sum of his recent behavior.

"Then why'd you leave me?" He hadn't meant to ask the question. She'd avoided it so many times in the past, he figured she'd steer the conversation clear of that territory again. So when she opened her mouth to answer, he felt another wave of emotion. She was knocking down her barriers. For him.

"You got too close," she said simply. "I wanted to help you. I was attracted to you. But, with you, it was more." She looked away and clamped her mouth shut as if she'd been about to reveal too much.

A surge of masculine pride that he'd been the one to affect her, such an amazing woman, nearly made him lightheaded. His thumb brushed her cheek and she turned her face back to him. He hated the uncertainty he saw there. "And now?"

"I still don't like it." She bit her lip. "But you seem to blow away my willpower."

He'd have to have enough willpower for the both of them—until she felt strong enough to recognize that being together would be a wise decision. As much as he wanted to make love to her, to show her that he didn't view her any differently because of her past, he wouldn't have her backing away later, saying she hadn't wanted to get in that deep.

He'd wait for her decision. And it would be all or nothing.

CHAPTER 15

Monday, 7:14 a.m.

As daylight slanted through the drapes, Diego unfolded himself from Becca's couch and dedicated extra time and attention to stretching his cramped muscles. Despite his protesting limbs, he felt better than he had in months. Becca was just on the other side of the wall. They'd broken down the barriers between them.

He'd had a hard time settling his body so he could sleep, thinking of a responsive Becca who seemed to want him to absolve her body as well as her heart. Though he might not have spent the night in her bed, and she'd seemed confused that he hadn't pressed his advantage in the early morning hours when he'd kissed her good-night, thanking her for trusting him with her story, he was certain he was on the right track. Things felt...*right.* As if he were precisely where he was supposed to be at the moment.

Except that she still thought she'd hurt his career. And she might be right. At the precinct, Herrera and other officers were looking for any excuse to blow the whistle and get him thrown off the force. He couldn't blame them.

As much as he hated to admit it, Becca could be right. She could ruin his future as an NYPD detective. Suddenly, his heart didn't feel as light as it had a minute ago.

"Hey." Becca muttered the halfhearted greeting as she trudged sleepily from her room. He'd remembered her as a morning person, but last night must have sapped her energy. Her hair stood at spiky angles like a lead singer in a punk band.

"Good morning. Didn't sleep well?"

She headed straight for the kitchen and the coffeemaker. "Overslept, actually. We leave in half an hour for the SSAM meeting. Unless you changed your mind and booked a flight home?"

He reached around her for the refrigerator door handle, purposely brushing against her shoulder. She shifted away. But he was in the mood to test her limits again. He loved a challenge, and he wouldn't let her put up roadblocks anymore. They'd come too far. "You shouldn't be so eager to get rid of me. I make a pretty mean omelet."

She looked tempted. Yesterday, the way to the hearts of Becca's family members had been through their stomachs. He doubted the apple fell far from the tree. In fact, the first conversation they'd shared was in a New York City deli, over pastrami sandwiches. He recalled the way she'd licked away a dab of mustard.

His gaze now went to her mouth, which was drawn in a tight line. He wanted to smooth a fingertip over it. She'd been through the wringer in the past three days—hell, in the past eight years. He wanted to whisk her away to a deserted beach where there was only the two of them and a whole lot of healing sunshine.

He removed a carton of eggs from the refrigerator. "Let me feed you."

"I can feed myself. I've gotten along all by my lonesome all these years without some big strong man to take care of little ol' me." She batted her eyes and fluttered her hand in front of her like a fan.

He leaned closer. "Big and strong, huh?"

She shoved at his bare chest, branding him in a split second. His heart thumped harder at her simple touch. "You *would* focus on the nonessential part of that statement."

He leaned a hip against the counter and snatched up the cup of coffee the moment she'd finished doctoring it to perfection.

"Hey!" she protested. "See—if I were on my own, I'd have a piping hot cup of coffee in my hands right now." She took the eggs off the counter and put them back in the refrigerator. "Unfortunately, we won't have time for a fancy breakfast this morning."

"That's a shame. I would have enjoyed cooking for you." He took a sip from the cup, then handed it back to her.

She moved out of grabbing distance like an animal hoarding a treat. "Don't you like living alone, too? I thought you were the perennial bachelor."

"I'm not sure that's me anymore." His small apartment in New York City was all he'd needed when he'd graduated from college and taken a job, but home had still been his mother's house, where he'd grown up, and where the family still gathered on a regular basis. Not having his own home base hadn't been important until recently, and he couldn't figure out what had changed.

Maybe everything had changed. His niece had died, his best friend married and was settled down in another city, and Diego had met a woman who rocked his world in every way possible.

And who could be the end of his career.

"I'm just not satisfied anymore." He realized with a shock he hadn't been able to identify the feelings that had kept him up at night, but that was it. He wasn't happy.

She froze with her cup halfway to her lips. "What do you mean?" She stared at him as if he were crazy. Maybe he was. There was a compulsion to stick by her. And imagining what it would be like to be with her every day for the long haul...it didn't sound so bad.

He shrugged as if the thoughts and emotions she'd awakened in him were no big deal instead of a mental kick to the head. "Maybe I'm lonely, too. Besides, I like working with you."

"It's temporary," she reminded him. "You'll be back in New York by this time next week. I'm not even sure why you'd want to be here. Especially now." She looked away. "You should get back, before someone at your station realizes who you're slumming with."

"I'm pretty sure you're just looking to pick a fight."

She was trying to create distance again by making him out to be the bad guy. Well, fuck that. He'd hammer away at her defenses until she admitted that what they shared was something real. Something valuable. Something worth figuring out.

And he had all week to do it. Contrary to popular belief, he was a patient guy—when he wanted something bad enough.

Monday, 7:32 a.m.
South Side, Chicago

"MOTHER?" THE FAN RAPPED HIS KNUCKLES LIGHTLY AGAINST Mother's bedroom door. All was quiet. He pushed the door open a crack. "You okay?"

"Go away." Her gruff response was muffled by a pile of blankets. Beneath them, she lay immobile on the bed.

His adrenaline kicked in as he realized what this meant—and what the next few weeks of his life would be like if he didn't act quickly. He'd thought he'd have time, that leaving to take care of his own needs hadn't been a problem, but this cycle was happening faster than ever. "Did you take the medicine the doctor prescribed?"

"Doesn't work."

He bit back disappointment. "You have to take it for two weeks, at least, before it starts working. Remember what he said?"

"I stopped taking it this weekend, when you left me. It made me feel sick. Leave me be. Don't you have work to do?"

He did, which made it all the more imperative to get her on her feet and off to her own job. He couldn't concentrate when she was around, especially when the blackness engulfed her and the mother of the new bride was already requesting he get the wedding pictures to her ASAP.

He stood and pulled some scrubs from the clean laundry basket in the corner. She hadn't folded her laundry, yet another sign that she was going downhill fast. "You'll feel better once you're up and moving. And you should give the pills a chance. You have to be consistent, and patient." As a nurse, he'd thought she'd recognize the need to stick to her doctor's plan. But when she got this depressed, she couldn't see reason.

She burrowed further under the covers. "You must hate me."

He smothered a tired sigh. This routine, too, was familiar. "I don't hate you."

"You left for three days."

"Two. And you had work, anyway." He couldn't keep the exasperation from his voice.

She peeked out from under the covers. "I don't know why you put up with me."

He sat at the edge of her bed. "We're a team. When you're down, I am too." It was the same thing she used to tell him when he was in the hospital with an illness.

Even that didn't provoke a smile. He'd have to go to extremes again. The only thing that made her happy, that created an upswing in her mood, that stabilized her for a few months, was when she became the center of positive external attention that reminded her of her value.

Everyone needed a purpose.

He put on a bright smile. "How about I come by the hospice with a picnic lunch? You can introduce me to your patients."

She sat up a little straighter. "I suppose it has been a while since you've been by. You haven't met half of this latest group." The hospice had a revolving door, its residents going there to live out their final days in comfort.

"And it's supposed to be warmer today, with plenty of sunshine. I'll bring sandwiches and we can eat outside." The hospice had a garden and patio area for the residents to enjoy, though most of them preferred the quiet solace of their rooms, as if they risked bumping into the grim reaper if they made their way out into the hall.

They just might, at that.

Monday, 8:49 a.m.
SSAM Offices, near South Side, Chicago

THE SCENT OF BECCA'S GRANDE SKINNY MOCHA WITH FULL-strength whipped cream filled the elevator as she and Diego entered on the garage's sublevel. On the way to SSAM, she'd stopped at a coffee shop for a second dose of caffeine, topped with extra sugar and fat—because it was going to be that kind of day, on practically no sleep.

She pressed the button for the fifth floor, where the SSAM offices were located, though Damian owned the entire building and there was a training area, small shooting range and gym in the basement, just above the parking level. Beside her, Diego was quiet, his scowl distracting.

"I would have bought you a coffee." She thought to tease him into a lighter mood.

She was striving for that lightness herself. After the shock of finding James murdered, the exhaustion of talking to the police, and then telling Diego the whole sordid story before falling to bed at a miserable hour, she was going to fake it until she could make it.

And that included pretending she wasn't hurt that, after telling her deepest, darkest secrets to Diego, he'd tucked her into bed and left her by herself. Was he ashamed of her? No man liked to hear that a woman he'd been with had been arrested for murder.

"Had enough at your place." Diego eyed her drink. "I can't believe you're having another."

"You're my bodyguard, not my mother." Definitely not a lighter mood.

"Partner."

"Excuse me?"

He shot her a look. "I'm your partner."

We'll see about that. The more time he had to think about what she'd confessed, the more eager he'd be to put some distance between them.

Still, Diego had told her earlier that he'd accepted this mission because of her. Because she was *worth it.* Did he still believe that, now that he knew the truth?

In the lobby, the reception desk was empty. Catherine was likely setting up for the meeting. No chance Becca would be able to bounce her confusion off of a dependable sounding board.

She took a bolstering sip of coffee, then used her palm and a security code to gain access from the lobby to the main offices. Diego followed. In the conference room, Damian was talking with Einstein, SSAM's computer expert, and Lorena, one of their mind-hunters. Catherine was seated, her laptop ready to record notes from the meeting. But her gaze was on the five Ziploc bags laid out side-by-side on the conference room table. More specifically, on the one that contained the copy of *The Scarlet Letter.* Becca sent her a sympathetic glance.

"I believe we have the necessary personnel here." At Damian's statement, everyone took their seats. "Originally, my goal was to inform you about this possible threat to SSAM, and to decide whether SSAM's so-called *fan* is benevolent or possibly...more. In the last twenty-four hours, however, his threat level has been confirmed. He's a killer, and, worse, he thinks he's killing to help Becca, clearly not thinking about how it might hurt her."

Catherine's gaze, her eyes round as saucers, met Becca's across the table. "What?"

"The Fan texted me," Becca said. "He led me to an apartment where he'd killed a man, supposedly for me." There was no judgment in Damian's eyes. In fact, she saw only acceptance and understanding. Did he know about her past?

"Let's discuss that part in a bit," Damian said.

Lorena cleared her throat. The mindhunter was fifty years old, but with her creamy, unblemished olive skin, she appeared a decade younger. "I've already requested the notes from the crime scene where last night's victim was found. The CPD also contacted us this morning to confirm the woman in the picture sent to Diego was a prostitute named Fanta. Her body was discovered late Friday night. As to the other parts of this case, I've read the notes and seen the pictures that the Fan sent, and have created a profile, but I think everyone should see the evidence and judge for themselves."

Damian gestured to Catherine. "If you could pass the photocopies around..."

Catherine pulled a stack of folders from a side table and passed one to each person. Inside were photocopies of the messages Damian had received. They dated back almost as long as Becca had worked at SSAM. And they'd always been signed from the SSAM Fan. Also attached were copies of any photographs, links, or articles that had been sent. The Fan apparently enjoyed his research, and had sent extensive notes about a myriad of cases over the past four or five years, from what Becca could estimate. Also inside the folder was a packet of printouts.

"What are these?" Becca asked.

"Transcripts of the videos the Fan sent," Damian said.

"Videos?"

"He'd find clips on the internet, or things on the news that he thought might be of interest, and send the links."

"I've combed through them," Lorena added. "So far, no common themes jump out at me other than he's trying to mimic us by pursuing bad guys."

"Like a cop wannabe," Becca said.

Lorena nodded. "Except that he has a more philosophical slant. His emails went into great detail about why a suspect could be the murderer. Our first indication that the Fan's behavior is changing was the communication he sent Damian last week. The email read: *Life is not always roses...especially white ones...sometimes it's just thorns. But then, you, of all people, know that. Justice, God's will—those are the real reasons we continue on. Your SSAM Fan.*"

Lorena gave Damian a sympathetic glance. "Leaving roses at Samantha's gravesite is a weekly ritual. Whoever sent this knows Damian's routine. Previously, the Fan had been interested in understanding criminal behavior. Last week, he showed a different side. And then he started contacting Becca, finding a personal connection with her." Lorena gestured to Becca to read her note.

"*My admiration for you knows no bounds,*" Becca read. "*We're on the same team, fighting the good fight. Keep doing your important work for Damian, and for Sam, like this afternoon. Ever yours, The SSAM Fan.* This was the first time he contacted me," she added. "And yet, he's professing he'll be ever mine."

"He's trying to establish a connection," Lorena said.

"Because he admires you," Catherine added, then frowned. "Which is probably why he thinks I should be wearing a scarlet *A*."

"I agree about the admiration part," Lorena said. "And, given James Powell's murder, and admitting he committed the crime for you, he's gone beyond admiration. Again, he's trying to form a connection with you, Becca. But what's interesting is the personal nature of these statements. With Damian, he's talking about justice, of the legal kind. Or so we thought. When the Fan targeted Catherine, accusing her of adultery with that scarlet A reference, he's indicating justice of a more moral kind. Adultery isn't illegal. He's looking at the personal hurt she is supposedly causing Becca."

"Which, for the record, is completely unfounded," Catherine added vehemently.

"Which makes it all the more chilling," Becca said. "He's judging things based on limited information, yet he feels entitled to comment on anything in my entire life."

"He's trying to understand these moral conflicts. To sort it out for himself."

"To figure out what's right and wrong?" Becca blew out a breath. "I thought most people had a grip on that by the time they were teenagers."

"Read the inscription of the book," Damian encouraged Catherine with a gentleness in his tone that indicated he knew, deep down, Catherine was scared.

She read from the photocopy in her folder. "*You might as well wear a scarlet A on your chest. Don't hurt her again.* No signature."

Lorena turned to Becca. "Given that you were at the wedding with another man, you'd think he'd be focused on his rival. Instead, it's more of a protective thing. He's more concerned with how your friend, a SSAM employee who should be above such behavior, is acting toward you, supposedly stealing your man." Lorena's gaze moved thoughtfully between Becca and Diego. "He doesn't seem threatened by Diego, either."

"Maybe he's just cocky," Diego muttered. "Thinks he'll have Becca all to himself if he impresses her enough."

"You might be onto something." Lorena turned to Damian. "I'd recommend reviewing applicants to SSAM positions for the last five years. Becca's cop wannabe comment has merit. And he seems desperate to belong here at SSAM. For whatever reason, we've caught his eye. He wants to impress us, particularly you and Becca. And his odd behavior is escalating. He's also growing more comfortable, and probably left that gift on the table at the wedding reception himself."

"I'm still waiting for the video from the hotel security and the wedding," Einstein said. Like a laser, he was focused energy, his strong fingers tapping on the table. His mussed brown hair and day-old scruff, most likely from endless hours on this case, gave him a sexy nerd look. "Noah and Vanessa are on their honeymoon, but Vanessa's mother has already contacted the photographer they hired. With those pictures, we hope to identify anybody who didn't belong. I'm also working on tracing the Fan's email address, as well as the text he sent Becca, but so far, he's using junk email addresses and throwaway phones."

"He's technologically savvy," Lorena said.

"So replying to his text wouldn't do any good?" Becca asked.

"Until this guy's ready to let us know who he is, or how to contact him, I don't think we'll get anywhere."

"Unless we can somehow invite him into our SSAM family?" Becca asked. "That seems to be what he wants, right? To be part of our group?" She picked up her phone. "This is the text he sent me last night. *I did it all for you. We're in this together. Come see, and hurry. 1845 Grand Avenue, Apartment 1203. —Your Fan.*"

"He's become your fan," Lorena said, looking thoughtful. "He wants to feel like your partner." A curtain of straight, midnight-black hair fell across her cheek as she bent to read the text of the note from the wedding. "*Congratulations to the happy couple. And congratulations to Becca for this lead. It's been a pleasure, even from afar, to watch the SSAM family celebrating how life goes on, even when those lives are painted with death and destruction. You give me faith in happy endings, and justice for all.* Even then, he was showing that he's following Becca's investigation, and applauding her for her efforts."

"What was on the DVD that was inside the box?" Becca asked, looking to Einstein. The SSAM computer expert was likely the one responsible for analyzing it. He cued the video to show on the flat-screen television hanging on the wall at the end of the conference table. Becca gasped.

Einstein nodded at her reaction. "Thought you'd recognize that guy."

"Who is he?" Diego asked.

"Tony Moreno. Someone you don't ever want to meet," Becca said. On the screen was a man. No, not a man. A monster. Someone she'd put away last year for raping and killing five women. She suspected there had been many more victims, but five had been enough to put him away for a long time. It had been her most difficult case yet. "What's the video about?"

"Our Fan took it upon himself to interview many of SSAM's monsters," Einstein said. "The thing is like a promotional video for our agency." Einstein turned the volume up.

The interviewer's voice was calm and confident. "Why did you do the things you did? Unburden your conscience."

Tony's gold-toothed grin showed no remorse. "I could say my daddy beat me. Or the public school system failed me. Or I could tell you the truth. I did it because I wanted to."

Becca shuddered and Einstein paused the video. Criminals without conscience were the worst of all, but they were also why she loved her job. Taking them down.

"So, let me get this straight," Becca said. "He wants to be part of us, leaves us these so-called gifts, but doesn't tell us how we can thank him? How can I invite him to get closer?"

"Maybe you don't," Diego said. "Maybe you're supposed to prove yourself, and your interest in partnering with him, by building trust." His gaze held hers at the word *trust*. Letting go and giving control to others was a lesson fate seemed determined to teach her lately.

"What about the Circle?" Becca asked. "He seems determined to follow my every move there. I think he knew my moves because he hacked my emails. It's the only way he would have known some of the things he knew." Like her meeting with Selina.

"I'll see what I can do about that," Einstein said. "But that might be a way to contact him, if we need it."

"As for the Circle investigation," Lorena said. "He may be trying to prove his worth to the agency by helping solve Sam's murder. Einstein and I have had a look at the pictures Becca sent of the cell walls. No sign of Sam's name there, but I've got a friend at the FBI matching names to a missing persons' list. So far, she's been able to match about a dozen missing people from over the past fifteen years. Two of them were, indeed, from Chicago, and from about a decade ago."

"How did they get to New York City?" Becca asked.

"That building in Brooklyn was a holding pen, of sorts," Diego said.

Becca felt like her head might spin off her shoulders, trying to piece it all together. "So why did the Fan kill Fanta, and why use the Circle's brand? Do we know if she was killed by him?"

Becca jumped as her phone vibrated on the table. Every eye in the room moved to the screen.

"Is it him?" Damian asked. Something dark vibrated in his voice.

Becca picked up her phone and read from the screen. *"Did you like my gift? See how we'd make a good team?—Your Fan."* She looked up. "Should I try to reply?"

"It's worth a shot," Einstein said.

Damian nodded. "Try it."

Becca read aloud as she typed. *"Teammates, or partners, don't frame each other. You left me to take the rap."* She glanced at Lorena, who nodded, and Becca hit Send, crossing her fingers that he hadn't discarded the phone yet. They needed to lure him out. If she could just get a conversation started...

"He replied," she said as the phone vibrated in her hand.

"What did he say?" Diego asked, leaning close.

"I'll fix it." Whatever that meant, it sounded ominous.

"Let us know the moment he contacts you again," Damian ordered. "In the meantime, Einstein and Lorena, review past cases to see if any of the other criminals Becca helped put behind bars have been released, contacted for interviews, or if any of the victims' families would have reason to start sending us notes. Pay close attention to those in the Chicago area."

"Want us to check into SSAM applicants over the past few years?" Becca asked.

"I'll be doing that myself. In the meantime..." He waited until Becca met his gaze. "You and Diego swing by the Metropolitan Correctional Center."

Diego sent her a questioning look.

Just her luck. "We're talking to Tony Moreno."

CHAPTER 16

Monday, 12:15 p.m.
Golden Oaks Hospice, South Side, Chicago

"It's a bit chilly for a picnic, but if we sit in the sun, the warmth should be sufficient." He helped Mother into her coat.

"It'll be fine." Her cheeks held a glow he hadn't seen in weeks. Her attention darted about in a subtle way, as if cataloguing which of her coworkers and patients might be observing her son doting on her.

He zipped his own jacket and hoisted the picnic basket in one hand, linking his other arm with hers. "Warm enough?"

Outside on the patio, he lent her a hand to help her down the stairs, alerted her to an icy spot, and escorted her to the picnic table. Wood, thank God. Stone or metal would have frozen his balls off.

Mother nodded. "Warm enough. You're so thoughtful. I don't deserve it."

"That's ridiculous." He settled her on a bench with a plaid lap blanket from his car and set the picnic basket on the table. When depressed, Mother fell back on self-pity for attention. It was his least favorite phase. But soon, others would be pitying her and taking the load off of him.

One death, one shining obituary, and Mother would be in the spotlight again. Because of him.

And because of him, Becca wouldn't be troubled by the police, once he called them with his anonymous tip about a large man leaving James Powell's place. He'd be one step closer to becoming Becca's partner.

"None of my friends have children who are so thoughtful," Mother said. "Of course, none of them have boys who still live at home at age forty."

He stiffened against a wave of anger. Was she trying to push his buttons? No, of course not. She had no clue about how he was seething inside. Or about the turmoil that she'd churned up the past few days. She didn't know the hunger he felt, and what it cost him to seem normal. And that *she* was such a key piece of his normality. And of his abnormality.

Or did she? Sometimes he wondered.

As if on cue, she gave him the information he needed to choose his next victim. "I'd like you to meet Hank. He should be up from his nap after our lunch. He naps more and more frequently. Body giving out, you know..." Her voice trailed off. She avoided his eyes.

Did she know?

She picked at her chicken salad with a fork, not really eating. In this phase, she rarely did.

"Tell me more about him," he encouraged, and listened with rapt attention as she rattled off a series of inane facts. *War veteran. Widowed two years ago. Grew up in these parts. Cancer's about eaten him through to his bones. In such pain, even with medication.*

When she was done, she gave him a look that said, *So what are you going to do about it?* Maybe she did know. Maybe she did understand, and simply looked the other way because he did it all for her.

No, not all for her. Like turning a valve to release pressure, a good kill made him feel great for a while... relaxed and at peace. And there was no denying that part of him enjoyed making these ordinary people— and even the useless people like Fanta—rock stars in the eyes of others. Just as much as he liked giving the hardened criminals such as Tony a voice. After all, you couldn't understand the good without the bad.

The only people who understood that were at SSAM.

Of course the killers SSAM hunted were nothing like him. He was a sociologist. A cultural scientist. And someday, scientists everywhere would appreciate his documentation of the stark difference between good and evil, and all the grays in between. Why else had God let him survive all his childhood illnesses? Some had been so painful, he'd begged to die. Yet he'd always survived, because of Mother's care. He owed her.

He handed her a soda. "I look forward to meeting Hank."

She reached over to pat his knee. "Such a good son. Did you bring your camera? You haven't interviewed this latest group."

"It's in the car."

"They always have a glow after you talk to them about their lives."

Like you, they like the attention.

After their picnic had been dutifully picked at—neither of them particularly hungry, but faking it for each other—he escorted Mother inside. Two women who worked the Monday afternoon shift were hanging out in the kitchen.

"Hi," the pretty nurse named Mary said. He'd met her the last time he'd been here, a month or so ago. She clutched a half-eaten energy bar and eyed their picnic basket with a wistful smile. "We were just enjoying a rare quiet moment before we start distributing the afternoon meds. And then, of course, the evening routine begins."

"He knows how things work," Mother snapped.

Mary looked stunned and the silence stretched on for several long seconds. Mary was new, but clearly the type of nurse others looked up to as a leader. Was this the source of Mother's recent depression?

Mother patted her hair as if tucking away her unwanted anger. "My son would like to visit with some of the patients."

My son. As if anybody here didn't know who he was by now. Sometimes it was difficult being her whole world. He felt the weight of it, and once more was buoyed by the thought he'd soon have a partner. It was almost time to reveal himself to Becca. She should be thrilled with his latest coup...killing the man who'd gotten away from her when she'd been trying to find justice. She'd appreciate that.

"Our tenants would love to visit, I'm sure," Mary said brightly, as if her feelings hadn't been wounded. Maybe they hadn't. She appeared a tough sort.

"I thought I'd start with Hank."

"That would be great. When he's lucid, he's ornery. But I think it's mostly loneliness. He could use some new people to talk to."

"I'd be happy to," he said. "Let me get my camera and I'll see if he wants to do an interview."

There was admiration in Mary's gaze. "That's quite the documentary you're putting together."

You have no idea.

"I'll get Hank up and by the window where the lighting is better," Mother offered. "A change of scenery will be good for him, anyway."

He retrieved his camera from his trunk, giving her time alone with Hank to get him where she wanted him. He'd often wondered if she'd become a geriatric nurse because she could manipulate people more easily. She definitely liked people depending on her— almost as much as she liked them doting on her. When he'd grown up and started community college, she'd entered a major depression. It had been years before he'd realized how entwined their lives were, and what his responsibility was where she was concerned.

After several minutes, Mother reappeared. "He's still a bit sullen, I'm afraid." She placed a hand on his arm. "Poor guy would be happier in the afterlife, I think."

His pulse kicked up. Again, he wondered how much Mother saw, how much she knew. At the open door to Hank's room, he knocked, but there was no answer. Steeling himself against the odor of the ill who were at death's door—or inching over the threshold of that door—he entered.

"How's it going?" He walked to the table where a hunch-backed Hank stared blankly at a puzzle with only the border finished. He wondered which of the nurses had completed that task, since Hank obviously couldn't care less. The box showed two kittens peeking out of a basket of flowers. *Jesus, how demoralizing.*

Hank looked up at him and grunted as if he'd read his thoughts.

"That good, huh?" He slid into the chair opposite him and eyed the pieces. There was so much sunny yellow it was depressing.

"Never changes," Hank finally said. It took him a moment to realize Hank was responding to his initial question.

"Some people find comfort in routine." The platitude grated on him, even, but he was testing the waters. If he could get Hank to open up about his past, about his life, it would make his obituary, and the documentary, that much more interesting. He had already begun composing the man's final opus in his head.

Hank's gaze moved to the camera bag. "What's that?"

"It's a service I provide to the hospice," he said. "I interview people, let them tell their stories. The good, the bad, the ugly. Send the videos to the family, if they want. I'm hoping to make a movie someday."

Hank grunted again, then turned to look out the window.

"I hear you served in the military," he tried again. "Were even in a war or two. Bet you have some great stories."

Hank met his gaze with a rheumy one of his own. "If you're gonna stay, you can't talk."

He cleared his throat. "Right. But if you want to talk..."

"I *want* silence."

"You don't want to be popular? I would have thought a war veteran like you would have liked the notoriety, the acclaim." *Someone to notice him.* Wasn't that what everyone wanted, deep down?

A low rumble that sounded like a growl startled him into looking up at the other man. Hank was laughing. With a great, hacking cough, the man cleared the phlegm and gave a body-shaking laugh. Except his old lungs could barely squeeze out enough air to support the effort. Hank was wheezing a moment later, and the Fan slapped him on the back, not entirely to help.

"Did I say something funny?" he asked.

"Life is funny. Except when it isn't. And then you die. You young people don't understand that."

The Fan bristled. He understood more, saw more, than anyone damn well knew. Soon, they would see. "I think I understand quite a lot." He snapped the stem of a flower into place in the puzzle.

For some reason, this prompted another round of raspy laughter from Hank.

"Haven't heard Hank that happy in ages," Mother said as she entered the room carrying a key ring. Hank's private medicine cabinet was kept locked up tight. With quick efficiency, her nimble fingers removed prescription bottles from the cupboard and lined them up next to Hank's little sink.

Just like when, as a boy, the Fan had been sick. He'd had more than his fair share of illness as a child. It was one reason his mother had encouraged him, even after he'd reached adulthood, to stick close to home, where she could take care of him.

Except, somewhere along the way, the roles had reversed.

Hank was still wiping water from the corners of his eyes. The laughter would serve one good purpose, anyway. Nobody would ever expect that a man who'd gone to the trouble of making Hank laugh would later come back and kill him.

"Time for more meds," Mother said, sounding more chirpy. She opened a bottle and shook out a pill. "We have to be extra careful with this one. Too much could kill a guy."

Hank grunted. "Like anyone would care."

"This will likely make him sleepy." She turned her back on the sink, with the open pill bottle and watched Hank take the pills.

"I should hit the road," the Fan said, standing. He bent to give Mother a kiss on the cheek. "See you at home?"

"Yes." There was a sparkle in her eye. Or was that his imagination?

"I'll come back soon," he told Hank. "And I'll bring my camera in case you change your mind about that interview."

The man didn't even look up, just stared out the window, probably hoping to die. His wish would come true soon enough.

Monday, 12:57 p.m.
SSAM offices

AFTER HOURS OF REVIEWING THE MESSAGES THE FAN HAD LEFT FOR Damian, Becca sat back in her office chair with a groan.

Diego looked up from where he was reading his own copy, in the chair across the desk from her. "We only have another hour before visiting hours at the prison. Let's grab a quick lunch, and you can tell me more about Tony."

"He's not exactly lunchtime material." The thought of talking to him again turned her stomach. She lifted her coffee cup. It was empty, which didn't alleviate her crankiness. "Lunch is already dutifully consumed."

He looked horrified. "Several cups of coffee are not enough sustenance to survive."

"Whipped cream is dairy, and packed with calories. Milk is also dairy, and some protein. Chocolate is a vegetable. Caffeine should be included on the list of essential vitamins. That's a fairly well-rounded meal."

He shook his head. "And you thought I needed someone to take care of *me* last summer. If I'd had any idea..."

"You'd what? Have given up your bachelorhood to care for me into my old age and beyond?" Becca scoffed and pushed to a standing position, then arched her back and stretched the muscles in her neck.

"Is that what you wanted?" Diego watched her walk by, then stood and followed her out of her office and down the hallway. "A lifetime commitment?"

She snorted, barely glancing over her shoulder at him. "Hardly." That was the complete opposite of what she wanted. She'd wanted a fling. Something temporary, so she wouldn't have to worry about her past getting in the way. But then it hadn't been enough. It had gotten complicated.

She pushed open the door to the lobby and waved to Catherine, who was in her seat behind the reception desk, talking with someone on the phone.

"Where are we going?" Diego asked as she headed for the elevator.

"Food truck across the street. Best tacos in town."

"I thought you weren't going to eat lunch."

She climbed on the elevator when the door slid open. "You need to keep your strength up."

"And you?"

Her throat constricted just thinking about what adventures their afternoon had in store. "I'm not sure I can eat."

Diego followed her off the elevator, then stepped ahead to open the door to the street. "This Tony Moreno sounds like a horrible person."

"I'm not sure he's human. But I've learned to block the monsters out. Most of the time."

Because it was personal, James Powell had become a nightmare she'd had to deal with on occasion. The killers and repeat violent offenders like Tony were locked away in her mind after she'd literally locked them away. Unfortunately, memories of those monsters, too, crept out on occasion. Often, she'd wished she had someone to talk to about those times. While Catherine understood on some level, she wasn't out, living the day-today gritty existence of a SSAM agent. Becca suspected Diego would understand, if she chose to talk to him.

Becca had just accepted the soft taco Diego ordered for her and taken a bite when her phone rang.

Diego's eyebrows went up. Around his own bite of taco, he said, "Want me to answer that?"

She chewed and swallowed quickly. "Not on your life." He would have had to dig into her front pants pocket, where she'd stuffed the phone before leaving her office. His fingertips would have brushed parts that longed too much for just that—his touch. And he'd made it clear, both in words and by the way he'd walked away from her last night, that he wasn't going to touch her in that way. At least, not while they were working together.

With a knowing grin, he took another bite of lunch while she quickly swiped at her fingers with a napkin and dug out her phone. It was Einstein calling.

"I was able to trace the threatening text Damian received Saturday morning," he said. "The one that was meant to have you back away from the Circle investigation. It was sent by Eve Reynolds. She's a budding investigative journalist based here in Chicago."

Becca had heard of her. About the same age as Becca, Eve was striking in both her strong physical presence on camera and a voice that was sultry but commanding. Her stories had regularly made local news, and possibly national news a time or two.

"What's going on?" Diego asked as he polished off his taco. Becca's was forgotten.

She put the phone on speaker. As it was after the usual lunch hour, they were nearly alone on the street corner. "Is Eve investigating the Circle?" she asked Einstein. "Is that why she wanted me to back off? And why didn't she just come to me?"

"I'll leave that to you guys to figure out," Einstein said. "But I did notice this particular reporter—who is quite beautiful, by the way—has a particular aversion to you."

"Me? What do you mean?"

"In addition to her occasional on-air segments, she hosts a news blog that covers hot topics. You're the topic *du jour*. I've notified Damian. I'll send you the link."

Stunned, Becca could only mutter a quick thank-you before hanging up and checking her inbox via her phone. His email with the link had already arrived.

Diego crowded in close, so he could read over her shoulder. When the world beneath her feet seemed to be shifting at whim, he was a solid mass she could count on—at least for another few days. But as she read the blog post, she wondered if she should push him away before he got any closer. And when she clicked Play on the embedded video, her fears were confirmed. Her past had just caught up to her.

BESIDE HIM, BECCA WENT RIGID AS EVE'S VOICE CONDEMNED HER through the podcast linked to her blog.

"A so-called agent named Becca Haney, who works with a mysterious agency named SSAM, was nearly arrested for the death of James Powell last evening. The CPD has reason to suspect Haney. Powell claimed she was a jealous liar who framed him years ago. She had sufficient motive, and was found on the scene of the murder when police arrived. So why does she remain free? Because of her connections." A picture of Damian Manchester filled the screen. "SSAM founder and wealthy businessman Damian Manchester has friends in this city, as well as connections that money can buy. But who will buy justice for James?"

"Bitch." Becca paused the video. "She doesn't care that everything Damian does is to put killers behind bars. To protect people. Or that James hurt dozens of women."

Diego took the phone from her. "Let's see what else she has to say. We have to know what we're up against."

"We?"

"Partners, remember?" He pressed Play.

"Tune in tomorrow for an exclusive interview with James Powell, filmed just hours before his death," Eve said. "I promise I won't rest until this is examined further. SSAM and its agents shouldn't get special treatment because they proclaim to help others. They must obey the rules, just like the rest of us." She looked confidently into the camera as she signed off.

"She interviewed James hours before his death?" Becca shoved her phone into her pocket and hurried to cross the street to the SSAM building. "Could she have killed him?"

"Doubtful." Diego matched her strides. "Why would she tell the world that she'd been with him the night of his murder?"

Inside the lobby, she headed for the elevator and pressed the down button, then exhaled shakily. "My parents are going to see this. She must be one hell of an investigative journalist to know they detained me last night."

Diego took her by the shoulders and turned her toward him, resisting the urge to shake her, or kiss her. Anything to get the blood back into her face and revive the passion in her spirit. This Becca, a defeated Becca, was not a woman he recognized. This was the scared Becca beneath the tough exterior.

"You're not the vindictive woman she hints at in this video," he said, willing all of his confidence into the words. "Your family will know that—if they even see this. I'm sure Einstein and Damian are working to take this down."

But Becca didn't seem to hear the message. She looked away as the elevator arrived. "Sometimes there's nothing that can be done."

He took his hands off her shoulders, sensing an invisible wall going up between them as they got on the elevator and descended to the parking level.

Becca unlocked her car and got in, but turned to face Diego instead of starting the ignition. "Why would someone who prides herself in uncovering the truth and achieving justice derail an agency set up to fight for those very things? And why does she want me to back away from the Circle investigation so badly she'd send a threat to Damian?"

"You think she's dirty? Maybe the Circle is paying her to slam you?"

She shrugged. "She's got some kind of an agenda. Why else would she interview James Powell unless she was targeting me? It wouldn't be the first time the Circle paid off people for their own gain."

"Dirty cops, you mean?"

Becca's eyes widened. "I wasn't talking about you."

"It's okay. I had to take money to appear I'm on their side, but I doubt that's why Eve's doing it. We'll talk with Eve and straighten this out. This is slander." Diego couldn't stand the thought of Becca being hurt by James Powell again, this time from the grave.

"It's not slander if it's true." Becca's voice was resigned.

"We'll get to the bottom of this and make it right before tomorrow's post."

"What does it matter what else she'll say? My career, my life, my family...they could all be ruined with this innuendo. Just like yours would be by being associated with me."

Diego couldn't stand the despair in her eyes. He reached out and cupped her cheeks, feeling the sting of cold. She must be freezing, but her thoughts were obviously far from here. "I can help."

"Nobody can help. They couldn't then. You can't now. It's time to tell my family. After we talk to Tony. This day just gets better and better."

Monday, 2:45 p.m.
Metropolitan Correctional Center

A GUARD LED A SHACKLED INMATE INTO THE ROOM AND SECURED HIS handcuffs to a bar on the table, ensuring Tony Moreno couldn't touch them.

Tony grinned widely as he spied Becca sitting across the table. "Well, if it isn't my little spitfire." He spit at her and the guard lunged, but Becca held up a hand. The saliva hadn't hit her, anyway, and she was made of sterner stuff.

"It's okay," she said. "I've survived worse than sitting across from this asshole, though his stench might be my greatest challenge yet."

Tony laughed at her provocation. "You're all talk, little girl. You haven't seen anything yet. I've got friends. They'll take care of me."

"Friends? In your chosen occupation, there's no such thing." There was no honor among thieves or thugs.

Tony leaned his elbows on the table and dropped his voice as if imparting a secret. "There is in the Circle."

She hid her surprise. "And what would you know about an organization that's been defunct in Chicago for years?"

"I know that's why you're here to talk to me. A certain someone has promised me a lifetime supply of cigarettes if I share what I know with you." His gaze slid to Diego. "And only you."

"So, share. You can start by telling me who this certain someone is."

"Uh-uh-uh." Though cuffed, Tony shook a finger back and forth. "You don't get his name until you give me something."

"I could just get a look at the visitor logs."

He smirked. "Be my guest. My fan is smarter than that. He's got a fake ID. Disguises himself, too. He's pretty smart."

Fan? It seemed her fan wasn't hers, and hers alone. "What do you want?"

"Cigarettes. He promised you'd bring cigarettes."

She looked at Diego and shrugged. Diego pulled out his wallet. "I've got cash."

"Enough to buy a carton?"

"Enough to buy two cartons if you tell us everything," Diego promised, though it twisted Becca's stomach to be doing business with this guy.

"No deal. Cigarettes are a more valuable currency. And they have to be from *her*." Tony leered at Becca. "I want her begging for what only I can give her. Come back tomorrow with three cartons. You might want to bring kneepads."

CHAPTER 17

Monday, 7:25 p.m.
Jefferson Park neighborhood

Slipping behind the driver's seat, Becca blew out the breath she'd been holding all afternoon as she and Diego left her parents' home for the second time in twenty-four hours. "They took that well."

"They love you," Diego said from the passenger side.

She smiled, feeling weepy again. She'd shed enough tears while talking to her parents. Matt had canceled his evening meeting to be there, too, and then embraced her in a huge hug that told her just how relieved he was that her past was now out in the open. Years ago, Matt had helped shield their parents from news of Becca's arrest. That her university was several hours away had helped, providing a buffer from the press hounds in Chicago. But Matt had been burdened with her secret, which had weighed Becca down with guilt. She couldn't bear to think of doing the same thing to Diego if they were to have a relationship.

"You sure you don't want me to drive?" Diego asked. "You look beat."

"I feel better than I have in a long time." She shifted the car into reverse, but before she lifted her foot off the brake, she paused to look at him. "Thank you. It was easier having you here." And it cost her everything to admit that. She'd held him back for so long. Letting him in was like exerting a muscle that wasn't used to regular exercise.

"You were there for me. I'm glad I could repay the favor." Diego slipped into a thoughtful silence that allowed her to hide her thoughts as she drove them back toward the city. Unfortunately, the silence didn't last long enough to get back to her apartment for the night.

"We need the results of Sam's exhumation," Diego said. "If that's Samantha's body, this investigation into the Circle is putting you at risk for nothing."

"Where the heck did that come from?" She glanced sideways at him.

"I don't like the way Tony was looking at you."

She smiled. "Like I was the one who put him behind bars?"

"No, like you were the one he'd like to visit first when he gets out. Do you know what he'd do to you?" The vehemence in his voice surprised her.

"I know exactly what he'd do to me. The same thing he did to other women. He's a misogynist who blames me for his fate. But he's not getting out. Ever. Unlike James, he's been sentenced to several lifetimes behind bars, without the opportunity for parole. More importantly, we need his information on both the Circle and the Fan."

He looked out his window, avoiding her gaze. "I'm well aware of that, but there are current investigations underway that are better prepared to handle it."

"And yet they haven't gotten anywhere in twenty years."

"I wouldn't say that. They just haven't gotten to the principal, the head of the snake. We need to catch him if we're going to shatter this organization."

"And if it really was Samantha's body that was recovered all those years ago and laid to rest, that doesn't mean the Circle didn't have something to do with it."

They were near her exit on the freeway. Becca glanced in the rearview mirror as white light filled the interior of her car and bounced off the rear- and side-view mirrors. An oncoming car was gaining on them.

Diego turned in his seat. "Pickup truck. Bearing down fast and doesn't look to be letting up."

"Think he's drunk?"

"Driving pretty straight to me."

Yeah, that was what she'd thought, too. Straight toward them.

"Do you have your gun?" Becca asked. "Mine's in the glovebox."

His face was hard with determination as he removed his weapon from his ankle holster and checked the ammo. He did the same with her gun and set it near her hand. There was nobody else she'd rather have by her side, no better partner. He knew the risks, the danger, and how to face it head-on.

"Is there a busy area around here?" Diego asked. "Maybe he'll back away."

"The next exit is still a mile away."

"Get there as fast as you can. We'll try to lose him there."

As if the driver of the pickup heard them, he swerved suddenly into the left lane. But instead of passing them, he drew up along Becca's side of the car. That was when she saw what he aimed in their direction. They weren't the only ones who were armed.

"Gun." Becca spoke with calm as her training took over.

"Affirmative." Diego took out his phone and dialed 9-1-1 with one hand while the other held his pistol, but Becca was between him and their pursuer.

Diego identified himself to the operator and requested assistance, giving their location. Becca doubted they'd be there in time. The truck beside them was determined to keep pace. In the dark, she could only make out certain features of the driver. From the light and shadow, she'd guess he was a bald man with facial hair and wide shoulders. The truck's cab was higher than her little car. The angle would be to their disadvantage if Diego needed to defend them with gunfire. But then, maybe the driver couldn't shoot at them, either. There were no other cars within a hundred feet, but Becca didn't want to be responsible for anyone else getting hurt.

The exit was just up ahead. At the last possible moment, she pulled into the exit lane, but the truck braked and swerved into place behind them.

Diego unbuckled his seatbelt and swiveled in his seat to look out the back. He faced front again, and adjusted his side mirror for a better look, then pointed to a grocery store parking lot. "Over there. We'll get lost in the crowd and hopefully, he'll give up. It's too risky for him."

But Becca didn't pull in. They were in her neighborhood now, and she knew an empty lot where there'd be as few people as possible.

"What are you doing?" Diego asked. "He's gaining on us."

"At least he won't go on a shooting spree in a crowded area." The street here was one lane in each direction. It would keep him behind them.

Unfortunately, their pursuer didn't mind a challenge. With no oncoming traffic, he pulled alongside them. A loud pop sounded as shards of glass from the backseat window on Becca's side went flying. One winged her cheek and she felt a slice of pain.

"Get down!" Diego tried to press on the back of her neck so that her head was lower, but she had to see to drive. She peered just over the steering wheel, looking for a safe place to escape.

"Returning fire," Diego warned. "I'm going for the tires." He steadied his arm against her seat and aimed, but their pursuer let off his gas pedal to fall behind.

It wasn't a reprieve. He swerved and rammed her door with his front right side. She gripped the wheel tighter and managed to keep control of her VW. But the impact on her door set off the air bags, which released with a suddenness that had her head slamming back into her headrest. Thick, warm fluid flooded her left eye, stinging and blurring her vision. She blinked it back, closing the eye when the irritation continued.

"Brakes or gun it?" She could barely see, though the air in the bag was deflating. Her left side hurt. Her neck ached. And her head was throbbing.

"He's backing off."

She pressed on the brakes and steered the car toward the side of the road. As the airbags deflated, she shoved them out of the way and saw the rapid flashing of blue-and-white lights as a CPD SUV pulled alongside them.

"They must have scared him away," Diego's voice, so calm and deep, flowed through her like a river.

"We're safe, then?" She put the car into park and slumped in her seat. "You might want to take over for this next bit." She was reaching for her seatbelt when the blackness hit her.

Monday, 10:27 p.m.
Mercy Hospital

DIEGO WATCHED BECCA AS SHE DOZED. GOD, HE HOPED SHE WAS just sleeping. It was late and she'd been through a rocky few days, so she *should* be sleeping. Unfortunately, she'd had a lapse of consciousness for a minute at the scene of the accident, so the doctors were keeping an eye on her.

Even when awake, she'd been quiet for the past couple hours as they'd waited for the ambulance, waited at the hospital for the doctor, waited as they stitched up the small gash at her temple and tended to the bruises that were starting to bloom on her left arm, and waited for her to be released.

So much goddamn waiting.

He felt like he'd been spending most of his life waiting for her. And he would continue to wait, if only he could be sure she wanted him to.

He rubbed his hands down his face. They both needed rest. The past four days had been packed with adrenaline highs with little recovery time.

Fuck. It should have been *him* driving. The rational side of him reasoned that the driver might simply have pulled alongside the passenger side to take his shot, if it was Becca he was after, but then she would have had a better angle for defending them against their assailant. From what he remembered, Becca was a damn good shot.

"You're getting wrinkles." Becca's voice stimulated yet another rush of chemicals into his system—this time endorphins from his immense relief.

He reached out and brushed his fingertips over a spiky lock of her hair, smoothing it down. Like Becca, it refused to stay put. "Yeah, probably gray hairs, too."

She touched the bandage at her temple, then winced. "Does it look that bad?"

He huffed out a humorless laugh. "You had blood all over your face and head, and blacked out. Your skin was cold. You were pale as death." For one long, horrible moment, he'd thought she was dead. He hadn't dared to move her, choosing to wait for the paramedics in case she had a neck or back injury. The police officer who'd been the first on the scene had humored Diego by repeatedly checking her pulse to assure him she was still alive.

Her hand closed over his on the edge of the bed. "Were you having flashbacks to..."

"Natalee? No." He supposed that was progress, but he'd had a flash *forward* to a future without Becca and it was bleak enough to scare the shit out of him. Later, when he could organize a coherent thought again, he'd figure out what the hell those feelings meant. For now, he swallowed to ease the tightness of his dry throat.

"That's good." Unaware of the tumult inside him, Becca smiled softly. The smile disappeared as her eyes widened. "You didn't call my family, did you? I don't want to worry anybody."

He felt the sudden urge to throttle her. To make her aware of exactly how worried he was, how helpless he'd felt. About her. Not because of his past, but because it was *her.*

"I didn't call them," he said. "But only because the doctor assured me there was nothing life-threatening, and I figured you'd been through enough today. That you wouldn't want to have to explain this to them, too."

"Thank you. At least they left me dressed," she said as she swung her feet over the side of the bed.

"Where do you think you're going?"

She looked at him like he was missing a few cookies from his cookie jar. "Home. And we need to get cigarettes and set up an early meeting at the prison. If the Circle did this because we were talking to Tony—"

"Wait just a goddamn minute. First, I already called Damian and he's arranging with the prison staff for a special meeting with Tony first thing in the morning. Second, you were hurt so bad you lost consciousness—even if only for a minute, it was scary as hell—and now you're thinking of jumping back into this investigation with both feet, blindfolded?"

"You're angry?" She seemed surprised, which only made him angrier.

"I learned a thing or two about you while you had your little *siesta.*"

She licked her dry lips. "What did you learn?"

"While the doctor stitched you up, I took a look at your medical history. You were brought in with a head injury before, from which you also lost consciousness. And there was another time you had a couple cracked ribs."

"Nobody hurt me that time, that was my own f—"

"You don't seem to put your safety first, almost as if you don't care. But *I* do. I care."

She snapped her mouth closed. She might be speechless, but his body was shaking like a train gaining speed. He'd been holding this in for too long, and he was just getting started.

"Your file is an inch thick," he said. "They might as well have a revolving door at the emergency room marked exclusively for Becca Haney. Do you have a death wish?"

She stood suddenly. At least she seemed steady on her feet— feet she shoved into her boots. She reached for her jacket.

"You're really leaving?" Frustration gnawed at his gut. "You didn't hear a word I just said, did you?"

The doctor's arrival saved Diego from pleading with her to find her sanity. "Well, I see the patient has regained consciousness."

"And stubbornness," Diego added.

Becca's chin jutted up as if in illustration of his point. "I'm ready to go home. I feel fine."

The doctor smiled indulgently. "That's because we injected the area around your wound with a numbing agent. You'll probably have a hell of a headache when it wears off."

"I'll take aspirin as directed. Now, may I go?"

Diego was wasting his breath, and his eye-roll. She wasn't even looking at him.

The doctor's pleasant demeanor turned serious. "This is the third time you've had a head injury in the past two years."

"That you know of," Diego muttered.

"I've always been fine right after." Becca's gaze moved between the two of them warily, like a caged animal. "There were no complications."

"That doesn't mean it won't be different this time." The doctor turned to Diego. "But she hasn't lost consciousness again since the accident."

"She was unconscious just a minute ago," Diego pointed out.

Becca put her hands on her hips. "I was resting. I'm tired, and my own bed is just what the doctor should order."

"Now that she's conscious," the doctor said, "I'll have the nurse check her vitals one more time. If she's okay, I'll send her home, provided you stay with her overnight. She needs someone with her in case she has complications."

"I'm right here." Becca waved her hand. "You can talk directly to me."

The doctor turned to her. "Yes, I know, but I deemed him the clearer thinking of the two of you. At least at the moment."

Monday, 11:35 p.m.
Becca's apartment

WITH HER CAR IMPOUNDED AS PART OF THE INVESTIGATION, BECCA and Diego took a cab back to her apartment. She was still fuming about Diego's handling of her as if she were a child, but as he tenderly helped her into the building, she realized her anger was a façade, holding her together until she could collapse on her own. The memory of that gun aimed at her, of the window shattering and the crash...she'd been scared. In that moment, she'd wondered if she'd live, or, worse, what she'd do if she did survive, but Diego didn't.

Outside her door, Diego propped her against the wall as if she were a doll and made her wait while he checked the place out.

"Satisfied?" she asked when he returned. The scowl still darkened his features.

"Not nearly, but there are no bad guys waiting in your apartment."

He'd wanted them both to stay at a hotel, worried that the Circle would continue to come after her, but Becca refused to be cowed. They had to be the ones responsible for running them off the road. Tony had threatened as much back at the prison, with all that talk of his friends watching his back. But what kind of message had they been trying to send? Don't talk to Tony? Because Tony was already doing plenty of talking on his own, to the Fan.

"I'm going to give Tony a piece of my mind tomorrow." She locked her door and stripped off her coat.

"You sure you have enough left to spare?" The growl in Diego's voice raised Becca's hackles.

She turned to square off with him. "More than enough for him *and* you."

"It's not your mind I want."

She heated in an instant, her nipples pebbling beneath his heavy-lidded gaze. The way Diego looked at her—anger layered with concern and desire like some rich, complex dessert that promised to be a delectable treat—was hot enough to melt the armor around her heart.

She put her hand to his cheek, running the pad of her thumb across one of the dark smudges under his eyes. His exhale of breath ruffled her hair. She couldn't resist soothing him further, pressing a kiss against the base of his neck, then moving upward to his throat. At his sharp intake of breath, a different need hit her. The need to comfort gave way to the need to feel his hot mouth on her chilled skin. She went up on tiptoe and pressed her lips to his.

"What are you doing?" he growled, not moving an inch.

Her lips curved against the edge of his jaw, then shifted to press another kiss to his lips. "Seducing you. I thought that was obvious."

He lifted her against his body, tucking his head into the crook of her neck and holding her still in his arms for a long moment. A shudder rippled through him and seemed to bring him to life.

With long strides, he walked her to the couch and set her down. By herself. She blinked up at him.

"What's obvious is that you're avoiding talking about what's real again." He crouched in front of her so they were at eye level. "I want the *real* Becca. The one who's as into me as I'm into her. Not the Becca using sex as a way to distance herself from her feelings, or to try and forget about what happened tonight, or that I failed to protect you."

Her jaw dropped. "Failed? I'd have been alone and unconscious if you hadn't been there tonight to call the police and dissuade our attacker with your gun. I'd probably be dead."

He paled beneath his olive skin. "Don't say that."

"Then stop saying I'm using sex. I'm simply tired of thinking. I want to feel."

His eyes turned stormy. "Then stop saying what we had last summer was *just fun.*"

She put her palms on his beard-roughened cheeks. "I was wrong to say that. At the time, I was trying to push you away. You're my partner." *In so many ways.*

His brown eyes sparkled with interest, but he was still uncertain. Kneeling in front of her, he put a hand on either side of her on the couch. His thumbs brushed the outside of her thighs.

"I want you, Becca, but I can feel you holding back. If I take you to bed, I want all of you."

That was asking a lot. She'd spent years keeping her heart safe. Was he asking for that, too? Or maybe he knew she was still keeping a part of her past from him. "I've told you everything you need to know."

He leaned closer. "But not everything I want to know."

"What else is there?" She'd become mesmerized by the need in his eyes.

"That you have feelings for me, just as I do for you."

"That's emotional blackmail." She wasn't ready to give him her love. It was too great a risk. "Not fair, Sandoval. Especially since you already demolished my willpower."

He gave a husky laugh. "You have plenty of willpower. Too much, if you ask me."

There was only one thing keeping her from making the final leap, and that was the thought of ruining Diego's future with the final secret. "One of us has to. You're trying to rebuild your world. I'd only tear it down again."

The edges of his mouth turned down in irritation. "Stop worrying about others and do what's best for you. I'm man enough to handle my choices, whatever the consequences. I've made some pretty serious mistakes, if you'll recall. Nobody's perfect. Certainly not me. And I didn't expect you to be, either." He'd brought their faces closer together with each word until she was only a breath away. "It's time you let go. Tell me how you feel."

Let go. Of the past, of the truckload of guilt she carried with her, or of her hang-ups about them being together—hell, of everything.

DIEGO COULD SEE HER MIND WORKING, TURNING OVER WHAT HE'D said.

Let go. He willed her to heed his advice and let him in. Fully. Because he was no longer content with rekindling an affair. He wanted more, whatever that *more* was.

It had to be her choice to admit she wanted him for reasons more than just adrenaline letdown or the need to feel alive. It might be his ego taking control, but he needed to know she felt something for him. So he hovered just a few inches away, inviting her to kiss him, aching with the need for her to surrender to him.

Finally, her gaze met his. "I care about you, Diego. So much it scares me."

That was good enough for him. As if of one mind, they breached the gap and joined their mouths. With a whimper, her hands slid from his cheeks downward, the fingers skimming his torso in a light touch that had his heart hammering, trying to leap out of his chest. When her hands reached the waist of his jeans, he sucked in a breath, hopeful he was reading her signals correctly. Her heart was in her eyes when their gazes met. Suddenly, she seemed like a woman ready to give him everything. Again. Including her heart.

Even if she didn't realize it, he could see in her eyes—and in her attempts to keep him free and clear of the past that tainted her—that she loved him.

The responsibility of accepting such a gift hit him like a battering ram in the chest. His own feelings swelled and filled him with desire for this resilient, giving woman. He didn't know what he'd done that earned him this second chance, but he'd seize the opportunity with both hands.

Her fingers dipped beneath the edge of his shirt and spread across his chest. He closed his eyes, focusing on her questing hands, her hot, wet mouth, her citrus scent, her little moans of pleasure and impatience—she wreaked havoc on all his senses. He groaned, pulled her to her feet while mindful of her sore arm, then lifted her and carried her into the bedroom.

"You're not too hurt?" He gently placed her on the bed, his gaze moving over her arm, and then to the bandage at her temple, a reminder of what he'd almost lost tonight.

She grinned wickedly, turning his concern to desire again. "I wouldn't miss this for anything."

She tugged him down onto the bed, then rolled him to his back so she could straddle him. Reaching between them, she undid the button and zipper of his pants, then raised up enough to wriggle him out of his clothing. Happy to oblige, he lifted his hips. His erection bumped her hand and when she seized the opportunity to touch him, taking him in her hands, he nearly exploded with pleasure.

He groaned. "Slower. I want to enjoy you."

She let go long enough to help him pull his pants and boxers from where they were caught at his ankles. He arched up to pull off his shirt, then almost shattered as she replaced her hands with her mouth, trailing kisses and licks back up his legs until she —*thank you, Lord Jesus*—found his hard-on. She locked on as Diego hissed out a breath.

THE SALTY TANG OF DIEGO FILLED BECCA'S NOSTRILS AS SHE NIPPED and sucked and nibbled his honey-toned skin. She lingered at his erection, enjoying the way he tried not to move under her minis-trations. It became a challenge to make him lose control, and she'd always loved a good challenge. She pleasured him until he had her head in his hands and was trying to pull her up his body.

A growl vibrated deep in his chest. "You drive me crazy."

She wanted to go crazy with him. So when he urgently tugged at her, she let him pull her up his body and then flip her to her back so he was in charge.

He made quick work of removing her clothes and tossing them on the floor. "Condom?"

"Side drawer." She heard the triumphant smile in her voice and wondered at his power over her. Being with him, this way, had always been healing. Always good.

He grabbed a condom and was kissing her again within seconds. His hot palms teased her nipples, kneading them into tight beads, building the ache inside her, an ache that hadn't been satisfied since she'd last been with him.

Returning her sweet torture, he licked and nipped his way up to her neck, seeming to savor every sweet spot until she was a melted, boneless mass. Her pulse leaped as he pressed his mouth to the sensitive curve of her throat. Then the world tilted when he filled her. He became her only axis, the only thing that kept her from spinning out of control entirely. She sighed with delight and locked her legs around his hips, digging her ankles into his behind.

God, this was good. This was right. Why had they wasted so much time?

"*Querida*," he murmured against her lips as he slid into her again. Slowly, he tortured her. His reverent tone resonated throughout her, touching her soul.

His tongue danced with hers while the tempo of his thrusts increased to match, building her inner tension into a tight ball preparing to explode into a supernova. She bucked upward to meet him halfway, deepening their contact.

She wanted all of him. Too much wouldn't be enough.

She locked her fingers in his hair and held on while he drank from her, pumped into her. One of his hands claimed a breast, his thumb flicking at her nipple. The contact, in sum with all the other parts, was enough to send her over the edge and she cried out his name. With a groan and final thrust, he followed her over the cliff.

Monday, 11:40 p.m.
Golden Oaks Hospice

THE SSAM FAN LOVED A GOOD STORY. SOMETIMES HE HAD TO embellish a bit, but it always came out great in the end. Something that would grab his viewer by the throat and shake him or her a bit, force some emotion.

Take Hank. Vietnam Vet. Father of two grown children and grandfather of three young kids—none of whom came to visit him in the outskirts of Chicago, though they lived only an hour away. Hank was a loner. By choice? To protect himself? Or because his family didn't give a shit?

It was those pieces of Hank's background that would make him interesting to the public. The *good* image of a *good* man. The pieces his family never saw.

The more his victim from the hospice was appreciated for the good he'd done, the more the sacrifice was worth it. And the more attention Mother would receive when Hank passed along.

From the doorway to the old man's room, he watched Hank. The smell of something industrial strength designed to mask the smell of piss and other unpleasant bodily functions clearly didn't do its job. To the Fan, it was part of the story.

He'd researched the man over the past few hours. Not only a war veteran, the man had been a prisoner of war. The poor, forgotten ex-POW had now been left to rot by his unappreciative family in what was, frankly, another type of cell. Another type of hell.

Thanks to Mother, Hank had been fed and bathed and tucked into bed for the night.

And would be tucked into a coffin by morning.

Also thanks to Mother leaving her key ring on the counter at home, he had a copy of the key to the rear door, the one right next to Hank's room.

It wouldn't take long. A pillow over the face, in Hank's sedated state, would be no struggle at all. His blood rushed with anticipation. His chest rose and fell a little faster.

Tonight, Mother would receive the call. The staff knew to phone her when the end was near. Or had already been breached.

In the morning, he'd see Mother's bright smile again, like sunshine breaking through the storm. Over breakfast, she'd talk as if she didn't know what he'd done. *Remember Hank? The nice gentleman you met with yesterday? I have sad news.*

Except it wouldn't be sad. He'd hear the thread of excitement underlying Mother's words. The affirmation of her purpose. The same rush he'd get tonight.

Mother was a caregiver, and knowing she'd helped another soul receive comfort before heading to the great beyond would invigorate her. It would be time to make arrangements. Contact the family. Help them rally beyond their grief and organize Hank's memorial.

He held the pillow to Hank's face. It didn't take much effort. Only a twitch here and there and the old man faded away.

In the morning, the Fan would finish composing the story of the brave veteran, ex-POW, who'd died peacefully in his sleep, a cuddly kitten puzzle barely begun on his table.

CHAPTER 18

Tuesday, 7:12 a.m.
South Side, Chicago

Upon opening his emails as he waited for Mother's morning tea to steep, the Fan was taken aback. He'd set up alerts that notified him when certain key words had been used somewhere on the internet. This alert led to Eve Reynolds's slanderous blog. Her video, posted yesterday morning, had not only slammed Becca and Damian, but it had received numerous comments supporting her viewpoint against so-called vigilante justice. The cretins commenting had swallowed the story whole, without question.

As he read the comments, outrage burned so hot he could feel it creeping up his neck and into his cheeks. Eve was an instrument of the devil, attacking Becca and Damian's agency when they were working to better society. The Circle did bad things for all the wrong reasons, and deserved to be taken down. Hell, Tony himself would admit that.

But what really got his blood pumping was the subsequent

video blog, dated early this morning. Eve had filmed herself again, this time asserting that the incident that led to Becca's injury would never have happened had Becca followed proper channels of justice. She'd implied that Becca had gotten what she deserved.

Injury? He quickly scanned the internet for more details. Frustration stemmed from concern as he searched for updates on Becca's health. There was nothing.

He felt sick. Had he been the one to put Becca at risk? The Circle had come after her, probably because she was tracking down his leads. If she'd viewed his gift from the wedding, she knew he'd talked to Tony, and she'd probably talked to Tony too by now. Eve's blog had stirred the pot, but he knew any endangerment was ultimately because of him. Just as she'd been arrested when he'd killed James for her. He'd fixed that blunder with an anonymous tip to the police, throwing them off the trail, and he'd fix this too.

After a quick listen at Mother's bathroom door, where he heard the shower running and her whistling—a sure sign that the call that had awakened him a couple hours ago had been from the hospice, informing her of Hank's passing—he moved to the front porch for privacy. He called several hospitals, but nobody had Becca Haney listed as a patient. At least, nobody would admit it. It was possible she was under an assumed name. Perhaps there was a better way to inquire about her health. He dialed the number he'd memorized months ago.

"Hello, you've reached the Society for the Study of the Aberrant Mind. This is Catherine. How may I direct your call?"

Picturing the attractive woman who'd danced with Becca's date at the wedding, he experienced another wave of anger. It seemed Becca was dealing with betrayal on every front. She didn't deserve that. And certainly not from him, her partner. He'd make things right.

But the purpose of his call was to assure himself of Becca's safety, so he shoved his anger below the surface and put on his polite voice. "Hello. I'd like to speak with Becca Haney, please."

"Who may I say is calling?"

"It's regarding a case," he said. "I'd rather remain anonymous."

"I'm sorry, but she's out of the office."

Was she in the hospital? Was she injured that badly? He paced the porch. "Is there some way I can reach her?"

"I can take a message."

"It's urgent."

"I can note that in the message." *Stupid, stubborn woman.* "Or I can connect you to Diego Sandoval's temporary voicemail."

Sandoval was here? *He* was helping Becca?

"No, thank you." He hung up and banged a fist into the frozen deck post in frustration.

Damn. Was she lying in a hospital somewhere, needing him? Was she so embarrassed by Eve's rants that she was in hiding? Or were Catherine and Diego, yet again, getting in the way of Becca's success by interfering?

His insides roiled with unexpressed feelings he had to wrestle into submission. After several calming breaths, he went back inside and poured Mother's tea, then put two slices of sourdough into the toaster. When she came to the table, it looked as if he had everything under control—at least on the outside.

Inside, he was making plans. The woman responsible for attacking SSAM needed to pay for this. There was no reason for Eve to go on the attack. She had plenty of stories to chase down, yet she was determined to hurt Becca. But if there was one thing he knew, it was how to take care of the people he loved.

Tuesday, 9:00 a.m.
Metropolitan Correctional Center

WITH THREE CIGARETTE CARTONS IN TOW, BECCA AND DIEGO

returned to the prison to meet with Tony. He arched an eyebrow as Becca plunked one carton on the table, out of his reach.

"Surprised to see me?" she asked.

"A little." Tony's dark gaze went to the bandage at her temple. His hand shook slightly as he gestured to the cigarettes. Nicotine withdrawal or fear? "Can I have one of those?"

Diego remained near the door, having agreed with Becca that she should again take charge of this interview. She had the personal connection with Tony. Besides, she knew all about how to work with men who preyed on women. She'd learned a lot in the past eight years.

"You failed," she said. "And the Circle knows you're talking to me, they know I'm here again today. And, quite possibly, they'll soon know you were talking to other people. You may as well tell me who interviewed you." As she spoke, she slowly unwrapped the carton and released a pack, tapped out a single cigarette, then handed it to him. In his visitor log, there were repeated entries for a Jack Johnson, but the contact information listed turned out to be false. It was a cover for the SSAM Fan, no doubt. She needed the man's real name. And she needed what information Tony could give her about the Circle's operations in Chicago.

In short, she needed entirely too much from Tony.

Tony reached for the cigarette and put it in his mouth. Though she wouldn't light it for him, he seemed to relax at just the touch of the cancer stick to his lips.

"Tell us what you know about Samantha Manchester," she said.

"Her again?"

"I presume our mutual friend asked about her."

"He did, and he got what he wanted, what you want.

You'll have to partner up with him if you want the rest. His words."

Partner up. Their Fan was seriously delusional. But also smart enough to track down a lead on a decades-old murder. How had she missed that Tony was connected to the Circle? She'd been too focused on the details of the case she'd been involved in to see the bigger picture. Besides, the Circle wasn't a blip on her radar at that point in time. They weren't even supposed to be operating in Chicago.

"What did you give him?" she tried again.

"If you want to know, you'll have to talk to him."

She scooped up the carton she'd laid on the table.

"Hey!" Tony tried to reach for them, but his hands were cuffed.

"We had a deal." Becca held the carton up. "You talked to your friend, so why not talk to me?"

"It's a matter of principle," he said wryly.

"That would be great—if you had any principles."

"Neither does your interviewer. In fact, he's killed a couple people that we know of, and possibly others that we don't know about."

This time, surprise registered in Tony's expression. "More than just Fanta, huh? Didn't know he had it in him."

"How did he know you were linked to the Circle?" This time, Becca handed Tony an entire pack of cigarettes.

"Not sure how he figured out the connection, but he's been coming for a while now. Months. Always brings his camera and likes to hear me talk." Tony laughed. "Which is fine, because I like to talk, especially about my conquests."

Tony leaned forward, into Becca's face, though his shackles prevented him from actually touching her. "You may have caught me for a few murders—"

"And rapes." She hid a shudder. Being this close to him was bringing back memories of the crimes she'd studied to track him down.

He smiled. "And rapes. But that's just a drop in the bucket, sweetheart."

Chills ran up her spine, but she refused to react. "So tell me the rest." She'd try appealing to his ego, since it had worked so well for the Fan. "What have you hidden from the world?"

"I worked for the Circle. That's all I'm saying."

She slid the carton of cigarettes within his reach. His fingers twitched. "What did you do for the Circle? Did it have to do with human trafficking?"

"That's all I'm saying," Tony repeated. He sat back in his seat, a grin splitting his too-handsome face. "The Fan knows. He's got it all on tape. He said he'd be waiting for you when you figured it all out. That's all I'm supposed to say."

"So this is a test?"

He shrugged. "Whatever he has in store, you'd better be careful. By my count, you don't have many lives left, pussy cat."

Tuesday, 3:00 p.m.
SSAM offices

DIEGO AND BECCA MET UP WITH DAMIAN AT SSAM.

"No luck contacting Eve?" Becca asked.

"She's not responding to our calls." Damian's annoyance was clear. "Still working on the cease and desist motion to remove her video blog from the internet."

Becca understood the frustration, because she felt it too. Eve's clip denounced everything they stood for, everything she would have thought a journalist like Eve, rumored to have integrity, stood for. So why was she doing this? What was her connection to the Circle?

"Maybe you can kill two birds with one stone," Diego said.

"What are you suggesting?" Damian asked.

"Post a comment on Eve's blog. Something that defends SSAM and invites her to contact you if she wants the correct information."

"And the second bird?" Becca asked.

"If Damian posts something indicating how hurtful Eve's post is to you, maybe the Fan will come out of the woodwork, too. He certainly seems protective of you."

"That he does," Damian said, his gaze thoughtful. "Let me run it by Lorena and see what she thinks."

Tuesday, 7:45 p.m.
Auburn Gresham neighborhood, Chicago

"You filmed without me?" Patrick could strangle Eve with his bare hands. They were partners. He had been her cameraman for nearly two years. Yet she'd filmed and posted the video diary entries without consulting him. All of it was aimed to hurt Becca, solely because she was getting to the truth about the Circle before Eve was. Jealous, selfish bitch.

Eve taking control hadn't been his plan when he'd arranged for the James Powell interview. She was only supposed to get the man to tell his story, so Patrick would have the video to send to the police. She wasn't supposed to latch on to some vendetta against Becca or SSAM.

"You've been busy." Eve didn't look up as she spoke. She skimmed through the comments on her blog. "Besides, it seems I did okay for myself. Nearly two hundred comments, including one from Damian Manchester himself. He's inviting me to interview him."

Patrick had seen it, all of it. He'd read every comment, mostly derogatory toward Becca, by people who only had Eve's point of view. And he'd nearly cheered out loud when he saw Damian's post defending their agency's mission, asserting Becca had done nothing wrong, and insisting Eve should get her facts straight.

Patrick stood in front of Eve's coffee table, but she continued to scroll through the website. "Do you know she was hurt last night?"

Eve finally looked up. "Who?"

"Becca Haney."

Eve looked back at the screen, dismissing his concern in an instant. "She's fine. She's been leaving me messages all day, asking me to take down the video."

At least Becca was okay—physically, anyway. Eve had still attacked her character, just as much as the Circle had attacked her body.

"Why would you do this?" Patrick asked in disbelief. "I trusted your ethics, your passion for justice."

She grew quiet, and he almost believed she wouldn't respond. "I have my reasons."

"Your accusations aren't even true. You're supposed to care about integrity and honesty. That's what investigative journalism is all about."

Eve frowned. "Sometimes you tell the truth that needs to be heard."

White-hot anger filled his vision. She was a hypocrite. She hadn't even mentioned him or his part in everything when she'd accepted an award last fall. "In other words, you speak whatever truth suits your needs. You're trying to pick a fight with an upstanding agency, not find the truth. Did that award you claimed for yourself mean nothing?"

She didn't know about his documentary project, and now he was glad he hadn't shared. When she'd been walking on air for weeks after that award, he'd bitten his tongue and played his normal part. But no more.

He was Becca's partner now. She'd appreciate him, and everything he'd done.

Eve didn't, and wouldn't, and needed to be punished.

"It's for a greater good," she said.

"Whatever the fuck that means."

Eve finally gave him her full attention. Her shocked expression was rewarding. "You're that mad that I did this without you?"

His jaw clenched so hard he thought it might shatter. He'd given her everything. Done everything she ever wanted. Their shared quest for truth and understanding was intensely personal for him. And what did she do? Threw it back in his face, saying she didn't need him. Jumped to rash judgments about people who didn't deserve it.

"I was about to film the next part of that video blog." She sounded hesitant now and closed her computer. She stood and went to a side table where she picked up some papers. "I've got the script ready to go. Found a juicy video that James Powell had hidden on his flash drive."

"The one I gave you."

"That's right." Her movements became jerky, nervous. "How did you get that, anyway?"

"I have a friend on the CPD. He took it from the scene of the murder." Patrick had found the thing himself, in James's desk drawer, just after killing the man.

"Want to help?" Her voice was unnaturally high. She was suspicious.

His hand slipped into his pocket, where a thin length of cord was coiled.

Becca didn't deserve Eve's unkind words. It was his job to protect Becca. Eve was ruining everything.

"I was thinking a retraction would be a better idea." He took a step toward her.

Eve must have sensed his intent, because she glanced toward the door and licked her lips. He sidestepped to put himself in the middle of her only escape route. *Not that way, sweetheart.* There was only one way out of this. *His.*

CHAPTER 19

Wednesday, 7:02 a.m.
Becca's apartment

Diego woke to something he hadn't felt in years. Contentment. He lay still, focusing on the regular rise and fall of Becca's chest as she slept, tucked against his side. His week was half over and he had no clue where this thing with Becca was going, but he hoped to figure it out.

Unfortunately, he couldn't spend the morning in her bed, thinking about the future, especially when a sense of urgency he couldn't explain pushed him to rise. He'd long ago learned to trust his instincts.

Not wanting to wake her, he slowly untwined their limbs and edged out from beneath her. With a sigh, she stretched and nestled into his pillow, a smile on her lips as she resumed her dream. Diego quietly tugged on some sweatpants, with an idea of making coffee and maybe seeing if he could scrounge up something for breakfast. Soon, they'd head to SSAM to see what Einstein might have found out about the location of Eve Reynolds. The woman hadn't returned their calls, despite Becca's frequent appeals. Maybe the need to talk to Eve was the urgency he was feeling. Or the need to figure out a way to have a future with Becca.

He stepped into the living area and gently closed the bedroom door behind him. And stopped short when he spied a stranger on Becca's couch, sitting casually, with one arm slung over the back as if he'd come over to enjoy a beer and a ballgame.

No, not a stranger. Diego tensed as he recognized the man. He'd seen him before, and it hadn't been under good circumstances. During an information drop when he'd notified the Circle of an impending drug bust, this guy had been in a corner of the room, talking quietly on the phone and sending glances his way. Almost as if the man had recognized him. Diego had assumed he was naturally suspicious and simply keeping an eye on people who came and went. But, even then, the man had the confident air of someone higher up on the food chain.

Diego had passed the guy's description on to Garrison months ago and hadn't heard anything about it. Hadn't thought about it again. And now the man was in Becca's living room in fucking Chicago. And Diego's pistol and his woman were in the other room. Shit. *Way to protect and serve.*

"I'm not here to hurt you," the man said. He remained seated, kept his hands where Diego could see them, and, in general, made an effort to appear nonthreatening. "Quite the contrary, actually. My name is Nico. I need your help."

New York accent, muscular build, unreadable expression. In short, this guy could have been Diego, in his undercover persona.

"Then you won't mind putting your weapon on the coffee table and sliding it toward me."

Nico immediately complied, using slow movements. That was one in the plus column. His sidearm was a beauty, too. H&K. Flat black with just a bit of shine. And then Nico went one step further and pulled a second sidearm from an ankle holster. An H&K P2000 SK subcompact. Diego had to resist a whistle. So, okay, trust between them now had a firm foundation. And the dude had good taste in guns. *Let's see how he stands up to the honesty test.*

Diego moved the weapons to the kitchen counter, then turned back to face Nico. "You work for the Circle."

Nico raised his eyebrows. "You remember. Or that's a good guess."

"I remember. But that was in New York. Why are you here?" Diego was supposedly a Circle minion, one with some connections in the NYPD. Had the Circle found out about him investigating in Chicago and sent someone to kill him?

"My work takes me to both cities."

"I don't have any information to share this week," Diego said, in case that was what Nico was here about. "I took the week off. Personal leave." He willed himself not to glance back toward the bedroom door, where Becca slept, naked and vulnerable. This leave was probably the most personal of his life.

Nico scowled. "I'm not here for the Circle, but we do need to talk about your role with them."

"What about it?" His muscles bunched, and though he had Nico's weapons, he had a feeling the man could be a serious threat if he chose. But then, so could Diego.

"I know your real role. I know about the task force."

Diego carefully schooled his face into a neutral expression. "Task force?"

Nico held his gaze for a long moment. "Good job, but I really do know. You're trying to take down the Circle, and hey, I'm all for that."

"Why would you want to take down the Circle?"

"Because I'm part of the task force, too."

Diego stiffened. That was complete bullshit. Diego would have known. Garrison would have told him if he'd come into contact with a fellow agent, wouldn't he?

"I know Garrison, and I know about Selina." Nico's quietly spoken statement stunned Diego. "I could have told the Circle where she is at any time. And what you did for her, that's how I knew I could come here, could trust you." A slant of his lips passed for a grin. "I don't do the white knight thing, but clearly you do."

"Let's say I do. Who needs a white knight?"

"I'm risking my job—hell, my *life*—right now," Nico said, rising, but still keeping his hands where Diego could see them. "But it's to save a friend."

Diego was reluctantly intrigued, especially since this guy seemed like the definition of *lone wolf*. "And in exchange?"

"I help you and Agent Haney take down the Circle."

Diego stiffened at the mention of Becca.

"I'm DEA. Deep undercover. I've been with the Circle for years, and I'm close to taking them down. Garrison wants to wait until we have enough evidence against the Boss."

"And all we have to do is help you find your friend? What's his name?" It couldn't be an easy task if this man was willing to take a chance letting Diego know about his undercover status. Either the job was dangerous, or the friend was important. Probably both.

"Eve Reynolds." Nico's eyes flashed like lightning as he said her name.

Definitely much more than just a friend.

BECCA HEARD THE LOW RUMBLE OF TWO MALE VOICES IN THE OTHER room. One was Diego's, but she couldn't make out their words. They didn't sound particularly hostile toward each other.

She hurried to pull some clothes on and took her gun from the safe in her closet, then waited on the other side of the closed bedroom door. She listened for any indication that he needed assistance. But then she heard, distinctly, Eve's name followed by total silence.

So she cracked the door open and slowly made her presence known—as well as the fact that she held a gun. Diego was facing another man, their stances practically mirror images of each other. She read tension in their lines, but not aggression.

"You know Eve?" Becca asked.

"I do," the stranger said, turning his attention to her. "I'm Nico." Just a first name.

"He wants our help finding Eve. She's missing." Diego was keeping his gaze on the other man, and there were two guns on the kitchen counter that weren't hers or Diego's.

"And are we going to help him?" Becca asked.

"That's the question." Seeing Becca's confusion, Diego explained. "Nico says he recognizes me as part of the task force—because he is also part of the task force."

If that were true, Nico was risking all kinds of danger by coming to them and revealing his undercover identity. Then again, he could be working for the Circle, trying to lure Diego into confessing the truth. "But you don't know him?"

"Only by sight. I saw him once at a Circle hangout."

"Eve is my friend," Nico said, appealing to Becca, but not begging. She suspected the man didn't know how to beg. The hardness in his hazel eyes indicated he'd seen the gritty side of life, possibly even lived it daily, and had come to expect shit to happen. His friend going missing was just one of those shitty things. "I know she was taken, and I know she posted a video blog about you, with the threat of more to come."

"I didn't take her," Becca hastened to assure him. "I had nothing to do with it. I didn't even know she was missing."

"I know."

"You do?"

"I talked to her about an hour before she disappeared. She seemed distracted."

"Well, she has been busy ruining my reputation."

Nico frowned. "She was doing that for me."

Diego tensed. "For you? Why?"

"I was looking for a way to get Becca to back away from the

Circle investigation. Her digging was making some people higher up very nervous, and I was close to getting the evidence I need. They were getting skittish enough that the Boss cancelled an important meeting with his uppermost tier of employees."

"What did Eve have to do with this?" Becca asked.

"I was giving her a story. She was going to bust the Circle wide open. Until then, she was supposed to distract you enough that I could wrap up what I needed. Last night, Eve and I were supposed to meet up. I haven't seen her since."

"Do you think the Circle took her?" Diego asked.

"No, it wasn't them."

"How do you know? They're capable of anything."

Nico shot him a dark look. "I know because I'm rather high up in the organization. I'd have heard about something like this." He didn't sound proud of that status.

"Unless they found out you're DEA," Becca pointed out. "They may have taken her to get back at you."

Something akin to fear and concern chased each other across his features before he frowned. "No. This is something different. I think it has to do with the damn blog posts she put up about you." Under his hard exterior, Nico's frustration and concern were clear. "I asked for her help, but I didn't realize it would put her in danger. I only wanted her to convince you to back away. So my question is —" Nico pinned Becca with his gaze, "—who has Eve?"

Becca blew out a breath. "I didn't know she was missing, but if it's related to her recent posts, it must be the Fan."

"The Fan?"

"A killer who's been stalking Becca," Diego said. "He's been acting protective of her, calling her his partner. I wouldn't put it past the guy to take Eve because of what she said against Becca."

Muttering an expletive, Nico sent a hand through his hair.

Wednesday, 9:35 a.m.

SSAM offices

DAMIAN KNOCKED ON THE DOOR OF LORENA'S OFFICE. SHE LOOKED up from her computer screen and removed her reading glasses. Black eyes gleamed with intelligence and a natural curiosity.

"Hey," she said, smiling in welcome. "Come in."

He moved farther inside but didn't sit down. "Hope I'm not interrupting."

"I was just looking through the applicant list from the past few years."

"Anything interesting?"

"There are a few. Thought maybe you could take a look through them and see if anything peculiar jumps out."

Damian took the file from her. "Becca should be in a little later. And she'll have company." Damian told her about the conversation he'd just had with Becca.

"You want me to check out Nico's story?" she asked. "I know someone at the DEA who could do some quiet digging."

"Don't do anything that could disturb his cover. I just want to know if he's being truthful." And if he was to be trusted. If they'd made a contact within the Circle, someone who'd been there for years and could give them a unique perspective on the human trafficking operations within the organization, their investigation into whether the Circle took Sam might move forward by leaps and bounds. "Nico knows where Eve lives. The three of them are heading to her place to see if they can find anything."

Her forehead creased in concern. "I don't want to see you get your hopes up. Even if the Circle took Sam, she might not be alive."

The words came from her heart, so he couldn't fault her for being cautious. She'd known him at his lowest—at least the lows he'd hit in the past fifteen years since she'd joined SSAM, soon after he'd created the agency—and she'd always sought him out with a word of comfort or support. Besides, he trusted her professional opinion. "If Nico has an inside track with the Circle, and if he can be trusted, it's worth helping him. He says he's close to blowing things wide open."

"That's encouraging." Her gaze was warm, as it always was when she reassured him. "And I certainly don't mean to be discouraging. I want you to find Sam's killer."

"I know." He turned to leave but paused, thinking he might ask her out for coffee. He'd wanted to in the past, but something always stopped him. Fear of impropriety. Or maybe it was self-preservation. He wasn't sure he could bear more rejection, more loss. He was about to take a risk when Catherine entered.

"There you are," Catherine said. "I tried buzzing you at your office. Your ex-wife wants to speak with you. It sounded urgent."

Whatever interest—real or imagined—he'd detected from Lorena was gone when he turned back to her. She was absorbed in her computer screen again. Disappointed, Damian walked to his office just a couple doors down and phoned Priscilla.

"Thank you for returning my call so quickly." Priscilla sounded as if she'd run to the phone, which was so out of character for his elegant ex-wife that his instincts went into high alert.

"Is there a problem?"

"I heard about the internet posts defaming SSAM. Why would anyone say you're using illegal means to hunt killers?"

He sighed. "It's not true."

"Well, I knew that, of course. I just wondered if I should give her a talking-to."

He smiled. The image of Priscilla, carefully coiffed and manicured, fighting someone for his honor eased some of his tension. "She was trying to discredit us. Or, more specifically, Becca."

"You don't sound worried."

Not about the agency, he wasn't. He was careful to keep a sterling reputation. SSAM was his life, and he took pride in the good it did. "Eve Reynolds has other reasons for posting what she did."

"Were you getting too close to something? Does it involve our daughter?" Priscilla sounded breathless. Hope did that to a person. It built you up before it stole everything from you, including the very breath from your lungs.

His chest squeezed in empathy. "I can't get into it."

"You have something new. I can hear it in your voice. What do you know about Sam?"

He hesitated.

"Please." Priscilla never begged. Which showed how desperate she was for closure, too. "As Sam's mother, I deserve to know what's going on."

"It's very likely nothing."

"I can judge that for myself."

He took a deep breath. "We may have a new lead on a case that could be related. But it's still a long shot."

The Fan. Tony. Nico. Suddenly people were popping out of the woodwork. People who might know something, but were also secretive and knew how to hide the bodies. He had to be careful how he handled them.

"And how does Samantha fit into this?"

"She would have been the type a human trafficking ring specializing in child prostitution would prey on." She'd been conveniently alone, happily distracted, and a beautiful, innocent girl when someone had taken her.

There was a long pause. "What would they have done with her?"

No way was he going into the gory details, but he could give her the ultimate outcome. "Some women or children they'll sell into the sex trade, or to work in sweatshops, in other countries, or to serve any number of needs, depending on the buyer. Some buyers are looking for pristine American girls. Some just want laborers or sex slaves. The traffickers ferry them up into Canada or down into Mexico, or even across the ocean to Europe or Asia. Babies, they sell to parents looking to adopt on the black market."

"Jesus."

Prayers wouldn't help, not that that was what she'd meant. But it brought a grim twist to his lips, since Priscilla rarely cursed on any level. Lorena, on the other hand, swore whenever the occasion called for it. She joked it was her Latina-Italian-Irish mixed blood, so she couldn't help herself. When her blood ran hot, her tongue was the release valve. Damian was shocked that his thoughts had him comparing the two women.

"So what's next?" Shaken by Damian's revelations, Priscilla's voice quavered. "And is there anything I can do to help?"

"We have to find Eve Reynolds. She went missing yesterday evening."

Priscilla was quiet a long moment. "Are you in trouble?"

"No, but we might be able to help. In return, I may have news about Sam soon. But there are no guarantees," he warned. "It's been twenty-some years."

"I'm well aware of that. I just... *My God*, Damian. If she's out there, alive, I wonder what she's been through."

And whether it would be better to be dead. That thought haunted him. Damian's mind had gone there many, many times in the weeks since he'd learned of the Circle.

"I know." It was all he could say. There were no adequate words. Whether she was dead or alive, Samantha very likely had gone through hell. But if she was alive, he would fight the beasts of Hades to get her back. "I'm doing what I can."

"Thank you. Please keep me posted."

He hung up and turned back to the pile of case folders on his desk. So many people, looking for answers, justice, peace. He'd help as many of them as he could, hoping to find his own in due time.

Lorena poked her head in his doorway, a curtain of ebony hair brushing her cheek. "Got a lead."

He waved her in. "Tell me."

"I was reading the comments on Eve's blog. There was one posted by a user named *SF* just a few minutes ago."

"SF? SSAM Fan?"

"I think so."

She came around his desk and leaned across him to bring up Eve's blog on his computer screen. He couldn't help inhaling a deep breath of her as she scrolled through the extensive comment list. Her hair smelled of some exotic island fruit. Mango, maybe.

She pointed at the screen and pulled away, oblivious to his momentary lapse in control. "There. Read that one."

The comment was a response to the one Damian had posted yesterday.

Eve Reynolds will regret the vile things she's said here. Damian does all he can to make our world better. His organization gets rid of the worst of the worst. The people who kill for no reason. And Becca is a sweetheart. I spoke to her myself, and she's a good person. The people who die are meant to die. They live on in the memories, in the tributes the living pay to them. What kind of tribute will you receive, Eve? And what crap will you spew when you unburden your conscience?

"It sounds like he does have her," Damian said. "Eve baited him, probably without even realizing the hornets' nest she'd stirred up."

"He says he's spoken with Becca personally. I wonder if telling her that will trigger her memory."

"Hopefully, before he hurts Eve." Damian felt excitement and concern war within him. Chasing a killer and racing against time was a heady combination, but it affirmed his life's purpose. He was going to catch the monster.

Wednesday, 1:00 p.m.
SSAM offices

THE CONFERENCE ROOM AT SSAM WAS FILLED WITH THE USUAL suspects, plus one. Nico seemed unable to smile, but whether that was a character flaw or related to the current circumstances and his concern for his friend Eve was up for debate. Becca was betting on the latter.

"He gave the initials SF," Damian said. "But we think that simply stands for SSAM Fan."

"And he's basically admitting he took Eve," Becca said.

Beside her, Nico's scowl deepened. The man blamed himself, but Eve had made her own decisions about how to go about this. He'd been stoic as they'd gone through Eve's apartment, looking for signs of foul play.

"At her apartment, there were signs of a struggle, and a cord that had slipped under the edge of the couch."

Across the table, Catherine shuddered.

"Fits the Fan's MO," Lorena said. "He strangled Fanta, the woman he branded with the Circle symbol."

"Eve's not dead." Nico's words were quiet and firm.

Lorena shot him a sympathetic glance. "No, probably not. He'd want to interview her first, I think."

"Why did he use the symbol on Fanta?" Becca asked. "If he wants to partner with me to help find out what happened to Sam, why would he use the brand?"

"It could be an identity issue," Lorena said. "He thinks he's one of the good guys, or he wants to be one of us, but he has a compulsion to kill. Or he wanted to get our attention, or Tony's."

"He does seem to enjoy interviewing people," Einstein said. "According to the prison logs, the Fan has been interviewing Tony, under the name Jack Johnson, for months. His visits date back to before we knew there could be a connection between the Circle and Sam's disappearance."

Becca sat forward. "Maybe he's trying to understand himself and his own urges. Trying to make killing okay in his mind."

"I was thinking that, too." Lorena tapped her pen against the table as she thought. "We have a killer with a conscience."

"At what point will he trust me enough to let me initiate contact?"

"Maybe try Eve's blog, as we did with Damian. Obviously, he's been monitoring the comments. If you left another one, this time indicating you understand his motives, he might feel comfortable enough to contact you again."

"But he needs to know hurting Eve won't be okay with me. With us." She shot a glance at Nico, who was looking even more grim.

Nico realized she was watching him and spoke up. "Better yet, find him and let me tell him personally."

"What about the Fan's reference in the blog comments to having spoken to you before, Becca?" Lorena asked. "Do you remember talking to anyone who may have seemed odd or out of place?" She read part of the blog comment. *"And Becca is a sweetheart. I spoke to her myself, and she's a good person."*

"If we've spoken, it might have been brief. I just don't know." Becca racked her brain, trying to picture faces and recall voices that might not have caught her attention at first. But trying to force the memory seemed to make it more obscure.

Lorena continued reading the Fan's latest comment. *"They live on in the memories, in the tributes the living pay to them. What kind of tribute will you receive, Eve? And what crap will you spew when you unburden your conscience?"*

Suddenly, Becca sat up. "Wait. That's it."

"The tributes?" Lorena's eyebrows came together.

"No, that last part. He mentioned that on the back of the photo he left for Diego, too."

Diego pulled the photo out and read the back again. *"Unburden your conscience. Tell me no lies. A circle binds her forever..."*

Lorena nodded. "The unburdening fits with his documentary, trying to figure out the lines between good and evil."

"No, it's where I heard that line before," Becca said. "It was the photographer from the wedding. Vanessa introduced us, when I bumped into him outside the elevators at the hotel and nearly knocked his camera from his hands. He told me not to *burden my conscience* with guilt about it. I don't remember ever exchanging names."

Catherine slid a folder across the table to her. "Those are the pictures from the wedding photographer. There's a CD with all of the digital images on them too."

"You finally got them."

"Yes, and I went through them already," Catherine added. "But I didn't see anybody who didn't match with the guest list."

Becca flipped through smiling photographs of the wedding party. "Because the face we were looking for was behind the lens. How did Vanessa hire this man?"

"Vanessa's mother. He apparently approached her with an impressive resume. She looked at some of his work for some big-name magazines and newspapers and hired him."

Becca searched the CD case for the photographer's name, then grabbed the stack of personnel files that included applicants to SSAM, flipping through until she found the same name. She tapped her finger on the application. "Patrick Bigelow. That's the name of the photographer and it matches one of the SSAM applicants. He applied several years ago, even before Tony's arrest."

Damian turned to Einstein. "Check if the address he gave on his application is current. Call the CPD and fill them in. Have them send a couple officers to meet us there."

CHAPTER 20

Wednesday, 1:20 p.m.
South Side, Chicago

"Y ou're a wildcat, I'll give you that." Patrick wiped from his face the water Eve had spit at him. "I was trying to be hospitable. You don't have much longer on earth. I would think you'd welcome a little kindness. But then, I forgot you're no longer a reasonable woman."

Patrick scowled through the tiny window in the cell door. It was an old root cellar, and three walls were still dirt. It was also conveniently located off the basement of his house, which he'd soundproofed years ago when he'd started making his videos.

When Eve opened her mouth to scream, he slammed the little window shut, closing her into darkness, keeping her sounds muted.

A moment later, he opened it again.

"I can be reasonable," she quickly said. Her words were raspy from her damaged throat. In her apartment, he'd held the cord tight around her neck until she was unconscious, enjoying the surrender he'd seen in the stubborn woman's eyes. He bore her claw marks on his hands with pride. She'd fought back but he'd been stronger. Even if she'd screamed now, the sound wouldn't have reached anyone's ears but his, but he wanted her to recognize who was in charge. "I won't scream. I promise. Tell me what you're doing, Patrick. Why did you take me? What are you trying to do?"

He chuckled. "There's the investigative journalist I know."

Her chin shot up. "Until the day I die, which isn't going to be today."

"We'll see. Your viper's tongue finally got you in trouble. Usually, that's perfect for our agenda, but you started using it to hurt people I care about."

"Who?" Her brow knit in confusion. Of course, she wrote so many stories that maybe she couldn't remember who she'd recently attacked.

"*Becca Haney*," he said with disgust. "The SSAM agency. Don't you remember what you posted just yesterday? If only you'd waited for me to help film it, I could have stopped you before you went too far. Now, it's too late." Anger had him starting to close the partition again.

"No, wait!"

He paused before closing it.

"Of course I remember," she said. "You're friends with Becca? I didn't know. *How?* Help me understand."

It was something his therapist might have said, back when he was seeing one nearly twenty years ago. His college guidance counselor had recommended it, sensing the pent-up anger that had come out as passive aggressiveness against fellow students. Nothing had soothed him until he'd finally accepted his gift and made his first kill. He'd started small, with one of Mother's patients. The effect on Mother had been an amazing side benefit. Then he understood everything—including his purpose in life— very, very well. Now, he had only to explain how his gift benefited society, to be accepted.

"The agents at SSAM are my friends. They're good people."

"I'm your friend," Eve hastened to say. "We worked together for two years. I know I couldn't pay you much, but I don't deserve this."

"It's not about money. Once again, you don't get it. You never really saw me, or what I did for you. Becca, on the other hand...people like her, like me, like SSAM, rule the world, and you don't even know it. We decide who lives and dies. Who is punished and who walks free. We judge people worthy."

"So they decided to let you walk free?" Her hand went to her sore throat.

He smiled. "Bet you're wishing you hadn't spit that water back in my face."

She nodded. "I am. I'm sorry."

So agreeable. He liked this new Eve. The old Eve would have choked on an apology. Maybe he would shed some light for her. Then again, Mother expected him to escort her to Hank's memorial. He couldn't disappoint her, not when it appeared she was finally starting to feel better again. Still, there were a couple things that had to be done before he left.

"I need you to do something for me," he said.

"What?" She was nearly breathless with the desire to please him, probably thinking it would save her.

"I have to leave for a few minutes. When I get back, we're going to have a little talk."

"About Becca?"

"About you. You spend your time digging up the roots of the people you go after in the public eye. Now, it'll be your turn to unburden your conscience. Dig deep and make it good. It'll go in your obituary."

"Obituary?" The word was a croak in her parched, tortured throat.

"I like to add a personal touch. Something my viewers wouldn't know about."

"Viewers? They watch me, not you."

He felt anger welling up again and suppressed it. "I've been working on a documentary. Good versus evil. The great debate. So be thinking about your answers and give me something good." He laughed. "Or evil. Whatever floats your boat. The viewers will decide for themselves, anyway."

Wednesday, 3:05 p.m.
Woodlawn neighborhood, South Side, Chicago

"You have information for us?" Becca's question to Einstein over the phone had Diego turning his head from where he sat in the passenger seat. For nearly thirty minutes, they'd been watching the house at the Woodlawn address Patrick had given on his SSAM application. There had been no sign of movement inside. She could only hope Patrick had been truthful back then, when he'd wanted to impress his future employers. And that he hadn't moved since. But they didn't know what they'd be walking into, thus they wanted Einstein's intel. On the other side of the street, down a few houses from the one they watched, two CPD plain-clothes officers watched, too.

"I confirmed Patrick's last known address. Who's a rock star?"

Becca could practically hear Einstein grin through the phone.

"Eddie Vedder?"

"Me. I'm the rock star, at least today. There is a Patrick Bigelow paying the utility bill at the address listed on his SSAM employ-ment app. Should be a house in a quiet suburb."

The house they'd been watching was definitely quiet, sedate in its 1950s brick frame with the small porch.

"He's thirty-eight and lives with his mother, Joyce," Einstein said.

"Oh." Beside her, Diego sent her a questioning glance and she put the phone on speaker.

Einstein laughed at her surprise. "He's a bit of a mama's boy, supposedly. Except that he's deadly. Three unsolved cases in the general vicinity of that neighborhood in the last five years might be linked to this guy, and I'm not done looking yet. Nobody anybody would raise a stink about, but they all suffocated or had signs of strangulation. Lorena thinks the guy was just getting started."

"What makes her think Patrick Bigelow was responsible for all of those murders?"

"He wrote the obituaries for the newspaper. We talked to the editor, who says the guy fancies himself as doing a service for his community."

"Any other surprises you can warn us about?"

"No dogs or guns registered in his name." Einstein liked the team members to go in as prepared as possible, God bless him. But that didn't mean they shouldn't expect the unexpected.

"The CPD officers have agreed to let you take the lead on this, at least to lure Patrick out. Then he's all theirs. Still waiting on a warrant from the judge to get into the home."

"The CPD can have him. As long as we don't need him to find Eve."

"Oh, and the specs for that house indicate it has a basement. Nothing good happens in a basement. I'd start there."

As Einstein hung up, Diego nudged her arm and nodded to the street in front of them. A station wagon slowed and turned into the driveway of the Bigelow home. The garage opened, then closed as soon as the car was inside.

"I didn't get a good look at the driver, did you?"

Diego shook his head. "Too far away."

"Guess we're going in for a closer look."

They checked their weapons, then tucked them out of sight on their bodies. Diego reached across and cupped the back of Becca's neck, pulling her face to his for a kiss that smoldered with heat and urgency for a brief, intense moment.

His lips were only an inch from hers when he spoke. "Don't do anything risky." As if kissing him wasn't risky enough.

"But Eve—"

"I mean it. Put your own safety first for once. I don't want anything to happen to you."

She bristled. She'd do what the mission required, within the safest parameters possible, as she always did. As they got out of the car, the police officers did as well, joining them on the sidewalk. After a brief discussion of the layout and objective, the officers agreed to wait in the wings while Becca knocked on the door and attempted to gain entrance to the home. The priority was ensuring Eve's safety, so she'd rather not have to wait for a warrant. Diego, however, was by her side as a woman in her early sixties with gray-and-brown hair pulled into a no-nonsense bun at the crown of her head, which stretched the wrinkles from her face, scowled through the open doorway. She had yet to take off her coat.

"Hi," Becca said, trying for a bright tone. "Are you Joyce Bigelow?"

The woman looked hesitant but answered. "Yes, I am."

"I'm looking for your son Patrick."

Her gaze shifted to Diego, who was standing behind Becca like a brick wall that had baked in the sun all day, imposing and immovable, but also warm and solid. Perhaps Becca should have insisted he guard her from afar, but she felt better knowing he had her back.

"Who are you?" Joyce asked her.

His worst nightmare. Becca bit her tongue against uttering the words she wanted to say. She wanted to shove the door open and hold a gun on Patrick while they searched for Eve. But Joyce was an unknown. Becca feared Eve might be in danger. If they could gain entrance to the house, granted by the owner, however...

Telling Joyce a shade of the truth might encourage her to help them locate her son, as well as get her out of the house and out of harm's way before they went in after him.

"I'm Agent Becca Haney, from SSAM—" Before she could explain the acronym, Joyce's brow creased, her features turning stormy.

"You need to leave," Joyce said.

"I just want to talk."

"Patrick doesn't want to talk to you." Something flashed in Joyce's eyes. "You're ruining everything. I've seen the emails. You're taunting him, teasing him." She looked Becca up and down with distaste.

Jealousy. That was what Becca saw in the woman's expression.

"I don't mean to tease." Becca smiled. "I'm here, aren't I? He said he wanted to be my partner. Please tell Patrick I came for him."

Joyce's gaze again moved to Diego. "Looks like you already have a partner."

Shit. Becca pulled the woman's attention back to her by giving a tired sigh. "Patrick asked me to come. Is he here or not? Or should I tell him you kept us apart?"

"You'll never have him. Not fully. He's not going to kill for you."

At Joyce's words, Becca froze. Behind her, she could sense Diego tensing, preparing for action, if necessary.

"I don't understand," Becca said.

"He thinks I don't know, but I do. He's been talking with you. I saw the drafts of his notes on the computer, and his phone. He just wants to belong. For you to admire him."

That was a feeling Becca could understand.

"But I should be enough." Joyce's lips quivered so much she had to press them together for a long moment to gain control. "He belongs with me. My admiration should be enough."

"You love your son." Becca picked her words with care. It seemed the nut didn't fall far from the tree in this family. "And he'd do anything for you."

Joyce gave a firm nod, an unholy light in her eyes. "*Anything.* He killed for me. Can you say he did the same for you?"

A pissing match. Just dandy.

"How do you know he's killed for you?" Becca tried to keep judgment from her voice.

"I select them, he helps them along. They find peace. There's nothing wrong with that."

Oh, God. What had they stumbled onto? "Who finds peace?"

"My patients." Joyce sent her a look as though Becca was dense. "At the hospice home. He does what he does for *me*. Because I've done the same for him."

What? Inside, her thoughts were whirling at the speed of light. Outside, Becca strived for a calm and cocky attitude. "Actually, he's done the same for me. I'm here to thank him. I think he deserves my personal gratitude."

Joyce suddenly looked pale. "He didn't. He wouldn't."

"He's killed many people, Joyce. All to get my attention." Becca smiled as if she appreciated this. "Only, this last one might not be dead yet." She shrugged as if it were no consequence. "Before I reward him properly, I'd like to make sure."

"He wouldn't." This time, her words were a whisper.

"He took a woman named Eve."

Joyce was wavering. Becca could see the woman's hesitation in the way she glanced back over her shoulder. She wanted Patrick's love—in the form of murderous dedication—and the thought of Becca earning it instead of her was unacceptable.

"He wouldn't have." Joyce added a nod of certainty to punctuate the statement.

"Why not?"

"I've done so much for him. I'm the one who got him all the attention when he was growing up, every time he was sick."

Every time? It sounded like Patrick had been an extremely sick little boy. "Maybe you're right. Maybe I'm wrong. I suppose, if that's true, it couldn't hurt to look around? If Eve and Patrick aren't here, I'll leave you alone."

Joyce was caught in the middle. If she denied them entrance, it would be as good as admitting her fears and hurt her pride. If she let them in, she was allowing them to invade their privacy but would prove that she was Patrick's favorite and Becca was a nobody. She didn't seem to comprehend that what Patrick had done was illegal, and a warrant would soon invade his privacy, anyway.

"If you're worried that you're wrong..." Becca continued when Joyce hesitated.

Joyce stepped aside, indicating they could come in. The police officers waiting on the sidewalk stepped forward and joined them in the house.

"Where is Patrick?" Becca searched the living room for signs of someone else in the home. Flower-patterned furniture and kitschy knickknacks dominated the decor. A high shelf lined every wall, and was filled from end to end with porcelain dolls and figures, all dressed in nurse uniforms. Becca couldn't look at their glassy eyes without shuddering.

"He's out running an errand for me. We were at a memorial service most of the day—"

"Whose?" Becca interrupted.

"That's none of your business."

Becca shrugged. "Patrick will tell me everything later."

Joyce heaved a long-suffering sigh. "One of my patients died."

"You're a doctor?"

"A nurse, at the hospice home a few miles away." That explained the creepy figurines. "Patrick should be back any minute." Joyce followed them into the kitchen, where more dolls lined the top of the cabinets. To their left, opposite a small kitchen table, Becca spied a door.

"You won't find anything," Joyce said confidently.

Becca gestured to the door. "There's a basement?"

"Yes, but that's Patrick's space."

Bingo. "Mind if I take a look?"

Joyce looked conflicted. The woman was clearly starting to

doubt what they'd find. But she'd also committed to her story that Patrick had nothing to hide. Finally, she shrugged.

"Please wait up here." Becca made eye contact with one of the police officers, who stepped forward and spoke to Joyce, efficiently leading her toward the living room to wait. The other officer would accompany them into the basement.

With the flip of a switch at the top of the stairs, the windowless room was flooded with fluorescent light. They could see most of a rectangular room, walls reinforced with soundproof padding, but part of it was hidden by the angle of the stairs.

The officer drew his gun and led them slowly down the stairs. Instinctively, Becca's hand went to her gun, tucked in a shoulder holster. But there was no need. Patrick wasn't here. A moment later, Diego and the officer had checked the area and given the all clear.

"This place is as clean as an operating room," Diego said.

"Which makes me wonder what kind of operating this guy has been doing." But something odd caught Becca's eye—a brown area of an otherwise-gray concrete-block wall. It was behind a shelving unit, and as she moved closer, she recognized scrape marks on the cement floor, arcing outward from the base of the unit. She gestured to Diego to help her pull the shelves out of the way. It wasn't particularly heavy, and was probably manageable on one's own if one was Patrick's size. Behind it, inset in the wall, was a wooden door with a tiny window that locked from the outside.

But the cell was empty. If anyone had been held there recently, they were long gone. "She's not here."

Diego moved toward a set of utility shelves in a far corner. A television and camera were set up at a desk adjacent to the shelves. "Maybe there's a clue in here?"

Becca came to his side. "There have to be over a hundred DVDs here, like at Eve's place. If he catalogued all of his victims..."

Diego nodded, understanding. "But these aren't all victims." He examined the spines of the cases. "These are from various prisons in the state. Looks like he's interviewed dozens of criminals. Here's Tony's DVD."

Becca froze as she spied one marked with her name...and James Powell's. She desperately didn't want Diego to see it. "We should let the CPD catalog these and set up a watch for when Patrick returns." Or maybe it was time to post a comment of her own on Eve's blog and see where it led.

"In the meantime, the police will take Joyce in for questioning. Maybe she'll tell us where Eve could be."

Eve was still in danger, and every minute that passed made it more likely she'd become one of Patrick's victims.

Wednesday, 4:15 p.m.
Woodlawn neighborhood

PATRICK WAS IN LINE AT THE GROCERY STORE WHEN HIS PHONE pinged with an alert. His heart sped as he saw Eve's post had received another comment—this time, from Becca. He hastily snatched up his bags and headed to the car, where he could view the post in private.

It seemed to take forever for the blog to load on his phone. "Come on. Come on." He scrolled through the hundreds of comments to Becca's. She'd signed her name, clear as day, announcing to the world that she was innocent. And that she was ready to move on— with him.

SF, I can't tell you how much I appreciate your support, and every-thing you've done. I would love to show you my gratitude. It's rare to find such a dedicated partner.

His heart soared and blood pounded in his ears. Becca wanted to be his partner. It was finally time to reveal himself.

He sped home, slowing when he entered his neighborhood. A school bus blocked his way, and he waited impatiently as several high school students disembarked and crossed the street. As the bus pulled forward, Patrick followed, but his eyes were still on the group of kids. Which is how he saw the unmarked cop car with two men inside, across the street and down a few houses from his house. Their attention was also on the kids. Instead of pulling into his driveway, he continued past.

They were watching him, which meant they'd figured out who he was. It was fortuitous that his mother had asked him to pick up groceries on the way home from Hank's memorial. And that he'd decided to check on Eve, too, in her new location. Fate was on his side, but was Becca? Was her comment a lure? An idea sprouted— one that would test Becca's loyalty and bind them as partners forever. If she passed his test, their bond would be unbreakable.

Luckily, for what Patrick had in mind, all he needed was his laptop and video camera, which he always carried with him. Escaping their trap didn't keep the anger at bay, though. The police would now be watching the house, watching his mom, watching everywhere Patrick had ever been. Not that he'd be any of those places from now on. He didn't like being the hunted, and he damn well didn't deserve it, but it wouldn't be for long.

Especially now that he realized what the finale for his documentary would be. It would all be over in twenty-four hours.

CHAPTER 21

Thursday, 6:35 a.m.
Becca's apartment

Becca watched the glow of sunrise creep across the bed, and absorbed what calm she could from Diego's body curved protectively behind hers. She sensed he hadn't slept, either, but he simply held her in the quiet, seeming to know without her telling him that she needed comfort. There had been no news of Eve or Patrick's location. Despite Becca's comment on Eve's blog, inviting him to become her partner, Patrick hadn't contacted her again. But he might not even have access to the internet.

She hated that Patrick had control. She hated even more that she had no clue how to pass his tests, or prove she could be a good partner. Joyce Bigelow hadn't been helpful in the least, swearing to the police that she had no clue where her son could be. But she was playing the grieving mother to the hilt, like a queen diva.

Diego shifted against her and pressed his mouth to her temple. "Good morning, sunshine."

She turned in his arms to face him across the pillow. "I hope so."

His eyes searched hers. "It will be. We'll find Eve. Patrick will contact you today, I'm sure of it. He wants nothing more than to impress you."

It was how far he would go to make that impression that worried her. Would he kill Eve? Was she already dead? Patrick seemed to have disappeared into the ether. Whatever he had planned, it sounded like he'd learned from the best. In the middle of the night, she'd stared at the dark ceiling, replaying the odd conversation with Patrick's mother.

Becca sighed. "What do you think Joyce meant when she said she'd done everything for her son and now he was paying her back? What kind of mother encourages her son to kill for her?"

Diego tucked a hair behind her ear. "A sick one. But she's not in the majority. Don't lose sight of the good in the world. Like what we have." Desire darkened his eyes.

Yes, they had something good. But it would die a painful death unless Becca could find the courage to tell him everything. There were things she had done, back when she'd tried to find evidence against James. Things that could hurt Diego.

Diego pressed another soothing kiss to her cheek, then her mouth, and her doubts receded under a tide of longing. The memories of last summer were strong, and her feelings even stronger than before. The walls around her heart had been razed, allowing her the comfort of leaning on someone. On the other hand, there was nothing but pain if Diego couldn't forgive all that she'd done.

What would happen in just a couple days, when he returned to his life and she returned to hers? She wanted to voice the question. Then again, she didn't want to hear the answer. She didn't want him to have to choose between her or his career. What kind of future could they have if he was forced to make that kind of choice? And how could he make the choice unless she gave him all of the information?

Her mind went to the DVD she'd seen in Patrick's basement library. Even now, was someone at the police station viewing the evidence of her gullibility? She and Diego would join them in the viewing soon, as they'd been invited to work with the CPD, but how would she explain that tape? How would he feel about her after seeing the low she'd sunk to?

Because you're worth it.

Would he still think that after he knew the truth?

Diego's hand drifted lower, his fingers splaying across her belly. She lost herself to the moment, trying not to think it could be their last. His lips blazed a trail down her neck, stopping to lavish her nipples with equal attention before moving lower still. But she couldn't stand the thought of him giving her pleasure when she was still holding back.

With a nudge at his shoulder, she shifted him onto his back and reached for a condom, then rolled it into place. He hissed in plea-sure, but didn't seem content to let her take her time. She took his hands in hers, interlacing their fingers, and slowly sank onto him. He watched her face, his own tense with the effort to prolong the pleasure. The look in his eyes was so intense and honest that she bent down to kiss him, hiding her guilt from him. She increased the rhythm, letting it carry both of them away, letting herself forget.

After, as they lay there, catching their breaths, Diego slapped her thigh gently. "Get up and moving. We're going back to the correctional center."

Confused by the rapid change in subject, Becca watched him jump up and head into the bathroom. The sound of running water started a moment later.

She joined him in the bathroom. "The correctional center?"

He tugged her into the shower with him. "I was thinking. If Joyce won't talk, and we can't talk to Eve, and Patrick isn't taking the bait, who else knows Patrick well enough to share his secrets?"

"Tony?" She scrubbed her skin a little harder at the thought of having to face him again.

Several minutes later, showered and dressed, she checked her emails and found one from Lorena with an updated profile for Patrick Bigelow. They'd given her what new information they had yesterday.

"I don't know when that woman sleeps," Becca said. "She apparently interviewed Joyce while the police had her in custody last night."

Diego looked up from where he'd been checking his own emails on his phone. "She's just as dedicated as you are."

"*Munchausen by proxy*," Becca read aloud. "I've heard of that. It's where a person earns attention by hurting someone in their care, and continues the cycle because it's rewarding. According to Lorena, Joyce used to make Patrick sick when he was a boy, just so she could take care of him and get sympathy from her friends, family and hospital staff."

"Except this is by proxy, squared," Diego said. "Patrick kills patients in his mother's care so that she gets attention and sympathy. What does he get out of it?"

Becca read more of Lorena's email, and then summarized. "Joyce Bigelow suffers from severe depressive episodes. Can't be easy to live with a mother who struggles with that. Joyce pursued a career as a nurse because she enjoyed that environment." She glanced at Diego. "That explains the creepy nurse dolls at their home. Being a caregiver was rewarding, and then she craved the attention more often, like an addict. It became a vicious circle. When Patrick grew up and beyond her control and she didn't have that Munchausen-by-proxy outlet anymore, Patrick somehow figured it was his duty to fill in."

"He learned from the best," Diego muttered.

"He gave her what she needed, playing the dutiful son." Becca's stomach twisted. How many people had these two hurt? "Must be why he wants to be a dutiful partner to me now. He's learned to interact with the women in his life by taking care of them in this manner. He learned at an early age to give people what they want so they'd love him."

"He wants you to accept him. To love him."

At the end of the email were Damian's orders. "Our goal is to check out the hospice where Joyce works. Worked," Becca corrected. "Surely, she'll be fired if she had anything to do with her son's murderous tendencies."

"Imagine being her patient," Diego said.

"We don't have to." Becca had spied many DVDs in Patrick's collection that had been labeled Golden Oaks Hospice.

Thursday, 9:00 a.m.
Golden Oaks Hospice

THE HEAD NURSE ON DUTY AT GOLDEN OAKS HOSPICE AIMED HER smiles at Diego and fluttered her lashes ever-so-slightly, so Diego took charge of interviewing her.

Becca wandered away to give him time to question Mary, leaving Diego disappointed. He would have liked to see some response from Becca to another woman's interest in him. A bit of fire, a flash of jealousy. Something that told him she was feeling something for him. Something deeper, akin to what he was feeling for her.

Or maybe he was alone in his feelings. He'd been thankful to be by Becca's side when they'd entered the Bigelow house. The thought of Patrick going after Becca without Diego around to protect her...

Diego refocused as Mary flashed him a mouthful of perfect teeth in a wide smile. "What did you want to know about Joyce?" she asked.

"Whatever you can tell me."

"She's a good nurse. Attentive to her patients, always on time, and personable enough."

"I'm sure you trained her well."

Mary seemed to soak in the praise. "She was here years before I was."

"Have you noticed anything odd about the number of deaths among her patients?"

"For the most part, it's not surprising when someone here dies. We're here to give them care and support in their final days or months." Mary tapped her lips with fingernails that were neatly trimmed and lacked polish. "But there were a couple times I thought her patients died before their time. It's just so hard to tell. Death is unpredictable, even when it's near, you know?"

Diego flashed to his niece, killed way too young. For no under-standable reason. And Patrick, killing James and taking Eve... Sometimes the mind was twisted enough to try to make death do its bidding. He made a wordless sound of agreement.

"But Hank... His passing was rather sudden, I felt."

"Hank?"

"He died earlier this week. Joyce and her son came to his memorial yesterday. In fact, they did a lot of the planning. Very thoughtful, and helped the family out a lot. They were amazed at Patrick's video tribute."

Diego's skin went cold. Patrick and Joyce had found ready-made victims here. The patients were easy targets.

After a few more minutes of interviewing Mary, and some time with the patients who'd had Joyce as their nurse—who all sang her praises as very attentive, if somewhat quiet and moody at times—Diego found Becca sitting with an elderly woman in the communal living room area, laughing with her over something.

Becca looked up at him. "Done already?"

"Talked to everyone except this lovely lady." His gaze moved to the woman in the recliner. "Seems like I've been missing all the fun in here."

Becca's eyes twinkled. "You were. This is Virginia. She's one of Joyce's."

"Have been for a while now," Virginia said. "Outlived all the doctors' predictions." Her triumph was clear, as was the reason she had survived whatever it was that was trying to kill her. She had laughter creased in every line of her face. "Joyce is an excellent nurse. Her son, however, is creepy as hell."

"We were just starting to talk about Patrick," Becca explained to Diego.

"He seemed nice enough, at first. The third or fourth time he visited, though, he got a little weird."

"How so?"

"Felt like he was interviewing me for a position or something. Wanted my life story. I've been talking to the others around here, and he admitted this himself. He's documenting the good in life."

"What seemed off about that?" Becca asked.

"He was also asking a lot of personal questions, asking me to *unburden my conscience*, whatever the hell that means. Which is one of the reasons, I suppose, that I felt weird about the interview." She looked contemplative. "It was almost like he was too eager to dig up some dirt or something."

"What kinds of questions was he asking?"

"He asked about how I grew up, what I did with my life." She cackled again. "Guess a mother of five and grandmother of twelve wasn't impressive enough, though. Kept asking for more. Almost felt like he wanted me to be a superhero, supervillain, or make something up, whether it was good or bad. He wanted a good story."

A few minutes later, Becca stood in the hall with Diego and shivered. He reached out to stroke her arm. "You okay?"

"I can't help but think that woman's so-called boring life saved her. I read through a few of those obituaries Lorena sent with the profile this morning, and Einstein's notes." He'd been sending them quick summaries as he viewed Patrick's video library at the CPD. "Either this area of the United States was heavily populated with everyday heroes or Patrick had a way of embellishing."

"He should be a speechwriter for a politician."

"Yeah. Instead, he's preying on these poor people." She glanced back toward Virginia's room.

"We'll stop him." He ran his hand up and down her arm again. "He'll soon realize he's not the grim reaper he thinks he is. Or the Darwinian scientist. Or whatever hell other game he's playing."

She went still as a chime indicated her phone had a text. She looked up at him with dread. He'd do anything to wrap this case up and bring the warmth and energy back into those vibrant brown eyes.

He squeezed her arm in support. "Want me to read it this time?"

"Could you?" She reached into her pocket and handed him her phone.

"*Ten p.m., alone. Meet me where it all began.*" His jaw clenched. He was sick of this guy's games.

"Alone?" she repeated.

"We won't let it go down that way."

She blew out a breath. "I don't get it. Where did it all begin?"

"We have until ten o'clock tonight to figure that out."

Thursday, 2:00 p.m.
Metropolitan Correctional Center

WITHOUT PREAMBLE, BECCA SHOVED THE CARTON TOWARD TONY. "This is the last time you'll see me."

Every instinct told her there was no more time for Eve. This was her last shot at getting important information from Tony.

Patrick had given her a deadline of ten tonight to figure out where he was, *where it all began*, and she wasn't going to let Eve down.

Tony grinned. "That's what they all say. Then they play hard to get."

She tried to look unaffected by the monster in front of her. Over Tony's shoulder, Becca met Diego's gaze and he gave her a subtle nod of encouragement. Again, he was hanging in the background, letting her handle the situation. Trusting her. He shouldn't trust her. She'd lied to him. Or, she'd kept the final piece of the truth from him.

"I need to know what else you shared with Patrick."

"Patrick has all the interviews. Ask him."

"Yeah, well, Patrick's on the run."

Tony snorted. "Little shit. I should have known he couldn't stand the heat. We had a deal." Tony's eyes lit with a light that gave Becca the shivers, though she controlled them. "Did you find the recordings?"

"He had all kinds of DVDs, all kinds of people. To which recordings are you referring?"

Some of the light in his gaze dimmed and his smile faded altogether. "The ones of me."

"Huh. I don't recall seeing any of you." Becca frowned at Diego. "Do you?"

"Nope." Diego acted bored.

"That fuck." Tony slammed a fist on the table. He seemed to vibrate with anger now. "We had a deal. He was going to make me famous. Said he'd get several million to air my story."

"Hope you got that in writing," Becca said.

Her blasé attitude only fueled Tony's rage. She caught a glimpse of the violent man who'd killed many women but she held her ground. "I gave him what he wanted. He'll pay if he doesn't come through."

"What'd you give him? What did he ask for besides information?"

"Evidence." The cold smirk was back. "Something concrete that proved the Circle was involved in Damian Manchester's daughter's disappearance."

Becca felt the air squeeze from her lungs. This was it, the evidence Damian sought. What she'd been searching for over the past few months. "Did he pay for it in cigarettes?"

The grin widened, his gold teeth flashing. "Nah. He did a job for me. Offed a prostitute who was a loose end."

"Fanta."

Tony nodded.

Becca's gaze met Diego's and she swallowed to clear her mind again. "What did you give him in return?" she asked.

"I told him about a storage room I have. Mementos and shit. Guy's gotta reminisce every once in a while, right?" He glanced around the drab interview room as if recalling where he was.

"And what were you reminiscing about?"

"The women. The girls. And how we did it back in those days."

"The Cattle Call?"

Tony's eyes widened. "Guess you're smarter than you look. I gotta tell you, that's a relief. I'd like to think it took a smart person to take me down."

"Tell me about how you did it when you worked for the Circle."

"We'd take a few of them at a time, usually two or three, brand them and put them in cells. Boss had a sweet set-up. He'd charge hundreds of thousands of dollars for men with certain *discerning* tastes to log in to a secret website where they could view the girls, and then bid on the merchandise. The guys and I had a hell of a lot of fun making the girls act the part. It was like a game show. I figured Patrick would like that part, since he's so big on story details, survival of the fittest, and all kinds of life purpose shit that doesn't mean anything. These girls had to appear fit to be bought or die trying."

At least that explained how Patrick had known about the branding, and why he'd branded Fanta. Tony had talked about the

Cattle Call, and the Circle's evil deeds. "So he proved his loyalty to you by killing Fanta. He branded her for you."

Tony shook his head in wonder. "I had pegged him for a weakling who got his rocks off by hearing how tough guys got the job done."

"Where'd you get the girls, Tony?" Becca could barely conceal the hate in her voice as she imagined Samantha, young and alone, taken from the world she'd known and thrown into hell.

"Everywhere. Wherever we came across them. There were so many. Too many to count." His grin was back. "Certainly more than the cops charged me with. But I kept something from each, so I'd have something to remember them by."

"And you remember Samantha?"

"Oh, yes. She was unusual."

"How so?"

"She was a special request."

Becca could sense Diego wanting to draw closer. Something big was about to be revealed.

Tony met Becca's gaze with a sly grin. "Someone paid me big money to take her."

"Tell me who, and where." Was that her voice that was so breathless?

Tony shook his head. "I'll only tell Damian Manchester himself. I want him here, with my lawyer. I'm not giving the information away for cigarettes anymore."

CHAPTER 22

Thursday, 5:55 p.m.
Northwest Side, Chicago

The street his target lived on was quiet and cold, and Patrick stomped his feet in the dead grass several times to keep the blood moving. But with the winter cold came the early darkness that would aid his mission.

He'd called to see if she'd left for the day and had been immediately sent to voicemail. Given her vigilance at the SSAM desk, Catherine Montague must have headed home. He only had a little while longer to hang out in the cold along the side wall between her and her neighbor's home.

Once he had Catherine, the game would truly be underway. Eve had been impatient, both angrier and more lethargic as time went by, but she wouldn't have to wait much longer. It would give her time to rethink her priorities, anyway. The little bitch probably hadn't ever been spanked as a child, and now felt the world was entitled to hear her opinion. He used to think her opinion counted. Now he knew she wasn't trustworthy.

Like Jack Spratt, he'd tucked her away in a pumpkin shell where he could keep her very well. He snickered, then recovered his composure. The thought of seeing Becca, face-to-face, soon had him giddy, which could lead to mistakes. But there was nobody around to hear him. Catherine lived on a quiet street in a quiet neighborhood with old brick single-family homes. He wondered why a single woman in her late twenties would rent a house like this, especially on an administrative assistant's salary, rather than choose an apartment closer to town. Perhaps she'd confess to him tonight, when he helped her unburden her conscience.

A car approached and he ducked further into the shadows, pressing his back against the cold brick as the headlights of a vehicle flashed against the neighbor's wall, indicating Catherine had turned into her driveway. The sound of the garage door rattling as it slid upward confirmed he could slip out of his hiding place. He silently made his way along the outside wall of the garage and waited until he heard her car door close with a soft thunk.

Most people didn't bother to look back to see if the garage closed all the way once they'd pressed the button to initiate it, let alone watch to make sure nobody dodged inside before it was fully closed. He was betting Catherine would do the same.

The door began rattling again, this time on its way down. The garage door was still only halfway through its descent when he heard the interior door that led from the garage to the house close, indicating she had gone inside. Patrick bent in half to squeeze under, but lifted his feet high as he stepped across the threshold, so as not to trigger any safety mechanisms that would stop the door.

Ducking his head low, he pressed close to the rear of Catherine's Jeep Cherokee, letting the adrenaline settle a moment before he moved on. The garage grew quiet as its door finished its journey, shutting out the frigid evening air and leaving Patrick with nothing but an inner door between him and the next part of his project.

Very slowly, Patrick opened the door leading into the house. It didn't creak, and there was a small laundry area on the other side, with another open door that gave him a view of part of the kitchen. Though he couldn't see Catherine, she hummed as she moved about, out of sight but not far out of reach. His fingers caressed the length of rope coiled in his pocket. Soon it would be about her slender neck.

Thursday, 6:07 p.m.
Metropolitan Correctional Center

"I THINK IT WOULD BE BEST FOR ME TO WAIT IN THE OBSERVATION room," Lorena told Damian. She was at his side as they went through the security checkpoint at the prison.

He was touched that she had dropped everything the moment Becca had called him with Tony Moreno's demands. It had taken a while to get Tony's lawyer there, too, and to arrange for a private meeting with the prisoner after hours. But Damian had friends in high places, and had gladly traded favors to make this happen. He'd do anything to learn more about Sam's disappearance.

With a half smile, Lorena turned to Becca and Diego. "Fill us in."

Becca looked toward the interview room where, presumably, Tony was talking with his lawyer. "Tony likes to manipulate, so be on your guard. In fact, this whole thing might be a game for his amusement."

"But you think he has something valuable?" Damian said, daring to hope. He trusted Becca's instincts.

She blew out a breath. "I hope I didn't bring you here for nothing, sir, but I think he does have information about Samantha. He mentioned he takes trophies from his victims."

Damian was surprised. "We didn't find any evidence of that when you caught him last year."

"No. He apparently kept a storage room he gave Patrick access to, in exchange for Patrick proving himself to Tony by killing Fanta. Tony would have been in his mid-twenties at the time of Samantha's disappearance, he's a hardened criminal with a record stretching back to juvie, and records show that he's lived in Chicago all his life, so it's not unbelievable that he could have been involved in her disappearance."

"But?" Damian sensed there was a flip side to this coin.

"But we think he could also be snatching at his last chance to make some kind of deal," Diego said. "He knows who you are, and is aware of your connections and wealth. He thought Patrick would be his road to fame and fortune, but that appears to have fallen through. The Circle must know he's been talking to Patrick, and now to us. He doesn't have many friends left, by my count."

Damian's gaze moved between the pair. "You think he's making things up to get something from me?"

Becca shrugged delicately. "Hard to tell until we see what he's asking for in exchange. Couldn't hurt to talk." She glanced at the clock on the wall in the waiting area. "We don't have a lot of time, sir. We need to know where Patrick thinks *it all began*."

Lorena reached out and slipped her hand into his, then gave it a supportive squeeze. Her fingers were long, smooth and warm within his. "I'll be listening and watching from the other room." The prison had a surveillance video feed hooked up to watch from an adjoining security office.

Becca and Diego entered the interview room with Damian but stayed on the fringes. Tony grinned and Damian hated him all over again. Had this monster grinned at his daughter like that, just before he stole her away? Damian didn't want to think what other crimes this man might have perpetrated on his daughter, or anybody else. It filled him with a rage he struggled to subdue.

"You requested to see me, Mr. Moreno?" Damian managed to

keep a cool exterior as he sat opposite the man without offering his hand.

Tony's lawyer cleared his throat. "My client is prepared to give you some valuable information if you sign this document."

Damian pulled reading glasses out of his pocket and put them on. He scanned through the paragraph that laid out what Tony expected of him.

"As you can see," the lawyer summarized, "this agreement indicates you will attempt to arrange for Tony Moreno's transfer to a more comfortable high-security prison in a state far from here."

"He doesn't specify where."

"Anywhere," Tony said, speaking for the first time. "As long as it's out of the Circle's reach. And I want a personal bodyguard or extra security, or whatever you can arrange, until I can ship out."

Damian doubted anyone was outside of the Circle's reach. "Why?"

"They'll kill me once they know I've been talking. I thought Patrick was going to be my ticket to safety, exchanging my interviews for a book deal that would keep me in enough money to buy protection within these walls. He duped me." Tony's voice vibrated with anger. His muscles flexed beneath his orange jumpsuit. When they put Patrick in jail, he'd better pray he wasn't near this man. "Nobody gets away with that."

Tony's gaze flicked to Becca and Diego, then back to Damian. "You want answers that only I have. I need a deal only you can provide. The ball's in your court."

"I'll do what I can to get you transferred. You have my word."

"That's not good enough."

Unflinching, Damian held the man's gaze. "It's all I can promise. I don't have ultimate power here. I only have connections of whom I can ask favors. My offer ends in—" Damian pulled his sleeve back to look at his watch, "—one minute."

Tony slammed a fist on the table. "I'm not giving you something for nothing."

"I'm in a bit of a time crunch. And you can bet I'll try to get you moved if you talk to me. I want to know what you know. And that means keeping you alive."

Tony looked at his lawyer, who nodded. "Deal," Tony said. "But if you don't come through—" His lawyer put a hand on Tony's shoulder, keeping him from completing his threat.

Damian pulled a pen out of his pocket and signed the document, then pushed it across the table to the lawyer. The lawyer scooped up the document, nodded to Tony, then left the room.

"I told him we'd want privacy for this," Tony said. He seemed to forget Becca and Diego were there. They'd faded into the background.

"Did you touch my daughter?" Damian couldn't control the tic in his jaw at the thought of Samantha's possible pre-death torture. Of course, if it turned out that wasn't Sam's body...

"I didn't touch her," Tony said, solidly meeting Damian's gaze. "Nobody did but the client."

"And I'm just supposed to believe that?"

Tony shrugged. "Believe what you want. Someone paid big money to have her. You want the man responsible for your daughter's death?"

Like he wanted his next breath.

Tony smiled, apparently seeing the answer in Damian's nonverbal cues—the tightening of his jaw, the widening of his pupils, the hitch in his breathing. He struggled for a calm demeanor when his brain was screaming to reach across the table, rip out Tony's taunting tongue and shove it down his throat.

"Then follow the money," Tony said.

Damian had no patience for cryptic messages. "You had to have told Patrick more than this. What did you give him?"

"Sam's necklace." Tony's statement seemed to echo in the room.

Damian's chest hurt so badly he thought his sternum was caving in. He blinked, trying to control the painful reaction to the memory of Sam wearing the gift he'd given her. She'd very rarely taken it off. They'd held back the details of Samantha's jewelry from the media, hoping, when it hadn't been found with her body, that it had been kept by the killer, and would become a useful piece of evidence one day. It looked like that detail was about to pay off.

BECCA HID HER NERVOUSNESS BEHIND A STERN LOOK, TRYING TO BE invisible as the two men squared off verbally. But when the necklace came up, she couldn't stifle a gasp. Tony really did have something to do with Samantha Manchester's disappearance. Surreptitiously, she tried to glance at Damian to see how he was taking this information. His jaw was clenched, but otherwise, he was calm. He had to be reeling inside, but he was determined to get the answers he deserved.

"Describe the necklace," he ordered.

Tony shrugged. "I could have showed it to you, before Patrick got hold of it."

"Describe it," Damian ordered again.

"Silver chain, little silver butterfly with pale pink gems in the body. The wings were made out of a whitish gem that sparkled like a rainbow."

"Opal. Her birthstone." Damian spoke to Becca without turning to look at her. He couldn't seem to tear his gaze away from Tony. "I gave it to her for her twelfth birthday. She wore it always."

"And it wasn't found on the body?" Becca asked.

"No." Damian still nailed Tony with his gaze.

Tony smirked. "And neither was the matching bracelet, was it?"

Damian's fingers gripped the edge of the table. "What do you know about a bracelet?"

He shrugged. "It had the same charm, only smaller. A butterfly with the same gems."

"Where is it now?"

"The man who paid for her has it, I'm sure. Unless it was found with the body."

A muscle leaped in Damian's jaw. "Is that my daughter's body that we buried, or is it someone else, meant to mislead us?"

Tony's grin faded, and he finally looked to be taking this as seriously as they were. "That's her body."

Becca stifled a gasp. Samantha *was* dead. There was no more hope for Damian—except to find her killer.

Damian closed his eyes for a brief moment, then turned an intense look on Tony. "Why?"

"You'll have to ask her killer that."

"How do I know you didn't kill her?"

"I was only paid to take her. I stashed her in the usual place for a day."

"What place was that?" Becca asked, sensing they were getting to the information she needed to find Patrick. He'd told her to meet him where it all began. That she'd find Eve there. Could he mean the place where Samantha had been taken by the Circle, where the crime had begun that had ultimately led to Damian starting his agency—the agency Patrick had become such a fan of?

"A building with holding cells in the basement," Tony said.

"Just like in New York," she said. "The Cattle Call."

"Makes sense," Diego said, emerging from his silence. "The Circle has a set way of doing things. They find what works for them and repeat it in other cities."

"Give me an address," Damian ordered Tony. "I'll get you your protection."

"YOU THINK HE'S TELLING THE TRUTH?" BECCA ASKED WHEN TONY had been returned to his cell and she and Diego stood outside the interview room.

"I do." Diego looked down the hall to where Damian's head was bent close to Lorena's. She was saying something forcefully, but they were too far away to hear. Given the way her hands were fluttering about, it was important.

Diego turned his gaze to Becca. "You okay?"

"I will be once we find Eve."

"Lock Patrick away. Save Eve. Find Samantha's killer. You can do it all, can't you?" His gentle smile said he wasn't being sarcastic.

"You bet your ass I can." Now that they had an address, she could do anything.

"I'd place that bet." He looked at her mouth as if he wanted to press a kiss there. Her lips tingled with anticipation, but he didn't bend to claim his kiss. "We should find Nico and fill him in."

Becca glanced at her phone to check the time. "We've got a few hours. Damian will have Einstein track down the blueprints for the building. Maybe we can study it and get an advantage."

Damian came toward them at a fast clip, holding a phone to his ear. "Let me know when you're sure," he said to someone on the other end. Lorena was following in his wake.

Becca got a chill at the look on Damian's face. Had they found Eve's body? "What's wrong?"

"That was Einstein. He's been trying to get in touch with Catherine for the last hour to see if she could help view more videos at the CPD. She promised she'd make herself available, but she's not answering the phones at SSAM or at her house."

Becca's skin tingled with certainty that something was wrong. It wasn't like Catherine to be unreachable.

Thursday, 9:54 p.m.
South Side, Chicago

NICO JUTTED A CHIN TOWARD THEM. "ARMED?"

"To the teeth," Diego said. He had a gun at his hip and another at his ankle. And a rebar knife at the other ankle. For balance.

"The CPD is standing by in their positions. And I'll be there the moment you need anything," Diego said into the mic, looking toward the other alley where Becca had moved to test the connection, putting some distance between her and the car he and Nico were sitting in.

"Gotcha." Becca responded through the mic sewn into the collar of her shirt.

The equipment was working then. They'd gone over and over the plan, but it had been hastily put together and there were always unknowns walking into a situation such as this at the last second.

He looked down the street to the building Tony had indicated had once been a front for the Circle's illegal activities, including the Cattle Call operation. Tony had told them they'd shut it down years ago, when Damian had been searching for information on Samantha's disappearance, offering a monetary reward that many people in this neighborhood couldn't refuse.

Had they guessed correctly? Was Patrick in there now, with Eve and Catherine as his prisoners, and was he planning to put Becca through the same thing? Diego knew how capable she was, what a skilled agent. Hell, he'd depended on it during his niece's case. But a fist gripped his heart at the thought of this operation going sour. And he hadn't even had a chance to do more than send her a supportive look before she'd gotten out of the car. They were on Patrick's timeline now, nearing ten o'clock.

Becca returned from the alley but avoided standing too close to the car. She adjusted the scarf around her neck as if she were bundling against the cold, but it was really to hide any lip movement as she communicated with them while approaching the building.

"Ready?" Diego asked.

"Absolutely," Becca said. "I know you have my back."

AS BECCA WALKED THE QUARTER-MILE FROM THE ALLEY TO THE abandoned apartment building where she expected Patrick to be, she channeled her adrenaline into one thought. *Save them.* Her head seemed to chant the mantra with every step.

Right foot. *Save.* Left foot. *Them.*

She was on a march to save Eve and Catherine, but also to get justice for Samantha and any other man, woman or child Patrick or the Circle—or any other criminal—had touched or ever would touch.

Patrick was right about one thing. It was good to know one's purpose in life, and for a moment she felt a glimmer of empathy for him. Good versus evil. He'd been lost, and his quest for understanding had led him even further astray.

Then again, he'd made some evil choices that couldn't go unpunished.

And what about people who made good choices and still got punished? People like Nico, and Eve and...*her.* Becca wanted to run back to Diego and tell him she was done punishing herself. She was ready to tell him the entire story, beg his understanding and explore what they could have together.

Those things that were barriers before are still there. Her conscience, or maybe it was her heart, kept trying to tell her things would be better, kept trying to hope that Diego would see the good Becca and not the things she'd done.

Then again, he wasn't thinking with his head when they were together. It was a whole other part of his anatomy that reacted to her, and that passion was strong. But it wasn't lasting. Eventually, what they had would burn out, and at what cost? He would lose his career, his future, his reputation. Worse, he would hate her.

Becca couldn't do that to him.

"Did you know tomorrow is Valentine's Day?" Diego's voice said through the tiny earbud she was wearing, hidden in case Patrick was watching.

"Valentine's Day?" She hadn't looked at a calendar in days.

"In a couple hours." Humor laced his voice.

She smiled, but was getting too close to the building to risk moving her lips to talk. What was he trying to say?

"I love you." Diego's words were clear, yet she must have heard him wrong.

Her step faltered, and the silly grin dissipated behind her scarf.

"You're going to drop that on your woman now?" Nico's tone was incredulous. "Not cool, Sandoval."

"And on a party line, no less," Einstein broke in from his headquarters at his house, which was wired to tap or hack or whatever he did best.

"I've been trying to tell her for a while now," Diego defended himself. "I just couldn't find the right time."

Becca blew out a breath of frustration. So he chose now, when she couldn't see him, couldn't hold him.

"I didn't want you to run away again," Diego added.

The cracked, weedy parking lot she crossed was desolate, with areas of ice where snow had melted and refrozen. It echoed the feelings inside her. She'd warm to Diego, then be forced to refreeze when she remembered her guilt.

"I know you can't reply, but we'll talk when this is over." Diego's statement was confident. Would he be so sure of his feelings when he knew the truth?

"Head in the game," Nico said gruffly.

On the front door of the abandoned, crumbling apartment building was a circle with a ring of fire like on the wall of the building in New York, but smaller. She wouldn't have seen it if she hadn't been standing right there. "Video camera," she muttered as she eyed the camera attached to the upper right of the door, tucking her chin to her chest so it was even less likely anyone watching in the dark would see her lips move. Patrick was watching her from behind the safety of a camera lens. The team had been right to let her come alone and keep their distance, though she'd had to fight them on it. Patrick was testing her.

"Use the code word," Diego said. "If you need anything —*anything*—we'll be there in seconds."

He was scared for her, she realized. And it wasn't because he wasn't confident in her abilities. He respected her, but he also loved her. And love was a risk.

Love.

A little thrill went through her at the word. But the tiny word carried great responsibility. If she let anything bad happen to her, it would hurt him. And hurting Diego was not okay with her.

She stepped up to the large metal door and knocked. Her phone buzzed in her pocket. She pulled it out to read a text from Patrick.

Leave your coat there. Lift your shirt and then your pants legs so I can see you're unarmed.

"You don't trust me," Becca stated aloud so her backup would get the gist. If Patrick was watching her, he might be listening, too.

She stripped off her scarf and coat and dropped them on the ground, then pulled up her shirt and pants legs, to reveal to the camera that she had no weapons. Silently, she cursed Patrick for putting her in a position of weakness, but she had skills in hand-to-hand combat that still gave her the upper hand.

She apparently received his approval. The lock on the door clicked open as if controlled electronically, and she was able to enter the building, but there was nobody inside. She hesitated for a moment on the threshold. Though Diego and Nico were only a couple of minutes away, would it be time enough to get there if she couldn't handle Patrick?

The gutted apartment building was so much like the one she'd entered in New York City, the one where Selina had been held, that Becca had flashbacks to that cold day. To the names on the cell walls. Was that what awaited her? More names? The echoes of more victims?

It was dark with only a few flickering candles lit, like an emergency exit path, along a hallway that led to another door. Beyond had to be the stairs to the basement. She hesitated at the precipice, uncertain what surprises awaited her on the other side, but having enough of an idea that her survival instincts were kicking in, keeping her from going even one step further.

"Go on," Patrick's voice encouraged over a speaker.

Startled, she jumped, then spied a tiny black dot beside the door frame, a hole where a spy camera was likely aimed at her. She felt a cool draft at her ankles and looked down at her feet. Tendrils of fog reached from beneath the closed door and wrapped about her legs as if they'd pull her under. Patrick liked drama. Then again, he was a filmmaker of sorts.

Bracing herself, mentally running through the various martial arts holds she could use on an attacker of his size if he were on the other side of the door, she turned the knob. The fog machine was right inside, on a landing, so that the makeshift fog spilled down the stairs that led into a dark basement. Candles lit every other stair, glowing through the cloudlike waves that curled and engulfed them. She couldn't see beyond those dozen or so stairs.

Then a light switched on. A red spotlight illuminated a cell door, identical to the one in Brooklyn, at the base of the stairs. *More drama.* Becca picked her way down the stairs toward the object within that light. A scratching noise started on the other side of the door.

"Eve?" Becca was suddenly uncertain. "Catherine?" There was a lock on the door. A strong one.

Like in Patrick's basement, this door had a small window at the top. He'd apparently copied the Circle's methods in his home decorating. Becca slid the window open. A hand—scratched, bloody and streaked with dirt—reached through, and she jumped back, a scream lodging in her throat.

"Please get me out," a raspy voice said.

Eve. Becca's heart clenched and she scrambled back to the window. "Eve Reynolds?"

"Yes." Her hand was replaced by what Becca could see of a face

—a nose and a pair of vibrant blue eyes. In the red lighting, she looked ghostly.

"I'm Becca."

Eve gasped softly. "Becca?"

"A friend of yours is very worried." As she whispered, Becca scanned her surroundings for another camera. She was certain Patrick was watching all of this, his own private performance. Where was he? Nearby, in the building, or off site watching from afar?

Eve's eyes flashed with blue fire. "Where is Patrick?"

"Watching." Becca touched Eve's fingertips where they curled about the edge of the window. They were filthy, the nails broken as if she'd tried to claw her way to freedom. Then she remembered the dirt walls in Patrick's root cellar. Perhaps he had held Eve there for a while. "And he's got a plan for us."

Eve seemed to notice the red spotlight and the fog for the first time. The whites of her eyes flashed as she glanced to her left. "The other cell. He brought in another woman a couple hours ago."

"I'm sorry you got mixed up in this," Becca whispered, feeling somewhat responsible.

Eve gave a harsh laugh and swiped at her nose. Her hands were shaking, probably as much from adrenaline as food depravation. "My own fault."

"I'll be right back." Becca moved to the next cell, identical to Eve's. She slid the metal window open and peeked inside. Dark. The red light suddenly turned off, shutting her into darkness, just before a blue light nearly blinded her. It was aimed directly at the second cage, encouraging Becca to explore.

Becca caught the outline of a woman within. "Catherine?"

CHAPTER 23

The body moved, pushing itself up from the floor. "Becca?" Catherine's voice triggered a flood of relief, quickly followed by concern.

"It's me." Becca nearly cried, watching her friend struggle to her feet. Catherine was okay, but when her face appeared in the window, a large purplish bruise covered one cheek and more marks lined her neck.

Catherine put a hand to the bruise. "I'm sure it looks worse in this light. Blue's not my color." That she could joke at a time like this surprised a laugh out of Becca.

"You're strong." Becca whispered fiercely. "You remember that."

"Don't worry about me. Kick this guy's ass."

Becca would, as soon as he presented it to her. First, she was going to have to lure him out of his hole. She turned to face the cavernous basement, knowing Patrick had to be watching. "I'm here. What's next?"

The blue light turned off and a yellow one came on, highlighting the third and final cell in the basement. This door was open.

Patrick's voice echoed in the basement. "Get in and close the door."

FROM A BLOCK AWAY, DIEGO SAT NEXT TO NICO AND LISTENED IN. The windows of the car fogged with their body heat. Einstein was listening from his computer station at his house.

"We got eyes yet?" Diego asked.

"Working on it." Einstein was hacking into the video and computer lines Patrick had established. Nico had a computer laptop open in front of him. The man had seemingly come back to life when he'd heard Eve's voice.

"Get in and close the door," Patrick's voice said. He was ordering Becca to make herself his prisoner. The ultimate trust test.

Diego tried to ignore the desire to storm in there and grab the weasel by the throat. The urge to rip him to shreds was strong.

"You guys hearing this?" Becca whispered.

"You're doing fine," Diego said, after switching the mic so she could hear them. "We got you. We'll get you all out safely."

Diego heard Patrick repeat his orders to Becca, just as the image on Nico's computer screen changed from black to... "Holy shit," Diego muttered. "Is that fog?"

"Gentlemen, we have eyes." Einstein sounded satisfied.

Nico grimaced. "Fog and the crazy lighting will make a rescue op a bit murkier."

"Any idea yet if Patrick's on the premises?" Diego asked Einstein.

"Affirmative," Einstein replied. "He's there. The CPD sniper unit using infrared spied him passing an upstairs window, but no clear shot."

Diego's gaze met Nico's. "The moment he moves to the basement, we move in."

.   .   .

BECCA WAS CALLING HERSELF ALL KINDS OF STUPID FOR LETTING herself get locked inside a cage. Hell, she'd locked *herself* in willingly. The feeling of four close walls, with only a tiny window as her connection to the outside world, squeezed the breath from her chest.

Until she remembered her auditory connection to Diego. He'd said the words she'd never expected to hear. *I love you.*

Almost as if he realized she was worried, Diego spoke through the mic. "I'm here with you. We've got eyes and ears on you now and we're moving closer to the building. Patrick's in an upstairs room but on the move."

Be careful. Heavy footsteps echoed on the stairs. The door to her tiny window swung open a moment later, and the man she'd bumped into in the New York hotel, the one who'd seemed so polite and *nice* as he thanked her for catching his camera, stood in front of her.

He grinned. "You're finally here."

As if she had a choice. "Wouldn't miss it. Now that I'm here, why don't you let my friends go as our first act of good faith?"

"You mean your enemies."

"I mean the two women who you made my responsibility by dragging them into our affair. I thought you wanted to be my partner, my friend." Her accusation rang with disappointment.

He frowned. "Only if I can trust you to make the right decisions." At least now she knew where she stood on the trust scale—hovering just around zilch.

"Decisions about what? I'm locked in a cage. Pretty sure there are no decisions under my control at the moment."

Becca didn't like the grin that spread across the portion of his face that filled her window.

"That's where you're wrong. You're going to make some tough choices today. Good versus evil. Society versus the needs of man. All the questions that plague men on a daily basis."

Not most men, Becca would wager. But this one certainly

wrestled with it, if his video collection was any indication. *Think like a mindhunter.* What would Lorena say about all of this? What would she do?

The same thing a security expert would do. Find his weakness, exploit it.

Patrick's weakness? He wanted to feel important. Recognized. Like he was holding the secret to life in his hands. He wanted to *belong.*

"I thought your documentary interviews were stunning. How did you get all of those people to talk to you?" Becca stepped closer to the window, putting them on more friendly, intimate footing. As if there wasn't a steel door between them and he had the only key.

His demeanor seemed to shift. His grin widened and he seemed to quiver like the whiskers of a rat. "You watched them?"

"As much as I could in such a short period. Pretty impressive collection of data. I've dealt with criminals on a daily basis and never gotten even one of them to talk to me the way they did to you. You must have a special charm."

"I always thought it was a gift."

"It is. And the way you knew just what questions to ask to get at the heart of the matter..." She looked at her surroundings as if she'd just remembered where she was, then steadily met his gaze. "I'd love to discuss this more. You must be a wealth of information."

"We can talk just fine as we are."

"I feel more comfortable if the person I'm having a conversation with trusts me."

Patrick smiled. "Me, too. Which is why we'll soon get on with the games."

"Games?" Becca didn't like the sound of that, or the eager gleam that came into his eyes.

"You didn't think I'd brought the three of you here for nothing, did you?" He laughed and a chill went down her spine. "But first, I have to set the stage. And you've got to get ready for your audience."

She swallowed and looked about nervously. Was Diego hearing all of this?

"A select group of people from around the world are able to watch this via internet. Don't worry. I screened my viewers carefully. They get to vote on who lives and who dies, but not until you each state your case."

"HE'S IN THE BASEMENT," EINSTEIN TOLD DIEGO. "I'M SWITCHING the broadcast to your phone now. He's got all three women in separate cells, adjacent to each other."

Einstein had not only hacked into Patrick's feed, but he'd found a way to block the feed from the external cameras so that Diego and Nico could approach the building undetected from the front, and CPD officers from the rear. Guns drawn, they made their way through the dark, moonless night to the door Becca had entered.

Before they crossed the weed-choked lot, he glanced at the video Einstein was sending to his phone. Outrage flared as he saw the tiny cages on the screen. They were just like the one in which Selina had been held. "Where's Patrick now?"

"Somewhere in the basement, but off screen for the last thirty seconds."

It made sense since he'd said something to Becca about *setting up* for the show. Diego didn't like the sound of that at all. He motioned to Nico that they'd approach the door.

"He's making the internet feed live," Einstein said.

"Are you able to see what he's broadcasting?" Diego knelt at the door to inspect the lock.

"Working on getting into that exclusive club now." Einstein's confident tone indicated he'd be able to do it soon.

On his phone, Patrick's image appeared on the screen for a moment as he adjusted a camera angle. He disappeared just as quickly, then spent a couple minutes bringing three chairs into the viewing area. The chairs were wooden ladder-backs with armrests.

"Almost ready," Patrick called, presumably to the women.

"Diego?" The sound of Becca's whispered voice rippled through him. "He's making me change clothes. We're going to lose our connection. I won't be able to talk directly to you."

Diego stilled. Shit. The mic through which she communicated was sewn into her shirt. "I can hear you as long as Einstein remains tapped into Patrick's broadcast. I'm right there with you."

THE SCREECH OF A KEY BEING INSERTED INTO A CELL DOOR HAD Becca standing up to face Patrick. She'd had to discard her mic, and chose to leave the earpiece behind as well. Now that he was close, he might see it, and she couldn't risk breaking his trust. But, damn, losing Diego's voice in her ear left her feeling vulnerable. *I'm right there with you.* She tried to focus on his final words.

"Turn around," he ordered. "Put your hands behind you and back up until your fingers are by the opening. When I open the door, I'm going to tie your hands together. If you try anything funny, I'll kill you and the other women here and now." He flashed the blade of a knife.

She did as instructed, putting her wrists together against the small of her back. Her cell door opened, but only a crack.

After he had the zip-tie secured, he gestured for her to come out. "Don't be shy."

She'd put on the ridiculous skin-tight satin and gold-sequined outfit, but she certainly didn't want to parade around in it in front of this guy. She gestured to her dress. "Are we going back in time to a seventies disco or something?"

"The world would have been a better place if we lived in a seventies sitcom."

"Or eighties," she said, mainly to be on his good side. But also because there were no serial killers running rampant in the shows she'd seen as a kid. And no assholes like James Powell taking advantage of their prey. Only four big brothers teaching her how to be tough. Patrick gestured to a chair that faced two others at a V-like angle so that the camera would have a full view of all of the occupants.

"Sit." He moved aside, keeping his distance, possibly feeling threatened by her. *You should be.*

"I don't bite," she said.

"Sit down and stick your hands behind your back."

He bound her wrists to one rung of the chair with another zip-tie. She was at an awkward, painful angle in her seat and let out a moan.

"Sorry," he said, actually sounding like he meant it. "It's only temporary."

"What is this all about?" Maybe asking questions would give her some insight.

"You'll find out soon."

Satisfied Becca was restrained properly, he moved to Eve's door and unlocked it. He had to practically drag her out, she was so weak, but she still tried to kick at him as he sat her in the chair farthest from Becca and tied her in place. He'd selected a clean outfit for Eve, too. It was a low-cut red dress that showed dirty, skinned-up knees.

"Water might be nice," Eve muttered.

"Sure," Patrick said, so agreeable that Eve looked suspicious. "But if you spit it at me this time, you'll die." This was said with such calm normalcy that Becca felt a chill.

He brought a water bottle and held it to Eve's lips. "Can't have your tongue sticking to the roof of your mouth before your big Cattle Call debut. Although, you always said hot tea was the trick for you."

"With honey," Eve added.

Becca had to admire Eve's bravado, but the woman's eyes were wary. The words *Cattle Call* chilled her. If Patrick was mimicking the Circle's techniques, he'd be broadcasting to potential buyers. Did he mean to sell them to the highest bidder?

"You two worked together," Becca said, to keep the conversation going as her mind worked out the possibilities.

"He was my cameraman," Eve said. "But I had no clue who he really was." She met Becca's gaze, trying to convey a wealth of information that Becca surmised meant *tread carefully with this monster*.

Patrick had moved to Catherine's cell. "Come on out," he called as he swung the door open. She emerged, blinking at the colored spotlights and fog. The bruise on her cheek seemed to glow, especially with her hair drawn back into a ponytail. The white sundress Patrick had dressed her in, à la Marilyn Monroe, made her features even more stark.

Patrick finished tying Catherine to her chair, a foot from Becca, and stood in front of them to survey the display. "I dressed you this way for a reason, though you'll have to forgive the outdated clothing. It's all they had at the secondhand store."

"Vintage, darling," Eve said with heavy sarcasm. "It's all the rage right now."

"Not that our viewers will care about that." Patrick scooted Becca so that her knees were almost touching Catherine's. She tried to smile encouragingly at her friend, but Catherine was quiet and avoiding eye contact.

Eve was not. She was prepared to fully engage Patrick with the only weapon she had available. Her tongue. "Your so-called viewers—all two or three of them—probably only want to see the cleavage. Strapping us to these chairs is impeding that."

Patrick's mouth tightened and, apparently done arranging them to his satisfaction, he moved to pick up his camera and looked through the lens. "My viewers—which number closer to a couple hundred, for your information—care more about what I'm going to do to you than what you look like, though it helps that you're all very beautiful."

Patrick said this matter-of-factly, then set the camera down again to pick up a length of rope, tied into a noose, then slipped it around Eve's neck. He did the same to Catherine. He pulled a step stool from a corner and looped the ends of the ropes around hooks he'd attached to the exposed wooden boards in the ceiling, then tightened the slack. Eve and Catherine sat, ramrod straight, looking fearfully at each other.

"Don't move," Eve said. The women were trapped. If they moved more than a couple inches any direction, the rope would tighten.

"Good advice," Patrick said, then moved away to adjust some lighting, shining white spotlights on each of the three women. Despite the chill in the winter-cold basement, Becca felt a trickle of sweat slide down her temple.

"What about me?" Becca asked when he didn't move to place a noose on her neck. Not that she wanted one, but she was still striving to understand this madness.

"You're the star of the show. You decide who lives or dies." He clapped his hands together once, evidently happy with his morbid set-up. "We're ready to begin. You've seen my tapes. I always give my interviewees a chance to *unburden their consciences*, to determine for themselves if they're good or evil."

"I think you made that decision for most of them, when you selected them as candidates for murder. You deemed them unworthy to live."

"That was my purpose. It's why I survived all those illnesses." He picked up his camera and aimed it at Becca. The red light indicated he was filming, and the cord leading to the laptop on the folding table behind him told her he was feeding it to something—very likely his internet viewers.

"Your *mother* decided whether you'd survive or not."

Patrick looked up sharply. "She took care of me. Don't talk about her like that."

"She's a selfish woman. She hurt you to get attention. You fell for it, believing your purpose was to keep her in the limelight. You didn't decide your purpose. She did."

His fists were white with anger, but he made a visible effort to calm himself. "This time, Becca, you'll make the decision. Who will live and who will die?" He turned the camera on Eve. "Your enemy whose contributions to society supposedly have a global impact and who personally attacked you." He focused on Catherine. "Or a friend whose only impact is on your life, and maybe a few other agents at SSAM, who is supposedly there for you through thick and thin but tried to steal your date? You'll each make your case."

"But I've already selected," Becca said calmly. Her throat clenched for a moment as she imagined never seeing her family again. She'd lost her mic connection to Diego, so she couldn't even give him final messages to send to the people she loved. She couldn't even tell Diego she loved him.

Eve and Catherine turned surprised gazes to Becca. Patrick and his camera swiveled to her. "You have?"

"I choose myself."

DIEGO BIT BACK A CURSE, SINCE THEY WERE IN STEALTH MODE. Though Becca couldn't hear him, Einstein had managed to keep the feed going from Patrick's filming setup, so Diego heard the killer's insane demand, and Becca's response. Her readiness to sacrifice herself made Diego want to roar with frustration. He wasn't surprised that Becca would put her own life on the line, though. That was who she was, and he loved that about her. She helped the underdog, even when she was an underdog herself.

Nico had finally found a way in through a rooftop vent, since Patrick had barricaded the main door to the building. It had cost them precious minutes trying to find an alternative entrance. Luckily, Nico was familiar with the layout of the building.

Unfortunately, the door to the basement was locked. Patrick was organized enough to cover all his bases. Hopefully, not *all* the bases.

Diego nudged Nico aside. "I'll get this one."

It looked to be an ordinary lock this time. He'd kick it in if he had to, though that would hurt like hell and give Patrick advance warning they were there—enough warning to do some serious damage to one of his abductees. Thankfully, he had Becca's lock-pick tools.

Einstein broke into their communication. "Patrick's begun broadcasting live on his private site. I'm tracking his scumbag viewers for future reference. Probably the type to watch snuff films and child pornography, too."

Likely, they were among the clients on the Circle's human trafficking list. Had Tony given Patrick that information, too? With any luck, one of them might lead to the man who paid for Samantha Manchester to disappear.

"We can't go storming in there," Nico muttered, looking at the phone's screen where they still had images of the inside. "Eve and Catherine are in a precarious position with nooses around their necks. If he decides to knock their chairs over..."

Diego hoped Becca had the time to spare. *Hold on just a little longer. I'm coming.*

His phone screen went black.

Einstein cursed. "We lost video connection." They were flying blind.

CHAPTER 24

"You're ruining everything." A haze of red clouded Patrick's vision. He leaned against the table, where he could see the laptop screen but still film the women sitting a few feet away. The votes and comments were streaming in. He grinned. Eve wasn't the only one who could attract and enthrall an audience.

But he hadn't counted on Becca's stubbornness. She wasn't supposed to be a martyr. She was supposed to let him save her.

Already, the viewers were voting to give Becca her wish and kill her first. Their comments were vicious.

Give the bitch what she wants if she wants to be so noble.

I don't care who dies, as long as one of them does soon. I want the one in red for myself. How much?

The white one is an angel. The bruise on her cheek is a nice touch. She's mine. I'll pay you a million.

Patrick felt disgust well up inside. These men weren't interested in justice, or discovering truth. They were only watching for sexual gratification. Whether it came from degrading women or any other means, they didn't care. This wasn't what he'd wanted.

"You're not an option," Patrick told Becca. "That's not your purpose."

She shrugged. "I decide what my purpose is. And I'm not going to choose between these two fine women."

Fine? She had to be kidding. "Let's review the facts, because I'm certain you're remembering things wrong. Better yet, I want each of these *fine* women to tell you how they'd tip the scales between good and evil, and what *fine* punishment they think they deserve."

He put the camera on a tripod and went to Eve's chair. He gave the leg a swift kick that moved it back an inch and tightened the noose around her neck. "You're first."

Fear widened Eve's eyes as the rope turned her throat a blotchy red, but she could still breathe, still talk, though it was raspy from the last time he had put a rope around her neck. The bruises he'd left by partially strangling her would likely serve to excite his audience and remind them of the high stakes in this game.

"Unburden your conscience. State your case."

Eve released a shaky breath. "Becca, you don't know me, but I'm not a bad person."

He shook his head. "She knows what you tried to do to her. The whole world knows. Where's that golden tongue when you need it? Trust me, you need it now."

Eve's blue eyes were wide, the pupils tiny in the brightness of the spotlight as she lifted her face to Becca. The camera loved her. "I'm a dedicated person. Like you, I seek out the perpetrators of injustice and fight to right the wrongs."

"Good," Patrick murmured. "Keep going. Other than your video blog, will anyone miss you when you're gone?"

Eve shot him a glare. It was clearly eating her alive to have to defend herself to him. "I'm a daughter, and a sister. A friend."

She stopped and her eyes suddenly looked wild, probably because she'd just realized how few people would actually be personally affected if she were gone tonight.

Patrick turned to Catherine. "Looks like it's your turn."

Catherine looked straight into the camera, biting her lip. Then, something seemed to come over her, a calm awareness as if she'd made an important decision. "I don't deserve to live—or die—any more than anybody else. We've all done things we're not proud of."

"Explain, please."

"I'd rather not," Catherine said. "You can take it or leave it."

"Catherine?" Becca's voice was a plea. "Tell him you're a good person. You love with all your heart."

"But I'm far from perfect." Finally, she looked away from the camera and met Becca's gaze. Just as quickly, she looked at the floor, careful not to move in a way that tightened the noose.

"Nobody's perfect." Becca's confusion was genuine. Was Catherine simply trying to distract Patrick? Because it was working. But if that was the case, she was an awfully good actress, because Becca believed that, deep down, something was troubling her friend. Becca could relate. She had her own dark past to confront, and she wouldn't let it torment her anymore. If she got out of here—*when* she got out of here—she was going to get rid of that baggage once and for all.

"I think we've heard enough," Patrick said into the silence that had fallen over the group. "Let me check the voting. It might influence your decision."

As Patrick moved to check his laptop, Becca tried to make eye contact with Catherine, to encourage her to be strong. But her friend wouldn't meet her gaze again.

"I'm not going to choose anyone," she told Patrick when he looked up from his computer screen.

"I was afraid you might say that," he said. "Perhaps I can encourage you with a little video that reminds you what happened last time you tried to play the martyr."

Panic welled up as he pulled out a DVD case and slid the disc into his computer. It didn't matter that Becca had tried to hide her shame from Diego, or that she'd finally decided to share the entire truth with him when she got out of here. Patrick was about to make her past very public.

His finger tapped a key, and he turned the computer so that the three women could see.

No. No, no, no! She wanted to scream, to struggle in her chair until her hands were free and around his neck. But she could only sit and watch as a much younger, much more naïve Becca seduced James Powell, not knowing James had been filming it all.

Catherine's look was pure amazement, and then sympathy. "What's this?"

"Yes, do explain," Patrick said.

DIEGO PAUSED IN THE SELECTION OF A LOCK-PICK TOOL. EINSTEIN had found a way to direct Patrick's webcast to Diego's phone, and he and Nico could again hear and see what Patrick was filming. As could the three CPD officers who'd followed them inside and carried a hydraulic ram for busting open the door to the basement. It was the only barrier left, but breaking in so suddenly and loudly could put the women in danger. Still, his muscles bunched with the desire to do just that—to barge in and take out Patrick Bigelow. The only thing that stopped him was Becca hadn't said the code word yet, which meant she wasn't in grave danger—he hoped.

But it was the sudden silence that worried him now. He watched the screen, shocked to see a video of Becca making love to James Powell. No, not love. Just sex, he told himself. His stomach churned with outrage and frustration that Patrick would humiliate her like this.

"Explain to our viewers what's happening here," Patrick urged Becca.

Becca's voice shook when she replied. "When I was accused of murder, years ago, the police told me they had nothing on James.

That I was their prime suspect. They implied that if I could give them something more to go on..."

So she'd degraded herself to find justice for Amy? And then she'd lived with the humiliation when it hadn't worked. Diego wanted to howl at the unfairness.

"So you filmed this, hoping to get a confession?" Patrick prodded.

"He somehow knew what I was up to, and turned the tables on me," Becca said. "He got me into bed with the illusion he would tell me everything once he could fully trust me. So I did what I had to do."

Trust. That was why she didn't give it easily. Diego's chest squeezed, and he attacked the lock on the door with renewed vigor. He was going to get her out of there, going to save her from this asshole, and going to prove to her that there was one man in her life who was absolutely, without a doubt, worthy of her trust.

"I, FOR ONE, ADMIRE THAT," EVE SAID. "YOU DID WHAT YOU HAD TO, and it was unselfish."

Becca met Eve's and Catherine's eyes and found silent support that buoyed her sagging spirits. And they certainly didn't deserve to pay for her mistakes, so she drew strength from them and faced Patrick once more. "I'm not going to choose. None of us deserves to die. Except for you, Patrick."

His gaze moved over the trio of women. The smug satisfaction in his smile sent shivers skittering across Becca's skin. "It looks like our private audience has chosen for you. And I approve their selection. It fits the end goal. You'll get what you've wanted all along. You'll come out the hero, Becca. You'll save one of these women, the viewers see the other one die, and you walk free. Everyone wins, even the one who dies. In the documentary, I'll glorify her as an example of evil redeemed."

Which would leave Becca with nightmares for the rest of her

life. "No, thank you. I don't want to be a hero, especially to viewers like yours."

"You have no choice."

Like hell. She'd been considering her options, restrained as she was. While Diego and Nico might be moving into position upstairs, there was no way she could count on that. The chair was heavy, and her only weapon. She'd make it work. "You have to have a choice to be a hero, otherwise there's nothing heroic about it."

But Patrick was no longer listening. "The loser, is, unfortunately—or fortunately, given she volunteered herself earlier—Catherine Montague."

Catherine's expression was stoic as he approached. But as Patrick reached over her head to tighten the noose, Becca shouted the code word at the top of her lungs, hoping Diego could hear it. "Natalee!"

She barely had time to register the door high above her, at the top of the stairs, crashing inward as she burst into motion. Throwing her weight forward so she could gain her footing, she balanced the chair on her back and spun on Patrick, using the furniture as a weapon by running the chair legs into his back. With a grunt of pain, he stumbled into Catherine, which—*oh, God!*—tightened Catherine's noose so that she was gasping. But he soon regained his footing and came at her again.

"Stop!" Diego shouted. "We'll shoot you if we have to."

But Patrick wasn't listening, and the sudden movements had stirred up the fog that was still pouring forth from the machine. That, combined with the crazy lighting, made it hard to see what was happening. If Diego took a shot, he could hurt Catherine or Eve. Or her. Likely, he knew that, or he would have taken the shot by now.

"Get to Catherine first!" she shouted to Diego when the pounding of footsteps reached the base of the stairs. It had to be him and Nico, and probably a CPD officer or two, judging by the noise. She had to deal with Patrick charging toward her. Again, she bent over to support the weight of the chair with her back, swung around in a circle, and struck him in the gut with the chair legs as hard as she could.

Unfortunately, Patrick's adrenaline was also kicking in, and this time he kept his footing, lunging for her. "You're ruining everything! I did all of this for you, so you could unburden your conscience and live out your life's purpose."

In the background, Catherine was sputtering for air, unable to free herself because her hands were still tied. Eve was trying to support Catherine the best she could by using her legs to reach for Catherine's chair, but the noose that was still around Eve's neck prevented her from moving enough. But other people, men she couldn't identify with the bright spotlights in her face, were at the base of the stairs, so Becca focused again on Patrick.

"A hero? Just like you did for your mother? No, thanks. Besides, you two are a match made in hell. I want no part of that." Becca tried to hit him again, but Patrick grabbed the chair legs and shoved hard, knocking her to the ground. The wooden legs cracked and split as she landed. Pieces of wood jabbed into her flesh, and she desperately tried to free her hands, but the back of the chair had remained stubbornly intact and Patrick was on her in an instant, refusing to give her a moment to reset her defenses. He grabbed her hair and yanked her face to focus on his. His breathing was rapid, his beady eyes had become more pronounced as his pupils dilated, and his cheeks were blotchy with anger.

"Guess it'll be your day to die, after all." He wrapped his hands around her throat and began squeezing. Ironic that a man who'd been smothered by his mother all his life had learned to kill by throttling his victims.

In her peripheral vision, Nico was freeing Catherine. Where was Diego? She had the sudden, alarming thought that he'd been hurt somehow. Or hadn't come for her after all, once he'd heard and seen who she really was, and what she'd kept from him. But then two large hands ripped Patrick off of her. Or tried to. Patrick wouldn't let go of her neck. She began to see stars in the fog swirling around her. Pinpricks of light. Her world shrank down to the only thing she wanted—her next gulp of air.

Diego swore and there was a crunching sound as he punched Patrick repeatedly, until the man fell to his side, unconscious. Sweet air filled Becca's lungs as she gasped, ignoring the pain of her neck muscles. Diego pulled a knife from his ankle holster and sliced through her bonds, releasing her from what was left of the chair and freeing her hands. She took another breath, draping her arms around Diego's neck as he carefully scooped her against his chest. This breath was filled with his unique spice, tinged with sweat. He was shaking with fear and relief.

She lifted a hand to soothe his cheek. But, uncertain of his feelings, she let it drop. "I'll be okay."

"Damn right you will," he said gruffly. "I'll never forgive you if you don't come out of this alive."

She tried to laugh, wanted to explain everything, but her throat hurt and her good intentions came out as a moan.

Thursday, 11:45 p.m.
Mercy Hospital

IT WAS NEARLY AN HOUR LATER, IN HER HOSPITAL ROOM AT MERCY, when Diego returned to her. "How are you feeling?" he asked.

"Better. The doctor said I can go any time."

"That's good." He seemed hesitant to come fully into the room. Now that the dust had settled, was he having second thoughts, realizing what kind of person she'd been?

"How are Catherine and Eve?"

"Eve is staying overnight. She was dehydrated, but the injuries to her neck will heal. Same with Catherine."

"We were all so lucky." Becca looked down at her hands,

unwilling to see the doubt or judgment in Diego's gaze. The bed shifted as he sat down next to her.

"I understand why you were hiding the rest of your past from me," he said. "It wasn't your fault. You were doing what you thought you should do at the time. To help other women."

Her throat tightened. Could he really forgive her that easily? She looked up, seeing him through a haze of tears. She swiped at the moisture that clung to her eyelids. "He put it up on the internet for a while. Used it to support his case that I was a jealous lover. Made me out to be a fool and a murderer."

"He can't hurt you anymore."

"But he can."

Diego scowled. "How?"

"His video. If there are copies out there, it could still hurt the people I love."

"They'll forgive you. They know you, and that you aren't the woman in the video. You were acting a part. Your heart is pure, as are your motives. Just like mine are in the Circle investigation."

"I'm sorry I didn't see that right away." She took his hand and squeezed. Her eyes widened. "You're shaking. Are you mad?"

"Mad?" He looked surprised. "I was scared. Scared you wouldn't let me forgive you."

Her laugh was raspy. "Let you forgive me?"

"You can be a stubborn woman."

"Well, just this once, I'll let you have your way."

He leaned close and kissed her lips with aching tenderness. He gathered her to him, deepening the kiss for a long moment that chased all of her fears away.

"I was scared too," she whispered into his neck. He held her tighter. "And I love you, too."

He pulled back to look down into her eyes. "You do?"

"I do."

"I'm going to make you say that again," he said, bending to place a quick, hard kiss on her lips.

"Say what, I love you?" She'd say it as many times as he wanted her to.

"No, *I do.* I'm going to make you say that in front of a hundred witnesses."

She laughed. "With your family and my family, there will be at least two hundred."

CHAPTER 25

Saturday, 8:25 a.m.
Becca's apartment

Becca pretended she wasn't trying to overhear Diego's phone conversation as she sprinkled brown sugar on her oatmeal. Her throat was still sore and not ready for tougher foods like bagels, but she needed to refuel. Especially after the day and night she'd spent in Diego's arms. Damian had given everyone Friday off, and, it being Valentine's Day, Diego and Becca had spent the day celebrating their love, and reaffirming their good health. In bed.

But now, the world threatened to burst their happy bubble. Diego's flight was due to leave this evening, and they hadn't discussed where they would go from here. Their declarations of love had been made in the heat of battle, and several times since, and she knew their love was true. What she didn't know was where that left them. Either they were facing a long-distance relationship or someone would have to relocate, leaving their family and career behind.

They'd make it work, somehow.

Diego had moved into the living room to take the call from Garrison. "Yes, sir. I should be back on the job Monday morning. I'll check in with you then."

Frowning, he rejoined her at the table. "Sorry about that."

"No problem. Or is there?"

As if she'd broken through a haze of deep thought, he looked up in bewilderment. "No, there's no problem."

"Because if there was, we could talk about it. I'm a good listener, you know."

He took her hand and laced his fingers with hers. "I know."

"When you mentioned marriage..."

"I meant it," he insisted, squeezing her hand.

Becca's next breath was a little easier, and she smiled. "I suppose we'll have to talk more after the SSAM meeting, before your flight."

Saturday, 9:30 a.m.
SSAM offices

WITH A SENSE OF PRIDE AND EXHILARATION, DAMIAN WATCHED HIS team assemble. "Great job this past week," he told Becca, Diego, Einstein and Lorena. Nico had bowed out of the meeting, insisting he had to return to his real life. That real life included bringing down the remnants of the Circle, at least in Chicago and New York. He wondered how Eve Reynolds, who had been released from the hospital yesterday morning, fit into the picture.

"Where's Catherine?" Becca asked.

He'd received a visit at his home from Catherine yesterday. The woman was troubled, and not just by recent events. He'd known for a while that she had some things to sort out in her life, but she hadn't shared what those things were, and, for once, he didn't have the intel ahead of time. "She's taking a personal leave of absence from SSAM."

"What?" Becca was startled.

"She said to tell you she'll be in touch soon."

"Is she okay?"

"Health-wise, yes. Her injuries will heal, though I'm sure the experience will fuel some nightmares."

Catherine had never been a field agent. She'd been content behind the scenes, with the day-to-day business of running the company and managing the agents. And she'd been damn good at it. She would be hard to replace during her absence.

"Then she should be here with us, to process."

"She had other matters, personal matters, to take care of."

"More important than this?" Becca was incredulous. "When will she be back?"

"She didn't give an exact date. She said she wants to reclaim her life, on her terms. I take that as a positive sign. Patrick is behind bars," Damian continued, changing topics. "He'll be facing multiple counts of murder, and the CPD is still investigating every one of Joyce's patients, looking for deaths that seem suspicious. The current count is seven, so it's unlikely Patrick will ever be on this side of the prison bars again. Joyce will likely be facing charges, too."

"What about Samantha's case?" Diego asked. "Did anything from Patrick's videos help? Any leads on the Circle?"

Damian held up the necklace they'd found among Patrick's possessions. Its opal body flashed red, blue and green fire at him, and the wings reflected pink light as it dangled from his fingers. "Patrick took this from Tony's storage room. The police will be searching there for other items that might have been taken from victims of the Circle, and I'll personally be interviewing Tony further about his criminal activities." He frowned, recalling the conversation he'd had with Priscilla yesterday. The sound of her crying still tore at his heart. "I also received confirmation from the exhumation and DNA tests that it was Samantha's body that had been buried all these years. At least I know now, for certain, that she's at peace."

If only he could say the same thing about himself. But he was getting closer. He could feel it.

"But Tony said the Circle was responsible for her abduction," Becca said. "That he took her, but it was under orders. So either he's lying or the person who paid for her killed her?"

"That's something Lorena and I hope to learn from Tony. As long as he sticks to his side of the bargain and talks to us, SSAM will provide added security for him and I'll petition to have him moved to a prison in Texas." No matter how long it took him, he'd find the man who did this to Samantha. He'd been patient this long. He would wait twenty more years if it meant having satisfaction in the end.

In the meantime, he was going to seize life, at least a little bit. At least today. He'd ask Lorena out for that cup of coffee he'd been thinking about. But first...

"Diego, can you stay behind a moment? I'd like to talk to you alone."

DIEGO COULD SENSE THE POWER IN THE MAN BEFORE HIM. DAMIAN Manchester was equally confident and intimidating in a boardroom as when taking down a murderer. He was a man to look up to.

"Thank you for staying," Damian said as he closed the door to the conference room after excusing the others. "I won't take too much more of your Saturday. I believe it's your last day here, correct?"

"I have a ticket home tonight," Diego said. And he'd buy more tickets to come for a longer visit soon. He and Becca would have to figure out the technicalities. For now, it was enough to spend time with her.

Hands in his pockets, Damian rocked back on his heels, looking thoughtful. "I wonder what it would take for you to start calling *this* your home." His penetrating silver gaze met Diego's.

"Chicago?" Diego's heart thumped a little harder as he saw a light at the end of the tunnel.

"Chicago. SSAM. We're a family here. I'd like you to come work with us. I'll especially need your help as we negotiate the tricky terrain in this Circle investigation."

Diego thought about the family and job waiting for him in New York. His family would visit. They would simply be thrilled he'd found someone to share the kind of deep, abiding love the Sandovals respected. And the job? He'd worked damn hard to resurrect his reputation. To prove himself. But wouldn't he have more opportunity for that here? And with a man who respected him enough to offer him a job?

Diego met the other man's gaze. "I'm honored. The answer is yes."

Damian grinned as they shook hands. "We'll work out all the details soon. I assume you'll need some time to settle things in New York?"

"I'll have to figure things out with the task force."

"I think you'll find Garrison accommodating. SSAM may be coordinating with them from the Chicago side of things."

BECCA LOOKED UP FROM BEHIND HER DESK, SURPRISED WHEN DIEGO made a beeline for her, pulling her to her feet and sweeping her against him for a kiss that shot sparks from her lips all the way through her body to her toes.

Laughing, she pulled back to look up at him. "What's this about?" It had better not be a goodbye kiss. Not yet. She still had a few precious hours with him. She didn't even want to say the G-word out loud.

"I'm happy. A guy's allowed to be happy, right?"

"I suppose."

"We're going to have the perfect life together, starting now."

"Maybe for a few hours, yes, but—"

He put a finger to her lips. "You're not avoiding me any longer."

"But—"

"No excuses. I let you walk out of my door once. Never again. I'm moving here, and you'll be stuck with me."

"What about your job?"

"My job is right here. I'll be working at SSAM." Diego's eyes glittered with the excitement of new challenges, and a new start.

Damian had offered him a job? She thought her chest might explode with happiness. Butterflies, birds—hell, full-size eagles—swooped and dipped in her chest. Was it legal to be this excited?

"We're really going to do this?" she asked.

"I just need a couple weeks to wrap some things up in New York."

"How will your family feel about you moving away?" Guilt shadowed her happy moment.

"Mama will be fine, as long as I'm moving for a good reason. She wants me to be happy. *You* make me happy. You always have. I just didn't believe I deserved you."

She wrapped her arms around Diego again, pulling him close. "You asked me before if I wanted a big family."

"Yeah." His eyes darkened with heat. "But first, do you want a husband? You never officially said yes to my proposal."

"I don't believe I heard an official proposal."

He dropped to one knee in front of her. Suddenly, her breath was stuck in her chest.

"Becca Haney, will you accept me, faults and all, as your husband?"

"Only if you'll take me, faults and all." She tugged him to his feet. His hands were strong and warm in hers. Capable. They would keep her steady and hold her up as she and Diego moved through life together, just as she would support him. "Yes, I'll marry you. We'll be perfect in our imperfections. And that big family? It'll be part Haney, part Sandoval, part SSAM, and completely perfect."

"Partners forever," he murmured against her lips.

A SPECIAL SNEAK PEEK...

The Mindhunters Series continues...

ACCEPTABLE RISK
(The Mindhunters, Book 5)

A sea of bluebonnets along Interstate 35 reminded Catherine she was close to her final destination and eased some of the tension in her neck and shoulders. April in Texas was beautiful, and held the promise of the new start she was looking for—back where her life had gone off course years ago.

A few country love songs later, she was stiff again, her body and mind on full alert as she drove through a sketchy neighborhood on the west side of San Antonio. She pulled her Jeep Cherokee, along with the small trailer it towed, behind a strip mall that housed a clinic, an insurance office, a florist and a check-cashing and quickie loan establishment. Catherine had mapped out the location of Pecan Grove Community Health Clinic the moment she'd heard the news about Rachel's new job, wanting to picture what her sister's life was like so far away from Chicago, where they'd lived for the past few years while Rachel attended medical school.

The dust-and-grass scent of fresh spring rain hung thick in the air as she picked her way across a cracked and puddle-strewn parking lot. A quick storm must have moved through earlier.

Inside, the receptionist greeted her from behind a tall counter. "May I help you?"

"I'm here to see Rachel. Dr. Montgomery. I'm her sister."

Her smile bloomed. "Catherine? I'm Teresa." She reached across the counter to shake Catherine's hand. "Dr. Montgomery is expecting you. And you've got great timing," the woman continued, dropping her voice. "The police just left."

Catherine glanced around the waiting room, which held seats for about a dozen patients but was nearly empty now. An elderly couple sat in the corner reading magazines. "Police?"

"We had a threat. Someone called and demanded drugs. Prescription pill abuse is such a problem lately. The guy threatened to show up with a gun if we didn't have them ready when he stopped by." Teresa scoffed. "As if we did to-go orders."

"Tough neighborhood?" The graffiti, barred windows and plethora of potholes had certainly given her that impression.

"It has its moments, but usually the worst holds off until after dark. We try not to be here past six."

"Try?" Catherine struggled to absorb a chill that radiated from the nape of her neck. It was nearly six now.

"Go on back. She's taking a couple minutes before her last appointment to fill out charts. I've been trying to get her to take a break, but she likes to keep on top of everything." They'd learned a lot about diligence, adaptation and sacrifice in their upbringing. *Do or die.* "Maybe you'll have better luck. Exam room one."

Four exam rooms jutted off the short hallway just past the reception area. She found her sister hunched over a chart, her blond curls twisted into an efficient tangle at the back of her head, her hand moving at a furious pace.

"Handwriting legible yet?" Catherine asked from the doorway.

Rachel looked up and the furrow between her brows smoothed out as she grinned. "Only to me, probably." She kicked the stool out of the way so she could embrace Catherine. "I'm so glad you're home."

Home. Catherine's chest squeezed.

"I'm sorry I couldn't get away earlier to meet you at my place. Looks like you found me okay, though." Rachel pulled away. "Now tell me everything. What's wrong? Why the sudden move from Chicago?"

Catherine had prepared herself for the questions, but now wasn't the time to delve into that twisted tale. She hadn't told Rachel what had happened six weeks ago and she hoped she never had to share the experience. "Isn't it enough that I want to be near my little sister again?"

Rachel examined her further, a doctor looking for a diagnosis. Would she notice the dark smudges beneath Catherine's eyes? She'd taken extra time that morning to cover them, not wanting to worry her sister. "I wish that's all it was, but I thought you loved your job at SSAM."

SSAM was the acronym for a private organization known as the Society for the Study of the Aberrant Mind, and pronounced *Sam* in honor of the founder's daughter. For the past few years, as Rachel attended the University of Illinois at Chicago's medical school, Catherine had worked as SSAM's receptionist. It had been more than a job, however. She'd prided herself on being a support system for the incredible agents who apprehended the worst monsters society had to offer—serial killers and violent repeat offenders who'd evaded the justice system. Even operating from home base, she'd felt a part of something bigger than herself.

It had all been a lie. Even her name was a lie. She'd changed her last name from Montgomery to Montague before leaving for Chicago. It had been one more layer of insulation against someone discovering her past.

She looked away from Rachel's penetrating gaze. Though their features were similar—narrow nose, high cheekbones, elegant eyebrows and a bow-shaped mouth, Rachel's eyes were a mossy green while Catherine's contained more blue. Rachel's hair was a pure blond, while Catherine's was touched with hints of red.

But inside lay the real differences. Where Rachel was filled with a burning desire to help people, Catherine was numb and empty. She'd had difficult choices to make, ones she couldn't afford to regret, but she was tired of the lies. If only she could change what happened ten years ago…. Still, looking at a tired but glowing Rachel, every punch of acid rain that had eaten at Catherine's conscience was worth it. The payoff had been worth the sacrifice. She had to constantly remind herself of that.

"I do love SSAM, but it was time for a change." Before they discovered she was a fraud and a liar.

The sound of raised voices from the lobby was followed by a crash and a stern command from Teresa, ordering someone to leave before she called the police. Catherine's entire body trembled with a fear born of her recent trauma, even after weeks of therapy, but seeing her sister moving toward the door to confront the intruder brought out her protective instincts.

Catherine grabbed Rachel's arm. "Stay here."

"I can't. This is my clinic. I'm responsible."

"Let me check this out. You call the police." Catherine gestured to the phone in the corner. "I'll be careful. Besides, I'm trained to deal with unruly customers."

Another, louder crash sounded through the thin wall. Rachel headed for the phone as Catherine closed the door behind her and tiptoed to the end of the hallway, where she could peek around the corner. Teresa stood like a sentinel behind the chest-high counter. The man across from her had dark, wiry hair going in every direction, as if it were trying to escape his scalp. Lines carved his face like a craggy rock, indicating a hard, unyielding life. In contrast, his eyes were wild, his pupils dilated.

"I just need something to get me through until my next appointment." His voice was part plea, part I'll-do-anything desperation.

An empty pencil cup rolled to a stop in the waiting room and various pens and pencils were strewn across the linoleum. That had to be the source of one of the crashes. Still in their seats, the elderly couple huddled together, warily eyeing the man. What had once been a vase of flowers now lay shattered behind Teresa's desk —the other crash. Water dripped down the cabinets. A thin smear of red on Teresa's arm suggested a rebounding shard of glass must have nicked her, illustrating the threat of violence behind this man's demands.

Catherine's hand rose to her neck, but there was no noose there this time. She forced herself to breathe. Adrenaline trumped anxiety. *This isn't like before. He's just a strung-out man looking for a fix, not a serial killer intent on murder.*

"I can leave a message for Dr. Montgomery, and if you're due for a refill, she'll contact you, Lee." Teresa's voice was shaky. Her fingers slipped beneath the edge of her desk. Was there an alarm button there? Either way, Rachel should have connected with the police by now. Survival was just a matter of distracting Lee until help could arrive.

Lee's chin jutted out. "I saw the doctor's car in the parking lot. I'll wait. I'm not leaving until I get what I need." He thumped the counter so hard with his fist that Catherine jumped. So did Teresa. Her hand popped back out, and she held both of them up as if he'd aimed a gun at her. Guilt was all over her face.

"Can I help?" Catherine stepped forward, ignoring the fissures of fear shooting through her. The fight-or-flight response was meant to protect the body. Her body definitely wanted to flee, but her mind was on her sister and these other innocent people.

Lee turned to her. "Who are you?"

"I'm Dr. Montgomery's sister."

"You a doctor, too?"

"No, but I can see you need help." Lee had the pinched, pale appearance of someone whose entire body was wincing, contracting in an attempt to smother the pain. "What hurts?"

She stepped closer until she was only a couple feet away. Teresa's eyes were wide with silent warning, but Catherine had faced down the worst evil she could imagine and survived. Lee was only a temporary nuisance—with the potential to be more, she realized as she rounded the edge of the tall counter and saw the gun tucked into the front of his waistband.

"My back, my joints, my everything." Lee slapped a palm against his thigh as if punishing his body for its betrayal. "Your sister prescribed me something. It worked for a while. Now it's gone."

"Did you follow the directions on the label?" Rachel came out of the hall, looking a little short of breath, but her expression was calm and controlled, even compassionate. "If they're gone, Lee, you took too many, too fast."

"I had to. The pain..." His face crumpled.

As her sister stepped forward, Catherine shifted to stop her, placing herself between the pair. Rachel came to an abrupt halt, looking at Catherine in confusion. Catherine gave a slight shake of her head.

Lee's eyes narrowed on her, as if he realized Catherine was an obstacle keeping him from what he wanted, from what he *needed*. His hand moved toward the gun.

Pounding fear and memories she'd thought she'd left behind in Chicago—the throbbing in her neck that felt like a noose tightening, the flush of heat in her cheeks, the sharp intake of breath—rose up. She ignored the riot of emotions and focused, as her therapist had taught her, on the subject at hand. She was at a violent man's mercy once again, but this time, she had more than survival instincts in her toolbox.

She held her palms out as she took slow steps toward him.

"Sounds like you've been through a lot. I can help. I'm good at getting people what they need."

"I've told you what I need." His words built to a shout, and he tried to look around Catherine to Rachel. "You'd better have those pills out here in thirty seconds or—" As he reached for the gun at his waist, Catherine shot forward.

She grabbed his hand before it could connect with the gun and quickly shifted behind him, twisting his arm behind his back. His joints cracked in protest, his bones brittle in her grip. But he was a danger and had to be dealt with, so she held on tight. "Down on the floor." To encourage compliance, she nudged the back of his knee sharply with hers. She needed him horizontal before he formed a coherent thought and went to grab his gun with his other hand. At the moment, he was focused on the pain she was inducing. With a moan, he knelt.

"He's hurt!" Rachel rushed over now that Lee was subdued. "Stop!"

"Get his weapon." The calm in her own voice surprised her, but it buoyed the confidence that had been sagging for the past six weeks.

Rachel froze. "I didn't see the gun." She looked at Lee with shock and crouched to pull the weapon from his waistband.

Through the front window, she saw a couple of police cruisers screech to a halt. A moment later, two SAPD officers entered cautiously through the front door and quickly assessed the situation. Rachel held the gun out, letting it dangle from her fingers to appear nonthreatening. One cop rushed forward to take it as another took control of Lee. Catherine released her hold, rose to her feet and pressed a hand to her lurching stomach.

Rachel wrapped an arm around her. "Where'd you learn to do that?"

"Comes with the territory when you work for an agency like SSAM." And when you'd been through a situation you shouldn't have survived and didn't care to repeat. She watched one of the officers escort a handcuffed Lee from the premises as the other removed a notepad and began questioning Teresa.

Rachel's gaze turned thoughtful. "I think we have a lot to talk about."

More than you'll ever hear from me.

ACCEPTABLE RISK is available now!

ABOUT THE AUTHOR

Anne Marie has always been fasci-
nated by people—inside and out—
which led to degrees in Biology,
Chemistry, Psychology, and Coun-
seling. Her passion for understanding the human race is now
satisfied by her roles as mother,
wife, daughter, sister, and award-
winning author of romantic
suspense.

She writes to reclaim her sanity.

Find ways to connect with Anne
Marie at AnneMarieBecker.com.
There, sign up for her newsletter to receive the latest information
regarding books, appearances, and giveaways.